Praise for Joanna Rees

'If you like losing yourself in epic tales by the likes
of Penny Vincenzi and Lesley Pearse, you'll love this'
Woman

'Genuinely exciting, extremely well crafted
and long enough to be perfect beach reading'
Daily Express

'A gripping tale'
Glamour

'It's freakin' ace. Pack it in your hand luggage and
expect to spend a day of your summer hols reading . . .
and refusing all food, drink and conversation'
Heat

'An ideal beach read'
Books Monthly

'A riveting rollercoaster of a tale, full of intrigue,
high-stakes drama and compelling characters that
will keep you hooked from beginning to end'
Hello!

The
GIRL FROM
LACE ISLAND

Joanna Rees, aka Josie Lloyd and Jo Rees, is a bestselling writer of twelve novels, including rom-coms, blockbusters and big-hearted adventures such as *Come Together*, *Platinum* and *A Twist of Fate*. With nearly twenty years' writing experience, Joanna regularly teaches creative writing in schools and libraries and runs a successful novel-editing business noveleditors.com. She also records regularly for Radio Gorgeous. Based in Brighton, Joanna is married to the author Emlyn Rees with whom she has three daughters. They have co-written seven novels, including the *Sunday Times* number one bestseller *Come Together*, which was translated into twenty-seven languages and made into a film. They have written three bestselling parodies of their favourite children's books, including *We're Going on a Bar Hunt* and *The Teenager Who Came to Tea* as well as a light-hearted activity book encouraging people to stop being addicted to their technology called *Switch It Off*. Joanna is always delighted to hear from readers, so please visit her website www.joannareesbooks.com. She's also on twitter @joannareesbooks.

By Joanna Rees

AS JOSIE LLOYD

It Could Be You

AS JOSIE LLOYD, WITH EMLYN REES

Come Together
Come Again
The Boy Next Door
Love Lives
We Are Family
The Three Day Rule
The Seven Year Itch
We're Going on a Bar Hunt
The Very Hungover Caterpillar
The Teenager Who Came to Tea
Switch It Off

AS JO REES

Platinum
Forbidden Pleasures

AS JOANNA REES

A Twist of Fate
The Key to It All
The Girl From Lace Island

The
GIRL FROM
LACE ISLAND

JOANNA REES

PAN BOOKS

First published 2016 by Pan Books
an imprint of Pan Macmillan
20 New Wharf Road, London N1 9RR
Associated companies throughout the world
www.panmacmillan.com

ISBN 978-1-4472-6664-8

1 3 5 7 9 8 6 4 2

A CIP catalogue record for this book is available from the British Library.

Typeset by Ellipsis Digital Limited, Glasgow
Printed and bound by CPI Group (UK) Ltd, Croydon CR0 4YY

Visit www.panmacmillan.com to read more about all our books
and to buy them. You will also find features, author interviews and
news of any author events, and you can sign up for e-newsletters
so that you're always first to hear about our new releases.

For Tallulah

Author's Note

This book was inspired by a family holiday to Kerala in 2012. Emlyn and I had taken our daughter Tallulah to India ten years previously when she was two, and I'd written a piece for a Sunday newspaper about backpacking with a toddler. (Emlyn took a potty and twenty-two cans of baked beans in his backpack, as that was all that Lula would eat!) We went back a decade later with all three of our girls to the same places, and although parts of Kerala had changed beyond recognition, it was just as magical as ever. Honestly, I would recommend a Keralan holiday to anyone. It's called 'God's Own Country' for good reason.

It was when we were visiting a remote homestay and our fabulously eccentric hosts Laila and Jai offered us their ancient visitors book to sign, that I became entranced with the connection I felt to the strangers amongst the yellowing pages and the idea for *The Girl From Lace Island* was born. I must point out that Lace Island is entirely fictional, although there are many islands off the coast of Kerala. Any references to real places are entirely coincidental.

The
GIRL FROM
LACE ISLAND

PART ONE

CHAPTER ONE

Lace Island, off the south-west coast of India, 1989

Leila stretched out her legs on the rickety black bicycle and whooped as she hurtled down the dried mud track. To her right, the hot afternoon sun flickered through the tall palm trunks, the bright blue Arabian Sea glittering beyond the cliff's edge. Her voice was juddering now as she sped up, Rasa closing in behind her, his laughter loud as he bumped over the ruts on his bike.

Ahead, Leila saw the palm trees bending right down to the cool green water in the lagoon, the hummingbirds dipping to break the surface. The stifling afternoon air was thick with insects and the loud trill of cicadas. In the distance, she could see one of the long wooden night fishing boats moored against a row of timber huts at the water's edge.

Nearer the clearing at the side of the lagoon, Rasa's cousins and a few others were waiting to start their cricket match and they turned and cheered, egging her on.

'I'm going to beat you,' Leila called to Rasa, seeing the lagoon's edge coming up and instinctively slowing down.

'No. I meant all the way,' Rasa yelled, overtaking her with a clatter. She watched as his body tensed and he took off, flying over the edge of the lagoon, cutting off its corner and landing on the path on the far side with a bump.

'Not fair,' Leila called after him, annoyed that he'd changed the rules at the last moment. He knew full well that she'd lose her nerve as she did now, skidding to a halt on the very edge of the path, staring down at the clumps of weed in the lagoon and the slimy creatures that lurked between them. If she attempted the bike jump, like he had, she'd no doubt land head first in the slimy green water, and there was no way she could risk that. Bamu had told her he'd seen the crocodile in there last week.

She coughed in the cloud of dust they'd both created, seeing Rasa standing on the pedals, looking back over his shoulder at her with a triumphant grin as he reached his cousins and their friends at the clearing. He always won, she thought. But she couldn't hate him. Not with that grin.

Leila, out of breath, pushed her bike along the last part of the path towards the gang and leant her bike against a tree.

'You're late,' Bamu said, clapping Rasa on the back and raising his chin towards Leila in greeting.

'We were caught in lessons,' Rasa said, flinging his bike on the ground. It was kind of him not to tell the truth, Leila thought – that he'd sailed through the maths lesson, while she had struggled. It was easy for Rasa. He was the same age as her, but at fourteen, he just seemed to absorb knowledge, knowing instinctively how to apply it, while she struggled with everything.

This afternoon, Timothy, the young tutor her parents had hired, had finally snapped. He'd made them both stay in until the basics of converting fractions had finally sunk in, and had given the terrible warning that he'd already sent off to Cochin for the exam papers that both Leila and Rasa would be taking.

Leila knew it would be awful when they arrived, but right now she didn't have a care in the world – other than cricket.

Leila gave Rasa a grateful half-smile. He'd beaten her to the coconut grove, but he hadn't betrayed her in front of their friends, and that's what counted.

'You're first for bowling,' Bamu said, chucking the hard cricket ball to Leila. She quickly caught it and tucked it under her chin while she tied up her long black hair with a band from her wrist.

On the other side of the lagoon, she could see Tusker. The elephant had arrived with the ancient mahout, who was talking quietly to it, his long white hair piled into his cloth turban. The mahout had allowed Rasa and Leila to ride Tusker when they were little, but since the elephant's last musth, when he'd rampaged through the village and Chan, Leila's stepfather, had been called to help corral the elephant into the sea to cool off, Bibi, Leila's mother, had declared it too dangerous to let her precious only child near the giant beast. It was a shame. He looked so wonderfully stately, Leila thought, resolving to go later and see the mahout and give Tusker some watermelon. Anjum, the cook, would be sure to spare some fruit for Leila if she asked. He'd always had a soft spot for her.

She watched Bamu spread out the fielders, knowing Rasa would be first up to bat. She rubbed the cricket ball against the side of her shorts and looked towards the makeshift wooden stumps stuck in the hard ground.

Behind them, near the edge of the lagoon, were the huts where Rasa lived. She saw Parva, Rasa's aunt, hanging out red and orange saris on the line at the back of the house in the yard where the chickens pecked in the dirt.

Parva raised a hand when she saw Leila and smiled. She looked immaculate, as she always did, in a long green-and-gold chemise, a gold ring in her nose. Why Parva had never found a suitor to marry was beyond Leila. By the time she was Parva's age, she'd be married with children. Maybe old Tusker could be decorated for her wedding celebrations. *Now there was an idea.*

Rasa took the scuffed cricket bat from Victor and walked to the stumps. Observing him from a distance, Leila realized he'd grown without her noticing. His legs were longer, and he had much more hair on them than he'd ever had before. And he was getting a moustache, something Bamu teased him about, although Leila hadn't mentioned it. She wondered if he noticed changes in her too. She'd certainly been alarmed at what had been going on lately. Her T-shirts were suddenly too tight: her breasts and hips had begun to curve out. She didn't mind her new shape; it just felt unnecessary, when all she wanted to do was play cricket.

She walked away from Rasa, twisting her pumps in the hard mud in a comedy walk to make the others laugh, her jokiness masking the determination she felt. She would get Rasa back and bowl him out and show him that she was just as much one of the boys as he was. She stopped before her run-up and looked up the hill, where she could just make out the long, sloping red tiles of her house, the white wooden shutters, closed now against the sun, as if bathing in its warm glow. Leila's great-grandparents had built the sturdy plantation house at the turn of the nineteenth century, when they had tamed the wild palm trees on the island and cultivated the fertile land into the rich paddy fields where Bamu and the others usually worked in the early mornings.

She prepared herself, laughing with her team and watching Rasa knock the bat against his scuffed plimsolls, waiting. He called out a threat, like he always did, and Leila steadied herself for her run, but just as she started running, a familiar noise made her stop.

The small aeroplane made the forest tremble, and with the game momentarily forgotten, the children ran through the trees to the edge of the red cliff to watch the plane coming from the sea so low over their heads it felt like they could touch it. They all instinctively ducked and laughed, shouting at the noise.

Leila tried to see who was in the back of the plane, but she knew it would be Chan and the latest guests. She sighed, trying to smother her disappointment. She liked it when it was just her and Bibi up at the house. When guests came, things changed and her mother and Chan became entertainers, bending over backwards to charm the guests who stayed in the luxury bungalows by the beach. No demand was too outrageous, and although Leila knew it was their money that kept Lace Island going, she also resented the guests Bibi so readily put up with and their bad behaviour. There were always people frolicking on the beach half naked, married couples coming here with their lovers, actresses recovering from operations, politicians who needed to let off steam without the fear of camera lenses. And when they did, it meant that Leila was not allowed out to play cricket in the grove.

'Come on, Leila,' Parva called from the path, once the sound of the plane engine had receded and they had all returned to their makeshift cricket pitch. In the distance, Leila could hear it slowing on the small landing strip. 'Your mother will want you up at the house.'

'But I've only just got here,' Leila called back, glancing now at Rasa and seeing his hazel eyes boring into hers from beneath his dark eyebrows. She knew he shared her disappointment. He hated the guests arriving too. No doubt he'd have to miss his lessons to take them out on the boat to the coral reef that gave Lace Island its name.

'Come on, young lady,' Parva called again. 'Time to do your duty.'

'Five minutes. Just let me bowl out Rasa. Shouldn't take long.'

Parva smiled and Leila resumed her position. Running as hard as she could, she flung the ball at the stumps. Rasa's bat was a blur as it hit the ball hard and they all watched it soaring towards the lagoon.

One more bowl, Leila thought to herself, annoyed at Rasa's skill. One more was all it would take. She wasn't going to go up to the house, she decided. Not until she'd won.

CHAPTER TWO

London, present day

The high roundhouse kick smashed into the side of his head
with a satisfying smack. *Hell, yeah*, Jess thought, as her leg
came lightly back down to the padded gym floor. There was no
time to gloat, though. Not yet. Not with an opponent as unpre-
dictable as Kai. She watched him stagger backwards, but she
stayed where she was, then jumped back on her toes, her fists
raised to her chin, shrugging her shoulders to rearrange her
heavy white robe. *Come on, sucker. Show me what you got.* She
was aware of her taut muscles screaming, her chest heaving, but
she wouldn't finish yet. Not until he was down for good.

Kai continued backwards, his hand clamped to his ear, but
Jess knew damn well that he could be bluffing. She jumped
lightly towards him and back, and he took the signal. She saw
him straightening up, steel in his eyes, his tall frame towering
over her, all bets off now. Finally, he was taking her seriously.

She pounced towards him, her fists punching. One, two,
one, two. And another roundhouse.

'OK, break it up.' Tony, their kick-boxing master, strode
quickly across the mats, his tattooed arms stretched between
Jess and her opponent. 'I said, break it up!'

In respect, Jess slunk backwards, but her eyes didn't leave Kai's.

'Take it easy, Jess. Save some juice in the tank,' Tony told her, catching her arm and breaking her stare.

As always, she came to her senses when she saw Tony's familiar wrinkled face, his thick neck cushioned with one of the white gym towels.

'Just giving it everything I got,' Jess said, wiping sweat from her top lip with the cuff of her robe, trying to make light of the fight, but they all knew she'd been waiting to kick Kai's butt for a year. 'Like you always taught me,' she added pointedly.

'Yeah, well, fifty sit-ups on the mat. Go,' Tony said. 'Burn off some of that aggression.'

She noticed now that Tony had tired lines round his eyes, but even so, he'd always been the same – ever since she'd started coming here as a teenager. Not having known her own father, Tony was the only older man Jess had ever had in her life and she respected him. It was Tony who'd set her straight and given her a path. Tony who'd shown her how to channel her anger and stop directing it at the teachers. And most recently, it had been Tony who'd encouraged her to apply for her dream job as cabin crew. He'd even given her a reference.

Yes, he was one of life's good guys. And Jess knew there weren't that many of them around, which is why she exhaled loudly now and smiled, before giving Kai an exhausted high-five. At twenty-two, he was three years younger than her, and taller. His black face was shiny with sweat, but there was respect in his eyes now as he nodded to her.

'You trained her too good,' Kai grumbled to Tony as she spun on her heel and left the mats, and she grinned with private satisfaction. 'So, Jess,' Kai called out, and she turned, 'you put in a word for me with Angel, right?'

Jess sighed and shrugged sadly, needing to dispel the hope in Kai's eyes. If only it were that simple. If only she could tempt Angel into going out with someone like Kai. She had to admit that he was kind of cute. But then, blonde Angel with her teasing ways had always been attractive to men. Unfortunately, always the wrong sort.

An hour later, Jess was still thinking about Kai and their fight as she got off her bike by the tower block where she lived. It was dark; a freezing drizzle was making a halo round the weak street light. She expertly flipped the bicycle frame onto her shoulder and stepped round the remains of a takeaway spilt over the cracked path, deliberately avoiding eye contact with the three youths who circled on their tiny bikes like sharks on the scrubby patch of grass below the street light.

She braced herself, waiting for them to shout out some sort of sexist or racist abuse, but tonight, she was off the hook. She couldn't help feeling that their silence indicated a grudging respect, but it had been hard won. Not everyone who lived here was so lucky.

Holding her breath against the stench of stale urine, Jess pushed through swing doors into the concrete stairwell. She'd done her best to make their flat homely, but she couldn't escape the nasty aesthetic of the tower block. The local estate agents shouted about this area being up-and-coming, but many generations of the same families had lived here for years and they viewed the influx of City boys and hipsters with suspicion and, in some cases, contempt. Which was why there was graffiti all over the walls and the air stank.

She started up the concrete stairs, her senses on alert, never knowing if she'd make it up to the second-floor walkway without bumping into one of the hooded junkies who liked to steal purses, phones and bags whenever they got the slightest opportunity.

God, she couldn't wait to get out of here. And as soon as she'd passed her training, she would be. Because then she'd finally have a career. For the first time in her life, she'd *be* someone.

She let her thoughts slip into the comfort of her fantasy once she had finally made it as cabin crew. She imagined herself in first class, dressed in a smart uniform, and how it would feel to greet all those rich and famous people. She imagined closing the doors to the swanky 747, sealing herself in and jetting off across the ocean to Australia, Thailand, India – places that had never been in her reach before, but now felt so tantalizingly close.

Safely on the walkway, she put her bike down, raising her arm in greeting to her elderly Indian neighbour, who was pulling in her washing from the line she had suspended outside her front door. As she passed, Jess breathed in the delicious waft of curry that always came from her tiny flat and mumbled a hello. She was starving, she realized, her session at Tony's kickboxing gym having gone on for longer than she'd thought. She pulled her keys out of her puffa-jacket pocket and unlocked the front door.

'Oh. You're home,' Angel said, her head popping over the top of the sofa just inside the door.

That was rich, Jess thought, considering Angel, her best friend and so-called flatmate, had been absent without so much as a text message for three days.

Jess recoiled at the cloud of cigarette smoke and wafted the front door to let in some air. She felt annoyed that Angel had suddenly turned up and had already wrecked the flat, which Jess had only cleaned that morning. *And* she'd started smoking again. Jess wanted to scream with fury. Why wouldn't she ever learn? Who could afford to smoke these days? Not Angel. That was for sure.

She glanced into the kitchenette area to the side and saw that the bags of shopping she'd left in a hurry before she'd gone to the gym had been half emptied, badly cut bread and a mangled block of cheese left out on the side. But worse, worse than all of that was that Weasel was on the sofa. Nobody knew what his real name was, something unpronounceable and Slavic, which is why everyone called him Weasel. And he was a weasel. By name and by nature. Even the sight of the top of his shaved head made Jess's skin crawl.

'Shut the door. It's freezing in here,' he growled in his clipped accent.

Jess walked in and propped her bike up against the wall inside, then shut the door with an unnecessary slam to show Angel just how pissed off she was.

'You got the job?' Angel asked, a cruelty in her voice Jess hadn't heard before.

'Don't know yet. I have to be accepted onto the training course first,' she said, infuriated that Angel clearly hadn't listened to a word Jess had told her about the whole process she had to go through before she could fly. She'd been waiting every day for news of her cabin-crew training course. She'd passed the initial interviews, but now came the real test. Her nerves were completely shattered, the 'what if?'s churning round and round her head. A few sympathetic or encouraging words from her best friend would have been appreciated, but she saw now in the slightly triumphant eye roll Angel gave

Weasel that her friend couldn't care less. If anything, she wanted her to fail.

It was ironic, Jess thought, because when they'd been kids, it had been Angel who'd been the ambitious one, Angel who dreamt of being a TV presenter, Angel with the big plans, who was going to do something with her life. But now all she did was spend her dole money on lottery tickets and online bingo, each loss further sapping her self-esteem.

She looked a mess too. As Jess walked round the sofa, she saw that Angel was wearing stained leggings that had once been Jess's and an oversized hoody. Her badly dyed blonde hair was scraped back into a ponytail, and there were dark circles under her eyes, like she hadn't slept for days. She shoved her hands into her hoody pockets, but not before Jess had seen that she'd bitten her nails right down.

'So. Look who it is,' Weasel said, turning his attention momentarily away from the TV towards Jess, as if she were some errant teenager. Jess stared at the full horror of the mess on the coffee table and the detritus of joint-rolling and cigarettes. 'The fire exits are here and here,' he said, laughing at his own joke as he fanned out his arms. Angel had obviously told him about Jess's airline training.

Seeing that he'd annoyed Jess, he laughed nastily again, putting his feet up on the table. His boots were dirty and little crescents of mud were all over the blue rug. He took a sip from the can of cheap lager he was drinking and gave a loud burp.

Jess stared at Angel, her look saying, 'What the fuck?' and Angel's return look saying it straight back. Jess picked up her bag and stomped down the lino-covered hallway to her bedroom, trying to calm her fury. She heard Angel following.

She pushed open the door to her room. Her single bed was neatly made, with its white-and-blue duvet cover complemented by the soft beige throw she'd bought. One wall was covered in white cupboards and shelves she'd built herself to house her college books, and another large wall was filled by a huge picture of a desert island scene.

'Why are you being weird?' Angel demanded. 'I thought you'd be pleased to see me. You left enough messages telling me to come back.'

'What is he doing here?' Jess hissed.

'Why shouldn't he be? I told you – we're together. He's ditched that skank Maisie.'

'She has a baby. *They* have a baby.'

'So?'

'So?' Jess stared at Angel, exasperated. Where had her moral compass gone? Angel had always been better. Better than this.

How could she describe Maisie as a 'skank'? That was Weasel talking. Didn't she care at all? What about the baby? Because Angel more than anyone knew what it was like to grow up without functional parents. She'd been taken into care at three years old after her mother had broken down, unable to cope alone. And now history was repeating itself.

Something was wrong. Very wrong. And that's when Jess noticed that Angel's eyes were flickering, her gaze darting around the room.

'Oh my God,' Jess gasped, the realization hitting. 'Are you *using*? Please don't tell me you're using.' She grabbed Angel's arm, trying to force her to look directly at her, but Angel's gaze flitted away. Everyone knew that Weasel smoked crack. *Oh Jesus. He hadn't got to Angel, had he?*

'Stop being so judgemental,' Angel snapped, shaking off Jess's grip. 'I can do what I want.'

Jess bit her lip, feeling furious tears rising. Angel had been her entire family for as long as she could remember. Her rock. The one she'd always relied on. But it was like looking at a stranger now.

'Has he made you start?' Jess demanded.

'Oh. Oh,' Angel countered, grasping for excuses. 'That's rich. You don't know him.'

'I don't *want* to know him. You know who he is. Who he hangs out with. He's bad news. Look what he's doing to you.'

'At least he's someone. At least I've got someone. At least I'm not frigid like you.' Angel thumped her chest with her fist, and as her eyes, with their dark yellow shadows, met Jess's, she saw that Angel was desperate. 'Take a look at yourself, Jess. Ever since we were kids you've been saving yourself to walk along that stupid beach with Mr Right.' She flung her arm out at the poster. 'But let me tell you – he doesn't exist, OK? That's a myth. Especially for people like us. From where we come from.'

Jess felt Angel's words sting, but the betrayal in Angel's attitude was worse. How could she have given up just when life was starting? When it should be starting for both of them?

'You don't have to settle for him. You are so much better than that.'

'How?' Angel spat back. 'How am I better than that? I'm unemployed, unemployable. Nothing I've ever wanted has happened. Nothing.'

That's because you haven't worked for it, Jess wanted to shout. *That's because you've given up whenever it got tough. That's because you expect life to hand you everything you want on a plate and it doesn't work like that . . .*

Instead, she took a deep breath. 'You're making a big mistake. We can make a better life.'

'There's no "we", Jess. Not anymore.'

'Angel, please. Listen—' she started.

'Fuck you. Don't lecture me, OK? You think you're so much better than everyone around here, but you're not. You're delusional,' Angel shouted, and Jess backed away, scared by her tone and the cold look in her eyes.

CHAPTER THREE

Lace Island, 1989

In the cool of the house's dark, wooden hallway, Leila picked off a small yellow banana from the bunch in the basket on the carved mahogany dresser, desperate to tell Bibi about Tusker and how Rasa's ball had nearly hit the old elephant and how the mahout had said the elephant was ill and needed a vet. Leila had promised that Bibi would sort it out. Nobody went sick for long on Lace Island. Old Maliba, Rasa's grandmother, usually ground up herbs and plants from her Ayurvedic garden to make potions, but this time she had failed to cure the elephant. They'd have to send for a vet from Cochin. With a bit of luck, Bibi would let Leila use the telex machine in her office.

Full of plans and munching on her banana, Leila skipped along the corridor, the muslin curtains blowing in against the old teak boards, the black-and-white framed pictures of Leila's maharaja relatives staring down from the wall and through the screen with its old mosquito netting out onto the terrace.

The back terrace was where Bibi preferred to entertain, when guests left the comfort of their bungalows and visited the house on her invitation, the dining room often being too formal and stuffy. It was covered by a canopy from which electric lights looped, and in the corner was the bamboo bar area that Chan had built and of which he was particularly proud. The polished floorboards stretched further to a wooden balustrade, which looked down into the blue mosaicked pool below.

Dotted around were a few fan-backed wicker armchairs, some squashy beanbag seats and a hanging swing seat, which was Leila's favourite. Through the huge palms in the garden, there was a view down towards the lagoon, and in the distance, the sea, changed now to a deep blue in the late-afternoon light. There would be a lovely sunset later.

Chan, Leila's stepfather, was a small-boned man with a mane of glossy black hair, a thin moustache and twinkling brown eyes. Parva said he was the spitting image of her favourite Bollywood star, and he certainly knew it, Leila thought. It was Chan's star quality that had charmed grief-stricken Bibi back to life after Leila's father had been killed in a shark attack when Leila had been barely two. That's what Old Maliba had always said.

Leila couldn't blame Bibi for falling for Chan. He was good-looking and suave and more than willing to run Lace Island with Bibi. Now, his face lit up with a grin when he saw Leila and he threw his arms out wide.

'There's my girl,' he said, and as she went to him, he grabbed her and spun her round in a hug. Leila felt the familiar tingle of shame that she felt each time he greeted her when he'd been away. She couldn't quite find it in her heart to love him like she knew she ought to. Not that she'd ever tell anyone – even Rasa – how she felt. But the fact remained that Chan wasn't her father. She wasn't 'his girl', and him laying claim like this, like he always did, just made her more aware that something was missing.

'Leila, mind out,' her mother said. Bibi was standing watering her collection of spider plants in their circular holder with a small copper watering can. She was wearing one of her pink-and-orange kaftans, which she often wafted about in during the afternoons, but despite the shapeless garment, she still exuded glamour and a sort of regal air, her long black hair wound into a shell clip at the nape of her neck, her skin flawless. But it was Bibi's pale aquamarine eyes with their dark rings round the irises that captivated everyone. They smiled at Leila now.

'She's fine,' Chan said, putting his arm round Leila's shoulder and snuggling her in close. 'Look at our girl, Bibi,' he said. 'I go away for less than a week and she gets so big. Almost a grown woman. Let me see . . .' He held Leila's face for a moment and she breathed in his particular sweet smell, of cigarette smoke mingled with the pomade he wore in his hair and the lavender water Parva always sprayed on his shirts. 'Nearly as beautiful as your mother. Not quite yet.'

'Look at the state of you, child,' Bibi scolded, blushing at Chan's compliment and trying to smooth Leila's hair before rubbing her cheek to remove some dirt. 'You've been playing with those boys in the grove again,' she said with a tut. Leila glanced at Chan, who winked. They both knew that Bibi's attempts to make Leila ladylike were wasted. 'Go and clean up. We have guests. Tina and Teddy Everdene. They're all the way from England. As well as their friends Martin and Christopher Barber. They work in the theatre, apparently. Oh, and Christopher's . . . fiancée?' Bibi checked with Chan.

'She probably will be by the time they leave here if he's got any sense,' Chan chuckled. 'She's a bombshell all right.'

Bibi gave him a sharp look, then turned to Leila. 'You must be polite to them.'

Leila shrugged in tacit acknowledgement, annoyed that her mother was so openly impressed by total strangers. Personally, she couldn't care less about these new guests or where they were from, her attention now caught by all the packages next to the armchair.

'What did you bring?' she asked Chan.

'Go ahead,' he said, pulling up the creases of his light blue trousers and sitting down on the chair. He lit a cigarette using the large amethyst lighter Bibi reserved for the guests. 'Take a look. There's plenty of treasures.'

Leila unwrapped the packages and Bibi joined her, standing over her as she emptied the bags.

'Did you remember saffron? Was Mr Singh at the market?' Bibi asked.

'Of course,' Chan said. 'He sends his regards. Oh, Bibi, look at this,' he said, leaning forward and passing her a package wrapped in thin pink paper.

Bibi looked warily at him as she unwrapped the silk shawl and gasped. 'How much did that cost?'

'Never you mind. Tell me you don't love it,' he said, standing now and going to her and wrapping it round her shoulders. Leila watched her mother cupping the soft, looping fringing along the edge of the scarf.

'We can't afford these luxuries, Chan,' she said, but Leila could tell that she loved the scarf and loved her husband for buying it.

'What are these?' Leila asked, pulling out a large colourful box.

'Ahh. Those are fireworks,' Chan said, rubbing his knees and crouching down next to her. 'I got them on special offer. We can have them next Christmas.' He opened the box and pulled out one of the paper-wrapped fireworks inside. 'Full of gunpowder.'

'Then don't put your cigarette near it,' Bibi scolded. 'You'll send the whole place up.'

Chan put back the firework. 'Good point. In fact, Leila, don't you ever think of playing with these. They are highly flammable,' he said, his tone slightly mocking. 'You know how paranoid your mother is about fire.'

'With good reason,' Bibi said. 'You should be too,' she continued, taking the cigarette from Chan's mouth and stubbing it in the glass ashtray.

'Run and put them in the cupboard in the hall,' Chan said. 'You'll have to remember to dig them out.'

Leila packed up the fireworks and carried them back through the screen into the hall. She knelt by one of the large mahogany sideboards and slid back the door. Inside, the shelves were lined with yellowing newspaper from a different era, and they smelt of musty joss sticks. She tried to clear a space on the top shelf, which was filled with an odd assortment of objects, including a steel helmet that had belonged to a guest, candlesticks, coconut shells and some photo albums. Leila flicked one of them open now, pulling aside the brown tissue-paper leaves to see the formal black-and-white pictures of Lace Island twenty years ago.

There was her father, Ranjidan, on the beach, making a pose in his 1950s swimming trunks next to a long wooden surfboard. How could a man who had so clearly loved the water come to such an awful end? For a year afterwards, nobody had swum on the beach where he had disappeared and his bloodied shorts had been found. She looked at his grinning face, running her fingertips over the line of his cheekbones, a likeness in his face to hers she was proud to share.

Behind her, she heard voices in the hall. She peeped round the edge of the desk and saw a tall man and a woman by the front door, admiring the photos on the wall. The woman was wearing a light blue sundress with padded shoulders, a large pair of sunglasses perched on her frizzy hair.

The man had a purple checked shirt with a large patch of sweat down the back. He walked over and started flicking through the visitors book.

'Tina, darling, you must come and see this,' the man said. 'It makes very interesting reading.'

Like many of the guests on Lace Island, he looked rich, Leila thought. But he was pale, like he hadn't been in the sun for a while.

'Look at that,' he continued, pointing to an entry. She could hear the awe in his voice as he flipped over the pages, his wife peering over his shoulder. 'We're certainly in rarefied company. All sorts in here.'

The foreign guests were always the same with the visitors book, Leila thought, although she couldn't understand why. They were just names. People. Fine when they were here. Even better when they left.

But the guests seemed to love the guessing game with the visitors book and its unspoken connections. Because that was Bibi's rule: you could only visit if you knew someone who had been before and had recommended you. Lace Island wasn't in any brochures or advertised anywhere, and Bibi had banned the few journalists who'd visited from writing about it. That's what made it special and so safe. Only lovely people came, according to Bibi, as if loveliness were a secret thread that connected all the guests.

'Hello,' Leila said, shoving the photo album back next to the fireworks and standing up.

The woman, Tina, put her hand on her chest. 'Oh, my, you scared me,' she said with a laugh.

'You must be young Leila,' the man said, peering at her through his round glasses like she was a rare monkey. 'I've heard a lot about you.'

'Oh, Leila, I think you must be the luckiest girl in the world, if you ask me,' Tina said, stepping forward to take Leila's arm. 'Living here. It really is paradise, isn't it. Oh look, there's Vanessa,' she said, spotting someone coming through the open front door into the hall. Leila turned and saw a woman in a pink-and-white spotted halter-neck dress sashaying in. She had a mane of long, curly blonde hair and exuded a sort of glamorous film-star quality, as if she was lit up from inside. 'Nessa, darling,' Tina continued, 'come and meet Chan's daughter, Leila. She's just as lovely as he promised.'

Now the woman took off her sunglasses and smiled, and as Leila stared at her bright green eyes, she thought she was possibly the most exotic creature she'd ever seen.

CHAPTER FOUR

London, present day

The three glasses chinked together and Tony grinned at Jess and Kai across the scuffed wooden table. They were in their local pub celebrating Jess starting her training course. Angel should have been here too, but despite texting her, Jess had heard nothing for days.

Their row still weighed heavily on Jess's mind. She should hate Angel for all the things she'd said, but instead, she felt a gnawing sorrow and a sense of abject failure.

She should have seen the signs before, but she'd been so busy working that she hadn't noticed just how depressed Angel had become. And right now, after starting her cabin-crew training course and meeting so many interesting people, she felt as if the gap between them had just widened even more.

'It'll be hard work, but six weeks and then, hopefully, I'll be in the air,' Jess told Tony now.

'At least being thirty-five thousand feet in the air will keep you out of trouble,' he said, taking a sip of his pint.

'I wouldn't guarantee it,' Jess said.

'You'll have to look after that ugly mug of yours. No more fights. You listening, you two?' he said with a grin.

'Fair enough,' Kai said.

Jess smiled and took a sip of her orange juice. She'd only popped into the gym tonight for a quick session. She'd been so excited she'd had to tell someone, and she'd been pleased that Kai and Tony had wanted to celebrate with her.

But now that she was here in the pub, she was itching to get home to start on her coursework. There would be six modules and she'd have to pass each one in order to get accepted by the airline, and the competition was fierce.

'Any hot chicks on your course?' Kai asked, and Jess rolled her eyes at him.

'Plenty. I met one girl, Claire, who seemed fun. She's sitting next to me.'

In fact, if it hadn't been for Claire, Jess might never have had the nerve to go into the lecture room at all. But that's what had been so great about today. The feeling that for the first time ever, she belonged. That she was the same as those nice boys and girls from their secure families, with their normal backgrounds. It felt like she was on her way to a new future.

'Yeah, well, don't forget who your friends are,' Tony said, and Jess smiled at him.

'Course I won't,' she said, but even as she did, she knew that her heart had already pulled away. That she was already wondering what tomorrow might bring.

Later, after the pub, Kai walked her home. He stood with her by her door, but Jess could see the lights were off in the flat and Angel still hadn't come home.

'You should be proud of yourself, Jess,' Kai said softly. 'Really. Not many people have the guts to change their lives the way you have.'

'Thanks,' she said, meaning it. She was genuinely touched he'd said that.

She smiled, reaching into her pocket for her key, but suddenly, she was aware of how still Kai had gone. When she looked up at him, he was staring at her intently. Then, taking her completely by surprise, he leant down and kissed her softly on the lips.

'What was that for?' she asked, taken aback.

'I dunno,' he said, with a shy smile and a shrug. 'Sorry.'

Jess held his gaze, her heart starting to race. 'Don't be sorry. I'm flattered.'

Kai glanced along the walkway. 'You know, Jess, I wondered if you wanted to . . . you know . . .'

She stared at him, her breath catching as she saw the meaning in his eyes. Then she laughed, but he looked serious.

'I don't want this to complicate things between us,' she whispered in the dark, scared that her neighbour would come out and see them.

'It won't. We're friends, right?' Kai said, stroking her face with the back of his hand, the tender gesture clinching it for Jess.

She unlocked the door, smiling while biting her lip. This wouldn't be another mistake, would it? Like the dozens she'd made in the past? Because this new phase of her life meant she was leaving the old, hot-headed Jess behind. That tearaway teenager who used to take drugs and make trouble. That was all in the past. Back in the care homes that she and Angel had always run away from.

These days, she was different. She was being sensible. She'd turned over a new leaf since she and Angel had moved here. It was six months or more since she'd even entertained the thought of an unsuitable hook-up. She'd stopped sleeping with men because she could. She'd been saving herself.

But now, as Kai held her arm and pulled her towards him and kissed her again as the door of the flat closed behind them, all her resolve went out of the window and she remembered how nice it felt to connect to someone physically.

He kissed her again, more deeply this time, moaning with pleasure. Man, he was a good kisser, she thought, thinking of how often she'd fought Kai, how many times she'd embraced him, made contact with him – but never like this. But why never like this? she wondered, feeling something sexual stirring inside her. And what the hell? Today had been one of the most exciting of her life. Why not make a proper celebration of it, as Kai was suggesting? Maybe she wasn't as uptight and frigid as Angel had declared she was. Maybe, just maybe this was exactly what she needed.

'I thought it was Angel you wanted,' she said, as she grabbed at his shirt.

'I was only saying that to make you jealous. You have no idea how hot you are, Jess. I've fancied you for ages.'

He lifted her up, like she was as light as a feather, and she wrapped her arms and legs round him, feeling his hardness through his sweatpants against her.

'Which way is your room?' he asked.

Afterwards, Jess lay in her single bed in Kai's arms, stroking the soft skin on his arm. She smiled, amazed at how content the sex between them had made her feel.

'So what's the deal with the big beach?' Kai asked, nodding at the poster opposite.

Jess stared at the poster. 'It's always been a fantasy. You know, to go somewhere like that.'

She stared at the poster, not elaborating. She couldn't tell Kai the whole fantasy. That one day she wanted to get married on a beach just like that. And it wasn't about the guests or how it looked, like it was on those bride shows on TV. She wouldn't care about who else was there, only that he was there. Him. The man she loved. The one she hadn't met yet, but she knew one day she would. The one who'd be perfect for her. She saw herself staring into his eyes feeling . . .

Feeling what? Who knew? How would she feel, other than more ecstatic than she'd ever thought it possible to feel? Was *that* how it felt? Perhaps. But she could only guess. She'd never been in love. Never even come close.

'I keep it there to remind me that there's a big world out there.' She stared at it for a moment. 'Angel gave it to me for my twenty-first,' she confided. *Back when she gave a shit about me*, she wanted to add.

'Are you worried about her? You seemed worried earlier.'

'I am.'

'She's a big girl, Jess. She has to make her own mistakes,' Kai said.

'I guess. It hurts, that's all. We've always been like this, you know,' Jess said, crossing her fingers. 'Here. Look.' She reached down and pulled the old shoebox from under her bed. She opened the lid. Inside were her savings book and her favourite keepsakes.

She pulled out the Polaroid photo of her and Angel when they'd been ten standing outside their first orphanage. They looked like such ragamuffins. Always in trouble, but always with each other's backs. She held it up for Kai to look.

'That's cute,' he said, with a smile. 'Neither of you has changed. You got any more?'

'Nope. That's it,' Jess said.

She felt the shame of it now. The sadness that she only had the one picture. One measly token of her childhood. The truth was that they'd been too poor to have cameras, and Jess had moved around so much, never having the space or a room of her own to collect possessions. Besides, it hadn't been a childhood that had been worth documenting with photos in an album. Not like she imagined real families had.

'What else is in there?' Kai asked, looking at the box.

'Not much. Oh . . . there's this,' she said, pulling out the small jewellery box. Inside was a fine gold crucifix.

'I didn't know you were religious.'

'I'm not,' she said, 'but that's all I have from my past.' She stared at the fine links, wondering who would once have owned it. 'I arrived in the orphanage as a baby and this was among my baby clothes.'

Kai was silent for a moment and Jess felt jangled. To share this with him suddenly felt more intimate than the sex they'd just had.

'Don't you want to know?' he asked. 'About what happened? About why you were in the orphanage in the first place?'

Jess shrugged. 'As far as I know, she's dead. My birth mother. That's what I was told.' She rubbed her finger across the worn gold, as she had done countless times before, and her heart ached with a familiar longing and she sighed. 'I'd just like to know for sure, that's all.'

It was true. Even if it was sad, or awful, or tragic, just to know who her mother had been would fill the hole she felt inside. She wouldn't judge anymore. Enough bad shit happened in the world. Jess was old enough to know *that*. But if she could just know *why* her mother gave her up. Did she simply not care, or did something happen? Something that could have been put right?

'Why don't you find out?'

'It's too late,' she said, kissing the crucifix before putting the jewellery box back. 'There's no point in dwelling on the past.'

'If it was me, I'd want to know.'

'I've got other things on my mind,' Jess said, putting the lid firmly back on the box and replacing it under the bed.

'Me too,' Kai said, wanting to snuggle back down with her, but Jess was no longer in the mood.

'You know, Kai, I should really study. I've got to be up early and back at my course in the morning.'

'Oh, oh, sure,' he said, getting the message.

She got up, feeling bad as she watched him climb out of her bed. She stared at his long, lean limbs as he pulled on his boxers.

He turned to her as she put on her dressing gown, crossing her arms.

'You know, I like you, Jess. I have done for a while. You must have guessed. All our fights . . .'

'*That* was flirting?' she said, attempting to joke, but he was being serious.

'We could, you know, make a go of it. If you wanted, I mean? You and me?'

Jess looked at the carpet, her eyebrows knitting together. She felt bad now for sleeping with him. For leading him on. It had been a mistake, because she'd hurt his feelings. She could see that now.

'Save yourself for someone who will be here,' she said. 'I want to go and travel the world. It's what I've wanted my whole life.'

'But—'

Jess shook her head, before reaching up to hug him. 'I'm sorry,' she whispered. 'Tonight has been lovely, and the last thing I wanted was to hurt you, but I can't be any more than your friend, Kai. I'm sorry.'

He nodded, not meeting her eye, and when he left, he kissed her on the cheek.

But after he'd gone and she'd shut the door, Jess felt unexpected tears rising up in her. What if believing in fate and her gorgeous fantasy man was just a big joke? Maybe there was no happy ever after, or deserted beach with the man of her dreams. What if Angel was right and she was holding out for a fantasy that didn't exist? Certainly not for people like her.

Maybe she would be better off with someone like Kai. Someone who could be here for her in the real world she lived in now. But it was too late, she reminded herself. She'd already rejected him. She'd sent him packing when he'd been nothing but sweet and kind to her. All because she felt she deserved something better.

What kind of a horrible person did it make her?

She took a breath to calm herself. No. No, it would be OK. She believed in fate. She believed she was destined for a better future. It would happen. She would make it. She would. No matter what.

CHAPTER FIVE

Lace Island, 1989

The Everdenes had been up for Bibi and Chan's infamous cocktail hour each evening of their stay, but tonight, along with Martin, Christopher and Vanessa, they'd stayed past sunset, Anjum, the cook, having prepared a special banquet. Leila stretched out on her favourite cushioned chair on the terrace, her tummy full from the feast they'd just enjoyed, the taste of the sweet kulfi still on her tongue.

It was the perfect kind of night, the sky fading into a soft indigo, the warm breeze tickling the wind chimes hanging near the door, the air scented with the night jasmine that covered the terrace roof and the incense sticks Bibi burnt to keep away the mosquitos.

Leila flicked through the magazines that Vanessa had given her earlier, having declared that she'd finished with them. One of the perks of the guests staying was that they often gifted her their unwanted possessions – paperbacks, suncream, bikinis (which were always too big), T-shirts, designer sunglasses and hats. Leila collected them all, and from the second she'd spotted glamorous Vanessa, who, apparently, was set to debut on the West End stage in London, she'd been secretly longing for a haul. She hadn't been disappointed. Vanessa had given her three lipsticks and a blue mascara, as well as a sarong and a straw hat. She'd been hoping to get friendly and chat more to Vanessa about her life in London, but she hadn't seen either her or Christopher much. They'd kept themselves to themselves in their guest bungalow, appearing with shining eyes and holding hands, like they were having the best love-in of all time. Although, what beautiful Vanessa saw in balding Christopher, who was clearly twice her age, Leila couldn't begin to understand.

Now, she pored over the glossy pages, fascinated by the glamorous shots of the French actress Isabella Rosellini and that model Cindy Crawford, who Leila had seen before. And yet more shots of Princess Diana, who Leila always felt sorry for. Always having to be on show, when all she probably wanted to do was stay at home and play with her little boys. She wrinkled her nose, looking at all the pictures of the silly pop stars performing for the second Live Aid single. How could it be that people were still starving in Africa? Hadn't they fixed it the first time around? She flicked through some more, bored by the news.

Events on the other side of the world only held so much fascination. It was a comfort to know there was a world going on out there, but Leila was very happy for it not to bother her on Lace Island, although it seemed to be a constant source of worry to Rasa that she wasn't more curious about it.

He was desperate to go away and travel. He didn't stop talking about how he couldn't wait to go to London and New York and Paris. Leila supposed she would see the world all in good time, but when everyone came here and gushed about how wonderful Lace Island was compared to everywhere else, she wasn't in any hurry to go anywhere that wasn't as fascinating. Besides, it would break her heart to leave Bibi and Chan, not to mention her friends.

Mr and Mrs Everdene, who had been sipping Chan's lethal cocktails all night, had now lost their British uptightness. The gramophone was on and Chan was playing his clarinet along with a Chet Baker record, while Tina Everdene was dancing a strange, flailing Charleston-type dance. Leila watched from her corner seat, seeing Chan's clarinet charming her like a snake.

'I never dance,' she called out to Leila. 'But I can't help myself. Isn't your father wonderful?'

Stepfather, Leila wanted to correct her, but she knew she couldn't. 'Yes,' Leila said, and Chan winked at her.

'Come and join in!' Tina held out her hands to Leila, who got to her feet.

She saw Bibi and Teddy Everdene clapping as they danced, but she knew Bibi wouldn't get up and dance herself. She'd never seen her mother dance in public, or let down her reserve, but Leila, who was entranced by the wedding saris in her mother's closet, longed just once to see her do the traditional dancing that she'd done at her wedding to Leila's father all those years ago. That was back in the days when Bibi was in the bosom of her own family, but when she'd married Chan, they'd cut her off, and Bibi never talked about her relatives now.

The record finished and Tina bent forward laughing, her hands on her knees, out of breath. Behind her, the moon was rising like a huge yellow smile. On the dark horizon, the lights from the fishing boats blinked on the gold-black sea.

'Have you ever been somewhere so romantic? Or felt so free? It's just marvellous, Teddy. Marvellous,' Tina said, putting her arms on the balustrade and taking in the view, breathing in the hot night air. 'I can't bear to go home.'

Leila couldn't help but smile. This was often the guests' reaction to Bibi and Chan's hospitality. Suddenly, there was a familiar buzzing and just as Bibi said, 'Not again,' the electricity went out, plunging them into darkness. The needle on the record stopped, the music making a funny dying sound, which Chan finished with a flourish on his clarinet.

'This happens all the time,' Bibi explained. 'Leila?'

Dutifully, Leila fetched the oil lamp, lighting it, so that the party had a warm glow. Now, without the gramophone, the air was filled with familiar night noises – the hypnotic chorus of the nocturnal crickets and the occasional hoot of the forest owls, the chatter of the palm fronds as the breeze tickled through them and, in the background – almost as a secret – the low, gentle whoosh of the sea.

'What a shame,' Tina said to Chan. 'I was enjoying that so much.'

'Well, I can carry on, if you insist.'

Now the clarinet's plaintive air filled the night all around them. Christopher and Vanessa danced slowly together in the corner, staring into each other's eyes, and Tina held her hands together and made a cooing sound as if she'd never seen anything so romantic.

'So tell me,' Tina said, 'if it's not rude to ask, how did you end up living on Lace Island, Bibi?'

'Mummy inherited this island from her grandma,' Leila said, when she saw that Bibi was reluctant to answer. Bibi gave her a sharp look. 'What? It's true.' But she could tell that Bibi was annoyed that she'd shared so much personal information. Trying to get back on track, she continued Bibi's story for her. 'But Mummy was always going to live here. Right from when she was a little girl and used to come here with her grandmother. She has loads of brothers,' Leila confided, 'but they're all horrible, so Grandma decided that Lace Island would pass down the female line.' She said this proudly. Lace Island would be hers one day. It was her birthright and she didn't care who knew it.

'Leila,' Bibi chided. 'Don't be rude.'

'So Bibi lived here with my father and they had me . . .'

Leila saw Tina and Teddy exchange a shocked look. They obviously hadn't realized that Chan wasn't Leila's father. Bibi looked annoyed that she'd brought it up.

'He died. A long time ago,' Bibi said, glaring at Leila. She didn't want Leila to tell the guests that he'd been killed in a shark attack, otherwise they wouldn't go in the sea and their holiday would be ruined.

'Oh, I'm so sorry,' Tina said, putting her hand to her chest.

'Then she met Chan, who came to stay,' Leila said, as a peace offering, 'and they fell in love.'

'I refused to go,' Chan interjected, briefly, before going back to 'Moonlight Serenade'.

'How romantic,' Tina said.

'It is. They really should make a movie. Don't you think this place would make a perfect film set?' Leila said.

'That's enough. You know perfectly well I'm not having any film crews traipsing around here,' Bibi said. 'And now I think it's time for you to go to bed, young lady,' she added.

'But—'

'Go.' There was a moment of silence, then a crackling and the lights came on again. Someone must have turned on the generator in the basement. 'Oh good,' Bibi said, giving Leila one of her stern but affectionate looks. Then she squeezed Leila's hand and patted her face gently, and Leila knew that, as always, she would do as she was told.

Besides, with the lights back on, the magic seemed broken,

and dutifully Leila said goodnight to the guests under Bibi's watchful eye. She kissed Chan and he pinched her nose and winked at her. He knew she liked being part of the grown-up talk.

She dawdled, knowing that as soon as she was out of sight, she'd be out of mind. She wandered down towards the pool, planning to listen from below the balcony, where the night jasmine circled the terrace's struts.

Silently, she sat down on the edge of the pool, dipping her feet in the water. Insects danced, breaking its surface. Leila wondered if she'd get in trouble for stripping off and going for a swim, when Bibi had told her to go to bed. She breathed in and gazed up between the palm trees to where the black sky was glittering with stars.

Above her, she could hear Chan at the bar mixing another drink for Teddy. He'd have another himself, too, no doubt, even though he knew Bibi disapproved of how much alcohol he consumed. But he always said that it greased the wheels and made the guests happy.

'She's certainly a spirited girl,' she heard Teddy say. 'She's clearly very taken with Tina. I hope if we have a child, she'll be just like your Leila.'

'That's kind of you to say. We think she's wonderful, but she's growing up so fast. We have a tutor for her, but I'm not sure it's doing her any good,' Chan replied.

'Why don't you send her to school? There's plenty of good boarding schools in England. In fact, I am a governor for a girls' school in Surrey. I could make some calls. I'm sure I could secure her a place. It's a marvellous girls' school and just what she needs, if you ask me. Tina? Tina, what do you think about Chan and Bibi sending Leila to Hillmain?'

'Oh, Teddy, that's a brilliant idea.'

Leila's heart lurched, her legs stopping in the water.

'We could never afford the fees,' Chan said.

'I could enquire about a bursary. Pull a few strings.'

'We could not possibly ask such a favour,' Chan said. 'What do you think, Bibi? It would make sense, yes? Particularly now, when we're so busy over the spring.'

Leila waited for Bibi to laugh off the suggestion, to give one of thousands of reasons why it would be a bad idea.

'It's halfway through the academic year, surely?' Bibi said.

'That's not a problem. She could start in January. At the start of the term. I know the headmistress. I could send her a fax.'

Leila felt an icicle of dread plummet inside her. They wouldn't send her away. Would they? She stared up between the trees and there, suddenly, she saw a shooting star. Remembering Parva's advice from when she was little, to always wish upon a star, Leila squeezed her eyes shut. *Let me stay on Lace Island for the rest of my life. Please. No matter what. I'll do anything . . .*

CHAPTER SIX

London, present day

Oh God. This was just like a real fire.

Jess heard her breathing loud in her ears, the mask tight over her face, her ears ringing with the fire siren. It was training. *Just training.* She'd probably never be in a fire like this . . . ever. Even so, her heart pounded, knowing that any second, the door to the smoke-filled chamber would open and that she and Claire, her training buddy for today, would both have to crawl inside.

Keep calm, Jess told herself. She had to get through this and the medical, and then she'd have done it. She couldn't fail now.

This was the final module on her training programme and the one that she'd been dreading, although practising the raft evacuation in the freezing drizzle yesterday had been pretty tough. For the past six weeks, she'd been in the classroom for ten hours a day and then racing back to the flat to revise for the module tests, and so far she hadn't failed one. She'd learnt everything from the procedures for opening doors and going into the cockpit to what to do if someone went into labour on a flight, and she'd loved every second.

Jess was determined not to mess this up. She'd written out the trainer's mantras and stuck them to her wall: *I treat everyone as an individual; I do things properly; I look the part.* She was determined to prove she was a team player. And now she was so close to finishing her training, she wanted this more than ever.

She certainly looked the part now, she thought, in her boiler suit and mask. She felt herself sweating under the suit, the blouse of her uniform clinging to her, but she was determined to be strong. Not only for her but for Claire, who had been feeling wobbly all morning.

Poor Claire. She had a terrible hangover from the hen weekend she'd been on, she'd told Jess. Jess had been amazed she'd gone when there was so much revision to do, but Claire had said it was her best friend and she hadn't been able to get out of it. Jess wondered whether she'd have made such a huge sacrifice for Angel, but she couldn't imagine Angel getting married. Not now. Not to Weasel. Besides, Angel had been totally unsupportive throughout this whole training process. The last time they'd spoken, Angel had accused Jess of dumping her – which was rich, all things considered. She hadn't dumped Angel; she'd just embraced a new opportunity, but Angel clearly didn't see it like that.

She tried to read Claire's expression, but she couldn't behind the mask.

'You go in and crawl right through the cabin to the other end,' the instructor was saying. 'There are two dummies to locate like this,' he said, holding up two rubber dolls. 'You'll need to open the door in the dark at the end. You guys ready?'

Jess nodded, and she and Claire stumbled to the door. Then the instructor nodded and backed away and they were on their own.

Jess fumbled with the door into the chamber. Inside, it was entirely filled with smoke. Suddenly, Jess heard a scream behind her.

'What?' she shouted, through her mask.

Claire's eyes were wide with terror. She gripped on to Jess like she was drowning. Her feet were planted on the floor, her knees shaking. 'I can't do it. I can't.'

She began to sob and Jess gripped her shoulders. 'You can.'

'I can't. I can't do it.'

'We have to get to the other end. Just hold on to me, OK?'

Jess got down onto all fours, directing Claire to do the same. It was almost impossible to see anything in front of her. Instead, trying to keep her breathing steady, she progressed forward through the cabin, feeling beneath the seats and on them until she'd located the two dummies. All the while, she could hear Claire sobbing into her mask behind her.

Jess stopped at the far end of the cabin, gripping Claire's upper arms, staring into her eyes through the mask. 'We're nearly there.'

Sweating, she groped forward, opened the complicated aircraft door and slid it open. Pulling Claire through with her, they collapsed on the other side in the training corridor.

Jess pulled off Claire's mask. 'It's OK. It's all over,' she said, giving her a hug.

Claire heaved in a breath before smoothing her blonde hair. Her heavily made-up eyes were smudged.

'Don't say anything, Jess. Please. Don't. They'll fail me if they know what happened.'

Jess nodded, feeling torn, but she could see how desperate Claire was.

'How was that?' their trainer asked, coming into the room.

Jess helped Claire get to her feet.

'No problem,' Claire said.

'Jess?'

'Fine. It was fine. Here,' she said, handing over the dummies. She didn't look at Claire. How could she fake it so convincingly? She'd been having a full-on panic attack just minutes ago.

'Good work, ladies,' he said, putting a tick on the clipboard.

'You're a rock, Jess,' Claire said. 'I owe you one.' She laughed lightly, as if nothing had happened, then walked towards where the others were getting a debriefing in the coffee room.

Jess followed a little way behind, and in the corridor, Mr Spencer, the course leader, stopped her. 'Everything OK, Jess?' he asked.

His eyes bored into hers. Did he know that Claire had panicked? Jess felt her throat go dry, but she couldn't back out of her lie now.

'Sure. It was fine.'

She smiled confidently and then walked away to join the others. She'd get away with the lie. It was more important to back up a mate, wasn't it? And Claire was a mate. All her fellow trainees were. She was part of a team, and Jess would do whatever it took to back them up.

By the end of the week, Jess couldn't keep her rising sense of euphoria down. She'd been told she'd passed all the modules – even the complicated first-aid training. Just one interview more after her medical and she'd be cleared to fly. She couldn't wait to find out where she'd be going first on her practice flight.

Jess smiled at Mr Spencer as she sat down on the other side

of the desk in his office. She stared at the photographs of the training graduates adorning the walls. She was the last of her team to come here for the verdict and could feel her stomach dancing with butterflies.

'So. There's good and bad news.'

'Oh?' Jess wrung her hands in her lap.

'Your friend Claire failed the medical,' he said.

'She did?'

'I'm not at liberty to disclose the details, but she admitted herself that she'd had what she called a very "heavy" weekend.'

The hen weekend. Claire had been going on about her best friend's wedding since the beginning of the course. She wouldn't have taken drugs, would she?

'There were other reasons that she failed her medical. Not least of all her anxiety problem.'

'Oh?'

'You don't have to look like that, Jess. We know what happened in the smoke chamber. Claire told us. And she told us, too, that you covered for her.'

'I—' Jess began, then stopped. She could see from the look on Mr Spencer's face that covering for her had been a bad idea.

'You lied.'

Jess swallowed hard. 'I didn't think . . . I mean—'

'No. You didn't think. And we require all our cabin crew to do just that. To think about the safety of the passengers. If your crew are not up to the job, it's your duty to report it.'

'I know. I'm sorry.'

'Which leaves me with a dilemma,' he said, tapping his pen on the desk. 'You are one of my most promising candidates, but because of what has happened, technically I shouldn't pass you.'

Jess closed her eyes. She should never have lied for Claire.

'Please. Please just give me a chance,' she said. 'It will never happen again. I absolutely promise.'

Mr Spencer sighed. 'This will have to go on your training report.'

'I understand.'

'So you cannot afford to make another mistake.'

'I won't, sir. You'll see.'

CHAPTER SEVEN

Surrey, England, 1990

Leila stood in the lunch queue in the canteen of Hillmain School holding her metal tray, trying not to make eye contact with any of the girls. Even so, she could hear them behind her whispering and she stepped forward, pretending not to notice. Her blisters screamed on her feet in the horrible clumpy school shoes, and her back itched where the shirt and scratchy wool of her blazer rubbed. She wished she could dump her tray and run. But to where?

She still couldn't believe that she was actually here. In England. It felt as if the past week had been a nightmarish blur. She thought about Lace Island constantly, each memory gouging a terrible scar on her heart. It felt so far away, it *was* so far away, that it might as well have been on a different planet. When she'd been told to show where Lace Island was on the giant globe in the geography class earlier, it hadn't even been a tiny pinprick. And now no one believed it even existed.

She shuffled again in the queue, thinking of Bibi and the night she'd announced that she was sending Leila away. Leila had been waiting up for her, convinced that Bibi must have refused the Everdenes' offer, but as she'd slowly sat on the edge of Leila's four-poster bed, Leila had seen the truth in her eyes.

'You can't make me go,' Leila had protested, flinging aside the mosquito nets and staring at Bibi, who didn't seem at all surprised that Leila had eavesdropped on the adults' conversation.

Bibi had smiled gently and reached out to stroke Leila's hair, but Leila had ducked out of the way. She'd been too furious to be touched.

'You are a woman now, my love. And an intelligent one, at that. Don't be afraid of the world. Go out and embrace it.'

'*You* don't. You stay here. Why can't I be like you?'

Her mother had sighed. 'It's for the best.'

'But why? Why now? I'm doing well at my lessons. Well enough at least.'

'Timothy can't teach you about the world. You don't find that in books. You find that out by meeting people. Experiencing new places.'

'I don't want to. I like it here best. What's wrong with that? Why can't I stay here and learn with Rasa?'

'Rasa. Rasa. That's all you ever talk about. It's not healthy for you to have just one friend you do lessons with. And you are both changing. Very soon, things won't be the same.'

'They will,' Leila had exclaimed, unaccountably furious at her mother's insinuations.

'They won't. You are no longer a child, Leila. I should have sent you away long ago, but I couldn't bring myself to let you go. But now it's time.'

'How can you say that? How can you?' Leila had turned away from her mother and flung herself into her pillow and wept.

After that, she'd expected Bibi to relent, but she'd just

become more determined that Leila was going. Chan had helped her pack a trunk, bubbling with falsely cheerful promises, when all the time Leila's heart had been breaking.

Saying goodbye to Rasa had been the worst. As she'd left on the plane with the Everdenes, he'd arrived, out of breath on his bike, to see her one last time. She'd watched him through the small porthole, his eyes boring into hers, and she'd known that as painful as it was to her to leave, it was even more painful for him to have to stay.

She'd slumped into a tearful depression, hardly taking in the long, uncomfortable flights, or the busy train station in London. Tina had gushed all the way about what a wonderful time she'd have, how she'd make friends she'd have for life, but when Teddy Everdene had dropped her off at the school, Leila had known he was glad to see the back of her and that all their promises had been lies.

Because it was hell here. She didn't understand what was expected of her – only that she was continually in the wrong place at the wrong time. Most of the lessons had gone completely over her head, and as for friends? That was a joke. Everyone was treating her like she was some kind of freak. Nobody seemed to believe her about Lace Island, or how special it was. Instead, they called her names and teased her.

Now, she walked level to the canteen hatch. Her stomach was growling, but it turned as she looked at the food on offer. How did people eat this stuff? She longed for Anjum's dosas, and the idli and sambhar he made especially for her. What she wouldn't give to be in the kitchen at home now, with its cool marble slab and the smell of ginger and nutmeg.

'Look, it's the darkie,' she heard the one with the grey teeth say to the fat one. 'No foreign curry here, love. Have some proper English stew.'

Leila fought down her sense of injustice at their all-too-familiar casual racism, as the dinner lady deposited some grey-looking gristle in gravy on her plate. As they laughed at her, she longed to hurl her tray at them. How dare they speak to her like that?

But she knew it was useless. And she knew that if she didn't eat this, then like the last few nights, she'd be so hungry it would be impossible to sleep.

Not that sleeping was easy in the freezing dormitory. She was in the cubicle that nobody wanted, nearest the house-mistress's office. Mrs Gorrall had a ferocious reputation and had thankfully largely ignored Leila so far, but it seemed that certain rules were for some of the pupils and not for others. Edwina, for example, was queen bee in their dormitory and never got into trouble for whispering late into the night with her friends, whereas Mrs Gorrall had confiscated Leila's book when she'd caught her reading past lights-out. She'd been enjoying the book, too.

Miserably, Leila moved on and then collected a black-cherry yoghurt and a glass of orange squash before surveying the long lines of wooden tables where the girls sat opposite each other, chatting. She couldn't understand why they laughed at her behind their hands. Was it something she was doing? Or wearing? On Lace Island, she'd always been accepted and loved by everyone. Even the guests who came were friendly to her, so what had changed? What was so wrong with her?

She walked towards a table of some of the younger girls in the year below, smiling shyly, but they shifted up to close the gap where she could sit. Pretending not to notice, she moved on, spotting an empty table on the far side of the hall.

She sat down alone, staring at the yellow dumpling float-ing in the stew, feeling the girls' stares on her back. And then she noticed Edwina, Elaine and Georgina, the bitchy girls from her dorm, walking down the canteen towards her, in formation. She could see the intent blazing in Edwina's eyes, but she ignored it.

Edwina swung her leg over the bench opposite Leila, and Georgina and Elaine sat either side of Leila, who shifted uncomfortably. What did they want? Why were they crowding her?

Edwina was blonde with freckles over her nose and was wearing a metallic-pink lipstick and blue eyeshadow that clashed with her brown eyes. Her school shirt was unbuttoned one button too low in order to display her ample cleavage.

'You not speaking?' Edwina demanded. 'You mute or something? Cat got your tongue?'

Leila felt fear ripple through her.

'Please leave me alone.'

Edwina laughed loudly, doing an impression of Leila. '"Please leave me alone."' Elaine and Georgina joined in too.

Now Edwina took some photographs out of her pocket and put them on the table. Leila's heart contracted, recognizing the photos straight away. They were from her diary. They were the only pictures she had of home. Of Rasa and her friends. Edwina must have been into her cupboard and found her diary. How dare she?

'Look at this one. He your boyfriend, is he?' Edwina taunted. 'Is he from *The Jungle Book*?'

'Look, he's wearing a dress,' Georgina added.

Edwina picked up the photograph of Rasa in his white dhoti, putting it to her lips and smearing her lipstick over it, pretending to kiss it. Her eyes danced with contempt over the top of it.

Leila launched herself across the table, trying to get the

photo from Edwina, but she dodged out of the way, ripping the photo in two. Leila grabbed Edwina's long ponytail and yanked it so hard she fell backwards off the bench, taking Leila with her. Leila found herself on the floor on top of Edwina. She could hear the shocked hush ripple around the room.

'Uh-oh. You just made a big mistake,' Edwina taunted, delighted. Then she flipped Leila over and punched her in the face.

CHAPTER EIGHT

Switzerland, present day

Jess rearranged the bottles on the duty-free cart, enjoying the sensation of making it look perfect. She liked this part of the flight best, when the meal was over and everyone was excited about landing. So far today, everything had gone well, and now, over fifty flights in, Jess was getting the hang of being cabin crew.

It was like being on stage. And with each new journey she felt like she really was shedding her old self. She'd stopped apologizing for flunking school, stopped making excuses about her age and all the failed jobs she'd had up until now. Instead, she behaved like the other crew did: like she deserved this.

And OK, yes, there were annoying things about the job, like the fact that she said hello and goodbye to each of the passengers on the way in and out, yet only a handful returned the favour or thanked her. Or the out-of-control kids who repeatedly pressed the service-call button, or the people who tugged on her skirt as she walked past to get her attention, but Jess didn't mind at all. Despite the long hours and the fact that she hadn't had time to go to the gym once, Jess knew that this was absolutely what she wanted to do for the rest of her life.

Tony had been right. Being thirty-five thousand feet in the air was keeping her out of trouble. At least, it was keeping her away from Angel, which is what mattered most.

Glancing out of the tiny window, Jess could see the Alps glistening with snow way down in the distance. She pictured all the people skiing down there, all the families like the ones in the cabin behind her. Nice middle-class families who didn't have to deal with crack-addict flatmates.

Jess had been doing this route to Geneva for just over a month now, but she'd never had the chance to stop over long enough to get to the slopes. The thought of whooshing down a mountain appealed to her, just because she'd never done anything like it in her life. Maybe on this stopover, she could find a way. Although maybe not with Gina. She didn't look like the adventurous type, Jess thought, glancing across at her colleague.

'You ready?' Jess asked.

'Yep. Coming now,' Gina replied, her eyes not leaving the magazine.

Jess had met girls like Gina on the crews she'd worked with before. Life for Gina-types was simple, Jess concluded. She was here to cruise the aisles in the hope that one day, a husband might appear in seats A to F. Jess was sure that like lots of the other stewardesses, the second she landed, Gina would be straight on the dating apps on her phone, swiping to annihilate or approve potential hook-ups. It all seemed so brutal to Jess. Like sex and love were commodities.

What happened to old-fashioned romance? And not sleeping with someone on the first date? Sex was great, but surely there was so much more to life than that?

'What's so interesting?' Jess asked.

Gina was shorter than Jess, her hair tied up in a blonde

bun. She smelt overpoweringly of the latest Armani perfume as Jess leant in and looked over her shoulder down at the magazine.

'Look at her, there,' Gina said, pointing a manicured nail at the picture of an American celebrity's latest surgical enhancement.

'Why do people do that?' Jess said. 'She used to be so pretty.'

'It's because she's rich.'

'If I was rich, I certainly wouldn't do that to my face,' Jess said.

'Well, you wouldn't have to, would you?' Gina replied. 'You're pretty as you are. Actually, she reminds me a bit of you,' Gina said, in her Essex accent, remembering the job at hand and walking to the trolley, smoothing her uniform pencil skirt over her hips. 'Not now, but before,' she added kindly. 'She's got that "every girl" thing going on. You know, not European or South American or Asian. I'm not being racist or nothing, but she's sort of in between. Like, um . . . what's her name?'

Jess frowned and smiled, bemused at Gina's backhanded compliment.

Gina rolled her eyes. 'Can't remember. It'll come to me. Where are your parents from, anyway?'

Jess was saved from making up a lie by Duncan, their senior cabin-crew officer, who appeared round the grey curtain. 'Will you two stop gassing and get on with it?' he said, flipping the curtain to the side and fastening it with poppers.

Gina and Jess shared a look. He'd been in a mood since they'd come on board. He had a sheen of sweat on his balding head.

'They are a right bunch today,' he told them, in his strong

Scottish accent. 'I don't know what you gave out earlier, but the guy in twenty-seven is drunk. Watch out.'

Jess looked at Gina again, who gave her a shrug. Neither of them could remember serving the guy. Together, they headed down the narrow aisle between the passengers. Gina could certainly turn on the charm, Jess noticed, and before long, they'd clocked up several good sales between them.

Then Jess heard a slurred voice and she turned to see a man standing three-quarters of the way down the cabin. His arm swung out towards her. The drunk in twenty-seven. Duncan hadn't been kidding. The guy was off his head, Jess noticed, and upsetting the polite passengers around him.

'Hurry it up. I need a drink,' the guy shouted again. Jess, sensing the discomfort of all the passengers around her now, quickly directed Gina to push the trolley further down the aisle so that she could position herself next to the guy.

'Sir, sir, could you please sit down?' He had a tattoo on his neck and a rough crew cut, but Jess wasn't fazed. Where she came from, drunk guys like him were a common sight. They didn't usually get their act together to board an aeroplane, though.

She leant towards him. Alcohol fumes were thick around his head, like a swarm of bees. 'Please sir, sit down.'

Something about her stare subdued him and he sat back down. Gina poured a whisky and Jess topped it up heavily with water.

'What a prick,' Gina said, as they passed to the end of the cabin. 'Hang on, we're out of hot water,' she said, picking up the jug. 'I'll go.' She pulled the cart into the far galley so that she could get past and set off up the aisle. Alone now, Jess re-arranged the cart, checking the money was safe and tipping it from the plastic cup into the tray in the cart.

Just then, she heard someone behind her. It was the drunk guy. She turned just as his hand groped between her legs from behind.

'You want it, don't you?' he slurred.

Jess knew there were protocols, but she ignored them now, gut instinct kicking in. In a second, she'd elbowed the guy in the ribs, then smacked him backwards. She watched, horrified, as he fell away from her, flailing, before hitting his head on the unit and falling to the floor.

Jess gasped. She stared at the man who'd just come out of the toilet cubicle. He looked at her and then at the drunk man flat out on the floor. Then suddenly Gina was there, bustling past him.

'What did you do?' Gina asked, her hand flying to her mouth.

'He . . . I didn't mean . . .' Jess said, crouching down near the man.

Duncan was walking down the aisle now, having sensed the commotion. 'What's going on here?'

'That fucking bitch. She fucking punched me,' the man said, glaring at Jess, who recoiled. 'I'm going to sue you. I'm going to sue you and this airline. That is grievous bodily harm.'

'Watch it, son,' Duncan said.

'He groped me,' Jess explained to Duncan, outraged. 'I was defending myself.'

'She's lying,' the drunk guy said, and Jess stared at him, seeing his eyes glinting with malice. He was enjoying this. Enjoying having the upper hand.

'This is not how we deal with things,' Duncan told Jess very pointedly, doing up the poppers on the curtain to shield the man from the curious passengers.

'But—'

'When we land, you will have to fill out a report.'

'But I—'

'She's new, I take it?' the drunk guy said. 'That bitch is out. And you – you'd better call a paramedic for when we land. I think I've got a spine injury.'

CHAPTER NINE

Surrey, 1990

As the school secretary opened the large white door to the headmistress's office, Leila sniffed, dabbing her swollen cheekbone with the icy green kitchen roll the school matron had given her. She stumbled forwards into the large room, with its thick yellow carpet covered in part by a plastic runner – presumably to stop the pupils' feet marking it. There were ornately framed oil paintings of hunting scenes on most of the walls, as well as a large bookcase full of old red and green leather-bound books. Through the bay windows between their heavy gold curtains, Leila could see the rain plopping into puddles on the Cotswolds-stone terrace. Beyond the fat stone balustrade, a green carpet of lawn gave way to playing fields. In the distance, she could see two teams of girls playing lacrosse. The muffled sound of the game and the girls' gruff shouting was just audible, along with a shrill whistle. The games teacher, Miss Sussman, had laughed in Leila's face when she'd politely enquired whether there was a cricket team at Hillmain. She'd been told that cricket was for boys.

She directed her attention to the desk, as the headmistress rose from her seat, hoping that she would be sympathetic, hoping that after she'd heard the truth, she'd discipline Edwina and her awful friends. But Mrs Grayson-Smith wasn't a friendly sort of person.

She had a pinched, pale face that looked like it had rarely either seen the sun or laughed at a good joke. She had powdered cheeks, and a double set of pearls were visible at the high neck of her frilly white blouse. She was wearing a brown tweed suit with large shoulder pads and half-moon glasses on the end of her nose, which she peered through at Leila now.

'I know I'm in trouble,' Leila began, 'but—'

'Young lady' – Mrs Grayson-Smith took off her glasses and fixed Leila with a laser-beam stare – 'you will wait until you're spoken to. And if you will insist on talking, you can address me properly. As "Headmistress",' she continued, momentarily closing her eyes and doing a kind of head-wobble shudder as if having to lower herself to cover such basics was a disgrace. 'And you'd be much better off losing that foreign accent of yours,' Mrs Grayson-Smith said. 'We try to speak the Queen's English here, and you sound, well . . . odd.'

'I'll do my best,' Leila said, trying to put on a proper English accent, but it felt all wrong. Like she was doing an impersonation of someone uptight and weird. Or like she was doing a skit for Rasa, telling him a joke on the porch of his hut on the far side of the paddy field. She held the image in her head. Of the bright green sun-drenched paddy fields of home.

The headmistress glared at her, as if she thought Leila were being sarcastic, and then she sat down in her chair. Leila heard a low growl and saw a small white terrier stretch in a basket on the far side of the desk. It plodded out from on top of its blue cushion and barked at Leila, who recoiled.

'Mortimer, sit back down right now,' Mrs Grayson-Smith snapped, in a voice so terrifying the dog whimpered and skulked back to its basket, casting a mournful glance at Leila. 'Well,' she concluded. She looked towards Leila and then at the dog, as if it had made some kind of character decision about Leila with which she now wholeheartedly agreed.

She took a deep breath, as if trying to control her patience. 'So . . .' she began, 'how do you explain yourself?'

'It should be Edwina who is in here in trouble, not me, Headmistress,' Leila protested. 'She started it.'

'First of all, I will not tolerate snitches,' the headmistress snapped. 'Secondly, I will not tolerate violence in my school. I heard you behaved like a savage *beast*. In the canteen. In front of all the girls.'

'I didn't. I—'

The headmistress held up her hand. 'I can see very well now why the Everdenes were so adamant that you be educated and turned into a proper lady, although on current form, I think that may well be impossible.'

'You don't understand,' Leila protested. 'Edwina stole my things. She's just a bully.'

'Edwina is one of our most promising pupils,' Mrs Grayson-Smith snapped, her bust rearing up. 'As I said,' she continued, 'I will not tolerate snitches. That will not help you to fit in. If I were you, I would seriously consider changing your attitude.'

Why wouldn't the headmistress listen to her? Didn't she want to know the truth? Leila simply couldn't understand why she wasn't being given a chance. Bibi had always listened to her. Always been fair. But this horrible woman wasn't even giving her the opportunity to tell her side of things.

'Do you realize how lucky you are that we've offered you a place at this school? Because I have to tell you that here at Hillmain, we have a long heritage of educating real princesses,' the headmistress continued before Leila had a chance to speak. She emphasized the word 'real' pointedly, as if she didn't believe that Leila's mother was descended from a maharaja at all, or that Leila was in any way special.

'And do you know how we do that so very successfully?' she asked. Leila sensed it was another rhetorical question. She shook her head meekly. 'I'll tell you, young lady. It is by treating everyone equally. If you remember that and you stay in your place, then I'm sure we can furnish you with an education. Dismissed.'

Leila rubbed her palms on her skirt and rose. 'I think you're being very unfair. You can't see what's going on in this school underneath your nose. Edwina is a bully, and as for everyone being treated equally—'

'I said, dismissed,' the headmistress said pointedly.

'You know, if you want to expel me, it's fine,' Leila said. The words were out before she could stop them. But she meant them. It was true. 'All I want is to go home.'

The headmistress fixed her with a beady eye. 'Then that's exactly what you *won't* be doing. And, Leila? Don't ever answer back again.'

Outside the headmistress's office, Leila felt her knees shaking and she let out a stifled sob. She'd hoped the headmistress would listen to sense, would see Leila's point of view and how unfairly she'd been treated, but instead Leila had made an enemy of her too. And now she had no idea how to fix it.

Did she mean it? About Leila not going home? For how long? What if she was stuck here, in this prison, forever?

She noticed a girl in the corridor studying the long rows of school photos. She turned when she heard Leila and pulled a lollypop from her mouth. She had a mass of frizzy ginger hair and freckles over the bridge of her nose.

'She give you a roasting?' the girl asked, and Leila nodded, trying to hide her tears. She turned her head away, unable to face another girl being mean, but she didn't seem to be going away. She walked closer and put her hand on Leila's arm. 'You just got to learn to play the system.'

'But how?' Leila asked desperately.

'Read books about sex and play lacrosse,' the girl said matter-of-factly. 'That's what the popular girls do. Not that I care. I'm just marking time in this shithole until I can get a break in the music business. I sing,' she said. 'Follow me.' She quickly started to walk away and Leila took a deep breath, wondering whether to trust her or not.

The girl stopped and turned. 'Come on,' she said, flicking her head. 'I know where Edwina put your photos. I'm Judith, by the way. Let's go nick your stuff back from that bitch.'

CHAPTER TEN

Switzerland, present day

The bar in the Geneva hotel was crowded, the air warm and heavy. Jess almost lost her nerve and retreated back to the lift, but she really didn't want to be alone in that soulless room, and she was too stressed out to watch TV. Anyway, she'd had an Instagram from Gina of the drink that was waiting for her. She glanced around the plush bar. In the far corner, a frizzy-haired woman in a blue sequinned dress was singing jazz standards, accompanied by a guy playing a shiny grand piano.

It was all so civilized and nice, but already Jess felt that this whole scene had slipped away from her. That she was watching herself from the corner of the room.

She stepped out of the way as a couple walked past her.

'The bus to get to the lift for the beginners' slopes leaves at nine,' the man was saying. 'The hotel said they'll lend us boots and jackets and skis, and organize a day pass.'

Jess considered what she'd overheard as she continued through the bar. This was probably her one and only chance ever to make it to the ski slopes, but it was already too late. She'd blown it. Tomorrow, she'd been told, she'd most likely be out of a job.

Gina was sitting over by the fireplace on the sofa, flicking her long blonde hair over her slight shoulders. She was with people Jess had never seen before, but even out of uniform, it was obvious that they were cabin crew and, from some of their faces as Jess approached, that she had been the subject of their discussions.

'Over here,' Gina called, and Jess waved.

One of the guys stared at her and budged up on the sofa to make room for her, but Jess deliberately ignored his advance. There was no way she'd even consider getting together with someone she worked with. Instead, she perched on the arm of Gina's leather armchair.

'Here's your drink,' Gina added, pressing a sweating glass of clear liquid into Jess's hand. 'I bet you need it after that.'

'Cheers,' Jess said gratefully, raising her glass to the assembled group.

'I was just saying how brave you were,' Gina gushed. 'You don't mind us talking. We are like family after all,' Gina said, justifying her gossiping.

Jess tried to smile, wanting to believe that the group of strangers were 'like family', but they weren't. And certainly not the kind of family she needed right now. She missed Angel. If only they were speaking, then Jess would have rung her up and told her everything. Angel would have been on her side. But Angel didn't care less, she remembered. She'd probably be thrilled that Jess had been brought back down to earth with a bump.

She looked around the group now settled on sofas and chairs round the cluster of low tables that were crammed with empty glasses. She recognized the looks on the faces of the heavily made-up girls and the perfectly preened boys. Girls who were up for fun and easy sex. Girls who had one eye out in the busy hotel bar for someone to pique their interest. But still, they were a tribe, and Jess so desperately wanted to be one of them.

'You should have seen her, though,' Gina said, leaning towards the girls across the table. 'She was amazing. Totally kicked his ass.'

'So . . . what happened?' one of the girls asked.

Jess glanced between her and Gina, who was several gin and tonics down by the looks of things and locked in with the crew for the evening. It was nice that she'd earned Gina's respect and the other girls were impressed, but it didn't matter now. Not after what the captain had said: about her being inexperienced and dangerous. About how some people – i.e. her – just weren't cut out for the job. That her training record showed that she had problems with the truth. That was the part that had outraged Jess the most.

Jess thought back to Captain McVeigh's red face and his thinning auburn hair. He was clearly a man who was used to being in charge, and it had taken all of Jess's self-control not to answer back. She wasn't going to start bitching about him now. She wouldn't give him that power.

'It was nothing. Just had to fill in some forms so they cover themselves if they get sued,' Jess lied, flapping her hand and taking a slurp of her drink through the straw. Vodka. A strong one. She didn't usually drink, but the burn of the liquid felt welcome now. 'It'll all blow over.'

'Thank God for that. I thought Captain McVeigh was on the warpath,' Gina said.

'I've flown with him before,' one of the girls said, leaning forward conspiratorially. 'He's a right one for inappropriate hands, if you know what I mean. And a drinker, they say.'

Jess tuned out as they continued gossiping, draining her

drink. She offered to buy another round, walking numbly over to the bar to order.

She stared over at a family who had clearly just come in from the slopes. A man with blond hair was in a light blue ski suit, which complemented his tanned face. A blond boy of about eight was next to him, and the man bent down and spoke quietly to him, before nodding over in Jess's direction.

'Just give Daddy one moment. I'll be there in a sec,' Jess heard him say. Then he moved round the bar towards her. 'I was on the flight this afternoon,' the man explained.

'Oh,' Jess said, embarrassed. He was the guy in the loo. She recognized him now.

'I saw what he did. That man, I mean. I was impressed by how you dealt with it. If it had been me, I'd have flattened him too.'

'That's nice of you to say, but try telling my boss that,' Jess said, with a self-deprecating smile.

The man narrowed his eyes. 'Yes, I couldn't help noticing as we left the plane that there was some . . . form-filling?' he guessed. 'I could tell them I saw what happened, if that would help?'

'You're very kind,' Jess said, 'but I doubt it would make any difference. There were protocols I broke, apparently.' She felt unexpected tears welling up. Caught up in the man's kind stare, she felt the anguish that she might lose her job and everything she'd worked so hard for doubling.

'Well, listen, I run a recruitment business in London. Here,' the man said, as he dug a wallet out of the pocket of his ski jacket and fumbled inside for a card. He handed it over. Jess took the card and read the embossed gold words on it. *Andrew Browning, CEO.*

'I do a fair bit of work with some of the bigger airlines,

and I should imagine that if I put a word in, I could certainly help you out if you felt you wanted a different position?'

Jess stared at him, hardly daring to take in what he was saying.

'I'm not promising anything, of course,' he added.

'No, of course. I'm very grateful,' Jess said.

'I think common sense should prevail, don't you?' Andrew Browning asked. 'Give me a call . . . ?'

'Oh, Jess. I'm Jess.'

'Jess,' he said, with a smile.

'Thank you. And thank you for this,' she said, holding up the card.

'I'll be back in London next week. Let's talk then.'

After the encounter with Andrew Browning, Jess's mood lightened and she joined in with the others, enjoying their anecdotes and the sense of camaraderie, as they bitched about passengers. Soon, the others had decided to go into town to a nightclub, but having spent all of her money on drinks, Jess said she was going to bed.

As she was making her way to the lift, however, she saw the captain from the flight earlier across the bar. Captain McVeigh. And he'd clearly been drinking. She sped up when she made eye contact, her pulse quickening when she saw that he'd got up and was following her to the lift. Jess jumped into the open lift ahead of him, but just when the lift was closing, the captain's hand stopped the door at the last moment. He grinned at her, his eyes cold, as they were suddenly alone in the lift together. In a moment, they were travelling up.

Jess squeezed her hands together, feeling embarrassed.

'You know, it was a shame about today. You're a very pretty girl,' the captain said.

Jess's eyes widened, amazed that he'd said something so forward.

'You know, I *could* make all this nasty business go away,' he whispered, moving in closer towards her and rubbing his finger up her arm. 'Why don't we go to my room to discuss it?'

Jess stared at him, astonished at his proposition. She flicked his arm away. 'Did you not listen earlier? I do kick-boxing.'

The captain laughed. 'Yes, but you can't assault *me*. I'm your captain.'

'You think I'm going to have sex with you?'

'Why not? That's what the others do to get ahead. You've got to learn to . . . let's say . . . practise diplomacy . . . if you want to get anywhere. Come on,' he said, in a cajoling tone. 'You're hot. And I like a bit of mixed-race pussy occasionally.'

'Oh, man,' Jess said, looking up at the ceiling, knowing the shitstorm she was in had just got a whole lot worse. 'You just messed with the wrong girl.'

CHAPTER ELEVEN

Surrey, 1990

'Flush it again,' Leila heard before Edwina pushed her head roughly into the toilet bowl.

'Stop,' she choked, as the water gurgled all around her, filling her ears and nose. She squeezed her eyes shut, trying not to think about the disgusting skid marks on the bowl, only concentrating on not breathing. She flailed, trying to hit Edwina behind her as the water flooded around her. Instead, she hit Georgina, who, as ever, was Edwina's accomplice.

Finally, when she could bear it no longer, her head was suddenly jerked back, clear of the bowl.

'What's going on in here?'

Leila gulped, water streaming down her face, her knees burning from being on the cold vinyl floor, her chest hurting from where she'd been pressed against the porcelain toilet bowl.

Edwina froze, Leila's ponytail gripped firmly in her hand, her eyes blazing, as they both listened to Mrs Gorrall, the housemistress. Her eyes flicked down at Leila's, daring her to make a sound, then up to Georgina's, who now looked terrified.

'Nothing, miss,' Edwina said, her voice sweet.

'Who's in there with you?'

'Just Leila, miss. She's got a few tummy problems again. Can't get used to the food. I'm looking after her.'

Leila sneered at Edwina, hating her with every fibre of her body.

'Well, hurry it up, you two. It's lights-out in two minutes.'

They waited, hearing the door close; then Edwina let go of Leila's hair, before shoving her head roughly towards the bowl.

'Don't you ever touch my things again,' Edwina snarled, her beauty-queen good looks bent into an ugly scowl.

'I didn't. I told you,' Leila lied.

Edwina ignored her, turning on her heel and marching out of the cubicle, followed by Georgina, who did a copycat sneer down at Leila.

'Clear up the mess you've made,' Georgina said. 'Before Gorrall sees. There's water everywhere.'

Then she was gone, the cubicle door banging. Leila slumped back under the toilet-roll holder, pulling down some tissue to wipe her face. Her pyjamas and dressing gown were soaked through. She ineffectually balled up the loo roll and mopped up the puddles of water on the floor, trying to ignore the stench. She felt herself wretch, toilet water still caught in her throat. She leant forward and heaved over the bowl, but nothing came out, just a choked sob.

It had been another bog flush, but it was worth it to have annoyed Edwina so much. And she'd done it. She'd successfully rummaged beneath the colour-coordinated stack of Benetton jumpers in Edwina's cubicle and stolen the cigarettes. And, as everyone knew in this place, cigarettes were the only currency worth anything.

She got up and made it out of the toilet and tipped the

tissues angrily in the bin. Then she washed her face, dunking her head under the tap, feeling the tepid water on her neck.

'Are you OK?' Judith whispered, sticking her head round the door. She handed her a clean towel. Leila took it, then piled her head up in a towel turban and took a breath, looking at Judith in the mirror. She nodded and pulled a triumphant grimace.

'Well done,' Judith said with a grin, and Leila knew it had all been worth it.

Twenty minutes later, after lights-out, Leila crept along the dorm to Judith's cubicle. She glanced behind her, but Edwina's end of the dorm was quiet. Further along the corridor the other way, the TV in Gorrall's room threw blue shadows up the wall.

Judith was waiting for her.

'Here,' she said, 'help me move this.'

Together, they shifted Judith's bed as silently as they could. On the wall behind it, Judith picked at one of the corners of the tongue and groove, the section came away, and there was a grille on the other side. Carefully, Judith unwound the screws holding the grille and pushed it away from her. Kneeling on all fours, she stuck her head through the hole, then came back in.

'All clear,' she said.

Nervously, Leila shuffled into the small space behind the bed and through the hole into the school corridor. How often had Judith used this route to leave the dorm? she wondered. And what about the others? Did they all escape while Leila was in bed? She was starting to get a sense of a whole other tier of school life she'd never imagined.

'Hang on, I've got to put the grille back,' Judith hissed, as she followed Leila onto the scuffed carpet of the corridor.

She put the grille back, and Leila stood up, getting her bearings. The weak security lights at the end of the corridor flickered. Leila pressed herself against the wall, her heart pounding. She'd never done anything this naughty in her life.

'Come on. The fire escape is this way,' Judith said, setting off at a tiptoe run along the brown vinyl floor. Leila followed, watching as she pressed down on the heavy fire-exit bar, which gave way. Then they hurried out onto the top of the metal fire escape.

Leila felt the cool night air snake beneath her nightdress, but she was warm with exhilaration. She looked out at the playing fields, which were shimmering with a light dew in the moonlight, and her breath caught in a cloud.

Leila grabbed Judith's arm and nodded to where the gym door opened.

'Sussman,' Judith whispered. 'She's on patrol. Don't let her see you.'

They waited, seeing the games teacher walking along the path towards them, and slunk back into the shadows. When she passed beneath them, Judith nodded at Leila.

'Come on. Up here,' Judith said, and they climbed up towards the roof.

Leila checked the pocket of her fleece dressing gown to make sure the cigarettes were still there.

Safely up on the roof, they sat down, looking out onto the whole school, bathed in silvery moonlight.

'We did it,' Leila said, taking the packet of Marlboro cigarettes and offering them to Judith. 'That was close with Sussman.'

'You don't want to get caught by her,' Judith agreed.

'She gives me the creeps.'

'So she should,' Judith shrugged. 'Every school has a perv, and she's ours. She touches up all the pretty girls.'

Leila was shocked. 'Why doesn't anyone say anything?'

'You can't. Grayson-Smith is in cahoots. Last girl who complained was gone. Poof. Just like that. Out of the building in less than ten minutes.'

Leila shook her head, reeling from this latest titbit of school injustice.

Her hands trembled as she flicked the red plastic lighter. She'd seen Chan smoke all her life, but before now, it had never occurred to her to do it herself. But this was the only way to secure Judith's friendship, and seeing her inhale, Leila knew that all the danger, the bog flush, everything had been worth it to finally have a friend.

She inhaled, the smoke making her choke.

'Take it in your mouth like this,' Judith said, instructing, and Leila followed as best she could. Judith smiled. 'You'll get the hang of it.'

Leila concentrated hard, determined to get the smoking thing right. She couldn't imagine what Bibi would say if she could see her now. Or Rasa, for that matter. They'd both be horrified that she was smoking up on the roof and breaking all the rules, but they didn't know what it was like in this hellhole. If taking up smoking was what it took to survive, then that's what she'd have to do.

'So come on, then,' Judith said. 'Tell me about this private island of yours.'

Leila coughed, then muffled another cough, as Judith blew a perfect smoke ring into the night sky. Grateful for an excuse to talk and not have to smoke, she began. She told Judith all about Bibi and her father dying and how Bibi had married

Chan. She told her about her friends and playing cricket in the coconut grove and about the guests too.

'Do you get anyone famous?'

'I guess so. They don't act like they're famous when they're with us.'

'It sounds very glamorous.'

'It's glorious,' Leila said, with a sigh. She didn't know whether Judith believed her or not, so she added, 'Maybe you'll get to go there with me one day.'

Judith gave her a strange look and Leila realized she'd overstepped the boundary of their friendship. They were silent for a while; then they fell into talking about Edwina and Judith suddenly became animated. Edwina was, after all, her favourite subject. But Leila felt sad that she didn't want to hear more about Lace Island, and talking about it had just made her more homesick than ever.

'You know that Georgina lost her cherry to her brother's best friend at a party at the Hurlingham Club.'

'Her cherry?'

'Her virginity. You know, sex.'

'Oh.'

'She said it was amazing. That's why Edwina likes her so much. Because Georgina tells her what she gets up to and takes her to all the best parties. They've got tickets to the Gatecrasher Ball in London, and Georgina has already been fixed up with an earl's son. She's definitely going to do it with him, she says,' Judith said.

'But she's only fourteen. Isn't it illegal?'

Judith laughed at her. 'Don't be silly. Everyone has sex. That's the only way to be popular.'

'Have you had sex?' Leila asked incredulously.

'No. But I probably will in the Easter holidays,' she said matter-of-factly.

Leila inhaled on her cigarette, digesting this information. Since she'd been at Hillmain, she'd learnt all sorts of facts about sex that had shocked her. She only had the most basic knowledge from Bibi about the birds and the bees, but now she was starting to see that sex was an elaborate game that adults played. And she had a lot to learn.

'Who with?'

'My brother's friend Harry.'

'Does he know?' Leila asked.

'Of course. Anyway, he's a boy. Boys think about sex all the time.'

Leila thought of Rasa. Did he think about sex all the time? And if so, with whom? With her?

She inhaled the cigarette smoke. 'Do you think it will hurt?' Leila asked. 'You know. The first time?'

Judith shrugged. 'Don't care. I just want it done. Then I can be in the club.'

Leila nodded, admiring how pragmatic she was, but she couldn't quite bring herself to embrace Judith's approach. Surely sex was supposed to be magical and amazing? She thought back to the very old book of Kama Sutra engravings in the mahogany sideboard in the dining room back at Lace Island and how she and Rasa had giggled over them as children. But that seemed a very long time ago now.

The memory of Rasa's face filled Leila's mind. What would he say, she wondered, if he could hear this conversation? She'd always known he'd hungered for experience, but did he know she hungered for experience now too? What would happen, she wondered, if she told him how she really felt?

CHAPTER TWELVE

London, present day

In the kick-boxing gym, Tony held the red leather cylinder as Jess punched it with all her might.

'So what did you do?' he asked, his thick eyebrows furrowing together.

'I did what you trained me to do. Gave him a hefty.' She smacked the cylinder hard. 'In the bollocks. He won't be accosting too many more cabin crew anytime soon.'

'And they fired you for that?'

'No. I didn't mention it. They' – she punched again, thinking of the letter from the airline in her bag – 'fired me' – she felt her muscles screaming – 'for assaulting a passenger.'

'OK, that's enough,' Tony said. 'Take a breather.'

Tony gripped Jess's shoulder as she stood up, her chest heaving. She ripped the Velcro on her boxing glove with her teeth and set her hand free. Tony undid the other glove for her. She'd hoped a good session in the gym would make her feel better and release some of the anger, but it hadn't. She felt wrung out and exhausted but just as bitter.

'Here,' Tony said, lifting up the water bottle and squirting some into Jess's mouth. She gulped at it greedily.

'I don't know. Maybe I *should* have had sex with him. Saved my job.'

'No. You did the right thing. He's a scumbag. You should report him.'

'And who's going to believe me? Not after the passenger incident. And my training record. It's just not fair.'

Tony laughed wryly. 'When did you think life was ever fair? Who told you it would be?' he countered in a familiar mantra. 'You make your own way, kid. That's it.'

'But after everything. All that work. I'm fired. I hardly got going. Maybe it's me. Maybe I'm not cut out for—'

'Listen to me and listen good,' Tony interrupted, his brow furrowing again. 'You don't give up. You've hit a setback, but think. There must be a way.'

Jess wiped her face and told Tony about the guy who'd given her his card.

'But he was posh. I mean seriously posh.'

'So? You can scrub up with the best of them. Call him,' Tony said, fixing her with one of his firm stares. 'Take a risk. It may just pay off.'

'He was only being nice. He's a stranger.'

'Stop being so suspicious of everyone. He's a businessman. He wouldn't have given you his card if he hadn't meant it.'

'But—'

'Have a little faith in yourself, Jess. You know what you want. Where you're headed. Make it happen.'

'OK. You're right.' She nodded and Tony squeezed the top of her arm.

'That's my girl.'

The next morning, Jess jolted on the Tube as it came to a stop, hating the feeling of the hostile passengers around her. She stared at the playlist she was listening to on the phone in her hand, but the light-hearted hip hop filling her head through the buds in her ears couldn't stop her feeling anxious. After Tony's pep talk yesterday, she'd called Andrew Browning's office and they'd given her an appointment for first thing today.

She tried to ignore everyone around her as the Tube stopped and more passengers boarded, cramming her in even more tightly. She got out at Oxford Circus, finding herself trapped in the crowd pushing up the stairs. She hated this feeling – of being an ant in such a big city.

What if Andrew Browning couldn't help her? What then? What if she *was* only an ant? Destined to be anonymous. Or, worse . . . crushed.

No. She had to stay positive, she counselled herself. That's what Angel once would have told her.

She came out of the Tube station now onto Oxford Street and breathed in a lungful of familiar London air, glad to be back at street level.

Jess stared at the buildings, remembering how they'd come here as kids to try and pickpocket, but had been distracted by all the shop windows instead, awed by the clothes and the people. They'd spent hours in the big Top Shop trying on clothes they could only dream about buying, and Jess had stopped Angel shoplifting. But then, like a celestial reward, Angel had found a ten-pound note in the gutter and they'd gorged on McDonald's.

Jess looked at her phone again. Still nothing from Angel. It hurt that they still weren't speaking. The last time she'd seen Angel, nearly ten days ago now, she'd looked like hell – her skin grey, her hair greasy – but Jess had felt unable to say anything. She'd sensed that Angel had been defensive and had wanted a fight, as if Jess were the enemy. And so Jess had stayed quiet, keeping their conversation to a minimum. She hadn't told her that she'd been fired. She hadn't been able to bear the fact that Angel would so clearly relish telling Weasel and laughing at Jess behind her back.

But it still hurt. It hurt that she had no one to wish her luck today or hold her hand, when she was in so much trouble. When this felt like the last roll of the dice. Her only chance to get back on track.

She stared at a woman with her daughter next to her, excitedly deciding on the direction they'd start shopping, and her heart ached with a familiar longing. Where was her own mother? Where was her mother when she needed her most?

Jess stood with the crowds rushing around her and composed a text to Angel. She was cabin crew, even if she didn't have an actual job to prove it right now. She had to look out for her friends. That was the first rule. To be compassionate and treat everyone as an individual. Which is why she swallowed her pride now and typed, *Call me, babe. Am worried. Love you. Xx*

Then, steeling her nerves and tugging at her smart jacket, she set off for Andrew Browning's offices.

CHAPTER THIRTEEN

Surrey, 1990

'She hates me,' Leila said, staring at Judith, not able to express how hopeless she felt. 'She says my parents don't see the point in me going home for Easter and I can stay in school. But it's a lie. She wants to torture me.'

They were in the changing rooms after PE, the steam from the showers making the air sticky. Leila could hear the other girls laughing and joking in the communal showers, but despite being muddy and cold, she knew that there was no way she was going in there. Not to be taunted and ridiculed.

Judith and a few others were also getting dressed, not leaving their clothes for a minute, in case one of Edwina's disciples stole them and threw them outside on the muddy pitch.

'I know you're upset,' Judith said, 'but maybe old G-S is right. By the time you get there, it'll be time to come back again.'

'But that's the point. I won't be coming back. I hate it here. I can't bear it,' Leila said, tears coming now. 'I've never been away from home for this long before.'

Judith put her arms around Leila sympathetically. 'Don't

say that. It's not so bad here. Listen, I'll call my mum. See if she'll let you come home to ours.'

'You would?' Leila said, pulling away and wiping her eyes, embarrassed at her outpouring of emotion.

Judith nodded; then her look changed. 'Oh God. Watch out. Here comes Sussman,' she said, turning her back and ducking her head.

Leila busied herself, desperate to get into her clothes, but she was only half dressed by the time Sussman had stridden towards them.

'Leila, is everything OK?' Miss Sussman asked. She was wearing a bottle-green tracksuit, the silver whistle on the shelf of her breasts. Her breath stank of instant coffee, and Leila saw the wart on her cheek had sprouted even more hairs.

'Yes, miss.'

'Then hurry up and get dressed.'

'Sorry, miss.'

'I haven't seen you at lac practice.'

Leila cast her eyes down. How could she go to lacrosse when Edwina and Georgina ruled the team? Besides, lacrosse, or lac, as everyone called it, made absolutely no sense to Leila. It appeared to be a wild game to her, with no boundaries or sidelines, and rules that made absolutely no sense.

'Make sure you join up after Easter. I'm determined to discover your potential.'

She stared at Leila, then she turned and, putting her hands behind her back, strutted towards the showers.

'She's such a perv,' Judith whispered with a giggle. 'I think she's got the hots for you. You should watch out.'

Leila closed her eyes, feeling sick. She had to get out of here.

*

81

Judith's parents' home was a ramshackle, noisy townhouse in Notting Hill and was full of guests when Judith and Leila arrived. Judith showed Leila up the wooden stairs, with their threadbare orange carpet, to her draughty room in the attic, where it was so cold she could see her breath. But she adored the house, which was full of books and dogs and framed theatre posters for the shows Judith's father had produced.

Over supper, Mrs Hobson seemed intrigued about Lace Island and all the guests that came, and when Leila dropped a few names, including Christopher Barber, there was a sudden collective hush. She saw Mrs Hobson's wine glass freeze half-way to her lips, and she threw a surprised look at her husband. Leila felt all eyes on her.

'You met Christopher?' Judith's father said. 'You're sure?'

'Maybe it was a different Christopher,' Leila said shyly, worried by the attention she'd garnered. She felt her cheeks burning in the hot kitchen, the coq au vin Judith's mother had served sitting uncomfortably in her stomach. 'But he definitely said he was in the theatre.'

'Well, we're all off to his play tomorrow night,' Judith's mother announced. 'Your father's latest enterprise,' she added to Judith, sounding sceptical, but one of the other guests raised a toast and declared it would be 'splendid', and more wine went round the table.

As the dinner went on, the adults talked about people they knew, but Leila was distracted by Judith's brother, Toby, who stared at her whenever she talked, and his friend Harry.

'My brother fancies you,' Judith informed Leila in a whisper, as they cleared the cheese plates onto the side by the sink. 'He wants to get off with you.'

'But he doesn't know me.'

'So? This is your chance.'

'He's your brother.'

'I don't care. I'm going to Harry's room tomorrow night.'

Leila had never been to the West End of London before, so she was entranced as she got out of the black cab on Shaftesbury Avenue. It was just like it was on the postcards, she thought. The bright lights of the theatre, the red London buses, the crowds of people on the street. She wished Rasa could be with her to see this too.

Inside the theatre, on the red seats in the front row of the balcony, she could sense the rising excitement of the audience, and she flicked through her programme, reading about *The Importance of Being Earnest*. But when the play started, she hardly understood it, and she was baffled by the audience, who seemed to hoot with laughter.

Judith nudged her. 'This is the famous bit,' she said, miming along with Lady Bracknell. '*To lose one parent, Mr Worthing, may be regarded as a misfortune; to lose both looks like carelessness*. Hilarious,' she added, laughing raucously with the rest of the audience. Leila smiled, but she felt lost. She'd already lost one parent. If she lost Bibi, it wouldn't be 'careless'; it would break her heart.

After the performance, Leila, Judith, Toby and Harry sipped lemonades at the theatre bar while waiting for Judith's father, who was backstage.

And that's when Leila saw Christopher Barber across the room. Christopher Barber from Lace Island. It was definitely him. Leaving the others, she confidently strode towards him.

'Hi, Christopher,' she said, interrupting his conversation with a woman in a blue trouser suit. 'It *is* you.' She beamed at him, delighted to see a familiar face, the memories of Bibi's moonlit terrace coming back in a sudden rush: Chan playing clarinet, Christopher dancing with Vanessa so romantically . . . how relaxed and happy everyone had been.

'I'm sorry,' he said, clearly astonished that she'd spoken to him. She saw something flash in his eyes. Was it fear? Confusion? He must remember her, mustn't he? It was impossible that he didn't recognize her.

'Christopher. You remember, surely? It's me. Leila from Lace Island.'

'Where? I don't know where you mean. Sorry. You must be confused.'

Leila stared at him, her mouth falling open. 'I'm not confused. You were there last year. With the girl. You remember. Vanessa. She gave me her sarong and straw hat. The girl with the long blonde hair and—' Leila stopped, seeing the thunderous face of the woman next to Christopher. Saliva flooded her mouth. Christopher's eyes blazed at Leila, who felt blood rushing to her cheeks. She'd clearly put her foot in it.

The woman made a small, sob-like noise. 'I knew it,' she yelled; then she turned and started running away from Christopher towards the door.

'Carol. Carol, wait,' Christopher called, setting off after the woman. 'It's not like you think . . .'

Leila stared after them, biting her lip. She felt Harry stand next to her.

'Oh God, that was so awesome. You totally dumped him in it,' he said. 'You know that's his wife, right?'

Leila felt tears pricking her eyes as his laughter rang in her ears.

Later, back at Judith's parents' house, Leila knew that she was in the doghouse, the whole evening having ended on a sour note. Judith's father was clearly furious and had made them all come back in cabs early while he tried to 'firefight', as he put it, staring at Leila.

Now, Leila sat upstairs in the snug with Harry, waiting for Judith, who had gone off with Toby to steal some cigarettes from the grown-ups. She stared at the chat show on the TV, but she was too miserable to watch it.

How was she supposed to have known that Christopher was married? Or that Vanessa was a secret? She tried to justify what she'd done, but she could only see Bibi's face in her mind's eye, who would be furious with her too. Lace Island was somewhere that people cherished for its discretion, and Leila knew that she had broken all the rules and put her foot in it. She saw now that she'd wanted to cash in on her status with Christopher in front of Judith's family. How wonderful it would have been if he'd told Judith's parents about Lace Island and confirmed everything Leila had told them, but instead she'd made a fool of him. Oh, it was just too awful, Leila thought miserably to herself. There was no way to make it any better.

'This Lace Island place,' Harry said. 'Can anyone go?'

'No,' Leila said, feeling uncomfortable. He was sitting right next to her on the sofa. She noticed that he was wearing after-shave. Was that for Judith's benefit? she wondered. Were they really going to do it later on? How could Judith want to? With him? He was covered in pimples, and now, as his arm snaked along the back of the low sofa towards her, she could smell the body odour from the armpit of his pink shirt. 'You have to be invited.'

'Would you invite me?'

'I guess. I suppose I could.'

'I'd like that,' he said, moving closer. He leant in towards her, trying to kiss her.

'What are you doing?' Leila said, struggling, but she only succeeded in pressing closer to him, and in a second he was on top of her on the sofa. At that moment, the door opened and Judith came in.

Harry sat up and Leila struggled up too. Judith's expression turned from a smile to utter horror in under a second.

'Leila and I were just having a chat,' he said, pretending nothing had happened, but he sounded ineffectual and weak. 'I'll go and see what Toby is up to.' He left the sofa and scooted past Judith in the doorway. 'See you later,' he said, with a little wave.

Judith watched him go. There was silence, apart from the low burble of the TV and his footsteps thundering down the stairs.

'I thought you were my friend,' Judith said, her voice shaking. 'But you're just a snake in the grass.'

'I'm not. I didn't do anything,' Leila protested.

'You led him on.'

'I didn't.'

'You did! All that Lace Island bullshit.'

'It's not bullshit.'

'It is. You totally humiliated yourself and my family at the theatre with that poor guy.'

'That's not fair.'

'I should never have trusted you. Never been your friend. Edwina was right about you all along. You're just a liar.'

'Judith, please . . .'

'I want you to leave and go back to school. Tomorrow. Because this friendship is officially over.'

CHAPTER FOURTEEN

London, present day

In the fuggy atmosphere of Mo's launderette, Jess sat flicking through a copy of the *Metro*, her knee jogging with nervous energy. It was late, the rain spattering against the steamed-up glass behind her, and despite the buds in her ears, she could still hear the thump and whir of the yellow machines around her.

She hated coming to the launderette, but the washing machine had broken in the flat, and she needed some time to process the interview this afternoon. She hoped she'd made the right impression, but it was impossible to tell. She'd never been in offices that posh, and Andrew himself had been immaculate in a pinstriped suit with a pink handkerchief sticking out of his pocket, like he was a member of the royal family or something. She replayed the whole thing now in her head, once more.

'So, how was the aftermath of the incident on that flight?' he asked her.

'Not good,' she admitted, before explaining that she'd been fired. She'd told him too about Claire and what had happened in training and how that had counted against her.

'I'm sorry to hear that,' Andrew Browning said, pinching

his lips. She was amazed he was listening to her, as if he was genuinely concerned.

'The thing is,' Jess continued, 'I don't think they realize how hard I've worked for this. It's not like it's been handed to me on a plate.'

Andrew smiled. 'I realize that. Don't be embarrassed about having – as you put it on your CV here – "humble" beginnings. In my long experience in recruitment, it's the people who start with nothing who achieve the most. What is important is that a future employer will see you as you are now. A beautiful, smart, streetwise young lady with – if you don't mind me saying – lots of potential for success.'

Jess flushed at his flattery, feeling a rush of emotion once more in his presence. A future employer? He seemed so sure there would be one. How could he be so nice? So able to say all the right things? They chatted some more, and he asked her about her motivation for flying.

'Tell me, are you trying to run away from something?'

Jess laughed, amazed that she was so obviously transparent. 'More a case of running away *to* something, if I'm honest. Although I'm not sure what. I just don't want to get sucked down into the life that some of my friends have. That's why I trained to be cabin crew. Someone once said that we travel not to escape life but for life not to escape us. That's what motivates me, anyway.'

Andrew Browning nodded and scribbled something in his leather-bound notebook.

'Where would you like to be in, let's say, two years' time?' he asked. His eyes were beady and Jess realized that this was her opportunity. That he was waiting for her to say something groundbreaking and clever.

She froze. How could she explain to him that she'd only

got this far in her future planning? As in this moment being the most daring she'd imagined. That her sitting on this chair meant everything to her. That he was her one lifeline. That if he didn't see the best in her or what she was capable of, then she was finished.

But just at that moment, Jess's phone rang and she cursed, apologizing as she pulled it from her bag. It was Angel. Of course it was Angel. Calling at the worst possible moment. She declined the call and apologized again.

'Two years' time . . .' she mused, trying to cover the embarrassment of the call and forcing herself to focus and not think about Angel, but a mixture of panic and relief reared up in her. If Angel was finally answering her messages, then she must be OK, right? She'd finally developed a conscience and realized that Jess had been out of her mind with worry. Well, she could damn well wait. It would do her good to get a taste of her own medicine.

'Where are you aiming?' Andrew asked her, his gaze entirely focused on her.

Jess felt years of conditioning grating against her. It was unthinkable to voice any kind of ambition in a care home, or to her peers. You dumbed down. Fitted in. Did what you could to appear as normal as possible. She wasn't used to articulating her desires to herself, let alone thinking about voicing them.

'I want to go all the way. Well, as far as I can, at least,' she added. 'But most of all, I want to travel. I want to see everything. Have amazing adventures. Go everywhere.'

'I always tell my clients to aim for the top. Someone has to fill the top slots. It might as well be you.'

He wrote something in his notebook before giving her a gentle smile. *It might as well be you.* Those simple words. As if it were that easy. But maybe it was for someone like Andrew

Browning and the people he mixed with. Maybe stuff just happened. It didn't have to always be a fight. Could life really be like that for her too?

Now, sitting in the launderette, Jess felt foolish for getting swept along by his enthusiasm and can-do attitude, for falling for his sales ruse. She was canny, yes, but she'd never really be able to beat the system. The only people who ever got to have that kind of life were the type who went to public school. Who were born rich. Who had class in their DNA. Like Andrew Browning.

No. Keep positive, she cautioned herself. She must never give up. That's what losers did.

She stared across at the huge drum of the washing machine, the suds whooshing inside and the red flash of her uniform skirt flapping inside like a flag. She might as well give it back clean. She checked the emails on her phone once more. Nothing from Andrew's office yet. But there would be. Of that she'd been assured.

The door of the launderette burst open, bringing Jess back to the present with a blast of cold air. Two young guys bustled through. They were from the tower block. The ones that hung out the front on their ridiculous bikes.

'You Angel's friend?' one of them asked, standing in front of her. Jess took her earphones out, already rising to her feet, a sickly feeling rushing through her as she met the kid's dark stare. 'You'd better come.'

Jess sprinted after the two guys as they ran back towards the tower block, but she knew, even before they reached the stairwell, that something dreadful had happened.

She could feel her heart racing as she followed them down the concrete corridor to an unfamiliar flat with a reinforced steel door. The stink made her retch and she covered her nose with her sleeve as she pushed open the door. Inside, the air was putrid, thick with dog excrement and stale bodies. The windows were covered with newspaper, casting a sickly yellow glow from the street light outside across the room towards where a lone body was slumped on the sofa.

Even from the door, Jess knew it was Angel and that her recent medical training was going to be of absolutely no use. She forced herself to walk inside, until she was standing above Angel. Her head was lolling against her chest, vomit staining her grey T-shirt. A needle was still stuck in a vein in her arm. Jess's knees crumpled and she screamed a silent 'No' as she saw the phone on the floor next to Angel's hand. She didn't need to pick it up to know that the call she'd declined this afternoon was the last one that Angel had ever made.

CHAPTER FIFTEEN

Surrey, 1990

The sound of the girls singing the hymn rang out in the sun-filled school chapel, but Leila was only pretending to sing. She could feel everyone watching her, as if she had a neon light pointing down on her.

It was the start of the new term and Mrs Grayson-Smith stood up in the pulpit as the rousing organ music faded.

'Welcome back, girls,' she said.

Leila felt someone beside her nudge her and she was passed a note. She opened it up. All it said was, *Snake*.

She glanced along the row, but all the girls were staring forward, pretending to listen to the headmistress.

Leila crumpled up the note and shoved it into her blazer pocket with the others. She tried to keep any sign of emotion from her face, but inside she felt hot tears rising up.

This was all so unfair. Since she'd got back from Judith's house, any hope that she'd started to fit in at school had been dashed. Judith had stubbornly refused to listen to the truth about Harry, and now Leila was so sick of her not believing what had happened, she'd stopped talking about it altogether.

But Judith refused to let it go and had spread rumours

about Leila. Worse, she was delighting in being part of Edwina's gang, parading around the dorm in Edwina's Benetton jumpers and whispering about Leila behind her back.

Three whole days had passed since they'd been back at school and Leila had hardly spoken to anyone, apart from her teachers, so it came as a surprise when she was asked to wait after the assembly had finished. She saw everyone giggling as they left to go to lessons and she wondered what kind of trouble she was in now.

She waited at the back until the chapel had cleared; then Mrs Grayson-Smith walked down from the stage, her heels clicking over the parquet flooring.

'I need to have a word with you, Leila,' Mrs Grayson-Smith said, holding a letter Leila had written to Bibi by its corner.

Leila stared at the letter and then at the headmistress. How dare she read her post?

'I hope you are not intent on slandering the reputation of this school,' Mrs Grayson-Smith said, 'after we have been so generous in accommodating you.'

'It's a private letter,' Leila protested, furious she'd been spied on. 'I can say what I want to my mother.'

'We don't encourage girls to express any homesickness. Their parents are the ones who suffer. They are the ones missing their children and doing all the work to afford the fees here. Do you not think your poor mother is missing you dreadfully, hmm?' she asked.

Leila felt her lip trembling.

'And do you think it's fair to send this snivelling letter telling her that you don't have any friends? Is that what she needs to hear on the other side of the world?'

'No,' she replied in a small whisper.

'I'm glad you agree,' the headmistress said, ripping up the letter and putting the quarters of the tear-stained paper in the pocket of her jacket.

'What you need, Leila, is some good English fresh air,' she declared. 'Miss Sussman has kindly said she'll make room for you in the training squad. You can report to her after lessons.'

Leila was still smarting about the letter as she joined the others on the playing field after school. She could see Edwina and Georgina nodding at each other, as if they were readying themselves to take her down.

Leila felt sick with dread as she ran onto the pitch, joining in with Miss Sussman's warm-up routine. She stood halfheartedly stretching and then touching her toes, feeling the hairs on the back of her neck standing up. Lac was so violent. She could almost feel Judith scraping her foot like a bull, ready for the charge. Ready to legitimately run Leila down. Which is when she realized that everyone had stopped and was pointing at her.

'Er, Leila, I think you've had a bit of an accident,' Edwina said, before bursting into laughter.

Leila felt humiliation wash over her as she looked down and realized that she'd started her period. Red blood had seeped through her gym shorts to the top of her thigh. She stared down, feeling hot tears of mortification fill her eyes. How could she have not known that her period was going to start today? She was always regular as clockwork, but she'd been so miserable in the aftermath of everything that had happened with Judith, she'd barely noticed her stomach cramps.

Miss Sussman blew her whistle to break up the commotion.

'You'd better clean yourself up,' she told Leila, leaning in close. 'Go and take a shower.'

Leila raced to her dorm and rummaged through the dirty laundry for some spare school uniform, then grabbed a towel and headed for the showers. It was weird being here all alone in the day, but at least there was no one around to steal her towel or her clothes.

She stepped under the stream of water, which for once was hot and not tepid, and washed her body down with soap, but she couldn't shake the cold feeling of dread inside her. It was bad enough to be an outsider, then to be cast out by her only friend, but now, the news of her humiliation would be all over the school.

Ever since she'd stepped foot in England, everything that could go wrong had, and things kept on getting worse and worse. She should never have left Lace Island. She should have insisted that she stayed, because, contrary to what Bibi believed, the world wasn't full of lovely people; it was full of bullies and liars.

Leila pushed her face into the shower, her tears mingling with the hot water. Then the sound of footsteps made her suddenly still. Leila tried to peek over the cubicle, but she couldn't see anyone in the steam. Had Edwina come to make her humiliation complete?

'Hello?' she called.

But there was nobody there. She redoubled her efforts to wash quickly. She couldn't bear anyone to find her in the showers, especially Edwina. She listened above the hiss of the water, but there was nothing. Maybe she was just being paranoid.

Quickly, she turned off the water, and in the sudden,

dripping silence, she gasped and turned as a large body reared towards her.

Miss Sussman.

Leila wrapped her arms across her chest, recoiling in shock.

'You need to hurry it up in here,' Miss Sussman said, staring at Leila's wet body.

'I will. I'm finished,' Leila said. 'One minute. I'll get dressed right away.'

But Miss Sussman didn't take the hint. She stood blocking the cubicle, staring at Leila, who felt herself flush all over.

'You have a nice little figure going on there, don't you,' she said in a quiet, creepy voice. Leila cowered away as Miss Sussman stepped closer, into the puddle of water on the shower floor. What was she doing?

Leila barely had time to work out what was going on before Miss Sussman had reached out her arm. Leila froze as her hand touched her hip and slid over Leila's wet skin. Miss Sussman made a low noise that sounded to Leila like a wolf's growl.

Terrified, Leila began to tremble. She stared at the whistle on Miss Sussman's chest, willing herself to grab it and blow it. But no one would come. And if they did, no one would believe her.

'Don't be scared,' Miss Sussman whispered, closer now, stepping fully into the shower and towering over Leila.

'Please. I just want to get dressed,' Leila whimpered, shrinking into the corner, her back pressed against the slimy, cold tiles.

'I don't want to hurt you. I just want to look,' Miss Sussman said, pulling Leila's arms away so that her breasts were exposed. Leila felt her eyes fill with fresh tears of humiliation as the teacher stared at her.

She squeezed her eyes shut, willing this not to be happening. She could feel herself trembling all over. She could feel cramps in her abdomen and knew the blood was coming again, dripping down the inside of her leg. She waited, knowing that Miss Sussman would touch her again, but she didn't. Leila opened her eyes and the teacher was gone and she was left alone, shivering and naked.

CHAPTER SIXTEEN

London, present day

Jess blew her nose as she stepped out of the chapel onto the steps of the crematorium, the walkway in front of her covered in flower tributes for the last person who'd been cremated. There had hardly been any flowers for Angel. She took a deep, shuddering breath and looked up at the clouds scudding across the dull sky. At least it had stopped raining, she thought, before remembering that today was her birthday. She turned, waiting for Tony and Maeve, his wife, to come out of the building behind her, but she already knew she wouldn't share this realization with them. Today was just too sad for any sort of celebration.

She dabbed the wodge of tissues against her eyes, glad that Maeve and Tony had come out to support her. And Kai had come too, shyly kissing Jess's cheek when he'd arrived. She still felt bad about the night they'd spent together, and she regretted hurting his feelings, but none of that mattered now.

It was two weeks since Angel's death, but it felt like Jess's life had stopped. Everything seemed to be in limbo, and each day had been a hellish slog of tough decisions. There'd been the paramedics, then the police; the press had even been involved.

Numb with grief, Jess had been questioned again and again, but there was only one question that actually mattered: if Jess had known Angel had a problem, why hadn't she done more?

It was a thought that had tortured Jess ever since she'd found Angel. She should have gone to the police ages ago and reported Weasel, or sought a counsellor to help out with Angel, but instead, she'd turned what amounted to a blind eye. Sure, she'd sent that last text to her friend, but she'd said, *Love you*. Not, *I love you*. Not, *You're my family and mean the world to me and I'm worried that something terrible is happening to you and you might feel alone and scared*. None of those things.

Her attempt at emotion had been glib. Worse than if she'd said nothing at all. And then she'd rejected Angel's last call. And now it was too late.

Of course, Weasel had gone. Jess had searched all over the estate for him, but he'd vanished. As had Maisie and the baby. Perhaps he'd just been using Angel all along. It was so cowardly to disappear, and it made Jess irrationally furious. People like Weasel were scum. Dealing in misery. Wrecking lives. If she'd hated drugs before, she now felt a personal vendetta against anyone involved with them.

Who made heroin? That's what she wanted to know. How had that muck even found its way into Angel's veins?

She stared out at the mourners queuing to go in for the next funeral, amazed to see one guy taking pictures with his camera. Why would you take pictures at a funeral? she wondered. She stared at him, alarmed that he was pointing his camera in her direction, but when she looked again, he was checking the screen on the back.

Maybe the next person was famous, Jess thought. Whoever it was certainly had a hell of a lot more mourners than Angel's death had mustered. It had been a shock to realize how few people actually cared at all about Angel. She saw the man who'd ushered them out earlier greeting the next mourners, his manner sincere but his eyes immune to the shocking conveyor belt of death over which he was presiding. Coffins in. People out. In the distance, the cars roared round the South Circular road.

It filled Jess with terror. Who would have come to her funeral if she'd been the one who'd died? The same people, maybe. Nobody else. How had she made so little impact in twenty-five, no, twenty-six years? It was terrifying to be so near to the edge of life. Where she could just drop off, like Angel had, and hardly anyone would notice. It made her want to claw away from it as fast as possible.

'It was a nice service,' Tony's wife, Maeve, said, in her lilting Jamaican accent, joining Jess on the steps and touching her elbow. She was a large woman, her soft skin hardly lined at all. She was wearing a purple flowery dress, which Jess suspected she always wore to church. Tony looked uncomfortable, as if he couldn't breathe in his done-up shirt.

'Was it?' Jess said. It had all been a blur. Angel had disappeared through the red curtain to Mariah Carey, which is what she would have wanted, Jess hoped, although that decision along with all the others had been exhausting.

'Come on. It's not your fault,' Tony said, putting his arm round Jess. 'Stop blaming yourself. You have to carry on. That's the best thing you can do now. That's what she would have wanted.'

As Jess packed up Angel's clothes in the flat later, though, she had no idea what Angel would have wanted, or what she wanted herself. How could she carry on now, when Angel was dead? Everything seemed pointless.

Exhausted, she went to her room, feeling the cold silence all around her, feeling the chill of Angel's absence. Outside, there was the faint sound of buses, sirens and a plane going overhead. People travelling, living, eating, loving, sleeping. The world was carrying on and yet hers had stopped.

She'd tried so hard to get ahead. She'd tried to follow her dream, but she'd blown it. Because she didn't belong. Angel had been right. There was no point in trying to be something she wasn't. It was all such a big joke.

No wonder Angel had thought Jess was a fool. People like Jess and Angel had been thrown away as babies. Nobody wanted them then, and nobody wanted them now. All her dreams had been just that: stupid fantasies. She'd never walk on a desert island beach, let alone with her ideal man. She'd never get out of this horrible estate. She'd never amount to anything.

She slumped to the floor, putting her head in her hands. She wasn't prone to this kind of self-pity, but for the first time in her life, she felt so tired and alone she grabbed a pillow and curled up on her side on the floor. Which is when she looked under her bed and saw that her shoebox had its lid off.

Her heart lurching, she pulled it towards her, thinking of the picture of her and Angel, but even as the box came closer, she knew something was wrong. She sat up, hardly able to breathe. Her savings book wasn't there, the photo of Angel and her wasn't there, and the jewellery box that had always housed her necklace was empty.

'No,' she gasped, tipping out the box, spreading out over the floor the few things that remained. But she knew that Angel or, more likely, Weasel had robbed her.

'You bastard,' she shouted, rage overtaking her.

She stood and picked up the box and hurled it at the wall. 'No, no, no,' she screamed. Not her necklace. Not that.

Crying, she tore down the poster of the desert island, ripping it into pieces, screaming with fury.

It was only after she'd torn it several times that she finally broke down. She wept herself to sleep. Everything was gone. Everything. All the dreams. All her hope.

The morning light was creeping round the blind when Jess became aware of her phone buzzing. Blearily, she sat up and pulled it from her pocket. She looked at the number and saw it was Andrew Browning. Desperately wiping her face with her cardigan, she blew out a breath and pressed the green button.

'Well, hello, Jess,' he said. 'I've left a few messages.'

Jess heard the enquiring tone in his voice.

'I'm sorry,' she said, her voice nothing more than a croak. It hadn't occurred to her to check her messages or emails. 'I had a family crisis. I mean, my friend . . . she . . . passed away.' She swallowed the big lump in her throat, remembering yesterday's sad funeral and the fact that Angel was dead.

'I'm so sorry. Is this a bad time? I can call back . . .'

'No. Please. I'm OK,' she said, trying to steady herself. But she wasn't OK. She'd never be OK again.

'I have an opportunity for you. I've got an interview for you with the airline I mentioned. Do you think you'd be able to get to Heathrow this afternoon?'

This afternoon? Jess stared at her reflection in the mirror of her wardrobe. She looked like shit.

She was about to refuse when she saw the ripped-up poster and remembered her misery last night and discovering that her necklace had been taken.

What was the point in mourning Angel now? In wallowing here? She had nothing holding her back now. Nothing. The past was over.

Bring it on, she thought. She would grab whatever life threw at her. Whatever tiny scrap. Today was a new day. The start of the rest of her life.

'Yes. Yes,' she gulped. 'Sure. I'll be there.'

PART TWO

CHAPTER SEVENTEEN

Lace Island, 1990

Leila stood on the metal steps that were pushed against the door of the small aeroplane, shielding her eyes against the glare of the sun and breathing in the tropical heat. It was late May and the weather was getting hotter, and soon, the monsoon season would be kicking in, but right now, it was glorious. She spread out her arms, looking over the tops of the palm trees and seeing the glint of the green fields beyond, wanting to shout with joy. *Home. She was home.*

But even as the heat warmed her, thawing her out for the first time in weeks, she couldn't quite feel the level of euphoria she'd hoped she might. She'd assumed that England would be washed away the second she touched down, but standing looking out at the shimmering heat haze on the dusty road and the scruffy wooden hut, she knew everything was different and that her experience had changed her in a way she couldn't put her finger on.

Perhaps it was just because she was older, she thought. Or maybe it was because when she'd left here, she'd thought that England would be full of the same lovely kind of people who came here to Lace Island. But she'd learnt the hard way that it wasn't. Christopher Barber had proved that, by pretending he'd never seen her before. And now, returning home, she knew that part of her faith in the goodness of people had died forever.

She wondered whether Bibi would be here to greet her or whether she'd be smarting over Leila's hurried return from school. Goodness only knew what slander Mrs Grayson-Smith had sent in her letter. After Leila had tearfully reported Miss Sussman's shower attack, leaving no detail out, the headmistress had been furious. Despite Leila's obvious upset, she hadn't believed a word Leila had told her. Instead, she'd railed at Leila, telling her she was impossible to educate, that she'd failed all her mock exams, that it had been a mistake agreeing to bring her into the fold at Hillmain and that she was a liar who would amount to nothing in life.

It had all been so shocking and hurtful, but just as Judith had said it had happened to the last pupil who'd complained about Sussman, arrangements had been made to send Leila home immediately to 'contemplate her behaviour'. Mrs Grayson-Smith had obviously wanted to see the back of her, and fast. The feeling had been entirely mutual on Leila's part. On the bleak, rainy morning she'd caught the taxi to the station, nobody had waved her goodbye or wished her well.

But now – *thank God* – Leila could start to put the whole ordeal behind her. She would stay here and resume her studies with Timothy. She'd help out Bibi and Chan with the guests and, with a bit of luck, never have to leave Lace Island again.

Grabbing on to the rail, she bounded down the rickety metal steps from the plane. Safely on the cracked tarmac of the small landing strip, she turned, watching the plane propellers slow down. She waved happily at Marc, the captain, and he winked back. He'd made the half-hour flight from Cochin especially for her, after her plane from London to Bombay had been delayed and she'd missed the scheduled flight that was bringing out the new batch of guests here yesterday evening.

She'd been lucky that she'd bumped into him at the airport and he'd agreed to bring her home. Otherwise, she'd have been stuck on the ferry from Cochin, which she knew from grim experience only came once a week and took six hours. She'd always had terrible seasickness on it.

Now the captain would be getting a free stay on Lace Island as a result of the favour, and his girlfriend, Monique, had been on the flight too. Leila had tried to make conversation with her, but she was French and very glamorous and more interested in reading her novel than talking to a child. Now, Leila saw her at the top of the steps, standing arms akimbo in her green wrap-over dress, which hugged her curves, and a large matching floppy sun hat. She was carrying a leather zip-up bag over her wrist, which Leila suspected was full of expensive creams and make-up. She wondered if she'd be on the receiving end of any posh freebies when she left.

Leila stared at her own shabby suitcase by her feet, thinking of her hurriedly packed belongings inside. It was ridiculous to have brought her thick school uniform to the other side of the world when she had no intention of ever wearing it again. She would ceremoniously cut it up, she decided. And then burn it.

'Miss Leila,' she heard, and turned to see Vijay, Rasa's father and Lace Island's self-appointed policeman, waddling out from the small, rush-covered hut. He was wearing a short-sleeved brown shirt and swatting flies with his stick as she approached. She'd never noticed before how stained his teeth were from chewing the red betel nuts, or how large his paunch had become. She heard him speaking in Malayalam, the local language, to a small boy Leila didn't recognize, who ran off.

Vijay checked the people going in and out of the island, but despite his uniform, he had very little actual authority. As Lace Island was privately owned, there was no need to check anyone's passports or paperwork, although Bibi did like to have an idea of who came in and when they left, and she trusted Vijay completely. Leila was so pleased to see him she flung herself into his arms. She tried not to gag at the stale sweat coming from his uniform.

'We welcome you back,' he told Leila, holding her away at arm's length, chuckling with an amused embarrassment. 'Goodness, you have grown, Miss Leila. You must make a point to go and see Maliba. She asks after you every day.'

'I will,' Leila grinned. Just hearing his voice and seeing the respect in his eyes filled her with comfort. She couldn't wait to go and see Maliba and hear all the gossip. She might even have her hands and feet painted with henna. From now on, life would be blissfully simple and easy.

'And Rasa will be pleased you are home. Bibi has been kind enough to keep the tutor on for him. He has been sitting his examinations,' Vijay said proudly.

That probably meant that Rasa was streaks ahead of her by now, she thought. How would she ever catch up? She had never considered how academically complicated her departure from Lace Island and sudden return might make things. But she'd work it out, she told herself. Besides, she couldn't wait to tell Rasa and Timothy about all the lessons she'd done in England. How she'd been totally out of her depth in RE, geography, history and Latin. Rasa might think that Timothy knew everything, but she'd discovered that education in England was a very different matter.

She heard a beep now and saw that the Mini Moke had arrived.

'Ah. Here he is now,' Vijay said.

'Rasa!' Leila dropped her bag and ran towards him.

As his scrawny arms went round her, there was a shyness to him that she'd never known. She stared up at him, wanting to touch his face. He had new hair on his jawline, and she noticed that he'd started shaving above the perfect bow of his lips, but his wide hazel eyes, with their impossibly long lashes, were just the same. They beamed out at her from behind his floppy fringe.

'Your parents are up at the house. They've got some new guests. Some American businessman. Adam something. And a couple from Rio.'

She could hear from Rasa's tone that he didn't approve, and she imagined that he'd witnessed the staff having to fawn over the new guests.

She watched now as Rasa hauled her suitcase into the back of the white Mini Moke. They set off and Vijay waved them off. Rasa stopped briefly to talk to Marc and his girlfriend, promising to be back shortly to take them to their bungalow by the beach. When had Rasa become so assertive? Leila wondered, impressed by his confidence. Was he this cool with all the guests?

Then Rasa swung the wheel round and Leila laughed and clung on to the bar as they bumped out onto the road along the coast that would cut up through the grove to the house. Leila stared ahead at the cracked tarmac, seeing a scrawny dog further up the road. Had there always been this many potholes? She jolted as Rasa negotiated the Mini Moke round them.

'It's very unusual for you to be home so early from the

school term, Aunty Parva says. Nobody has been expecting you.' There was both a question and an accusation in Rasa's voice. 'Is everything OK with that new school?'

How typical that he would assume that there was something wrong with the school rather than with her.

'I was homesick,' she said. At least that part of her excuse was true.

'But why? Nothing ever happens here,' Rasa said. 'Don't tell me you have given up on your education?'

She could see the concern in his eyes, but she resented it. If she could stay and do Rasa's job and let him go to school in England, she'd do it in a heartbeat, but she sensed that this wasn't the time to tell him.

She sighed, not answering, and hung on to the metal bar beside her, breathing in the delicious tropical air and staring through the palm trees at the side of the road. She felt wretched. Filled up with secrets that she didn't want either in or out.

'Leila?'

She turned to see Rasa glancing between the road and her, his eyebrows drawn together with concern.

'It's a long story. I'll tell you later,' she said, but she knew right then that she couldn't and wouldn't. She didn't want Rasa's view of her to be ruined forever – which it would be, if he knew the truth.

'Oh, it's so good to be home,' she said, trying to ignore the babble in her mind and stretching both hands up as they bumped over the track. She looked at the blue sky, only broken by a few high, wispy clouds. To her left, she could see the vast expanse of green paddy fields stretching out, a line of workers hunched over, harvesting the rice, each one like a colourful dot. Above the noise of the engine, she could hear the very faint sound of singing. An ox was in the field, stoically bearing the swarm of flies that buzzed round its nose.

Bamu and Victor and Rasa's other cousins worked in the fields, but now Leila wondered if they ever got bored. Maybe they wanted to study like Rasa did. She'd always assumed that they were happy picking rice and fishing and living a simple life. She'd thought the tiny village had a charm and simplicity that people envied, but after being in England, seeing the workers made Leila feel like Lace Island was just the same as the Middle Ages they'd all studied in their history class. The realization made her sit up straight.

'So . . . tell me everything. What's been happening?' she asked brightly.

'The usual,' Rasa said, but she knew he was confused that she'd changed the subject. 'It's been busy. More guests, so there's been a lot of work on.'

Leila frowned, aware that there was something Rasa wasn't telling her. She wondered why it had been so busy. Bibi was very careful to keep things manageable for the staff, but it sounded as if everyone had been stressed out in Leila's absence. She hadn't considered the dramas that had been going on here, with guests coming and going. Perhaps Bibi hadn't given her a second thought, but now that she was back, Leila was determined to help as much as possible.

Coming towards the coconut grove, Leila felt jittery nerves rising up in her. She wished there weren't guests at the house. She needed to see Bibi alone and to explain herself. And she needed to find out exactly what it was that Rasa wasn't telling her.

As the road wound round and up towards the house, they stopped, and Leila smiled as Rasa talked to the guys who were fixing the drainage system that led to one of the boreholes from which the island got all its water and which irrigated the paddy fields.

It was impossible to imagine that soon they would be ankle-deep in rainwater, and Bibi would insist that they collect every drop possible. Watching the men bantering with Rasa, Leila realized that she hadn't even considered where the water she'd taken for granted in England came from. No one did. It just appeared by magic from the taps. Hot and cold. On demand. And now she remembered the clunky shower in the bathroom along the corridor from her bedroom in the house here and how the spiders crawled up the drainpipe into the ancient bath.

Soon, the house came into view and Leila felt nerves and excitement competing inside her as Rasa stopped the Mini Moke.

'Thank you for the lift. We'll catch up later, if you like,' she said, hauling out her suitcase from the back.

'Leila.' Rasa leant across and touched her arm. 'I'm glad you're home.'

Leila felt her heart lift a little and she smiled at him. He'd missed her, then. After all.

'I hope everyone else is pleased to see me,' she said with a nervous grimace.

'Bibi will be,' Rasa said, with the familiar grin she loved so much. 'Go in there and front it out. You're her girl. You know that.'

Leila bit her lip, hoping he was right; then she waved him off and, leaving her bag by the bush, ran two at a time up the stone steps and into the house.

She raced through the hallway towards the screen door. Out on the back terrace, Leila could hear voices. A man was talking in a deep American accent.

'I have been to the Maldives, but the development there is already starting. In twenty years' time, the whole place will be overrun with hotels. You mark my words.'

Leila held her breath and pushed open the mesh door. Bibi turned at the familiar creak as Leila stepped onto the terrace, but as Bibi's eyes met hers, Leila saw dark circles beneath them. She started towards her mother, longing for the embrace that she'd missed so much, but Bibi's voice stopped her.

'We have a guest,' Bibi said, her voice laden with meaning. Leila was to behave herself. There would be no emotional greeting, or any attempt to talk about herself. That was the message and Leila received it loud and clear. She bowed her head, feeling a lump in her throat. Bibi was cross with her, then. Despite what Rasa may think, Bibi wasn't pleased to see her only daughter – she was furious.

Leila looked now across the rattan floor mats to where a man was relaxing back on one of the linen-covered cushions beneath the palm gazebo. He had blondish sandy-coloured hair, and his skin was deeply tanned. He was wearing an open loose white shirt and yellow shorts, which showed off the blond hairs on his legs. He surveyed Leila as he pushed the plastic straw protruding from the coconut he was holding into his mouth.

'Leila, this is Mr Lonegan. He's an important businessman from America.'

'Bibi, please. It's Adam,' the man said, getting to his feet and putting down his coconut. He was tall, Leila noticed, with very white teeth.

'This is my daughter, Leila,' Bibi said.

'Well, aren't you a delight, little lady,' he said, taking Leila's hand. He brought it to his lips and kissed the back of it, his eyes never leaving hers.

Leila felt a shudder deep inside her. It was his eyes. The way they seemed to devour her. Like Sussman's had. She pulled her hand away quickly and he chuckled knowingly, his eyes still not leaving hers as he sat back down, spreading out his arms, like he owned the place.

CHAPTER EIGHTEEN

Miami, present day

It was the middle of the night, and on board the flight to Miami, a soporific hush had fallen over the cabin. Most of the passengers were sleeping under their fluffy blue blankets, and Jess was in the galley, wiping down the units. Now, with a rare moment to herself, her mind flitted briefly to Angel, but it was as if she was testing herself, seeing how close she could get to the pain.

In the past six months, it had certainly dulled, that was for sure. And the guilt that had been so overwhelming when Angel had died had solidified into a deep sense of injustice about the way she'd been taken. Jess's efforts to find Weasel had come to nothing, and there seemed to be nobody to blame. Worse, everyone she'd spoken to around the estate seemed to treat Angel's death as just another everyday occurrence, as if she'd had it coming.

Jess had had some grief counselling, but it hadn't stopped her feelings of impotent rage. What's more, every day she felt guilty, knowing that she should be doing something to stop other people like Angel falling so quickly into such dreadful addiction. It felt particularly galling that someone somewhere was profiting from all this misery. But what could Jess do? Nothing. That was the painful thing. She couldn't do anything but get on with her own life.

And – very reluctantly at first – that's what she had done. Having to retrain with the airline had come as a complete shock, after the initial interviews that Andrew Browning had set up for her, but as soon as she'd started, Jess had felt a profound sense of relief to be part of a team again. She hadn't told any of her colleagues about Angel, and keeping her grief a secret had kept her sane. Because, up here, she could pretend that she was just like the other crew. That her easy charm was all for real. That her life was normal and that she deserved all of this, when most of the time, when she finished her shift, she felt like a huge fraud.

'Hey.'

A voice interrupted her thoughts and Jess turned to see a little girl standing shyly by the doorway. She was gorgeous. About six, Jess reckoned, with her brown Afro hair tied up in two bunches. Jess wanted to twirl them round her fingers.

'Can't you sleep?' Jess asked, and the girl shook her head. 'How about I make you a hot chocolate? Would that help?'

Jess stared a few seats down the aisle from the galley to where the little girl's mother was. The poor woman looked exhausted. She held up the hot-chocolate sachet and nodded her head behind her, and the woman nodded back and smiled.

'Do you want to have it in here with me?' Jess asked. 'You can sit in this special seat if you want?'

The little girl smiled and Jess lifted her onto the crew seat before making the hot drink.

'I'm Jess. What's your name?' Jess asked.

'Lisa,' the girl said.

'That's a nice name. My mum was called Lisa.'

'What's your mom do? Mine is an attorney,' Lisa said.

'My mum's not around anymore, but she was a travelling musician.'

'That sounds fun.'

Jess smiled, amazed at how easily the lie tripped off her tongue. Her travelling-mother-musician background held a certain appeal, and with each retelling, she liked to embellish a little more. Now, she told Lisa about her crazy fictitious sisters and how they'd spent months in America and moved from state to state, and how one of them had run away to join the circus.

She smiled at the little girl and crouched down as she sipped the hot chocolate. Jess couldn't help reaching out and stroking the little girl's head as she yawned.

'You look tired to me, sweetheart.'

The girl shook her head. 'I can't sleep. I'm too excited about the holiday.'

'In Miami?'

'We're going all over Florida and to Disney World too.'

'Aren't you lucky,' Jess said, but the girl just shrugged. Jess had only been in this job a month, but every flight she took astounded her. The people who flew with this airline seemed so civilized.

And this lot were nothing compared to first class. That was something else. Jess had only glimpsed the enormous first-class seats a couple of times, but they were enough to inspire awe among the other cabin crew. Eleanor, who was on this flight with Jess, had told her that only the best got promoted to cabin crew on first class. You had to get noticed, she'd confided in Jess, and work bloody hard in the meantime.

Jess had taken the tip-off to heart. Work was all she intended to do for the foreseeable future, for as long as possible.

It was only when she was flying that Jess felt alive. Only then that she could put on a mask and be someone that Angel had never known.

'Do you know what I do when I want to go to sleep?' she asked the girl, who stared at Jess with her wide eyes. 'I close my eyes and breathe in and out through my nose a hundred times, and each time I have to feel my breath tickling the end of my nostrils right here,' she said, touching the little girl's nose. 'It works, because I never get to a hundred. Shall I take you back to Mummy now and you can get really comfy and try it?'

She took the mug of hot chocolate from the little girl and held her hand. She returned her to her appreciative mother and did a quick scan of the cabin, but everyone was settled. Jess's colleague Eleanor was on a break, and the senior steward, Martin, was in with the captain, so she was on her own, but so far, so good. Everything was under control.

As she got back to the galley, though, she saw that she wasn't alone. A guy was leaning up against the doorway through to first class. He was wearing jeans and a blue checked shirt, and had dark hair, which he ruffled with his tanned hand. He had the shadow of a beard, which only accentuated his high cheekbones and deep blue eyes, peering intently at her from under his thick, dark eyebrows. His bare feet were tanned too, she noticed, with manicured toenails, but even in such a state of scruffy, middle-of-the-night undress, he had a certain air to him. Of class and wealth. The chunky gold Rolex on his wrist gave it away.

'You were very sweet with her,' he said to Jess. He had an accent. Australian? Jess couldn't be sure.

'All part of the service,' Jess said, realizing that the guy must have been there all the time, just out of sight, and she hadn't noticed. 'What can I get you?'

'A beer, I think. I just need to stretch my legs. I might try your sleeping trick.'

Jess turned away and opened a beer for him; he refused a glass and Jess felt unusually flustered, wondering what to do next. She hadn't seen anyone this good-looking on a flight – ever. As she handed the bottle over and their eyes met, she felt an unexpected tug of sexual desire that took her completely by surprise. She hadn't even thought about men or sex since that night with Kai, which seemed like years ago now. Since then, she'd shut herself off, steadfastly refusing to give out any signals that could be misinterpreted.

Because since Angel had died, everything had been different. Since she'd ripped down the poster of her dream desert beach, Jess had given up on her idea of fate. Of the notion that her dream man might make an appearance.

Instead, she'd concentrated on taking one day at a time and keeping her head above water. She hadn't thought once about the future. And she certainly hadn't entertained the thought of *flirting*. Which is what this guy clearly was doing.

'I'm Blaise. And you're Jess, I hear,' he said.

Blaise. What kind of a name was that?

He had a nice smile. Perfect teeth. He didn't stop staring at her and Jess blushed, wondering if he'd believed her made-up story about her travelling-musician mother.

'You're going to Miami? On holiday?' she ventured, tearing her gaze away from his. He was still looking at her over the top of his beer bottle. She turned away and straightened her jacket, trying to come across as professional, but her body language suddenly seemed awkward and wrong.

'Just on business for a few days,' Blaise said.

'I've never been to Miami,' Jess admitted, although why she felt she had to tell the guy she didn't know.

'It's cool if you know where to go,' he said. 'You should let me show you around.'

It was such an openly flirtatious invitation, so presumptuous, as if they'd had a much longer conversation, Jess had to laugh.

'You want to show *me* around Miami?' she checked.

'Why not?'

'Because . . .' Jess trailed off, her embarrassed laugh turning into a blush now as Blaise stared at her. 'Because,' she battled on, 'you don't know me.'

'That can be changed,' he countered. She liked the way the corners of his eyes crinkled. 'Call it a whim, but I know what it's like to be alone in hotels somewhere far from home; you just want to get the sense of the place you're in.' He smiled at her again and Jess noticed a dimple in his cheek. 'You look like the kind of girl who likes exploring. You have a travelling background, after all. It's probably in the blood.'

At that moment, the plane hit a sudden patch of turbulence and Jess was thrown towards Blaise, who caught her, stopping her from falling. The seatbelt signs pinged on and the calm, soothing voice of the captain asked people to return to their seats, but Jess stayed trapped in Blaise's embrace.

Up close to him, she could feel his steady heartbeat through his shirt. She stared at his neck, not daring to meet his eyes. He smelt delicious, of an expensive, musky kind of aftershave.

She coughed and pulled away, embarrassed. 'You'd better get back to your seat,' she managed, her voice cracking.

Blaise smiled. 'See you around, then, Jess,' he said. 'I meant it about taking you out.' He raised his bottle to her. 'Think about it.'

Jess smiled, flustered, as he went back to his seat. She straightened her jacket to go and check the cabin and get everyone's seatbelts on. She was thrown off course by another dip of turbulence, but nothing could faze her, or wipe the confused smile from her face.

For the rest of the flight, she could feel Blaise's presence, even though she couldn't see him, and she wondered if he was as shaken by their encounter as she was. When the plane landed a few hours later, she tried to take a peek through to first class to see if he was leaving, but she was on door duty, ushering out the passengers.

As she said goodbye to each of the passengers, she gave herself a reality check. Out of the bubble of the aeroplane, she was just a nobody. Someone a guy like Blaise wouldn't even notice. Besides, she had never flirted with anyone on a flight, unlike so many of the other crew she'd worked with. Hooking up with Blaise was absolutely out of the question.

It was a meaningless encounter. End of.

But still her mind refused to let it go. Rich, drop-dead-gorgeous Blaise. What could he possibly see in her? Nothing, surely. Except he'd offered to show her the sights of Miami. What if he'd meant it?

CHAPTER NINETEEN

Lace Island, 1990

It was dark by the time Bibi summoned Leila for the inevitable showdown. As she entered her mother's room, Leila knew it wasn't going to be good.

Bibi was sitting by her huge mahogany desk on the wooden swivel chair. Chan stood over on the other side of the room, next to the large wooden radio, which hadn't worked for years, feeding seeds through the bars of the birdcage that housed Bibi's yellow canaries. Chan had always taken care of himself, but tonight his glossy hair was greasy and unkempt.

Leila stood in the middle of the rug, not making eye contact with either of them. She'd always thought this room, Bibi's office, adjoining her bedroom, to be one of the most sophisticated in the house, but now she noticed how shabby everything was. There were water stains on the blue walls and a crack in the ceiling. The filing cabinet overflowed with paper, and the wiring near the light switch buzzed intermittently.

'Go on, then,' Chan said, stretching his arm out to Leila as if he were indulgently giving her the floor. 'You'd better start from the beginning.'

Leila glanced up at him nervously. He'd always been on

her side before now, but she could see that, like Bibi, he was tired. And he'd been drinking.

Leila patiently began her account of everything that had happened. About how she'd been bullied from the start at school, and how the teachers and headmistress wouldn't believe anything she'd told them about Lace Island. She didn't elaborate about Sussman, only saying that the PE teacher gave her the creeps and picked on her. She told them how the teachers refused to explain the lessons to her, choosing instead to ridicule her for her bad marks. And that she had no friends. That the girls had been horrible to her. They'd stolen her photos and diaries, and had flushed her head in the toilet and the teachers had done nothing about it. That the food had been inedible. She hardly paused for breath as her grievances came pouring out.

She saw that she was gaining ground and that Bibi looked horrified by everything she'd been saying.

'You think everyone is so nice,' she told Bibi, 'but they're not. They're really not.'

She told now about what had happened at the theatre and how nobody had believed her stories about Lace Island. And how Christopher had pretended not to know her.

'Oh, Leila,' Chan said, covering his eyes with his hand. 'How could you?'

'How could I what? I was just being friendly.'

'You embarrassed him. Clearly,' Chan said angrily, staring at her.

'I didn't mean to,' Leila said, feeling tears rising.

'You never think before opening your mouth,' Chan snapped.

Bibi held up her hand to stop the argument and there was a moment of tense silence. Then Bibi seemed to crumple into a sigh. She squeezed the bridge of her nose and Leila noticed a bruise on the back of her hand that looked painful.

'Why didn't you explain then, Leila?' Bibi asked. 'At school, I mean. They can't have been that cruel, or badly behaved. The teachers would have helped you.'

'That's what I'm telling you. Mrs Grayson-Smith didn't believe me when I told her what was happening. She refused to listen.'

Leila stared at the electric fan on her mother's desk, which was blowing air at a pile of papers held down with a brass elephant paperweight. The edges flickered like a palm branch in the wind. Bibi stretched and turned it off. Leila felt her eyes sting with tears as she watched the dusty blade slowing down.

'I'm telling the truth.'

'Are you?' Chan said, glancing at Bibi. 'You always used to tell tall stories when you were young, but we thought you'd grown out of it.'

'Please,' Leila implored, fighting back her tears. 'I'm not lying. Why don't you believe me?'

'I want to believe you, Leila. I really do. But how will you get on in life if you can't stick up for yourself? That's why you had to go away to school. To learn about the real world,' Bibi said. 'I can't believe you're back so soon.'

'I don't want to know about the real world if that's what it's like. You don't know how terrible it was,' Leila choked. 'I want to stay here and help you. I can be much more useful—'

'I have written to your headmistress,' Bibi snapped, 'demanding that she allow you to return.'

'Don't send me back. Please. I beg you.' She let out an anguished sob, her eyes appealing to Chan, begging him to listen, and she saw him finally relent. His face changed when he saw she was crying properly. He'd never been able to bear her being upset.

'We can't have this,' he told Bibi. 'She's clearly not happy.'

'What would you know about happiness?' Bibi's head snapped round to face her husband. Both Leila and Chan recoiled at the venom in her words.

There was a shocked moment of silence. Leila held her breath, waiting for Bibi to back down, but when she didn't, Leila glanced at Chan and he turned away.

Leila felt sick. She wasn't used to Bibi saying something so loaded and hurtful. And judging from the charged atmosphere in the room, she meant every word. What had happened while she'd been away? Why was everything and everyone different? And what had happened to Bibi and Chan? They were solid. *Weren't they?*

'Go to bed, Leila. We shan't discuss this again,' Bibi said. She fiddled with the gold chain on her neck, as if it could give her courage. 'The matter is settled. But since you are here, you can make yourself useful and stay out of trouble.'

Leila nodded, her chin trembling. Was Bibi telling her off to prove a point, because she felt she had to? Still she stared at her mother, waiting for her to crack. Waiting for the telling-off to be over and the hugs to begin. Then she would feel like she was home properly. But Bibi just sighed and Leila realized that it wasn't going to happen. She turned and shut the door of Bibi's office.

Outside, she flattened herself against the door, her ear against the crack.

'You've spoilt her,' she heard Chan say. 'That's why she can't be disciplined. We should have sent her away long ago. This island is no place for a child.'

'Don't you dare have an opinion now,' Bibi said. 'It's too late.'

'What are you doing?' Parva scolded, coming up the stairs and shooing Leila away. Today, she was wearing a simple mundu – a white sari – with a plain green shirt underneath. She had faded henna on her bare feet and hands. Leila wondered what festival or wedding she'd missed while she'd been in England.

'They're fighting about me,' Leila whispered, wiping her nose on her sleeve. She wanted nothing more than to throw herself into Parva's arms.

'You and everything else,' Parva muttered, breathlessly shooing Leila up the stairs.

'Everything else? What's going on?'

'Never you mind. You've caused your poor mother enough stress,' Parva warned. 'She doesn't need any more.'

Leila pondered Parva's comments late into the night, waiting for the gentle knock on the door she knew would come. She strained in the dark for the familiar creak of her mother's quiet footsteps along the floorboards outside, wishing that Bibi would come and sing the lullaby that she always did. Tonight, Leila would even let her brush her hair. Whatever it took to make Bibi happy.

But the longer she listened, the quieter the house became.

At two thirty, she woke with a start and, battling out of the swathes of yellowing mosquito nets round her antique four-poster, tiptoed across the moonlit room towards the window. There was a motorbike on the gravel outside, its engine idling. A man waited on the bike, his face only visible from the red glow of a cheroot. She caught a faint whiff of the acrid smoke as it dispersed in the night air.

She saw a sliver of light spreading out onto the gravel and, a second later, saw the top of Chan's head as he crept out towards the bike, furtively looking around him.

She heard a low murmur of voices as he and the man on the bike spoke; then the man handed Chan something – Leila couldn't tell what it was – hidden beneath a dhoti. Chan nodded, and as he turned away, Leila saw the terrible strain etched on his face.

CHAPTER TWENTY

Miami, present day

Jess walked into the reception area of the Miami hotel from the lift, telling herself with every step that this couldn't be happening.

But . . . oh my God, it was, she panicked, seeing Blaise standing by the fancy palm tree in the reception area. He was even more gorgeous than she remembered from the flight. She was so nervous she was tempted to turn on her heel and get back into the lift, but he'd already seen her. She put her hand up in a shy wave.

'There you are. You ready?' he asked. He was carrying two motorcycle helmets and wearing a white T-shirt with faded jeans, which showed off his taut muscles and scuffed brown boots. The receptionist was looking at him with wide eyes, but it was hard not to, Jess thought. He looked like he'd just stepped out of an aftershave commercial – *and he knew it*.

'For what?' she asked.

He shook the helmet at her so that she had to take it. 'Seeing the sights. Like I promised.'

She had excuses lining up in her head. She hadn't had any sleep. She didn't have the right clothes to go on a motorbike.

And most importantly, she didn't know a thing about him. Certainly not enough to put her life in his hands. But when he'd called up the hotel earlier and told her how difficult it had been to track down the airline's hotel, and asked if she was free this afternoon, Jess had been so overwhelmed and flattered that she'd agreed.

And it was no time to back out now. Jess glanced at the receptionist, who was watching her with unmasked envy. Her eyes were shining, willing Jess to go with Blaise. Her look said it all: that Jess would be a fool to resist someone like him.

Jess shook her head, rolling her eyes at her own pathetic resolve. Faced with Blaise in person, it was hard not to get swept away by his overpowering charm. Besides, what would she gain from not going? she reasoned. She wanted adventure, didn't she? That's what she'd told Andrew Browning. And here it was. What else was she saving herself for? It had been months and months since she'd had any fun. What harm would it do to have some now?

So she took the helmet and, knowing that she only had her credit card in the back pocket of her jeans shorts and a bikini on beneath, stepped out into the baking afternoon sun with Blaise and climbed aboard his black vintage Harley-Davidson, which the door porter was admiring.

They set off out of the concrete hotel driveway and onto the main road.

'Welcome to Miami,' Blaise yelled, before applying the gas and zooming away. She yelped and held on tight round his waist. She could feel the ripple of his muscles beneath the thin fabric of his T-shirt, and once again, she felt something sexual stir within her. But it was crazy, right? Blaise was a first-class passenger. Rich and handsome and clearly connected. He was – dare she even think it? – a *fantasy man*. So what was he doing with *her*? Could this really be happening? Was Angel up in heaven, Jess wondered, pulling strings?

She'd spent so many months putting on a mask, putting on her professional caring face, but now, for the first time in as long as she could remember, she felt genuinely excited. She grinned. A real grin, she realized, feeling butterflies again in her stomach. It was as if Blaise had levered open a door and the hot Miami sun was filling up the dark shadows, and she remembered how brilliant it felt to be impulsive. To be *herself*.

Except she wasn't being herself, she realized with a jolt. She was being the cool girl with the travelling-musician mother. How the hell was she going to explain that one? she wondered.

In minutes, they'd overtaken several sports cars as he headed out onto the highway and took the signs for Miami Beach. Jess knew the exclusive resort where all the rich people were was on an island, connected by bridges, and sure enough, soon they were crossing into the north of the island, where the hotels were impossibly expensive and chic.

She watched their shadow as they sped down Collins Avenue in the late-afternoon sun. Man, they looked cool, she thought, feeling suddenly like she was in a movie. To her left, she caught glimpses of the long white beach and the Atlantic Ocean sparkling in the sun, surfers riding the waves. *This was the life*.

She'd read a tourist brochure in the hotel about the famous sights of Miami, but nothing had prepared her for the wealth on display – the Porches and Ferraris and the manicured men and women who drove them. Soon, they were on Ocean Drive, with its restored 1930s art deco buildings in pretty pastel colours. Jess had read that the prime real-estate properties with their view of the ocean were worth a fortune and she could believe it. Who were these people who lived here?

People like Blaise, she reminded herself. She wanted to pinch herself for being here. She was an estate girl from London with just her monthly wage to her name, suddenly looking like she belonged. She wanted to whoop with the absurdity of it all.

They sped on, through the traffic lights and down to South Beach. Eventually, Blaise slowed and turned into the parking lot. Below them, the beach itself was crowded with people, all enjoying the sun and the glorious white surf.

They drove past the cars and stopped by a bar, and Blaise helped Jess get off the bike before hoisting it onto its stand. Jess liked watching his tanned, muscled arms, and she wasn't the only one. She watched a blonde bikini-clad girl sashay past, her eyes lingering on Blaise. But Blaise didn't seem interested in her false breasts and pert bottom. The girl threw an avariciously disapproving look at Jess.

'You want a soda?' Blaise asked. 'I'm thirsty.'

She nodded. 'Sure.'

She followed him to the bar and they sat on the high stools overlooking the beach.

'Looks tempting. I can't wait to go in,' Jess said, squinting at the water.

'We're not stopping here,' he said. 'I've got something else I want to show you.'

He ordered Diet Cokes and Jess realized the guy behind the bar recognized him. He glanced over at Jess as if he was checking her out, and his lips curled into a private smile. How many other girls had Blaise brought here? she wondered. She was still unsure about how this date – if you could call it that – was going. Or whether she should be here at all. Back home in London, she was so suspicious of people. Always on her guard, but now *this* was happening. She was sitting on Miami Beach with a total stranger, as if it were the most normal thing in the world. And not just any old stranger . . . Blaise.

She clinked bottles with him, feeling out of her depth and tongue-tied as he stared at her. There was so much she wanted to ask about him, but she didn't even know where to start.

'So—'

'Where—'

They started talking at the same time and both laughed, embarrassed. He nodded for Jess to go first.

'I just wondered how you know Miami so well. Do you work here a lot?' Jess inwardly cringed. She sounded so uptight, like she was asking him for his CV.

'I have business interests here I check in on.'

Business interests? What did that mean? Jess wondered, but Blaise didn't seem to want to elaborate or talk about work.

'It's kind of fun. I like it here,' he said, looking out over the beach.

'You know, I just can't place your accent,' Jess said.

'That's because I've lived all over the place. My mum's in Australia, my dad is – *was* – Italian, but my great-grandfather's family was Indian, believe it or not. I'm a bit of a mongrel dog.'

He said it like he meant in, but groomed Blaise with his swarthy good looks was anything but a mongrel dog. If anyone was a mongrel, she was. Not that she was going to admit that anytime soon. She tore her eyes away and looked out over the beach.

'There's so many people,' she said. 'I could sit here all day and watch them.'

'You like people-watching? Me too,' Blaise said. 'You can

tell so much about a person straight away. But you must know that in your line of work.'

'I guess,' Jess said with a shrug. 'You know immediately when people come on board what type they are.'

'Type?'

'Yeah, well, sort of,' she clarified. 'Just the way people talk to each other, or sit down next to strangers, tells you a lot about them.'

'Oh? And what did you find out about me, then?' he asked, as if reading her mind.

'That you're nosey,' she said, with a smile.

He grinned. 'Guilty. I prefer "curious", though. When I saw you talking to that little girl on the plane, I couldn't help spying on you. You were very sweet to her.'

'Thanks.'

There was a beat and Jess was unsure what had just passed between them. She wondered if he was about to tell her that she'd make a good mother, or something like that. Because if he was, then she'd have to correct him. In fact, she'd have to correct him on everything. She'd have to come clean and tell him that everything he'd witnessed was all an act. But right now, as his eyes connected with hers, she couldn't. She liked being the version of herself he thought she was.

A second later, he grinned and pulled his mirrored shades down over his eyes and she saw herself reflected back, the glamour of Miami Beach behind her. But she felt like she was looking into a camera lens and he held all the power. She wanted to tell him to take his glasses off, but she didn't know him well enough yet. She held his gaze, wondering what his eyes were saying, but his mouth was smiling. Like he liked what he saw.

'Drink up,' he said, draining his bottle. 'We're going.'
'Where?'
'You'll see.'

CHAPTER TWENTY-ONE

Lace Island, 1990

It was just gone dawn and Leila couldn't sleep, but Anjum was up in the kitchen, whistling. Leila sauntered along the back path towards the sound, but she hardly noticed the birds hopping in the bushes, or the pretty yellow butterflies dancing among Anjum's prized pepper plants.

She'd thought it would be so different coming home, but it was as if everyone was suddenly in a bad mood. Bibi and Chan, even Parva. Had she done this? she wondered. Was all this tension because she'd failed at school?

Perhaps it was because there were so many guests staying and Bibi was stressed with all the entertaining. The bungalows were full, and Parva and the other staff seemed rushed off their feet.

Anjum grinned at her as she walked in through the kitchen door. 'Good morning, Leila,' he said. 'You're up early.'

'I couldn't sleep. Probably jet lag.'

'You must be hungry after such a long journey.'

She shrugged. Food hadn't been much on her mind.

'Let me make you some breakfast.'

'Maybe later,' Leila said. She was going to cycle down and

see if she could talk to Rasa before the guests needed him. She fancied a swim in the sea. Perhaps that would wash away all her misgivings.

'You must eat. It's not like you to be missing breakfast. Were you like this at school? Because it's no good for studying to have an empty stomach.'

'School breakfasts were horrible,' she told him. 'All I craved was your masala dosas.'

He laughed. 'OK, OK, I will make you one, if you insist.'

Leila smiled and slid onto the high stool by the kitchen counter.

'Make yourself useful and strain that yoghurt for me,' Anjum instructed, pushing the metal bowl across the marble counter towards her. She picked up the heavy muslin cloth filled with yoghurt curd and watched it drip into the bowl.

Anjum took a bowl of batter from the ancient fridge and put a dollop of it on the crude griddle-stone above the gas-bottle flame. She'd always thought the kitchen was sophisticated, but compared to Judith's parents' kitchen, with its big electric oven and dishwashing machine, it now seemed primitive. She wondered how Anjum managed to produce so many incredible meals with such limited resources.

'So tell me what happened. Did you go to London?' Anjum asked, his voice laden with awe. She smiled at the way he said 'London'.

'Uh-huh,' Leila said. She thought about Judith and that awful night they'd been to the theatre. And about Harry. And how Judith had chosen not to believe Leila and how much that still hurt.

'All of that wonderful city to explore,' he said, a faraway look in his eye. 'I can only dream. Did you meet the Queen?'

Leila laughed. 'No. She wasn't around. But London? I

didn't like it that much. It's dirty and loud, and the people there are horrible.'

Anjum tutted. 'There are horrible people everywhere, Leila, if you look for them.'

'I suppose.'

There was a hiss as he expertly scraped the dough round the hot plate.

'What is the matter, Leila?' Anjum asked. 'Why are you looking so sad? That long face will curdle my yoghurt.'

'I don't know,' she said. 'Everyone seems to be so angry that I came back early.'

'You are a silly girl to waste an opportunity, that's all. Your mother will have lost a lot of money because of what you did,' Anjum said, giving her a sobering look.

Leila nodded, feeling small. She'd never considered that her mother would be out of pocket, but she must have lost the school fees, Leila realized. She watched Anjum make the perfect pancake she'd so craved, but as he slid it onto the plate with a little dish of coconut curry, she no longer felt hungry, and she ate miserably in silence, feeling awful about how much trouble she'd caused.

Later, cycling along the lagoon, on her way to find Rasa, Leila tried to make sense of her time at school. Should she have been different? she wondered. Should she have made more of an effort to fit in? Why couldn't she just have been accepted for herself?

Suddenly, a yellow-and-black tuk-tuk swerved round the corner into her path and Leila wobbled, falling towards the steep bank and then slipping down it a small way, falling off her bike into the mud.

'Hey,' she shouted, as the tuk-tuk's horn blasted and she

coughed in the blast of fumes belching out from the back. Further along the road, the tuk-tuk stopped.

'Are you OK?' she heard.

Leila scrambled up the bank. The American guy – Adam, wasn't it? – held out his hand to her and pulled her back up towards the road. She puffed, standing up, rubbing the mud from her hands. Now Leila saw the driver get out too, his huge bulk unfolding from the tuk-tuk. What the hell was someone like Adam doing taking a tuk-tuk ride in this part of the island, and at this time of the morning?

'I'm fine,' Leila said, as Adam gingerly stepped past her and retrieved her bike.

'We thought the roads were empty. We were probably going a bit fast.' He said it as an explanation, with an 'it can't be helped' shrug. It was a confusing type of apology – if it was an apology. The 'we' implied that he and the driver knew each other. 'Where are you going this early?' he asked, placing the bike next to her. It looked unscathed, but this bike had been in many similar scrapes.

'I'm just visiting an old friend,' Leila shrugged, uncomfortable with Adam's scrutiny. She flinched slightly as he squeezed the top of her arm.

'So long as you're OK.'

Leila stared between Adam and the driver, trying to fathom out what their connection could be. She took in Adam's wide smile, but his eyes were hard. There was something creepy about him, despite his attempt at open charm. She stayed silent, but he seemed unfazed.

'You know the island pretty well, huh? You should show me around.'

Leila nodded.

'Great. That's settled, then. Come and find me later. I'm in the beach bungalow.'

Leila brushed the mud off her hands and got back onto her bike, as Adam stepped back inside the tuk-tuk. As she looked over, she saw the scary-looking driver staring at her. His face was grim and she felt fear prickle all over her. She watched him tap a brown cheroot on a packet he was holding; then he flicked a match and lit it. Leila's heart thumped hard. Could it be the same guy who'd been to visit Chan in the dead of night? And if so, what was he doing driving Adam around now?

CHAPTER TWENTY-TWO

Miami, present day

Blaise was an expert on South Beach, but soon they headed north on the bike and the marina came into view. When the barrier opened, Blaise drove straight through with a cursory wave at the guy in the white booth.

But Blaise was that type of guy, Jess sensed. Someone for whom doors always opened, for whom barriers were customarily raised. She felt awed by how comfortable and easy his life seemed to be. It was just about as far away as she could imagine from any of the people she knew back home. Perhaps this was what life was like when you were very rich. She always assumed it would be, but witnessing it like this made her mind reel.

Jess whistled to herself as she looked over the rows of power-yachts lined up against the jetties. There must be millions of dollars' worth moored right here.

Blaise drove along the edge of the marina to the far jetty and then parked the bike. Jess looked back at it as they casually walked away. Wasn't he going to lock it up? Wouldn't someone just come and nick it? But Blaise didn't seem bothered. Perhaps the crime she was all too used to didn't happen in a place like this.

Jess followed him as he strode confidently up a little way along the wooden jetty and stopped.

'Here we are,' he said, holding out his arm towards the power-yacht moored next to him. It was huge, with a gleaming double deck and shiny white and teak steps spiralling between them. A couple of jet skis were on the upper deck with a fancy-looking hydraulic lift. It was clear that whoever owned this yacht was into their boys' toys.

'You can't be serious,' Jess laughed, as Blaise held her hand and she stepped off the jetty onto the white step of the boat. 'This is yours?'

'Not mine exactly, no,' Blaise said. 'It belongs to a friend, but I use it when I'm in Miami. It's the best way to see the sights. I promise.'

Jess was dazzled by the shiny whiteness of everything. Like it wasn't quite real. She saw herself reflected in the mirrored glass as Blaise slid it open and she felt again like pinching herself. 'Angel, you'd better be seeing this, girl,' she muttered to herself, feeling a pang of sadness that Angel wasn't here in person. Jess could very well imagine her squeal of delight and how excited she'd be.

'Come and meet my friend Nacho,' Blaise called, waving for her to follow.

She walked awestruck through the sumptuous galley with its cream and grey squashy sofas and cushions. Everything looked so clean and new. It was like being in the centrefold of a glossy yacht magazine.

'Ah,' she heard, and a small guy appeared from steps going down further into the yacht. 'How ya doin'?' he laughed, pulling Blaise into a friendly hug and clapping him on his back. He had white shorts on and very hairy legs, Jess noticed. His face was deeply suntanned, with craggy lines around his eyes.

'This is Nacho,' Blaise said, with a grin. 'This is Jess, my friend.'

Jess shook Nacho's hand. Was she Blaise's friend? Surely it took more than a handful of words to be a true friend. But then again, Blaise struck her as the kind of guy who made plenty of friends, easily. It was hard not to with this kind of lifestyle.

And she liked it. The possibility that she could be friends with Blaise. Did he do this with everyone he met? she wondered. Decide that he wanted to hang out with them and make them drop everything until they did?

'You like sailing, Jess?' Nacho asked.

'Um . . . I don't know. I mean, I haven't really been on board a . . .' she was about to say 'boat' but continued with 'yacht like this.'

She saw straight away that she'd passed some kind of test. If you wanted to hang out with the rich, then you had to speak their lingo. Wasn't that what one of the stewardesses had told her once?

'You'll love it,' Blaise said.

Where the hell were they going? She had no idea, but it felt too late to ask. Besides, she'd be fine, right? It felt weird to surrender herself entirely to Blaise, but she was in too deep now. Was she safe? she wondered, feeling a small pang of worry. She'd always been so cautious before, but no one in the whole world knew where she was, or who she was with. She was on a power-yacht with a multimillionaire in Miami. What could possibly go wrong?

CHAPTER TWENTY-THREE

Lace Island, 1990

Leila could see Rasa in the distance at the end of the jetty, leaning over in the wooden boat and pulling the string to start the outboard motor. Even from here, under the bowing palms, she smiled, sensing the frustration that would be on his face. That motor had always given him trouble, but Rasa was the only one who had the knack to fix it. She had thought that Chan had been planning to buy a new boat to take the guests out scuba-diving, but it clearly hadn't happened. The boat, which had long ago seen better days, was clearly still in use. It swayed in the water as Rasa balanced in it.

Leila ran lightly between the flowering mangroves down the sandy path to the beach. The white sand was already hot and she tiptoed lightly in her old leather flip-flops past the palm-covered makeshift beach bar and the rickety plastic sun-loungers. This was the main beach where the guests came to enjoy the water, and the beach bar had been Rasa's idea. BK, one of the shopkeepers from the village, came here in the mornings with sliced pineapple and watermelon when guests were staying, but other than his visits during the day, the long stretch of palm-fringed beach was deserted. Leila noticed a few empty plastic sunloungers that BK had tied to a palm tree over-night. They were brittle with sun-damage. They needed to be replaced too.

She looked out at the beach, the sand dotted with holes where the crabs had buried themselves, and a few shells glittered in the sun. The gentle white ripples broke onto the shore and she sighed, breathing in the hot breeze, her eyes feasting on that particular jewel hue of bright blue-green that she could never capture on her camera.

'Rasa,' she called, waving and shifting the string bag on her shoulder. Anjum had loaded Leila up with chapattis and a couple of fresh coconuts, and they bumped against her hip.

Rasa stood, shading his eyes from the sun as he heard her voice, and she ran along the jetty towards him, smiling and waving. He waved back, and she saw him unwind the cloth from round his head and wipe the sweat from his brow. He hitched up the white dhoti round his waist.

'Hey,' he said, smiling as she arrived, breathless, at the end of the jetty. 'I didn't expect to see you this morning.'

'Parva said you'd be here,' she said, sitting down and taking off her flip-flops before dangling her feet over the edge of the jetty. Below her, she could see rocks and sea cucumbers and shoals of darting yellow fish dancing in the current.

She didn't add that he'd been difficult to track down. That after her run-in with the tuk-tuk yesterday, she'd gone to his hut at the far end of the lagoon but had missed him. All day yesterday, she'd waited for him to appear on the beach, but then her mother had insisted that Leila help Anjum in the kitchen, and by the time she'd finished, it had been dark.

Leila looked at the scuba vests and tanks piled next to her on the jetty. In the boat, Rasa was bare-chested. His shoulders were slick with sweat and Leila felt an unexpected desire to reach out and touch him. If only they had the day to themselves and could take the boat out alone.

She looked out to sea to where the white line of surf broke on the reef. It was the most perfect day for diving. There wasn't a cloud in the sky, and all the things she'd been planning to blurt straight out – about seeing Chan and that man driving the tuk-tuk – stalled on her lips.

'Oh God, it's so gorgeous,' she sighed. 'Sometimes I forget just how breathtaking this place is.'

Rasa raised his eyebrows and then continued fiddling with the outboard motor. 'It would be nice if anything worked around here,' he muttered.

'Here,' Leila said, delving into her bag and pulling out the coconut. She handed it to Rasa, who took it gratefully. She took her own and put the straw in her mouth, sucking up the cool, refreshing liquid inside. It was this taste – this sweet, fresh green coconut juice – that made her feel like she was nourishing her soul. That along with Rasa's kind eyes, which connected with hers now. She felt so safe, suddenly, so relieved that she was here and alone with Rasa, that she wanted to cry.

'What's wrong?' Rasa asked, his brow creased with concern.

Leila put down her coconut and blew out her cheeks, annoyed and embarrassed at this sudden welling-up of emotion. 'I'm just glad to be back, that's all. Although nobody else seems happy I'm here. Bibi is so cross with me.'

Rasa sighed and turned his attention back to the engine. He didn't say anything and Leila knew him well enough to know that he was choosing his words carefully.

'I'm not sure, but I think they ran out of money. They must have, because nobody has been paid for months.'

He twisted a screw with a screwdriver, peering over the

engine, then pulled the starter motor. This time, the engine rattled into life with a belch of diesel smoke and a thundering rattle that broke the tranquil air. Below the surface of the water, a shoal of fish did an about-turn and swam quickly towards the shore.

'There she goes,' Rasa said, standing back with a grin on his face. He put the battered white cover over the engine, but the noise was hardly any less deafening. 'I will keep it on,' he shouted over the din. 'Warm it up.'

Leila frowned, annoyed that the engine had broken the moment. She mulled over the words he'd told her, trying to grasp their real meaning. She'd never even considered Bibi and Chan's finances before. She'd just assumed that her mother owned Lace Island and that the visitors paid for the upkeep. They didn't live a lavish lifestyle – not like some of Bibi's extended family were rumoured to have. They didn't have fancy clothes or demand banquets and cars. Lace Island didn't call for such extravagances.

But Leila had always assumed that they could afford everything they needed – effortlessly. That as long as the guests came, then the money would roll in. She'd thought, too, that Chan must have wealth hidden somewhere. He must have done to marry Bibi. Although she'd always claimed she'd married for love.

What did it mean if they'd run out of money? For a start, it meant that nothing was getting replaced. Leila could see that clearly enough for herself. But what about the staff? Everyone on the island was like family. Lace Island only ran because everyone felt they were here together. That was what made it so special. The sense of community. Of everyone having their place. And money didn't matter. Not in a place like this.

Only now she was realizing it did.

Maybe it was all her fault. Maybe, just as Anjum had suggested, Leila's school had cost a fortune. Maybe she really was to blame for everyone being in a bad mood.

If only she'd never gone away, everything would be different. If only she'd made more effort with Timothy and her lessons with Rasa. If only she'd put her mind to it and shown Bibi how hard she could work, then Bibi and Chan would never have sent her away. She could have done her exams with Rasa.

And now it was too late. Everything had changed.

'Wait up!'

Leila turned to see two people approaching from the jetty. It was that American guy Adam, and just behind him, in a flowing kaftan and floppy hat and large shades, was the Frenchwoman who'd been on the flight with the captain. Wasn't she supposed to be the captain's girlfriend? So why was she alone with Adam? Had she extended her holiday, while Marc went back to the mainland?

Adam was wearing blue shorts and a checked shirt, which had a large sweat patch across his chest. He was carrying a rolled-up towel under his arm. He hurried down the jetty and Leila stood. He grinned from beneath his American baseball cap.

'Ah, it's young Leila, if I'm not mistaken,' Adam said, taking off his cap. His teeth were dazzling in the sun. 'I was expecting you to show me the sights.'

Leila looked down. She felt Rasa staring at her, trying to digest this news. This implication that she already knew Adam well.

'I've been busy,' she mumbled.

'Is this your friend?' He said it with a horrible insinuation in his tone. As if he knew something about her and Rasa. She could feel Rasa's hackles rising. 'So, does that mean you're coming with us, Leila?'

She hated the way he said her name. She hated that everything about him seemed to be about causing mischief. The way he seemed to so effortlessly bamboozle her.

'Oh no, I . . . I just came to see Rasa.'

Feeling trapped, Leila glanced behind him at the French girl, who pouted in the sunlight, as if completely bored by her surroundings. She didn't want to be stuck on a boat with Adam and this woman, but as she looked at Rasa, she saw a plea in his eyes. Because he didn't want to be stuck alone with them either.

'Come on. Come with us. It'll be fun. I insist.' Adam said it like it was settled and jumped down into the boat. 'Rasa agrees. Don't you, old sport?'

'Why don't you, Leila? I could do with a hand,' Rasa said. She saw the look pass between him and Adam, and she knew that Rasa hated him as much as she did.

Leila stared back at Rasa; she knew that if he asked her, she'd go to the moon for him and back. But Rasa's attention had already been diverted. Leila watched his face as Monique arrived next to the boat, took off her hat and shook out her hair. She was clearly fully aware of how Adam and Rasa were looking at her and Leila felt a part of her shrivel. She was just the same as those girls at school. Rich and snotty – just like Edwina had been. Except this girl was worse, because she was a grown-up. For one moment, Leila pictured pushing the French girl off the jetty and into the sea.

But then Rasa and Adam both held out their hand and she stepped down into the boat as if she were a queen, and Leila was left to pass out the scuba jackets.

She braced herself. This was going to be a tricky morning.

CHAPTER TWENTY-FOUR

Miami, present day

'And that,' Blaise announced, 'is the best way to see Miami.'

Jess giggled as Blaise flung his hand out to show her the view of the whole of Miami Beach, as if he owned the lot. And maybe he did, she thought, gasping at the view. Everything was perfect – the white sand, the blue sea, the huge, glittering hotels, but right now, she was more interested in watching Blaise.

They were heading out to sea, and the breeze tickled her face as they sipped champagne. She wanted to pinch herself. So far, Blaise had been nothing but charming and funny, and he and Nacho had entertained her with stories of their fishing expeditions as they'd driven out of the harbour.

'You know, I heard the dolphins are around,' Nacho shouted, as Blaise led Jess to the cushions at the front of the yacht.

'Then let's go find them, Captain,' he called back, and Nacho put the throttle down.

Jess smiled, brushing a strand of hair away from her mouth as the yacht sped up and she shifted backwards in the cushioned seat as the force threw her back. She could see the front of the yacht slicing effortlessly through the waves. Moving this fast, so close to the water was exciting, but Blaise seemed to be taking it completely in his stride and carried on pouring champagne with a steady hand as if nothing was happening.

'Look at me,' he said, making a joke of it. 'Would I make good cabin crew?'

Jess laughed. Of course he would, she wanted to say. He could probably do anything he set his mind to. The only problem would be that the other crew and all the other passengers would probably just drool over him all day.

Because *he was gorgeous*. Jess couldn't stop thinking it. The more time she spent with him, the more attractive he became.

Stop it! Jess told herself. She was having a brilliant time, but she hardly knew a thing about this guy, and there must be a catch, right? He couldn't be this rich and funny and handsome and charming and like *her*. Could he?

He handed her a glass of bubbles and smiled.

'Bottoms up,' he said. 'Isn't that what they say in England?'

'Not where I come from,' Jess laughed, clinking glasses with him. She took a sip of the delicious liquid. Champagne had never really been her thing – not on an empty stomach – and she felt the hit of it almost instantly.

'So, Miss Jess . . .'

'What?'

'It's very tempting to interview you,' he said, in a jokey way. He sat next to her and didn't seem to notice that his forearm brushed against hers. The contact sent goosebumps rushing through her. 'I'm so curious.'

Why would he be curious about her? she wondered.

'About what?' she asked, enjoying the way he sat next to

her gazing at her as if she were the most interesting person in the world. He sank back onto his elbow, lying next to her. She breathed in the delicious scent of his aftershave. 'There's not much to know.'

She liked his feet, she thought, and his slim ankles. He looked like he worked out a lot. She wondered what he'd be like in Tony's gym, whether he'd be any good at kick-boxing. What would Tony say if he could see her right now? she thought. Her life in London seemed so impossibly far away all of a sudden.

'I don't know. Tell me about your sisters. About your life travelling around America growing up. I'm intrigued,' he said.

Jess was caught off guard and stared at him for a moment, feeling colour rising in her cheeks.

'You told the little girl on the plane. About your sisters,' he prompted.

Jess swallowed hard and then took another glug of champagne, stalling for time. This was the moment. Right now. She needed to come clean and confess. She needed to tell him how she made up different versions of her past to keep herself amused – maybe make a joke of it? But even voicing it that way made her sound odd. A phoney. And Blaise wouldn't understand. Why would he?

What possible need had he ever had to make up a different version of himself? He didn't look like he was the kind of guy with an ugly past to escape. He looked like he belonged in this privileged life.

It was her quirky lie that had piqued his interest. He wasn't going to be attracted to a girl like her from a scruffy, forgotten suburb of Outer London. He was attracted to the bohemian story she'd made up.

But looking at him, the sun twinkling behind him, making

his eyes more blue than ever as they peered at her over the top of his shades, she knew she couldn't break the magic. Not yet. She had to carry on with the lie.

'Well, it was an odd childhood,' she began. 'A long time ago, now. I don't have that great a memory, but I do remember it was fun.'

Without warning, a buried memory bubbled up to the surface, unbidden: the care home and the scratchy nylon duvet. With sudden, shocking clarity, she pictured herself as a small girl, alone and frightened, listening to the shouting of the staff and one of the other, older girls along the corridor. The banging doors. The boarded-up window that had never been replaced after someone had thrown a brick through it. How she shivered in bed, her nostrils filled with the smell of boiled cabbage from the kitchen and stale cigarette smoke, as she clutched the gold crucifix in her tiny palm, hoping it would keep her safe.

'Do you sing, like your mother?'

'Huh? Oh no,' Jess said, trying to keep the lightness in her voice. 'I play guitar. Just a little. That's all. Nothing like Mum.'

Still the memory came – the sing-song chants of the boys in the home. 'Paki. Nobody wants you, Paki.' She pictured Christina, the woman in charge. She saw her raising her hand, saw her hitting the child.

Hitting her.

And Angel screaming, pulling at her top to make her stop, and Angel getting whacked too.

She cleared her throat, looking out at the white skyscrapers receding in the distance. 'Mum was, well, she was quite a character. Certainly entertaining, although she never stopped singing. Or being on the move.'

She forced out the words, words and then more made-up words about being on the road, and with each one she felt like she was drowning in her lie. As she glugged more champagne, she became increasingly light-headed and name-dropped Bon Jovi and George Michael. She made up anecdotes about Austin, Texas, and Glastonbury, throwing in random facts she'd borrowed like a magpie from the profiles of people she'd only read about in magazines. And with every word, her lies moulded into something more tangible and she watched Blaise taking it all in, watching it set as the truth.

But it didn't matter, she told herself, trying to quash the nerves that made her feel shaky inside. She was just a casual dalliance for him. Someone to fill up some time in Miami. He was the kind of guy who picked up people all the time, right? In fact, he probably had a girlfriend, or even a wife. *Oh God . . . did he?* The thought brought her up short. She hoped not. She didn't want to be here for a day as wonderful as this . . . if that's really all she was for him. Some kind of game.

Because that must be what this was. And after today, she'd probably never see him again. So what she'd just told him didn't really matter.

It didn't matter.

'What about you?' Jess said, as soon as she could. 'Tell me about growing up.'

'It was fun. I was lucky. Mum and Dad were in love back then and we had a great life. I was the baby, with two older brothers and a sister, so I always got spoilt. Dad liked the high life, so we holidayed a lot.'

Jess listened as he talked about his perfect life, feeling like her made-up past was more ridiculous than ever. Because in contrast to all the lies she'd told, she could picture the simple truth of Blaise's life so well. Good-looking, well-educated teen-age Blaise, perfectly formed with his sense of entitlement fully intact. For a second, she wanted to sling her champagne in the sea at the unfairness of it all. He'd had the kind of life she'd fantasized about for so long. Why did it get to be him and not her?

'And what now? It sounds like you have it all,' she said, hoping she didn't seem bitter.

'I can't deny that I've been fortunate,' Blaise laughed, as he took a sip of champagne. 'My mother always told me I had a lucky streak. I seem to know a good property deal when I see one.'

'A handy knack to have,' Jess said. She wondered what kind of woman Blaise's mother might be. She imagined a rich, gin-soaked woman with plump lips and no wrinkles, all designer suits and bright lipstick, who would be perfectly at home on a yacht like this. She probably wouldn't take too kindly to her son dating an air hostess.

Dating? Jess caught herself. She was getting ahead of herself. Way ahead of herself. And anyway, it was too late. She'd already made up too many lies.

Your parents don't make you who you are, she reminded herself of her familiar mantra, even though people like Blaise thought they did. She was responsible for being who she was. That was it. End of. Whatever backstory she gave didn't change the present.

'Yes, it is. And what about you? Where are you up to, Jess? Have you achieved everything you dreamt of?'

Jess smiled and shook her head. 'Not even close,' she said.

'Oh. I see. You're more ambitious than I thought.'

Hadn't he thought she was ambitious? She couldn't read his tone, or what he was implying. If she'd told him the truth from the start, maybe he'd think differently. Maybe he'd be impressed that she was someone who'd worked her way up from nothing. Someone who'd never had a leg-up, or a daddy to make a useful call. But instead, she'd given the impression of someone who mixed with singers and musicians, for whom this crazy travelling lifestyle she had was a matter of course, a stepping stone on the road to somewhere else, when it was actually something she'd worked her socks off for. It was everything that defined her.

'I really like my job,' she said, sounding more defensive than she meant to. 'I want to continue to work my way up, you know. Go as far as I can in my career.'

'What does that mean? You want to work in first class?'

She couldn't gauge his tone. Was he teasing her? Undermining her dreams? 'Ideally, yes. Then get to be senior cabin crew.'

'What then? Would you work in management at the airline? People do that, I've heard.'

Why was he pretending he was interested in her career? It meant nothing compared to the things he did. Whatever they were. His 'business interests'. She wished he'd stop pretending to find her fascinating.

'I like flying. I mean, there's so many places I want to go. So many things I'd like to see.'

'Oh? Where's top of the list?'

'I don't know . . . New York. I'd love to go to New York.'

'Didn't you go there when you toured with your mum?'

He'd tripped her up and she blushed.

'Not really. Not properly. You know, to live,' she said. 'Besides, everything is different as an adult. Anyway, you don't want to know about my silly dreams,' she added, brushing the moment away.

Blaise's eyes bored into hers. 'Of course I do. I'd like to see if I can make any of your dreams come true.'

'How you guys doing up there?' Nacho called. 'You fancy taking the jet skis out before lunch?'

Blaise grinned like a little boy and she was pleased that the moment was broken. 'Sure,' he called back. 'Come on, Jess. I promise you you'll love it.'

Oh God, Jess thought. What have I done? He might just be the most perfect man I've ever met and I've ruined it all before it has even begun.

CHAPTER TWENTY-FIVE

Lace Island, 1990

The coral reef stretched in a horseshoe round the southern tip of Lace Island. Leila had first gone out on the diving boat with Chan when she'd been eight, but it had been Rasa who'd persuaded her to overcome her fear and dive. Even so, there'd always been that warning light of fear in her mind, thinking of the rogue shark that had killed her father, and she preferred the other dive site nearer the shore to this one.

Now, on the boat, she scanned the clear horizon, knowing it was ridiculous, but knowing too that she was waiting to see a dorsal fin break the glittering blue surface and confirm all her worst fears. But she knew better than to say anything.

As they chugged across the water to the reef, Rasa was still staring at the French girl, Marc's girlfriend.

'You know Monique, right?' Adam checked, unrolling his towel to reveal two large brown beer bottles. He grinned mischievously and then popped open the bottle with his palm on the edge of the boat, denting the wood. Leila and Rasa exchanged a look as he tossed the bottle top into the clear ocean. She hated men like Adam, and seeing him through Rasa's eyes made Leila despise him even more. What if one of the sea turtles ate that bottle top? She was about to say something, but she saw the minutest shake of Rasa's head. They were staff, he was saying. This wasn't the time or place to challenge Adam.

Leila watched as he took a swig of beer and then offered it to Monique, who shook her head. He licked the foam from his lip.

'You are lucky to live here,' Monique said, surprising Leila with her English. It was the first time she'd addressed her directly. 'I have done some shoots in the Maldives, but this place is more raw. More naturally beautiful.'

So she was a model. That figured, Leila thought.

'She's famous, you know,' Adam told Leila and Rasa. 'A world-famous model. All the top designers know her.' He looked at Monique with something very much like pure greed in his eyes, as if he was claiming responsibility for Monique's success. And that he too should be applauded for recognizing her beauty.

'No, Adam, I am not world-famous,' Monique said, but as she turned her nose into the breeze like a proud dog, she was clearly flattered. Leila said nothing, watching a look pass between Adam and Monique. She squirmed uncomfortably in her seat. He was openly flirting with someone else's girlfriend, and the fact that he was so blatant about it made Leila feel as if she was complicit in their secret affair.

She thought of the girls back at Hillmain and what Edwina would say if she could see Leila right now. What fools they'd been not to have believed Leila about any of this. They'd be in a geography lesson right now, while Leila was on one of the world's most beautiful coral reefs with a famous model. She should feel like she'd got the last laugh, except that right now, she didn't feel like laughing at all. Besides, those girls would already have moved on without her and have found someone else to bully.

She stared back towards the island. From out at sea, with this perspective, she couldn't see the paddy fields, the village by the small port or the landing strip. Instead, Lace Island looked like the proper desert island it was, the land covered in palm trees, the shore fringed by the whitest of sand. The only building she could see was the old lighthouse, its white tower rising up to the sky. She wished she could scoop the whole image up and swallow it and hold it inside her forever. What if Bibi really had lost all their money? What if they lost Lace Island and had to move away from paradise? What would happen to her then?

The thought made her shudder. Ever since she'd been tiny, she'd been planning her future here. Not in any specific way, just a deep-down assumption that she'd have her children here and look after Bibi and Chan as they got old. But what if that didn't happen? What if she had to go back out into the real world, where Lace Island didn't matter, where everything that happened here meant nothing?

As the water changed colour where the reef started below, Rasa expertly slowed the boat and cut the engine. Automatically, Leila reached for the anchor line and, without even checking, threw it over the side. They'd done this often enough together that she knew the drill.

She watched the line sinking, hoping it would make it to the soft sand at the bottom. The clear water below her was teeming with life, shoals of fish darting among the pink and yellow coral plants.

Soon, Rasa had helped Monique get her scuba jacket on, and Rasa guided her off the side of the boat, backwards into the water. Leila watched Monique swim away, her long legs sleek in the water, her hair fanning out around her like a mermaid's, and Leila was glad to be free of her presence in the boat and the cloying perfume she wore.

Adam watched Monique in the water for a moment before she turned and broke the surface.

'*Mon Dieu, c'est incroyable.* Come, Adam.'

Adam grinned at her and then flipped himself backwards off the boat, his arms crossed over his chest. Leila and Rasa watched him swim away.

'Good riddance,' Leila muttered.

'Are you going in?' Rasa asked her.

'Are you?'

'No. I'll stay with the boat. Help them out when they're ready. We must help the guests at all times,' he said, his voice laced with sarcasm. He hated Adam too, then. And it didn't sound as if he was as enamoured with Monique as she'd feared.

Rasa nudged her and she looked over to where Monique and Adam were, near the reef. From above, it was easy to see that they were close together and Monique's legs were twisting round Adam's as they sank in the water together.

'She couldn't wait to get her hands on him,' Rasa said.

'I thought she was with the captain?' Leila whispered, although it was ridiculous to whisper when no one could hear them.

Rasa raised his eyebrows. 'She is. Or was. Only yesterday Lonegan came here with the man from Rio's wife,' Rasa said, as he tied the small metal ladder to the boat. 'The same thing. He tipped me five dollars at the end of the day.'

'That's good, isn't it?' Leila said, but Rasa shook his head and pulled a face.

'He's paying for my silence. Men like that think they can have anything they want. You should watch him.'

'Me?'

'Have you not seen the way he stares at you?'

'He's not interested in me.'

'Why wouldn't he be?' Rasa said. 'You're far more beautiful than her.'

'But I'm only fourteen.'

'You think age matters to him?'

He was leaning over the boat and the reflection of the sunlight on the water danced on his face. She wanted to say something – to deny that Adam might possibly be interested in her, to claim that she wasn't beautiful – but she sensed that making him justify his compliment was the wrong thing to do and would only make her seem vain. She felt a strange emotion welling up in her.

Flattered as she was, was Rasa's warning about Adam justified? Was Adam staring at her in his greedy way? Like that very first time they'd met? For a second, she remembered Sussman and a chill ran through her.

'I saw him – Adam – with this guy I've never seen before. They nearly ran me over yesterday morning by the lagoon,' Leila said.

'What were you doing there?'

'I was looking for you,' she said, before blushing and quickly carrying on to cover the moment. 'It was early and Adam was with this guy. A tall guy. I haven't seen him before. He smokes a cheroot.'

Rasa's face was serious. 'Don't go near him.'

'Why? Is he dangerous?'

'I don't know yet,' Rasa said, in a way that implied that Rasa was spying on him himself.

'Where's he from?'

'Bamu told me that he comes from Burma. His name is Lee Shang.'

'What's he doing here?'

'Nothing good, that's for sure. Stay away from him, Leila. Promise me.'

Leila nodded, but her mind was whirling. The guy, Shang, was dangerous. She knew it and Rasa knew it. But Chan knew him too. If he was meeting Shang in the dead of night, then the chances were that Bibi didn't know about him. But what was Chan hiding?

'He scares me.'

'Don't show him your fear,' Rasa said, reaching forward and touching her hand. Their skin against each other and the flaking painted blue wood would make an amazing picture, she thought. 'I'll protect you,' he said. 'OK? No matter what.'

She stared into his eyes, seeing the amber dancing in the heart of them, and she knew that she was home. Whatever was going on, Rasa would find out and protect her. Together with him, she could handle anything.

'Oh look,' she heard. She broke away from Rasa's stare to see that Adam had popped up on the other side of the boat and had taken the scuba tube from his mouth. 'Love's young dream,' he said, grinning. 'Pass me that knife, boy,' he said to Rasa.

'What for?'

'There's some oysters down here. I want to see if any have pearls in for Monique.' He stared right at Leila. 'There's nothing I like better than teasing out a pearl.'

CHAPTER TWENTY-SIX

London, present day

Jess sat on the leather seat in the airline's offices, feeling sweat prickle her neck. She'd come here for her first interview seven months ago now, but it felt much longer. That was just after Angel had died and she'd been in a very dark place. But her job had given her a new outlook and she felt that all the hope she'd lost in those dark days had returned. She was clinging on to this opportunity for all it was worth, which is why she was so nervous to have been called in on her day off.

It was an unseasonably hot April day and the office fan was blowing a stream of hot air in her face. This was why she wanted to fly, she thought, looking around the office of the HR manager, with its wall of filing cabinets and glossy framed pictures of the airline's fleet. She couldn't imagine being able to handle a desk job in somewhere like this.

She wondered what kind of a man Stephen Pikeman was and why she'd been called in to see him. And then a thought struck her: maybe someone had reported her for going off for the day in Miami with a passenger. No, no, that was ridiculous. She was pretty sure she hadn't broken any rules. She could see who she wanted, surely? But maybe someone – one of the stewardesses, perhaps – had implied that she'd broken some sort of unspoken airline etiquette.

It would be pretty unfair to get chastised for going on a date with Blaise when nothing had happened. Well, not exactly nothing. There'd been a connection. A big one. Of that Jess was sure. But nothing physical had happened, despite the romantic sunset and the candlelit dinner he'd treated her to at his favourite Miami Beach restaurant. It had been nearly two in the morning when he'd dropped her back at the hotel, kissing her gently on the cheek, thanking her for a lovely day and saying he'd see her around.

Jess kept on going round and round the date in her head. In this sweaty, cramped office in London, she thought back now to the sunset, to the dolphins they'd seen and realized how impossibly romantic it had all been. He'd made her feel amazing, and it hadn't been all one-sided. She'd been able to tell he was torn. That he'd wanted to kiss her, but that he had held back.

She hadn't realized that he would prove to be such a gentleman. And it was that, more than anything else, that had captured her imagination and kept her awake all that night in Miami, mooning around to herself like one of the Disney princesses just down the road.

Even though it had been a one-time dream date, Jess knew that she should really stop obsessing about him. That life she'd glimpsed – the fast motorbike, the glamour of Miami Beach, the luxury yacht, the money – it wasn't hers. She didn't belong in that world.

And Blaise must know that. Because it wasn't as if he was going to call her. If he had been going to, he would have by now.

But he's been busy, Jess's dreamy self protested. *It will happen. It was fate. You were destined to meet him.*

She sighed heavily, furious with herself for this schizophrenic mind chat that had plagued her ever since she'd first clapped eyes on Blaise.

The truth was glaringly obvious: Blaise had been filling in time with her. If he wanted a girlfriend (and if he did want one, he probably already had one installed in a fabulous apartment somewhere), then it was highly unlikely that he'd ever fall for anyone like Jess. In all likelihood, he probably hadn't thought about her once since their date.

She jumped as the door opened and the human resources manager, Stephen Pikeman, walked in. She'd seen his profile on the airline's website, but she was not prepared for how tall he was in the flesh. He had a brown fringe, which he smoothed down with his palm.

'Don't get up,' he said, stooping to get round the desk. He had a sort of no-nonsense directness that made Jess nervous. Was this a chat about how she was getting on, now she was a few months into her job, or was she in trouble? It was hard to tell, but she suspected the latter. 'Sorry I'm a bit late. It's hectic here today.'

She watched as Mr Pikeman sat down with a sigh on his leather seat, which hissed beneath him. She felt her palms sweating as he rattled a few keys on his keyboard and his computer screen sprang into life.

'Phew, it's hot today, right?' he muttered. 'Well,' he said. 'Well, well, well. It seems that someone has put in a good word.' He fixed her with a searching stare. 'To tell you the truth, you usually have to have a lot more flying hours to be up for a promotion like this, but I have to follow orders from the top. So . . .' He smiled at her. 'I guess congratulations are in order.'

Jess shook her head, confused.

'Well, you can be happy,' he urged. 'You must have broken the record. There's a lot of crew who'll have their nose put out of joint about this, but if you're up to the job, then good for you.'

'I'm sorry . . . I'm not sure I understand.'

'You've been bumped up,' Mr Pikeman said, as if Jess were particularly dense. 'Unusual, yes, but not unheard of. You'll need to sign a new contract,' he added, sliding paperwork across the desk towards Jess. 'You can choose where you work. First class included.'

Numbly she took the papers, seeing her name at the top of the contract. How had this happened? Why had she suddenly been promoted?

I'd like to see if I can make any of your dreams come true.
Blaise.

She stared at the piece of paper in front of her, her heart pounding. This promotion meant she was in a different pay bracket. There wouldn't be that much more, but if she budgeted right, there'd certainly be a little left over each month. Money that she could save and put towards a deposit on her own flat. Money that would mean she'd never have to feel poor again. She picked up the pen, staring at the place where she was to sign her name, but she hesitated, guilt pulsing through her.

She didn't deserve this. Mr Pikeman knew it as clearly as she did.

'It appears you're starting right away,' Mr Pikeman said. He turned his attention to the screen and opened a complicated spreadsheet. 'Your rota is different. You're going to New York tomorrow.'

'New York?'

'Yep. The Big Apple. It's one of the best routes. Looks like you've lucked out.'

Jess was still jittery with nerves when she arrived for work the next day. As she met her colleagues in the flight briefing room, she felt sure they'd see through her straight away, but everyone was super-friendly. Even when she chose to work in first class. What the hell, she thought. She might as well.

'I'm Mac, the captain,' a good-looking guy in captain's uniform said, shaking her hand, as they walked out towards the terminal. 'Good to have you aboard, Jess. It should be a pleasant run to New York. Sue will look after you.'

Jess smiled at Sue, her other cabin-crew colleague. She was probably close to thirty, Jess thought, glad that she was flying with someone experienced.

'The New York run is always fun. We had Jay-Z last week. He was a riot.'

'I've never been . . . I mean . . . I just got promoted,' Jess gushed, instantly regretting it.

'Lucky you,' Sue said with a friendly smile. 'Congratulations.'

She didn't know, Jess thought. Whatever back-stabbing she was expecting wasn't going to happen today. She just had to go along with it, she cautioned herself, and pretend everything was normal. She could do it. Couldn't she?

When they arrived on the plane, Jess checked her phone one last time. She'd tried phoning Blaise several times yesterday, but his phone kept going straight to his voicemail and she wondered if he was deliberately avoiding her. When she left a message, she had almost told him what had happened, but at the last moment, she'd stopped herself. If Blaise was responsible for her sudden promotion, then she'd have to hear it from him himself. And then what? she wondered. She couldn't exactly get angry at him. Not when she'd had no choice but to accept the promotion. She hadn't had the nerve – or the proof – to tell Stephen Pikeman about her conversation with Blaise.

And maybe, just maybe, someone at the airline had put in a good word for her. Perhaps it hadn't been Blaise but a grateful customer. Stranger things had happened. But even as she told herself that, she knew it wasn't true. Blaise had interfered with her fate and now she had no idea what to do with that knowledge. Because nobody had ever given her a bump-up before. And it felt . . . it felt weird. Like she didn't deserve it. If she'd felt like an imposter when she'd first started, she felt even more like one now.

What if Sue and the captain and Leanne, her other colleague, realized that she had been promoted unfairly? That she didn't deserve this? That she wasn't good enough?

No. She could do it, she told herself. She'd have to bluff this out. Do the best job she possibly could. It didn't matter how she'd got here, only that she was here. She was just going to have to try her hardest and be as professional as possible. No slip-ups. No mistakes.

She tried to put Blaise out of her mind as she and Sue greeted the passengers on board. Everyone was so friendly and happy, and Jess wanted to pinch herself when she noticed two famous actors were sitting on her side of the plane. She wanted to jump up and down and point, but she stayed calm and professional, as if this happened every day.

'There's a gentleman in seat five asking for you,' Leanne said, as they met in the galley to get more champagne.

'Me?'

'Yes. He asked for you specifically. I'd get in there if I were you. He's, like, seriously hot.' Leanne gave her a meaningful look.

Jess laughed, walking down the aisle to seat five. The guy in it was leaning down getting something from his bag.

'Can I help you with that, sir?' Jess asked. 'I could stow that for—'

'No, it's fine.'

Jess gasped as Blaise straightened up, sitting upright in his seat.

'Blaise. Oh my God. What are you doing here?'

He grinned at her. 'I got your message. I thought I might accompany you to New York.'

CHAPTER TWENTY-SEVEN

Lace Island, 1990

Leila pushed her bike up the hill, the basket laden with peppercorn plants she was taking to Maliba from Anjum's kitchen garden. She'd offered to go for him, knowing that it would give her an excuse for her meeting with Rasa. They'd agreed to meet at lunchtime by the lighthouse, and she hoped that once they were alone, he would tell her what he knew about Shang.

She smiled to herself, wondering if the dress she'd chosen was too much for such a casual meeting. She'd had Parva oil and braid her hair late last night too, and she smoothed it now, hoping it looked as nice as it had done in the mirror earlier.

In all likelihood, Rasa wouldn't even notice the effort she'd made, but Leila hadn't been able to stop thinking about what he'd said on the boat. It was just the way he'd said it, the way he'd told her she was more beautiful than Monique. It had filled her up with sunshine. Was it possible that he meant it? That he liked her too, the way she liked him? Not that she'd ever really admitted it to herself before, but she'd stopped thinking of Rasa as her best friend and he'd become something . . . well, more. Something confusing, indefinable. Something that she couldn't ignore.

Now, as she approached the familiar path through the trees up to the lighthouse, she noticed deep ruts in the hard mud, and as she went further, the track widened into a road. She'd thought it would be a deserted track, but someone must have been up here in a truck. Maybe they'd been fixing the light.

Chan had kept the light maintained over the years, but he was always complaining about how temperamental it was. And there was one thing you didn't want, he always quipped – a temperamental lighthouse.

Like Bibi, Leila wondered why they kept the lighthouse going at all, when it used precious electricity. The boats that came from the mainland usually passed in the day, the shipping routes ran far to the north to avoid the coral reef, and there were never any boats in the seas around Lace Island at night.

Even so, Leila had always liked the lighthouse and had found something romantic in its searching beam. It felt comforting. As if the light was not only warning people at sea but alerting them to their presence on Lace Island. *We're here*, the light seemed to say.

When she was a kid, she and Rasa had come here with Chan, who sometimes let them go up to inspect the light. The view from the top was incredible, and Leila and Rasa had fantasized about building a camp up there and sleeping out under the stars, but Chan had always forbidden it, worried that she'd topple off in the night. She wondered if she and Rasa would climb up there today. She wondered if he wanted to be alone with her as much as she longed to spend time with him. Just the two of them.

Now, Leila stopped, suddenly aware of voices and of the noise of engines further along the track. She got off her bike, leant it against the tree and set off between the tall palms to investigate.

At the top of the hill, there was a black-and-yellow tuk-tuk – the same one that had run her off the road – as well as a large truck with crates in the back. Men were unloading the heavy crates into the lighthouse through the open door. She heard their gruff voices and crept nearer.

She looked behind her. The path through the forest was a dense green. Where was Rasa? Did he know about this? That all this was going on, here in secret, in the trees?

Shang was there. She heard his commanding voice and the men talking back, but she couldn't work out what they were saying. Careful not to be seen, she pressed herself against the smooth bark of the tree. Then she stared round once more. One of the guys walked round the truck and Leila saw that he had a black gun slung over his shoulder.

She ducked out of sight, her heart racing with fear. Why was there a man with a gun? This was Lace Island, she reminded herself, trying to calm down. Bad things didn't happen here, and yet her knees started trembling. Those men . . . Shang in particular, were terrifying. What were they unloading?

She could front it out – push her bike past and just wave a hand in greeting as if nothing was happening, but her instinct told her that was the wrong thing to do. She didn't want Shang to see her, or risk being discovered spying. Most importantly, she should warn Rasa.

Quickly, she set off back the way she'd come, ditching her bike in the undergrowth away from the path. She'd take a shortcut and go down the steep part of the hill towards the guest bungalows and onto the beach, and hopefully intercept Rasa on the way.

She scrambled down the steep slope, the weeds clinging to

her ankles, her mind racing. Rasa would know what to do, when she found him. He might be angry about what she'd found, though. After all, she had made a promise to keep away from Shang, but she couldn't help it that she'd come across him by accident.

What on earth was going on? Because whatever it was, Leila was fairly sure Bibi had no idea about it.

She looked around her desperately. What if she missed Rasa? What if he was coming the other way, from the village? No. No, he would be coming from the beach, she was sure of it. If she was quick, she'd find him.

But her plan to get to the beach this way wasn't as easy as she thought. Soon the forest floor was a tangle of mangroves she kept tripping on. She told herself not to worry about snakes and spiders as she trod through them, but the further she went, the more her legs got stung and scratched. It was too late to turn back, though. If she didn't get to the beach soon, she'd miss Rasa. She couldn't bear for him to get to the lighthouse and think she hadn't turned up. Or worse, arrive and get into trouble with that guy Shang. Rasa was absolutely the kind of person to demand to know what they were doing.

She slapped her arm where a bug had bitten her, annoyed that her dress was stained and her hair was now a sweaty mess. So much for looking her best for Rasa, she thought, as she fought through a spider's web, pulling it away from her face. It felt as if the undergrowth was trying to swallow her whole.

At last the sea came into view and the tops of the guest bungalows. If she could just make it past them and onto the beach, she'd be in the clear. If Rasa was still by the boat, maybe she could persuade him to take her out to the reef. All she wanted now was to be under water, in that blissful coral world, just with Rasa. That would blot everything out for a while.

And when they surfaced, everything would be better. She was sure of it.

She eased down the very steep part of the path, feeling herself sliding the last bit of the way, suddenly out of control. Frantically, she slipped, flailing her arms, stopping her fall by clinging to the branch of a palm tree. She gasped, her heart pounding, realizing how close she'd come to falling directly down towards the beach, twenty or more feet. She could have easily broken something, and now she circled her ankle, feeling how sore it was.

Below her, she could see one of the guest bungalows with its private pool behind. She would have to climb back up the branch of the palm tree and then somehow find a pathway down. She looked along the line of trees, wondering how the hell she was going to extricate herself and find a way to safety.

And then she saw the door of the bungalow below her open and two people come onto the terrace, kissing. Leila gasped when she saw it was Adam and Monique. She heard them talking and then Monique laughing.

Leila froze. If she made a sound, they'd only have to look up and they'd see her hanging right above them.

Marc, the captain, had been gone a few days, but he would be back, and what would happen then? If Monique was having an affair with Adam, would she call things off with him? Did she prefer Adam now, or was she being unfaithful behind the captain's back just for the thrill of it? How could she be so brazen? Or so cruel?

Leila couldn't fathom the games grown-ups played with each other, or what it was that Monique saw in Adam exactly. She tried not to look at them as they came out further onto the terrace, until they were right next to the Bali bed directly beneath her.

Leila could hardly breathe. The only thing she could do for the moment was to stay very still.

In a second Monique had whipped off the sheet tied round Adam's waist and Leila swallowed hard, shock making her flush all over. She'd never seen a naked man before. The size of his erect penis against his taut stomach was truly shocking.

But Monique wasn't shocked. She looked like she was very used to Adam being naked. Leila saw her reaching down to hold him in her hand, and then she kissed him deeply, her other hand clawing through his hair.

Leila watched, transfixed, as Adam, still kissing Monique, untied her bikini top and threw it to the floor. Leila felt her foot slipping and looked down, wincing. Gingerly, she moved her foot back, seeing her shin was scraped and bleeding where she'd fallen against the tree. She took a sharp intake of breath at the stinging, but Adam and Monique were far too involved with each other to notice.

She closed her eyes, willing herself not to look, but she couldn't help it. The gasps of desire felt like they were right in her ear as Monique and Adam kissed.

Monique, totally naked now, was sliding back on the soft cushion of the bed, right below Leila, who had a bird's-eye view through the threadbare rattan canopy.

Monique's breasts were large with dusky nipples, and her stomach was flat and soft. Leila held her breath as Monique parted her legs and she clearly saw the dark pubic hair between them. She was looking at Adam through half-closed eyes, like he should love what he was seeing. And he clearly did.

Now, Leila saw Adam hold his erect member in his hand. She felt her heart hammering as she watched Monique smile; then Adam moved upwards towards her face and she greedily ran her tongue over his tip before taking him between her lips.

Leila felt saliva flooding her mouth and she grew hot all over. She'd never seen anyone having sex and the scene before her was as repelling as it was fascinating. Is this what it was like? Is this what people did? Did they taste each other like this? Did they not feel shy? How could Monique take him in her mouth like that?

After a while, she saw Adam withdraw from Monique's mouth and shuffle backwards, opening Monique's legs wider with his thighs. He turned slightly and Leila froze, thinking he must be aware of her, but he didn't look up.

How could that fit inside Monique? she wondered. But Monique clearly wanted it. She lifted her legs and she saw Adam's eyes flutter shut as he guided himself inside her. Monique cried out before wrapping her legs round Adam's buttocks, and Leila heard them gasping as they moved together, the slats of the bed banging, Monique clawing Adam's back.

Leila squeezed her eyes shut. She felt frozen and yet molten at the same time, confusion threatening to drown her. She shouldn't be watching them. It was wrong, so wrong and yet . . . she couldn't help herself. Through one eye, she watched as Monique expertly flicked Adam over, and Leila saw him lying on the bed, his arms behind his head. She watched Monique lowering herself onto him, hearing the slick, slippery sound as she undulated her hips and ground down on top of him.

She saw Adam suck breath through his teeth, as if the pleasure were an exquisite torture. Monique flicked her long hair back over her shoulders, her lips parted as she fondled her own hard nipples.

They sped up now and she cried out and Adam sat up, burying his face in her breasts, both of them gasping as if they were in pain. Leila felt sick, longing for this to be over so that she could run away.

She looked up, the hot sunlight through the leaves blinding her, tears making everything blur. In the distance, she could hear the waves breaking against the shore. She longed to run as fast as she could across the burning sand and fling herself into the sea. She yearned to feel the cool water seep through her hair to her scalp, like an absolution. But she doubted that after witnessing this, she'd ever truly feel clean again.

CHAPTER TWENTY-EIGHT

New York, present day

Even now, after the meal was over, Jess was still giddy with butterflies. Blaise was here. Right in front of her. In New York. She feasted her eyes on him, effortlessly chatting with the waitress as she left dessert menus for them. Not that Jess could eat another thing after the most delicious ribs she'd ever eaten in her entire life. She smiled to herself to see how obvious it was that the waitress thought Blaise was hot.

She flashed a grudging look of respect in Jess's direction and Jess wanted to punch the air. She knew she had to play it cool with Blaise, but she longed to confess that she'd replayed their meeting in Miami over and over in her head, reliving the romance, the sunset, until it was burnt like a movie scene in her memory.

'This was a good recommendation,' Blaise said, pretending to take his hat off to her.

Jess grinned. It had been Sue who'd suggested this place in Brooklyn Heights Promenade, but it was clear that Blaise had had to pull strings to get a table at the last moment. She saw the queue of people waiting at the door.

'You want dessert?' he asked.

'You're joking,' she laughed. 'I'm totally stuffed.'

'Me too. I'm sure glad I caught that flight,' he said. 'That's the best meal I've had for weeks. Certainly the best company.' His eyes met hers and her stomach flipped over.

'About the flight . . .' she said.

'Hmm?'

'Can I ask you something?'

'Ask me what?'

Only, now she was on the verge of asking for the truth, Jess realized how stupid this might sound. What an idiot she was for even thinking this conversation might be a good idea.

'Nothing. It doesn't matter.'

'Go on.'

'Did you . . . ?' She fizzled out, losing her nerve. How could he possibly understand her feelings about her promotion? And what could she do about it now? She hadn't stuck up for her principles. She had signed on the dotted line. She'd even started her new job. Complaining about her promotion after the event seemed pathetic.

'I got promoted.'

'So I saw.'

'You didn't . . . I mean, this might sound crazy, but you didn't put in a word for me or something?'

Blaise stared at her, searching her face. His eyebrows furrowed. 'Do you think I did that?'

'I don't know. I don't know what to think. It's all so sudden. And you were the only one who knew I wanted to . . . well . . .' She fizzled out once more. This was ridiculous. *She* was ridiculous.

'No. I didn't say anything,' he said. 'To anyone. You can trust me.'

She felt relief surge through her. He hadn't tried to interfere after all. Whatever fluke had resulted in her landing her dream job, it hadn't been Blaise's doing.

'Uh,' she said, covering her face. 'I'm so embarrassed I said anything. Sorry.'

Blaise laughed softly. 'Maybe they like you at the airline. You ever think of that?' he said, and Jess thought of Tony and how he'd told her to believe in herself. What would he make of Blaise? she wondered.

'You're smart and beautiful,' Blaise continued. 'If I owned an airline, I'd want you near my best customers.'

Jess smiled, flattered by his words, but she still felt mortified. 'Oh God. You must think I'm—'

'I think you're great,' he interrupted, smiling across at her. Then he turned his attention to the jukebox, which had gone quiet during their conversation. 'You must know this one? Carole King,' Blaise said, popping a coin into the jukebox. 'Didn't you say your mum sang with her? My mum loved *Tapestry*, her second album. Played it over and over when we were growing up. But I like "Up on the Roof", which was on *Writer*.'

Here it was. The lie again. Coming back to haunt her. Just when she thought she was safe.

She smiled weakly at Blaise, who sang along.

'I always wanted a cool apartment after this song. In New York, where all my friends could sit on the roof.'

'And did you get it?' Jess asked.

'Sure. It's not a penthouse, though. Sadly.'

Was that where he was staying, then? Jess's mind was whirling. There was still so much she didn't know about him. Least of all how he'd managed to engineer to be here with her in New York.

'Shame,' she said, then regretted it immediately, although

he didn't seem to mind being teased. Come on. Be cool, she cautioned herself. Don't blow it or scare him off.

'So . . . is that where you call home?' she asked, wiping her mouth with her napkin and placing it on her plate. It probably hadn't been very ladylike to chow down the huge plate of ribs she'd just devoured. Blaise was probably used to girls who picked at their food and didn't eat carbs.

'I have a few places I keep toothbrushes,' he said, 'but nowhere has ever struck me as the place I want to stay forever. What about you?'

'I'm nowhere near close to finding home. I keep my toothbrush in my bag,' Jess said.

'Then do you want to see it? My apartment?' he asked softly.

'Sure,' she said, trying to mask her suddenly nervous flush. 'I fancy walking off those ribs, though.'

Blaise laughed and called for the bill. 'Good idea.'

'Can we walk across the bridge?' Jess said, relieved that she had a bit more time before they were going back to his apartment, and whatever might happen once they were alone there together. 'I used to watch *Sex and the City*. I always dreamt about going across it.'

'Then I'd be delighted to accompany you,' Blaise said.

As she strolled alongside Blaise on the wooden walkway, Jess thought the lovely stone arches of the towers at either end of the Brooklyn Bridge and the looping lights between them were even more romantic than the dolphins had been. If that were even possible. Blaise caught her arm as a cyclist shot past them and they stopped, looking out over the rail, the dark water way below. Blaise stepped in closer.

'You can see everything, look,' she said, awed by the

twinkling lights. From here, she could see the lit Statue of Liberty, the Freedom Tower and all the sights between. It made her feel simultaneously small and incredibly alive. Like she was part of this wonderful city.

He put his arms round her and pressed into the back of her, their heads side by side as they looked at the view. *He was hugging her*. Cuddling in close. Just like that. Like they'd agreed it. Like they *were* close.

She longed to turn in his arms and kiss him. She longed to tell him how much she'd thought about him. Instead, she closed her eyes, breathing in his closeness, wondering how this moment could possibly get any better.

'Come on,' he said.

Jess took his arm. He had his hands in his pockets and she liked the feeling of being connected to him like this. They passed a woman with a dog walking the other way and she smiled happily at them, as if they were a couple.

Were they a couple?

Was this what this was? What this felt like? She watched the city coming closer and she thought about what was going to happen when they got to Blaise's apartment. Suddenly, she stopped, furious with herself that she was about to do what she knew she would regret. But she couldn't seem to stop herself.

'Blaise, there's something I've got to tell you.'

'Hmm?'

'Just before . . . I mean . . . I don't want you to think . . .'

'Think what?'

She blew out a deep, pent-up breath. 'I'm just going to say it.'

'What?'

'That stuff about my sisters, my mum . . . it's not true. I

made it up. I'm sorry. You see, on the flights, I make up stories because I can be anyone.' She pressed her lips together, unable to look him in the eye. She couldn't bear to see if she'd lost him or not. 'I'm sorry. I had to tell you. I don't want you to carry on believing I'm someone I'm not.'

She opened her eyes. Blaise was staring at her.

'So who are you, then?'

She couldn't read his tone. He'd broken away from her, and his face looked dark as he stood opposite her. She'd blown it. She saw it then in his eyes.

'I don't know. I mean, I was taken into care when I was a baby. My mother died. Well, that's what I was told. I looked into it, but I couldn't find much out, so I'm not sure it's true. I had a crucifix of hers. The only thing . . .' Jess felt a great burst of anguish rising in her chest as his dark look bored into hers. 'And then my friend died and it was stolen and . . . Oh God . . . I'm so sorry. You don't need to know any of this and . . .'

She covered her face, humiliation and shame washing over her. She couldn't bear to look at him and have to explain. She felt the big canyon in her heart she'd tried so hard to paper over threatening to swallow her up with grief. She felt Angel in her mind telling her what a fool she was. That her honesty had always got her into trouble and now this was the crowning moment. She'd made a huge mistake coming clean.

But a second later, she felt Blaise's arms go round her.

'I'm so sorry. It sounds tough,' he said.

She pulled away, furiously wiping her tears. 'I don't blame you if you want to go,' she said, sniffing and trying to be brave. 'I don't know why you're even interested in me anyway. So maybe it's best if—'

'You want the truth?' Blaise said. 'Is this what this is about?'

She nodded.

'OK, well, the truth is, since the moment I saw you on that plane, I haven't been able to stop thinking about you. I think you're quirky and cool and unlike anyone I've ever met. Oh, and you have quite possibly the most beautiful eyes I have ever seen. And I don't care where you came from, only that you're here with me now.' Jess swallowed hard, staring into his eyes as he stepped towards her. 'OK? Is that enough reasons?'

She nodded, her chin wobbling, and she smiled.

'Good,' he said, holding out his hand for her to take. 'Then let's go.'

'No,' she said. 'I've got a better idea.'

Then she grabbed his coat lapels and pulled him towards her. And with his lips on hers, she knew that this moment had changed the course of her life forever.

CHAPTER TWENTY-NINE

Lace Island, 1990

The black crows hopped on the grass as Leila swam lengths in the swimming pool. Chan used to swim with her in the mornings, and sometimes Bibi had too, but this morning, the house was still quiet. Leila had heard their muffled argument late last night and heard Chan slamming out of the door, although she had no idea where he'd gone. There was no sign of either Bibi or Chan this morning, and Leila felt so out of sorts she knew only a swim would fix it.

She held her breath, pushing off the side, tasting the chlorine of the water. At the deep end, exhausted now, she spread her arms out against the side, circling her legs in the water. She half closed her eyes, the droplets of water making the bright morning sun glare. A gecko slithered past her, scuttling into the cracks between the stone slabs.

She turned and looked down at her legs, seeing how long they suddenly seemed to be. Her shin looked sore still, where she had scuffed it on the tree, although she had dabbed some of Maliba's famed Ayurvedic ointment on it.

She couldn't stop thinking about what had happened yesterday. How Adam and Monique had been together. And now, after a night's fretful sleep, Leila felt the conversation she'd witnessed between Monique and Adam only growing in significance.

'This is so good, but it can't last forever, you know. Marc will be back soon with the plane,' Monique had said.

'When?'

'I don't know. Maybe the end of next week. But after that, will I see you again?'

'If you come back here occasionally, then I'm sure we'll meet again.'

'Why? Are you staying here for good?'

'Sadly not. I will stay for a while longer, but I have business to attend to in the US. But I will be back. Lace Island will make me a lot of money one day.'

Why would he have said that? Leila wondered now. In such a smug way. What was Adam's business connection on Lace Island? Leila felt sure it had something to do with the lighthouse and Shang. Something to do with those boxes the men were guarding so closely.

Leila had tried to bring this up when she'd finally found Rasa late last night down by the fishing boats, but he'd been furious that she hadn't turned up to meet him. He said he'd waited for an hour by the lighthouse and then had been in trouble with his father, Vijay, for failing to help with one of the fishing boats Rasa had promised to mend.

Leila had explained what had happened. How she'd done her best to intercept him and warn him about what was going on, but how, on her way to the beach, she'd fallen into the trees by the guest bungalows and had seen Adam and Monique.

'You saw them? Actually saw them? They were together? Properly together, I mean?' Rasa had been horrified.

Leila had pulled an embarrassed grimace and nodded. 'It

was awful. I was totally stuck. If I'd moved then, they'd have seen me.'

'You should have gone away,' Rasa had said sharply. 'You shouldn't have watched them.'

'I tried not to,' Leila had said, feeling defensive, but inside she felt hot with shame.

'If he'd seen you—'

'He didn't.'

'You mustn't go snooping around. It's not right.'

'But something is going on,' she had persisted, telling him about how she'd overheard Adam talking about how he would make money out of Lace Island. 'Do you know what they're doing?'

Rasa had been unreachable after that, as they'd gone together with the lantern to retrieve her bike and to finally deliver the peppercorns to Maliba. It seemed to Leila that he'd been crosser about her inadvertently spying on Adam and Monique than he had been about Shang being at the light-house. When they'd gone with the lantern to the lighthouse, it had all been shut up, the same as Rasa had found it when he'd gone to meet Leila at lunchtime, and Leila wondered if he'd believed her at all about what she'd seen and the man with the gun and the trucks.

Leila had so wanted to be alone with Rasa, but his bad mood had ruined everything. Perhaps today he'd be easier to talk to.

In the meantime, maybe she should talk to Bibi. All of this was too much to process by herself. Her mother might be cross with her about leaving school, but she knew that Bibi loved her. And Bibi loved Lace Island too. If people were plotting something here, then Bibi must know about it.

Leila climbed out of the pool and wrapped herself in a

cotton throw, feeling suddenly clear-headed. She would ask Bibi straight out what was going on with the lighthouse and who that cheroot-smoking man Shang was.

But to Leila's surprise, just as she'd finished climbing the stairs two at a time, she saw that Chan was coming out of her mother's room and gently turning the door handle to shut it.

'Leila,' he said in a hushed whisper, as if he'd been caught out. She wondered why he looked so guilty.

'Is she in there?' she asked.

Chan nodded. 'Yes, but we should leave her to rest.'

'Rest?' Leila asked. She'd never heard anything so ridiculous. Her mother didn't rest. Not when it was time to get up.

'Yes. She's just . . . well, she's tired. That's all. Nothing to worry about. Don't go in there.'

'But—'

'Come and help me. The guests will be here later, and the terrace needs a good sweep.' He grabbed her firmly by the shoulder and led her to the staircase. She looked behind her once at her mother's closed door. 'I mean it, Leila. I don't want your mother to be bothered by anything. And I mean anything at all.'

'Why? What's wrong with her?'

He gave her a look and she suspected that he'd been having a conversation with Bibi about their fight last night and Leila knew it was probably better not to interfere.

Chan pulled her arm, ushering her away. 'Tell me what you've been up to,' he said. 'I've hardly seen you.'

'I've been around,' Leila said, confused. There was something odd about his tone. About the way he was speaking.

'Oh? Doing what?'

'Nothing much. Exploring.'

'Find anything unusual?' Chan asked, and Leila stiffened

as his eyes bored into hers. She'd never been scared of him before now, but the look he gave her made her heart thump very hard. Did he know she'd been to the lighthouse? Worse, did he know she'd seen Adam and Monique?

'No. Nothing,' she lied.

Chan held her gaze for a second longer, then turned away and lit a cigarette. And that's when Leila knew for sure: Chan was hiding something.

She would have to tell Bibi. And soon.

But getting Bibi alone was difficult. All morning Leila waited for her mother to get up, and when she did, she was in a fractious mood and sent Leila off on an errand to get Parva. When Leila got back, Bibi was talking to Anjum; then some guests came up to the house so that Bibi could show them around the kitchen garden. Surrounded, as she always was, by the affairs of Lace Island, Bibi seemed happy and in control, but Leila noticed a pallor to her she hadn't seen before, anxiety etched into the creases round her eyes.

It was almost evening before Leila got an opportunity to sneak out and find Rasa, but Chan stopped her just as she was getting on her bike and insisted that she help serve the guests. He seemed cross, as if she'd let him down, and he reminded her of her earlier promise to help him and Bibi out, although Leila couldn't remember making such a promise at all.

When Bibi arrived on the terrace, she looked like she always did, her glossy black hair perfect in its shell clip, her orange sari resplendent with gold embroidery, but now Leila saw her pausing by the screen door and wincing in pain.

She went to hug her mother, but Bibi stepped away, as if she couldn't bear being touched.

'Are you all right?' Leila asked.

'Of course I am. I'm fine,' her mother snapped, making Leila recoil. 'Why? Why do you ask that, Leila?'

Leila swallowed hard, her mother's defensive tone confirming her worst fears. 'Chan said you were resting this morning.'

'Did he?'

She saw her mother's sharp eyes scanning the terrace, looking for Chan.

'Ah, the beautiful Bibi.' It was Adam. He wafted in a cloud of strong cologne onto the terrace from the pool steps as if he owned the place. 'Leila,' he added, in a very knowing tone. 'How nice to see you again.'

'Have you had a pleasing day, Adam?' Bibi asked. Her charming manner betrayed nothing of the tension she'd shown to Leila just now.

'Not so much today, but yesterday was quite exhausting,' he said. 'Well, Leila will tell you.'

He sat in the canopied chair just as Chan also appeared at the top of the pool steps with bottles of tonic tucked under his arm.

'She's quite the little spy, your daughter,' Adam said to Bibi, after accepting the offer of a gin and tonic from Chan. 'If I didn't know better, I'd think she was way beyond her years. She certainly has a *hunger* for experience.'

Leila felt her heart thudding hard as his eyes bored into hers. He'd seen her, then. He knew that she had been up the tree all along.

Her cheeks pulsating with shame, she busied herself, hurrying to the sideboard for the snacks, avoiding both her mother and Adam.

Now, there were voices from inside the house and Marc and Monique came onto the terrace through the screen door.

She had her arm linked over his and was giggling at something he was saying. Leila didn't even glance in Adam's direction.

'Leila, I don't know what you've been doing, or where you've been going, but do not stick your nose into the guests' business. Do you hear me?' Chan hissed, suddenly by her side. 'Do not displease Mr Lonegan. He is important to us. Whatever he wants he must have while he's here. Anything at all.'

Even if that meant other people's girlfriends, Leila thought bitterly. She watched as Adam sat back smugly in his chair, surveying everyone as if this were his kingdom. When he caught her eye, he winked at her and raised his glass.

CHAPTER THIRTY

New York, present day

Jess had only ever seen apartments like Blaise's New York bachelor pad in movies.

'Wow,' she laughed, spreading out her arms as she walked out of the old-fashioned crate lift they'd just come up in and doing a twirl on the parquet flooring as Blaise turned on more lights.

'You like it?' he called, his voice strange in the open-plan space. The room was huge, three sides made entirely from glass, with views of the skyscraper next door. Three square cream pillars held up the double-height ceiling. There was a massive L-shaped sofa between two of the pillars, and low, artfully scuffed-up leather armchairs. On one side of the apartment, steps led up to a kitchen area with lots of exposed brickwork and expensive-looking cooking pans on display, and a spiral staircase led up to another floor.

'I love it. There's so much space,' Jess said, failing to mask her awe.

Her head was busy doing calculations. She'd had no real sense of Blaise's wealth before now and just how rich his property-development business had made him. So he had a motorbike in Miami and the use of a swanky power-yacht, and he flew first class, but this apartment made her start to realize exactly how rich he must be.

And he was clearly single. There was no doubt about that. There was no sign that any girlfriend had ever lived here. She was still buzzing from their chat on the bridge earlier, when he told her that he hadn't been able to stop thinking about her. And that kiss. *That kiss. Oh my God.* Jess bit her lip, stifling an exuberant laugh. He was only just about the best kisser in the world.

'Come and see this,' Blaise called. 'You'll love it.'

She ran across the floor towards him and he led her up the spiral staircase. He unlocked the door at the top and pushed against it, the expensive seal making the silence turn into the sound of the city. Outside was a wide balcony that housed several designer sofas and a black wood burner. Just the part in between the sofas and the chair was the size of Jess's entire flat at home.

'You said it wasn't a penthouse!' Jess exclaimed, laughing. 'I'd definitely say that we're up on the roof.'

How was it possible to live in this much space? To own it? Claim it, just for yourself? No wonder wealth gave you so much power. Jess could understand it now, she thought, as she went to the edge of the balcony and looked out over the roof-tops. It felt like she owned it all – like she could swoop down and claim anything she wanted.

'Do you do much entertaining?' she asked, nodding to the barbeque. She'd only ever eaten food from a disposable barbeque, but that looked like a seriously expensive piece of kit.

'Not really. Sometimes,' he said, with a shrug. He grinned at her, his hands in his pockets as if he were shy. Who exactly

did he entertain? she wondered. Who were the people sophisticated and cool enough to come here just to hang out? Movie
stars? Models? Probably. Certainly people who took an apartment like this in their stride. 'I haven't lived here long. So . . .
what do you think?' Blaise asked.

'What do I think?' she asked, laughing. 'I think it's amazing. Possibly the coolest place I've ever been.'

'Really? Then I must take you to some cooler places.' She
couldn't tell what he meant. Was he teasing her for her naivety?
She felt wrong-footed, but then he grabbed her round her
waist, pulling her into his embrace.

'So now that I've got you here, let me entertain *you*. Would
you like a nightcap?' he asked.

'Sure,' she nodded.

He walked towards a cupboard by the barbeque. 'Ah,' he
said, opening it to reveal a fridge. He pulled out a bottle of
champagne. 'That'll do.'

Jess wondered if he'd put the champagne in there earlier.
Had he known all along that she'd be coming up here to his
apartment with him, or did he always have a chilled bottle of
pink Dom Pérignon for moments such as these? He picked up
a remote and flicked it, and suddenly, there was music and
funky big-bulbed lights lit up, which she hadn't noticed before.
Adele's 'Make You Feel My Love'. One of her favourite songs.
She smiled. Could he read her mind?

'Ta da.'

'Smooth,' Jess said, walking towards him, nodding at how
incredible this all was. 'Very smooth.'

He gave her two chilled glasses from the fridge to hold,
and he opened the champagne and expertly popped the cork.

'What shall we drink to?' she asked, as he poured the
liquid.

'To fate,' he said. 'To us.'

She smiled at him, and as their glasses chinked together, she felt her emotions fizzing with excitement too. It was those blue eyes of his. They seemed to sweep her up, and she found herself grinning back at him, feeling completely alive in this amazing moment. Blaise took a sip of his champagne and then took her glass from her hand and put it down. 'I want to dance with you,' he said.

'I can't. I mean, I don't really dance—'

'You do now,' he interrupted her, sweeping her into his arms, so she had no choice, the lyrics of the song coursing through her.

She fitted perfectly into his arms, she thought, feeling his soft hand enclose hers. She laughed as he danced with her expertly around the balcony, not allowing her to trip up, the lights of the city all around them. And once again Jess felt like she was in a scene from a movie, it felt so magical.

'It's so nice getting to know you,' he said, smiling. She stared at the dimple in his cheek, wishing she could touch it. 'I've had such a fun night.'

She took a breath. He really had forgiven her, then, for lying to him in Miami. He really was accepting her just for herself. 'Me too. But . . .'

'But?'

'What's the catch?'

Blaise looked surprised. 'Why, should there be a catch?'

'Yes. There must be a catch. Because this doesn't happen to girls like me.'

'What doesn't?' he asked, twirling her away from him and back into his embrace.

'People like you,' she said. 'People rich and handsome and . . .'

'I'm just a guy,' he said, stopping and cupping her face. 'And yes, I have money, but I still want what everyone else wants.'

'And what's that?'

'To find someone and to fall in love,' he said, looking at her lips. 'To feel like fate has finally done me a favour.'

And, just as she'd felt on the bridge, Jess felt desire rushing through her. She held him tight as he kissed her, and then she was on her tiptoes, kissing back as passionately as she could. She could feel his hardness through his jeans.

'I didn't expect this to happen,' he said.

'Neither did I,' she said, staring at his lips, wanting them back on hers.

'Do you want to stay?' he asked. 'You don't have to. I don't want to—'

She put her fingers on his lips. 'Shhh. Of course I want to stay,' she said. 'I thought you'd never ask.'

'Then why don't we go somewhere more comfortable?' he said.

'I know. It's weird . . . all these windows,' she said, laughing and nodding at the skyscraper, as he held her hand. 'You can't tell who is watching.'

He held her hand as they raced back inside the apartment, and he grabbed her as they got to the bedroom. She was already pulling at his T-shirt, desperate to get her hands on his body. He kissed her passionately as he lifted up her shirt, and then he was pulling off her jeans.

He pushed her back on the bed, and she felt herself trembling all over as he kissed her stomach and the line of her white lacy knickers.

'You are amazing,' he breathed, as he pulled her knickers down and buried his face in between her legs. She felt his tongue on her and cried out. 'Oh my God, I want you so much,' he said.

Later, Jess awoke in Blaise's enormous bed, with its grey Egyptian-cotton sheets, and sat up. Blaise wasn't in bed with her. She stretched, amazed that she'd dozed off, before picking up the cashmere throw and wrapping it round her.

Wow. Her mind was reeling with how this New York trip had panned out. Because she'd slept with Blaise. Twice. She wanted to do a little jig, or run outside onto the balcony and shout it across the rooftops. Because sex with Blaise had been on a totally different level to anything she'd ever experienced before.

She had no idea how many girls he'd slept with, but when it came to sex, Blaise was nothing short of an expert. And it wasn't just that she'd loved him pleasuring her. He was just so gorgeous. His smell, his taut muscles, the way he felt when he was inside her, like they were a perfect match. And now, she couldn't wait to do it all over again.

She tiptoed out of the bedroom, into the living room. Blaise was in the far corner, talking on the phone. She ran lightly up behind him, wanting to surprise him. She stared at his back, longing to reach out and touch his muscly shoulders, longing for him to hold her close, for him to come back to bed.

He hadn't seen her, and she crept closer now, stifling a giggle; the chill of the apartment was making her skin pucker into goosebumps.

'Yes,' she heard him say. 'Yes, I'm sure. It's her—' He turned suddenly, his face shocked, his hand flying to the phone. His eyes locked with hers, and in that split second, Jess saw something she hadn't seen before. Like she'd caught him out. She took a step back.

She wrapped the throw more tightly round her, suddenly freezing. Who could he be talking to? *It's her*.

Was he talking about her? And if he was, what could he mean?

She felt fear ripple all over her, but Blaise's expression suddenly changed.

He gasped and laughed, covering the moment. 'You scared me,' he said to her, pulling her towards him. 'Sorry, man,' he said into the phone. 'There's someone here. I mean, yeah, I'm sure it's her *turn* . . .' He smiled at Jess, like she'd just witnessed a big joke. 'Well, just tell her. Mum'll understand. I gotta go, bro,' he said suddenly, ending the call.

Jess couldn't look at him.

'Hey,' he said, his voice totally normal.

'Who was that?'

'Just my brother. Family stuff. Mum's birthday's coming up.' He rolled his eyes, then grabbed her. 'Come back to bed. You gave me such a fright,' he said, laughing and putting his arm round her. 'My God, you're gorgeous. Come here.'

'I thought . . .' she began, searching his face for the proof she needed, but Blaise stared down at her innocently.

'What?'

'Nothing,' she said, telling herself she was just being paranoid.

He hugged her in tight and then kissed her hair.

It was nothing, she decided. He was amazing. And she couldn't wait to find out what happened next.

CHAPTER THIRTY-ONE

Lace Island, 1990

It was dusk and the air had been heavy and sticky with the promise of rain all day, but despite some distant rumblings of thunder, the sky above Lace Island had stayed resolutely blue, the sun scorching down. Now, the sun having dropped, the air was cooler, the mosquitos making a high whine as they darted around the lagoon.

Leila slapped one away from her neck as she walked to Maliba's house. She heard Rasa's cousins calling out to her from where they were playing cricket in the grove. It seemed like only yesterday that Leila and Rasa were playing with them, but now they all looked like young boys. She waved and smiled.

Maliba's house was the largest along the banks of the lagoon. It was painted green and blue like the others, and the front of it opened up onto the water. On the other side of the yard, Maliba's Ayurvedic garden was fenced off, and Leila could see an overgrown hedge bursting with purple-and-yellow flowers as she walked through the gate, careful not to let the chickens escape from the yard.

'It's Leila. Leila is here, Maliba,' she heard Rasa's youngest cousin, Mina, shout, and she grinned and ran from the back porch towards Leila, the door clanking shut behind her.

Maliba came out onto the porch, rubbing her hands, her blue-and-green sari spattered with white blotches of flour. She bustled down the steps, shooing the chickens out of the way. Leila saw her brown wodge of flesh between her camisole and skirt, but there was something very feminine about Maliba. Her grey hair was tied up loosely, strands of it falling around her face, but her knowing brown eyes were as bright as ever.

She held Leila's shoulders and Leila realized that she was now taller than Maliba, who had always been a towering presence in her childhood.

'Goodness me,' she smiled, before holding Leila's face, her eyes shining with affection. She kissed Leila on the cheek. She smelt of watermelon and wood smoke, but it was a homely smell that Leila loved. 'Even more beautiful,' she sighed, as if that were impossible. 'Come, come, come. I have been waiting for you and you've been back all this time and haven't been to see me.'

Leila apologized and followed Maliba into her kitchen, where the air was thick with the smell of frying chillis. Maliba was famous for her chutney and Leila's eyes started watering. Even so, it was a relief to be here and out of the house, where the tension between Chan and Bibi had been simmering all day. Leila hadn't been able to shake the feeling that Chan had been watching her, deliberately stopping her from being alone with Bibi. And now Leila had given up altogether. She'd have to get up early and talk to her mother in the morning.

Maliba fiddled with the oil lamp, until Leila took over.

'I can't see,' Maliba grumbled.

'You should get glasses,' Leila said. They'd all been telling her this for years, but Maliba, who believed firmly in her

Ayurvedic remedies for everything, refused to believe that her eyesight wouldn't fix itself with the right encouragement.

'How is your mother? I haven't seen her for a few weeks,' Maliba said, as the soft glow of the lamp lit up the basic kitchen, the walls covered with crude drawings that all the children had made over the years and given to Maliba, most of them yellow with cooking smoke.

'She's busy. There have been lots of guests.'

Maliba placed her arms akimbo, as if deciding something. 'I hope you have been helping. Poor Bibi has been working non-stop, and Parva hasn't had a day off for a month. Not to mention Rasa.'

She heard a note of recrimination in Maliba's tone.

'I guess it's good for business, though?' Leila ventured. 'All the extra work.'

'It would be if they got paid,' Maliba said.

So Rasa had been telling the truth. 'Bibi hasn't paid them? Are you sure?'

Maliba shrugged her shoulders, turning away as if she'd said too much. Leila didn't understand. Bibi was always fastidious about paying the staff on time.

'I'll ask her,' she said. 'There must be an explanation.'

'Don't you go bothering your mother,' Maliba said sharply. 'Now. You will sit and tell me all about England.'

Leila sat at the wooden table while Maliba fussed around her, filling up her cup with fresh mango juice, and Leila gave her a palatable, edited version of her time in England. Mina sat patiently, drawing a pattern on a piece of paper.

'It always rains there,' she told Maliba. 'Not proper rain like we have, but cold drizzle. You wouldn't like it. And the food is terrible. So bland. It tastes of nothing.'

But as she spoke, she felt as if something had changed. She

wasn't one of them anymore. She was Bibi's daughter who'd been away in England, as if her journey overseas had set her apart from them forever.

And with her sense of otherness came a new sense of responsibility. What if this awful Shang guy and Chan were planning something terrible that would hurt Maliba and her family? It was unthinkable that there was a man with a gun on this island where all these innocent children played.

'Look, Leila – Rasa is here,' Mina said, nodding at the door.

Maliba clapped her hands happily and looked at Leila. 'Just like you wanted,' she said, making Leila blush. The way she said it made Leila feel as if she knew her innermost thoughts. Or, more likely, Parva had been gossiping.

'Hey,' Rasa said, coming right into Maliba's kitchen now and putting down the smoked fish on the table. His eyes met Leila's and she felt something squirming inside her when she looked at him. Something that made her feel breathless and awkward.

Leila felt Maliba's curious and knowing eyes watching them both.

'You must be going,' Maliba told Leila. 'Give this to your mother,' she said, pushing a small brown paper package of powder in her hand. 'Tell her to dissolve it and drink three times a day.'

'What's it for?'

'Your mother will know. Go now, before it gets dark. Rasa will see you up to the road, won't you?'

Flung together by Maliba, Leila and Rasa walked on the short path down to the paddy field. The cow in the field turned and observed them with its big eyes as they darted along the muddy path to the line of trees.

'Let's walk along the beach for a while,' Leila suggested.

They crossed the road and ran down through the mangrove plants onto the hot sand. The sea seemed to be sighing after the heat of the day, gently whooshing as it dragged back the fine sand. Leila watched her and Rasa's footsteps sinking as they strolled in the ripples. It was always wonderful at this time of evening, the sun having sunk below the horizon, the water shimmering purple, the palms casting long, dark shadows.

Rasa picked up a flat stone and skimmed it over the water. It bounced several times.

'It's the last few days before the rains come,' Rasa said. His voice had a sad air to it. As if something was over.

'I don't mind the rain,' Leila said. 'All the guests will finally go. I like it here when it's quiet.'

'Do you? I can't stand it,' Rasa countered. 'I'd rather be anywhere but here.'

Leila walked on. His comment stung and he knew it.

'You can take my place,' she said bitterly. 'You can go to school in England if that's what you really want.' She couldn't keep her voice from sounding petulant. 'I don't know why you're so angry with me.'

Rasa stopped and sighed. He reached out and grabbed Leila's arm, forcing her to face him. 'Why don't we talk honestly for once?'

'OK,' she said, feeling nervous.

They walked on for a moment or two, and then Rasa said suddenly, 'What happened in England, Leila? I know you have a secret. Why don't you tell me? If I had a secret, I'd tell you.'

So that's what was bothering him? That she hadn't told him why she'd come back from school early.

'Whatever's bugging you, just tell me and we can work it out together, hey? What was so bad? It can't just have been the food.'

'No, it wasn't the food.'

'Then what?'

His eyes were so honest and searching, and she remembered then that Rasa was her one true friend. She'd been wrong to shut him out. Because she could trust him. She saw that now.

'Someone . . . someone . . .' She felt a great shuddering breath threatening to choke her.

'What?'

She cast her eyes down, feeling them bulging with tears, remembering the horror of Sussman in that shower cubicle, feeling the same revulsion.

'Tell me,' he pressed, holding her arm. They'd stopped now and Leila covered her face. 'Leila?'

'Someone – a teacher – they touched me,' she whispered. 'They . . . they . . . It wasn't what I wanted . . . I . . . They made me . . .'

She gasped, the tears coming now as the secret that had burnt through her and eaten her alive was purged like the creature it was onto the rippling white beach.

'Did he hurt you? Did he?' Rasa's voice was urgent.

Leila felt shame then. Horrible shame that she'd told him. She shook her head, sniffing away the tears. She couldn't tell him it was Miss Sussman. He would never understand, could never understand that a woman like that existed.

'Listen to me. Listen. It's over,' he implored. 'Whatever happened, it's done. And you're still you.'

Was she? She didn't feel like the same person who had gone away. Rasa might want to believe she was still innocent and untainted, but Leila knew differently.

'Don't ever let anyone touch you again. Unless you want them to. You promise?'

'I promise,' she said. She took a shaky breath.

'I'll toughen you up,' he said, playfully punching her shoulder, 'teach you how to fight.'

He was making a joke of it, but she knew that her confession had upset him.

She nodded and wiped away her tears. 'OK. I'm sorry.'

She tried to smile, but something inside her felt like the embers of her secret were still smouldering, still waiting to burst into flame. Telling him hadn't helped; it had just made her feel more alone. She knew that he was trying to be comforting, but he would never understand what being terrified felt like. He'd never been scared in his life. Why would he be? Everything here on Lace Island was in his control. And he was a man. Almost a man, in any case, and strong as an ox.

'I didn't want to tell you. It's so embarrassing. And I can't tell Bibi. And that's why I can't go back. Do you understand now?'

He nodded. 'You know you can tell me everything,' he said. 'We're best friends. Always will be.'

They walked along the beach as the light faded, but they were getting slower, knowing they'd nearly reached the place where Leila must peel off and go on the road back up to the big house. They were right near the rock that looked like a frog, and Leila leant her hand against it, feeling its smooth, cold surface.

'Rasa, why were you so cross with me yesterday, about seeing Adam and Monique?'

He sighed. 'I don't want your experience to be . . . of them,' he said. 'It should be special, shouldn't it? Sex, I mean. When it happens.'

Leila nodded, touched once again at how much he wanted to protect her innocence. She knew he was embarrassed to be talking to her about this, and they stayed silent for a long while.

'Look. The first star,' she said, pointing up into the sky.

She felt as if the air between them was charged with electricity. She turned towards him at the same time as he turned to her and she knew then that they were going to kiss. And this would be the kiss that would make everything right. She held her breath, waiting for their lips to touch, wanting it more than anything she'd ever wanted in her life.

But then the sound of engines out on the sea broke the moment. They both turned towards the noise, seeing bright lights shining out, temporarily blinding them.

'What the hell . . .' Rasa said, putting his arm up over his face.

He grabbed Leila's hand and they moved behind the frog rock. Two boats were coming quickly towards the beach, men jumping out of them. Gruff voices reached them on the breeze.

'Who are they?' Leila whispered.

She could see men now in the shallows unloading boxes. And then she saw the red tip of a cheroot.

Shang. He was there too. He was in charge.

She stiffened. 'It's him. Like I told you. Look, they've got guns.'

'Go,' Rasa implored her. 'Go back to the house now and stay there.'

'But—'

'They mustn't see us, Leila.'

'But—'

'I'll find out what I can.'

'Be careful, Rasa.'

'I will. I promise.'

His hand squeezed hers briefly, and then she turned and ran.

CHAPTER THIRTY-TWO

Dubai, present day

On the flight to Dubai, Jess stood in the galley, stacking the breakfast trolley, the air filled with the smell of scrambled eggs and coffee, but Jess, who usually loved breakfast, was too excited to eat.

'Sorry,' she said to her colleague Anneka, realizing she'd hardly paused for breath. She'd just finished her latest recounting of her whirlwind romance with Blaise. She knew how smug she sounded, but she didn't care. She couldn't help herself. She'd never had anything to crow about before. Never had anything that made her special. But now she had Blaise. And she couldn't help wanting to shout about him, especially when it made her colleagues so clearly jealous. She sympathized with them. It was hardly believable to her either.

'He certainly sounds like a dreamboat,' Anneka said.

And that was only the half of it, Jess wanted to tell her. In the month since New York, Blaise had done everything to see her as often as possible, rearranging his business meetings to coincide with her flights. It had been the most romantic whirlwind she could ever have imagined, and she was loving every second.

There had been a weekend in Italy, when he'd whisked her off to a vineyard for a wine-tasting in a sun-dappled farm-house. There'd been dinner at the poshest restaurant Jess had ever been to in Paris, followed by a heavenly moonlit walk back to a suite at the George V. An exclusive spa in Iceland had followed, when they'd stayed in an ice hotel and bathed in the thermal waters. With each retelling of everything that had happened, Jess still had to pinch herself, even though she knew it was real. She was grateful for the time away from Blaise when she was in the air and could let every detail soak in.

'He's picking me up when we land in Dubai,' she said. The steam hissed as Anneka filled up the steel jug with hot water. 'I'll probably stay with him for the weekend.'

'It's not a whole weekend. You'd better not miss the connecting flight back home.'

Jess rolled her eyes. 'Of course I won't.'

But she heeded the warning. Every time she saw Blaise, it was like her normal life went out of the window. She'd nearly missed the flight home from New York. Time seemed to speed up when she was with him. Like they were in this crazy bubble together, where the rest of the world just ceased to exist.

It didn't help that she always had jet lag and that they couldn't keep their hands off each other, making normal sleep almost impossible. Even now, being on this flight, it felt like all she was doing was biding time until she could be naked with him again.

Anneka laughed and nodded to Sarah. 'She's got it bad all right. I don't mind admitting I'm jealous.'

Jess smiled, but she knew that Anneka's jealousy was tempered by a hefty dose of scepticism. Jess could see it in her face. She could see it in the look she'd given Sarah just now.

'Listen, kid, I know you really like him, but just be

warned,' Sarah said, glancing at Anneka. 'There's plenty of us who have dated passengers, but it never lasts. They like us because we're pretty and sociable and have our own jobs, but for those guys ... well, they're looking for something else when it comes to settling down.'

Jess felt her heart thumping hard and her cheeks getting warm. She wanted so much to bite back at Sarah to stop being such a cynic, to prove that her relationship with Blaise was different.

She knew how it must seem to them, though. But if Blaise had just wanted to have sex with her and then dump her, he wouldn't have followed her to New York or taken her to any of the places she'd been. And yes, she knew she ought to play it cool, but she couldn't. It might be too good to be true, but it *was* happening right now. To her.

Blaise was leaning against the bonnet of a midnight-blue Porsche Cayenne when Jess wheeled her bag out of the terminal with Anneka and Sarah. He looked incongruous among all the Arab men in their white tunics and headdresses.

You see, she wanted to scream. Instead, she rushed over to Blaise, who scooped her up and kissed her. She felt Anneka and Sarah staring at her.

'How have you been?' Blaise asked, putting his arm round her. 'I've missed you.' He breathed in the expensive perfume she'd bought in Paris.

She felt herself lighting up from the inside as he wheeled her bag to the boot and put it inside.

Jess gave a discreet wave to Anneka and Sarah, and they smiled back, clearly impressed.

'Are they your friends? Do they want a lift?' Blaise asked,

and Jess was touched that he was always such a gentleman. But she didn't want to share Blaise with anyone.

'No, I think they're fine. Let's just go,' Jess said, getting into the passenger side. 'Wow, it's hot out there,' she continued. 'I can't wait to get out of this uniform.' She tugged at the red necktie to undo it.

'I can't wait to get you out of it too,' he said with a grin, turning the key. 'Look at you. Look at that super-spray.' He patted her hair, which was solid from the hairspray she'd used. She took great pride in looking perfect for her job, but she knew Blaise liked her much more natural.

'I know. I can't wait to get in the shower.'

Blaise expertly swerved out into the lane. 'I've booked us into the hotel by the mall. We don't want to be too far from all the shopping.'

'Shopping? Oh God, I'm useless at shopping,' Jess said.

Blaise glanced at her, his eyes dancing with laughter. 'You're a girl. Last time I checked, you were a girl. And you *don't* like shopping?'

Jess bit her bottom lip and shrugged. How could she explain that she didn't like shopping because she'd never had the money to shop? That she had no idea what did or didn't suit her. That she had only ever had the option to go with what was cheap.

'I want you to come to a business dinner with me next week when I'm in London.'

'Really?'

'Sure. Why not?'

There were many reasons why not, Jess thought, but she was still flattered that he'd asked her.

'I won't know what to say.'

'You don't have to say anything. Well, not if you don't want to. All you have to do is be yourself.'

Jess felt a jolt of triumph. If she was going to accompany him to business dinners, then he must be serious about her. 'But I've got nothing to wear.'

'Which is why we're going shopping,' Blaise said, as if she'd just justified his whole argument. 'And they do say that this is practically *the* best place in the whole world to do that.'

Later, as they strolled around the Dubai Mall, hand in hand, Jess couldn't stop grinning. This is what couples did, right? They shopped together. They held hands and snuggled like this.

She wanted to stand on a podium and hold her hand and Blaise's aloft, like an Olympic champion. Because that's how she felt. Like she'd won something incredible.

'You like it here,' he said, lifting her hand to his lips and kissing it. 'I knew you would.'

'It's fab. I never imagined somewhere this bling could actually exist. Look at all the gold,' Jess said, staring in at the window of a nearby shop.

'It's a bit gaudy. Come on. My friend Cara is working in Cartier. If ever there was a neck designed for diamonds, it's yours.'

'Oh no . . . really, I can't,' she protested.

'Come on. It's just up there. Don't you even want to try one on? It'll be fun. Come on.'

He held her hand tightly as she resisted and he pulled her towards the door.

The doorman tipped his top hat and smiled at Blaise. 'Nice to see you again, sir,' he said.

So Blaise had been here before, Jess guessed. With one of

his multiple girlfriends, she assumed. The girlfriends who did nothing but shop. *For diamonds.*

Inside, the atmosphere was hushed and immediately Jess wanted to giggle with nerves. She'd never been anywhere this classy in her life.

'Hey, Blaise,' she heard someone say, and turned to see a stylish woman in a grey suit walking in high heels across the thick red carpet. She had an American accent and a tease in her voice as she stared at Jess, flicking her glossy brown hair over her shoulders.

'Hey yourself, Cara,' Blaise said, kissing her cheek. 'This is the lovely Jess. And I hope you'll be able to help her overcome her fear of diamonds.'

'That's what I'm here for,' Cara said.

Jess listened, feeling embarrassed as Blaise told Cara how he wanted to show Jess off at a business dinner, while Jess added that she had yet to find anything to wear.

'I have just the thing,' Cara said, unlocking a cabinet and taking out an intricate necklace made of diamond-shaped flowers. 'This is pretty and elegant and guaranteed to go with just about anything,' she added.

Blaise put the diamond necklace round Jess's neck, lifting her hair to fasten it. Jess stared at herself in the mirror, putting her fingertips on the cold jewels.

'That's gorgeous,' Blaise said, his lips close to her ear. She looked at their reflections in the large oval mirror. 'Does something with your eyes.'

Jess was entranced by how sparkly the diamonds were. She remembered once shoplifting a plastic tiara and necklace from Poundland for one of the little girls, Trisha, in the home and how much she'd loved it. She wondered what Trisha would be doing now. Not trying on diamonds in Dubai. That was for sure. She'd most likely ended up like Angel, Jess thought with a shudder.

'Let's have it,' Blaise said, smiling at Cara.

'No, Blaise. No. I can't. I just can't,' Jess said, reaching for the clasp.

The necklace was worth more than she earned in a year and Blaise was treating it as if it was just a trifle. What would Tony think, she wondered, if he saw Jess accepting diamond necklaces?

'I'll be right back,' Cara said, clearly picking up Jess's panic and giving them some space.

'I don't want you to buy it for me, Blaise. Honestly,' she said, 'I mean it. It's too much.' As it was, she felt uncomfortable that he was the one who paid for all their hotel rooms and hire cars, even though he said he claimed them as business expenses.

'Why won't you let me buy you a gift?'

'Because this isn't a gift. It's a diamond necklace.'

'So?'

'It makes me feel . . . I don't know . . . It's just too much.'

'It's rude to refuse a gift. I insist.' She couldn't help feeling as if she'd transgressed some sort of social etiquette. 'It's just money,' Blaise said. 'It's no big deal.'

'It is to me.'

'Then sell the necklace, give the money away to the poor or the homeless or whatever it is you feel you need to do with it.'

She'd offended him. 'I didn't mean it like that.'

'Don't you want nice things?' She heard the implication in his voice. That she didn't have nice things. That if she was going to be with Blaise, then she needed to sharpen up, look the part and that her refusal was exasperating to him. 'Don't look like that,' he said. He pulled her into a hug and put his nose against hers. 'I'm just a guy buying you diamonds.'

'Oh, that is so typical,' she said, exasperated herself now. 'I'm very touched, but I don't want you to,' she said. 'That's the point. I want to be able to afford these things myself.'

Blaise stared at her, then turned away, defeated. 'OK. Then I *won't* buy you diamonds,' he said, putting his hands up in surrender. 'It's just very beautiful, that's all. I'd like you to have it.'

There was a tense moment of silence between them and Cara came back over. She'd clearly overheard their argument.

'How about we loan you the necklace?' she said to Jess. 'That way, you can wear it, then drop it back to our store in London.'

Wanting to save face and cheer up Blaise, she nodded. 'OK,' she said. 'That's an idea.'

'You are so stubborn,' Blaise said, as Cara went to pack up the necklace. Jess reached up and kissed his cheek. 'I bet you're not going to let me buy you an outfit either, are you?' he said.

'No. But you can help me choose,' she said.

Ten shops later, they left the shopping mall and headed down to the famous aquarium. As they walked hand in hand through the glass tunnel, Jess reflected on how much fun she'd had shopping with Blaise. She'd tried on loads of outfits and had eventually decided on a body-hugging black Louis Vuitton dress. It was the most expensive item of clothing she'd ever bought, but she didn't regret it. She felt great in it.

She had relented and let Blaise buy her some Louboutin heels to go with it, but she was pleased that she'd proved to him that she wasn't the kind of girl who wanted to spend all his money.

It was just so hard to feel on an equal footing with someone like Blaise, when he had so much more than her. But the girls on the plane had hit home. If their relationship was going to work, she had to prove to him that she wanted so much more than to be some kind of trophy girlfriend.

'Look at these fish,' she said, staring up through the Perspex. 'Aren't they amazing? It must be what it's like to go diving. I've always wanted to do that,' she said, pointing at the fish, darting among the coral plants. The colours were breathtaking.

'Then I shall take you.'

'I bet you're fabulous at it. Like skiing and everything else,' she pointed out.

'You're a quick learner. You'll catch up. I'll take you to the Barrier Reef. There's nowhere better,' he said.

'Australia? That's another place on my list.'

'We'll have to go there anyway so I can show you off to my family.'

'You want to take me to meet your family?'

'Don't you want to meet them?'

'Of course I do.'

She only wished she had family that he could meet too. But maybe Blaise's family would make up for her lack of relatives. She felt a shiver of something so tangible it took her breath away. To finally belong to a family, even if it was Blaise's, would be wonderful. She imagined family Christmases together, children running around and Jess being at the centre of it all. They walked on in silence for a minute longer, then stopped to look at the stingrays.

'So, at the dinner next week, when people ask . . . ?' he began.

'Ask what?'

'About us. I mean, they'll assume that we're together and

that it's serious. And I just wanted to check that's OK with you. I mean that they would think that.'

Jess smiled at him. She loved the patch of freckles on the indent of his neck and the white tan line on the bridge of his nose where his sunglasses had been. Of course it was OK with her.

'Is it OK with *you*?' she asked.

'Come here,' he said, grabbing her and trapping her, holding his hands behind her lower back. 'I want you to be my girlfriend. I want us to be together. Properly, I mean.'

'Me too,' she said. She felt like she could dive into his eyes.

'I know we haven't known each other very long, but the thing is, Jess, I think I've fallen totally in love with you.'

Jess gasped as she realized what he'd just said. Nobody had ever told her that they loved her before and she was awed now with how profoundly the words rocked her.

'I love you too,' she whispered, meaning it. Knowing that this was it. This was finally what she'd been waiting for.

She could feel her own heartbeat as she reached up and kissed him. She didn't notice the shadow crossing them as a massive shark swam overhead.

CHAPTER THIRTY-THREE

Lace Island, 1990

Leila woke suddenly as the gravel stone skittered across the wooden floorboards in her bedroom. She flung aside the mosquito nets and ran to the open window. Rasa was outside on the gravel staring up at her window, preparing to throw another stone.

She felt relief flooding through her veins. All evening she'd been on tenterhooks. Chan hadn't been at supper, and Bibi had been busy with paperwork and had insisted on the radio news being on. She hadn't even noticed that Leila was only picking at her food, waiting and waiting for Rasa to send some kind of message to tell her he was OK. Despairing and worried, she'd gone to bed early to read her book, and she was amazed she'd dropped off to sleep given that she'd been so anxious.

'Wait,' she said, leaning out of the window. 'I'll come down.'

She grabbed her robe and leather flip-flops and quietly opened her bedroom door. She could see Chan's door was open. She couldn't risk him finding her.

The only way to get out without being seen or heard was to climb down the vine outside her window. She pushed the chair underneath her door handle and then went to the window, pulling her hair into her T-shirt. She flung aside her robe, hitched up her loose pyjama bottoms and climbed out.

'What are you doing?' hissed Rasa. 'Are you crazy?'

'Shhh,' she laughed, suddenly remembering how she'd escaped at night in school with Judith. She felt the same sense of excitement now, only ten times more. Rasa had come to see her. He was here and all that mattered was getting to him.

She pushed her foot through the vine and secured the grip on the trellis, holding on to the window ledge.

'Careful,' Rasa called up.

Leila bit her lip, concentrating hard and trying to ignore the spiders she knew would probably be nesting in the leaves. Quickly, she hurried down the trellis, the plants rustling wildly.

'Shhh,' Rasa said.

'I know. I'm coming,' Leila said.

'You'll have to jump the last part,' he told her, and she did, crashing into Rasa, who staggered backwards. A light went on in Bibi's room.

'Quick,' warned Leila. 'Come on.'

She grabbed Rasa's hand and they ran round the house into the kitchen garden. All around them, the air was alive with the sound of insects. In the distance, there was the faint sound of music from a radio.

'Come in here,' Leila said, pulling Rasa through the gateway to the small stone courtyard. There was a bench under a bower at the end of the canopy of creeping vines. The air was filled with the scent of night jasmine.

They walked through the shadows to the stone bench at the end and huddled together, the moonlight shining through the vines, casting everything in a soft mauve.

'You're cold,' Rasa said, seeing that Leila was shivering,

but it was from excitement, not cold. She was self-conscious now, aware of her thin pyjamas and the fact that she didn't have any underwear on.

'I'm OK. What did you see?' she urged.

'They are taking something to the lighthouse,' he said. 'And that guy Adam, he knows about it. He's in on it too. It's not good, Leila.'

'I told you. I knew something was wrong.'

'You mustn't say anything. Not until we find out more.'

'What are they taking into the lighthouse? What could it be?'

'Whatever it is, they are guarding it closely.'

'They didn't see you, did they?'

'No, I don't think so.'

'I've been so worried.'

Rasa smiled. 'I'm fine. I'm just annoyed they came. When I was talking to you.'

She looked down, embarrassed that he'd brought up their earlier conversation.

'About that thing in school. I'm sorry. I shouldn't have told you.'

'Yes, you should. And I understand that it was hard. But I'm even more sorry that someone took advantage of you. That they didn't respect you.'

'Nothing . . . I mean nothing physically bad happened. Not really. Not, you know . . .'

'You still . . . you mean?'

Did it matter to him that she was still a virgin? That she was still untouched by any other man? He held her gaze for a moment.

'Did you mean what you said? About us being best friends?'

He nodded and still his eyes didn't leave hers. 'Of course. Why do you ask?'

'Do you think . . .' She fizzled out. She couldn't ask him if he'd ever consider being more than friends. If she asked him that and he didn't answer, then she would have lost him forever.

'Think what?'

'Nothing. It doesn't matter.' She got up to leave, crossing her arms across her chest. She had to go. If she stayed any longer, then she'd do something she regretted. 'Chan is still awake, and I know he's suspicious. If he finds out I'm not in my room, he'll come looking.'

'Don't go,' Rasa said, standing and catching her arm. As her eyes met his, he stepped forward, holding the top of her arms, and then it happened: he pressed his lips against hers for a long, delicious moment. Then he pulled away and stared at her. 'I'm sorry.'

'Don't be.'

'I've wanted to do that for as long as I can remember,' he said.

His eyes were searching hers, as if he wanted to look into the very depths of her soul.

'And I've wanted you to do it too,' she said, smiling. Then she snaked her arms round his neck and kissed him again. Tentatively, his lips opened against hers and their tongues touched.

Leila felt as if time had stopped and this perfect moment was what she'd been waiting for all her life. They kissed and kissed, and then Rasa pulled her into a long embrace, sighing like he felt as much relief as she did.

Laughing, he held her hand and they sat down on the bench. Leila rested her head against his shoulder.

'I thought about you all the time when I was away at

school. I got into a fight when one of the girls stole your photograph.'

'I have your photograph by my bed.'

'You do?'

'I think we belong to each other, Leila. I've always thought that. Haven't you?'

She nodded, feeling as though her heart was like a balloon and any minute she would just float up to the stars with happiness.

'Tomorrow, let's go diving. Just you and me and we can be alone,' he said; then he kissed her again.

The next morning, Leila couldn't keep the smile from her face as she wiped down the breakfast table. Rasa had kissed her. He was hers and she was his. It was no longer a secret between them but something real.

All of a sudden, life had become very simple. Whatever was going on with Shang and Chan, it didn't matter. Together, she and Rasa would find a way to stop it and to keep this island safe.

She noticed Parva, who was sweeping under the table, using unnecessary force. She kept glancing up at Leila.

'You'd better forget it,' she said, in a low, urgent voice.

'Forget what?'

'Forget those thoughts you are having about Rasa.'

Leila blushed. 'I'm not—'

'You cannot be with him,' Parva interrupted. 'Chan would never allow it.'

'It's not up to Chan,' Leila snapped. 'He's not my father.'

'He is married to your mother. You are his responsibility. And I can tell you now that he'll want a better match for you than the odd-job boy.'

Leila was shocked. She couldn't believe Parva was saying such a thing. She looked desperately up the corridor, worried in case Bibi or Chan might overhear this conversation.

'Rasa is not an odd-job boy. He's going to be a lawyer.'

'How?' Parva demanded, her hand on her hip. 'Who will pay for him to study? I certainly can't afford it. Neither can Vijay.'

'He'll find a way.' Leila stared at Parva defiantly. Her eyes prickled with unwelcome tears.

'I don't know what you two have been doing, or why you have that look on your face, but it will end in heartbreak. You'll see.'

Parva had just touched on Leila's worst fear. But whatever happened between her and Rasa, it had nothing to do with Parva, or Bibi, or Chan. Or anyone. She felt angry now that she and Rasa had been the subject of his aunt's scrutiny when nothing had happened. Well, almost nothing. What if they were all wrong and she and Rasa were meant to be together? What could they really do about it?

Nothing, she decided. From now on, Leila was determined to make her own decisions.

For the rest of the day, she counted the minutes until she could meet Rasa, sneaking out just after lunch with her swimming bag. She'd almost made it to where she'd left her bike in the grove when she heard the familiar sound of Chan's moped.

'There you are,' he said, coming to a stop on the path in front of her. His eyes were bloodshot. Had he been drinking again? As early as this?

'Where are you going?'

'Nowhere.'

'I have a job for you.'

'But—'

He reached behind him into a bag balancing on the back of his moped. He took out an official-looking brown envelope. 'I want you to take this to Mr Lonegan in his bungalow for me.'

'I'm late. I'm doing something else.'

'It will only take you a moment, Leila,' he said, his look stern. 'We are all here to serve the guests, and Mr Lonegan needs this.'

'But—'

'Take it. Whatever you're doing can wait. This is important.'

Leila grabbed the envelope and scowled at Chan before breaking into a run. She didn't have much time. If she was super-quick, she could just about make it to Adam Lonegan's bungalow and onto the beach where Rasa would be waiting, but she would have to hurry.

CHAPTER THIRTY-FOUR

London, present day

Tony was at the reception desk in the gym, counting the money from the till onto the chipped counter, his old boxing trophies in the glass cabinet behind him. The radio that usually blared in the background was off for once and Jess could hear the traffic on the busy London road outside.

It felt weird being back in London but not staying at the flat. Blaise had insisted on hiring a suite at the Dorchester, but with him so tied up with emails and work calls, Jess had snuck out to Tony's gym for a workout.

For the last ten minutes, she'd been busy explaining her absence to him and how she'd been flying around the world, but he didn't seem as impressed as she thought he'd be. Especially when she'd told him about Blaise.

'Boyfriend and girlfriend. That's something,' Tony said. 'Well, that certainly explains why we haven't seen you for a while. When do we get to meet him?'

'Soon,' Jess lied. She wouldn't be bringing Blaise here to Tony's gym anytime soon. She wiped her sweating face on her towel, realizing how old and tatty it was. She looked around her at the gym, seeing it through new eyes. Had it always been this dreary and shabby? The hole in the roof had got worse and one of the buckets of water below it was full.

She couldn't help comparing it to the gyms in the hotels around the world she'd been in recently. She wanted to blurt out all the details of the spa in Iceland, but she sensed Tony wouldn't want to hear it.

'I don't know. It doesn't sound like you've had much downtime to get to know him.'

Jess shrugged. 'When you know, you know,' she said with a smile, but Tony glanced up at her with a frown.

'All I'm saying is, don't go rushing into something and giving your heart away. It's still quite soon after Angel and all that business.'

'I'm not.' Jess felt defensive. Angel's death felt like years ago. Everything had changed since then. 'Tony, he's a multi-millionaire. Do you know what that means?'

'Uh-huh,' he said, putting a pile of battered five-pound notes in a leather pouch. He looked away and Jess sensed a sadness in him. 'He's still just a guy.'

'I didn't mean it like that. I don't like him just because he's rich. But nothing like this has ever happened to me. Him being who he is just makes life, well, easier. And he's so generous. I mean, he'd do anything for me. If I asked him, I'm sure he could get the roof fixed here.'

'Oh! You're spending his money for him now, are you? No, Jess, I don't need a handout from your rich boyfriend.'

She'd thought Tony would be pleased for her, that he'd be thrilled that her dream had come true, but as she accompanied him outside, refusing his offer of dinner at his flat with Maeve, she felt unsettled. She knew she'd handled it all wrong – shoving her rich boyfriend down Tony's throat – but he didn't understand how much Blaise had already changed her life. Why wasn't he more pleased for her?

Back at the Dorchester, Jess found that Blaise was still on his phone. She took a long shower in the sumptuous bathroom, then blow-dried her hair, waiting for him to finish.

She felt nervous about meeting Blaise's colleagues tonight and wished she knew more about his business life. He tended to brush away her questions, saying it was boring and he didn't want to talk about work, but Jess was desperate to know everything about what he did when they weren't together. Besides, his property business sounded exciting.

She glanced round the door, but he was still on the phone, and he held up his hand, telling her he'd be with her soon. Who could he be talking to for this long?

Maybe it wasn't a business call. Maybe he was talking to an ex-girlfriend. Jess gave herself a mental slap for being so paranoid and thinking such a disloyal thought. Blaise had never given her even the slightest cause to distrust him. But even so, she still only had a vague sense of his sexual history and past relationships.

'I don't want to talk about other partners. There's only you for me now,' he'd said, late one night in bed. At the time, Jess had thought that had been a romantic thing to say, especially since he seemed to mean it, but she couldn't help wondering why he was so secretive about his emails and calls if he had nothing to hide.

With time running out until they had to leave for his business dinner, Jess had no choice but to get dressed.

A short while later, she walked from the bedroom into the sitting room, her high heels sinking into the carpet. She saw

Blaise quickly shutting his laptop; then he stood up and did a long wolf whistle.

'Wow,' he said, grinning and stretching out his arms. 'You look knockout.'

'It's sparkly, right?' she said with a grin, fingering the diamond necklace. 'I'd better not lose it. I'll take it back tomorrow.'

'Er . . . well, that won't be necessary,' Blaise said, smiling at her with a guilty shrug.

'Blaise?' she protested. 'Oh God. Tell me you didn't.'

'I couldn't help it. I know you wanted to hire it, but it seemed a shame to give it back,' he said, coming over to her and trying to kiss her.

'You are impossible,' she said, slapping him. She didn't have time to argue with him over the necklace now, but she was cross that he'd disrespected her wishes. She saw now that she didn't have a leg to stand on. She should never have gone into Cartier in the first place. 'Come on. You've got to get ready,' she said, seeing he was still in his jeans. 'What have you been doing all this time?'

'Just emails. Business stuff.'

'Anything exciting?'

'Yes, actually,' Blaise said, surprising her.

'Oh?'

'I was talking to a business associate, Serge. He's invited us on his yacht in Ibiza.'

'Us?'

'I'm not going on my own to party in Ibiza. You'll come, won't you? Serge's yacht is off the clock. And his wife, Ivana, is brilliant. You'll have to book time off work. It'll be a holiday.'

'OK,' she said, but she felt nervous. How would she ever fit in on a mega-yacht?

*

In the limousine that Blaise had ordered, Jess sat in the back on the soft leather seat watching the lights of Hyde Park.

'Seeing London like this makes it look so beautiful,' she said. 'I usually cycle round it or take the bus.'

'I'd like to see the places you know,' he said. 'The places you hang out.'

'No, you wouldn't. Believe me.'

Jess stared out of the window. She couldn't take Blaise back to the flat. He had no idea where she had come from – and just how desperate it had been. The world she'd lived in and his world? Well, they just didn't gel. He would be horrified at the standards she'd so readily put up with.

Besides, the flat was too full of memories of Angel. The longer she stayed away, the easier it was for Jess to pretend that she'd started over and the past had gone.

'So, tell me,' she said brightly, changing the subject, putting all thoughts of the flat, of Angel, firmly to the back of her mind. 'Who are we meeting?'

'It's just some property investors. Associates.'

'Where's the property? Is this one you're doing up?'

Blaise looked at her as if weighing up whether to tell her or not. 'Well, it's all very confidential, but there's this island off the south-western coast of India. Not far from the Maldives.'

Jess smiled, her imagination whirring. India. How exotic. That was another place high up on her list.

'An island? Sounds glorious.'

'It will be. At the moment, it's wild.'

'So . . . can we go there?' Jess asked hopefully. She thought about the poster in her flat, the one Angel had given her. She looked at Blaise. Would he be the man who walked along the desert island beach with her? Was this really all her fantasies coming true?

'Well, once we own it.'

'You're going to get your own island?' Jess asked, her mind racing. 'What are you going to do with it?'

'We'll develop it into a luxury resort, most probably.'

'So you're buying the whole thing?'

Blaise twisted his lips and looked out of the window. 'Kind of more acquiring it. It's complicated.'

Jess had been expecting the business dinner to take place in a posh restaurant, or a private dining room, but to her surprise, the car drove the short way to a casino in Knightsbridge.

The entrance round the side of the building was dark and gloomy, and the man on the door had a gold tooth and a wire snaking up the side of his neck into an earpiece. He looked like he'd once been a boxer.

Blaise smiled nervously, taking Jess's hand and leading her to a plush lift with a red interior. She could see her diamonds glinting in the tinted mirrors. The lift went down, swallowing them into the depths of the building, and Jess felt a momentary flash of fear. This wasn't what she'd been expecting at all. She gripped Blaise's hand tighter.

They stepped out into what looked like a very private club, with dark leather booths. Jess saw a woman in a bikini writhing round a metal pole near a bar area, where a good-looking barman was polishing glasses. What was this place? She stared at Blaise, but he didn't meet her eye.

Surely Blaise didn't hang out with the kind of people who came to places like this. It was so seedy. What was happening?

They walked through the club to the booth right at the very end and Jess felt as if everyone was watching them. She might have got it all wrong, but she knew how to sense a criminal crowd. And this place had her hackles up.

Blaise's business was all above board, wasn't it? she panicked. He was honest and decent. So why were they here?

At the end booth, Blaise stopped and a man stood up, dressed in a grey pinstriped suit. He was Asian, with greying hair.

'Hello, Blaise,' he said. His accent was thick. 'You're late.'

'I'm sorry. I—' Blaise began, but the man suddenly turned and stared at Jess.

'So this is her,' he said.

Blaise scratched the side of his head. Jess noticed a sheen of sweat on his neck just above his collar. She glared at him, wanting to know what was going on and who the scary man was, but again Blaise didn't meet her eye.

'This is . . . er . . . Jess,' he mumbled. 'My girlfriend.'

'I am enchanted to meet you,' the man said, bowing his head slightly. 'Please, come and join me. Have a drink.' He gestured for her to sit in the booth. Then, without taking his eyes off her, he removed a thin brown cigarette from a packet on the table and lit it. He took a deep drag.

'Haven't you done well, Blaise,' the man said, before exhaling, and Jess felt the pungent smoke swirl round her neck, like a noose.

CHAPTER THIRTY-FIVE

Lace Island, 1990

Most of the other guests had left Lace Island and the bunga-lows on the beach were all empty except Adam's. Leila looked anxiously around her before rapping on the thin wooden front door. She hated Chan for making her come here, but what choice had she had? She needed to do whatever it took to stay under his radar, so that she could go diving with Rasa. She stared out at the blue horizon. Rasa would be waiting for her by now.

Her Rasa. After last night, he'd filled every second of her thoughts. She didn't care about Parva's warning this morning. Whatever happened between her and Rasa was nobody else's business.

The door opened, jolting her out of her thoughts, and Adam leant against the door frame, a beer in his hand.

'Leila. What a nice surprise. Come in, come in,' he said. 'You look pretty today, don't you. All dressed up for someone? For me?'

'I just came to give you this. I've got to go,' Leila said. She thrust the envelope at him impatiently.

'Don't look so scared. I don't bite,' Adam said, laughing,

his white teeth flashing at her, as he slowly took the envelope. Leila bit her lip, wishing he'd hurry up, hating being here with every fibre of her being.

Adam opened the envelope and took some papers part of the way out and nodded, before taking a sip of beer. 'You have to come in. I need to sign this and you'll have to take it back to the house. Come,' he said, cupping his hand and waving for her to follow him inside the bungalow.

Leila wanted to scream with frustration. She looked behind her, along the wooden path to the white sand of the beach. The palm trees leant invitingly down towards the water, crows pecking the bark. Rasa would be firing up the engine by now.

She could take the signed papers on the boat with her and give them to Chan later. She stepped inside the door, praying that Adam would hurry up.

'Why the rush?' Adam said, staring at her from where he'd pulled the papers out on a small wooden table.

'I'm late to meet someone, that's all. It's a busy day.'

'Aha. Oh yes. Your friend,' he said. His tone was mocking, and his eyes glittered with menace. Leila wished she hadn't said anything. 'Come, come, though, just a friend? I've seen the way you look at him,' he said, with a sly smile.

Leila cast her eyes down, annoyed at what he was implying. Rasa was nothing to do with him.

'I bet he wants you, that Rasa. I bet he wants you like I do,' Adam said, leaving the papers and beer on the table and taking a step towards her.

Leila backed away from him. *He wanted her?* He'd said it so casually, but she knew that he meant sexually.

'Oh, don't be coy. Since we're having this chat, you might as well know that I saw you watching me and Monique.'

Her hand trembled violently as it groped behind her for the door handle, but Adam moved fast. In a second, he'd slammed the door shut, making her jump back. He moved so that he was standing close to her now, pressing her back against the closed door. He brushed the hair away from her shoulder and kissed her neck.

'You are delicious,' he said. 'Like a peach. I want to eat you all up. I have since the first moment I saw you. And I think I'm more deserving than your fisherboy.'

His breath was hot and disgusting in her ear. She froze as behind her, she heard him pushing the bolt across the door. She squeezed her eyes shut, visions of Sussman filling her head. Because it was the same feeling. The same feeling of terror and helplessness.

She had to get away, but there was no other way out apart from the garden. She darted forward, aiming for the door, but Adam was faster, anticipating her move and blocking her escape.

'Don't play hard to get,' he said, grabbing her wrist. 'You've known all along that I intend to have you.'

Leila was desperate. 'Stop. Please. You're hurting me.' She tried to wrestle her arm away, but his grip tightened. How could she get out of here? How could she get to Rasa? Terror reared up in her as she ducked, trying to wrestle free, but he was too strong.

He wasn't going to let her go.

She tried again, a yelp of pure fear escaping her lips as she saw the intent in his eyes.

'Well, yes. I guess I will be hurting you a bit, but losing your virginity always does hurt a little, I'm told. You *are* a virgin?'

Leila's teeth started chattering uncontrollably as she spoke. 'Let me go. Please. I'll scream.'

Adam laughed, mocking her. 'You'll scream? And who will hear you, little one? Your fisherboy?'

Quickly, he let go of her wrist and grabbed her in a vice-like hold round her waist and moved her towards the bed. She kicked her legs, but he was too fast and too strong for her. She saw that there was a large brown suitcase open and neatly packed on the ottoman. A gun was on the top of the criss-crossed elastic. He threw her roughly onto the teak bed, where she bounced slightly and scrabbled backwards towards the soft pillows, but he was on all fours coming after her.

He pulled at the top of her shorts jumpsuit, breaking the strap, and she cried, hot tears bursting from her eyes. He yanked the string of her halter-neck bikini and pulled it down to expose her breasts. She saw a white fleck of spittle on his lip.

This couldn't be happening. *This couldn't be happening.*

Leila felt herself trembling violently as she struggled for breath. She squeezed her eyes shut, huddling her knees up against her.

Think. Think, she willed herself.

'Oh no. Look at me,' he said in a hoarse whisper, leaning in and pulling her chin. It hurt. She stared at him, wide-eyed with terror. His mouth was pulled back into an ugly grin, and sweat popped on his forehead.

He pulled at her blue jumpsuit, taking her bikini bottoms down with it. Desperately, she looked through the mosquito netting over at the gun on the suitcase, wondering how to get it, but there was no time.

In a second, he'd wedged her legs apart with his knees, and she saw that he'd opened his yellow shorts. He held his large erect penis in his hand, like it was a weapon.

'No,' she screamed out. '*No!*'

'Yes. Oh yes. This is what all the girls want, believe me. I know. You saw how Monique loved it. And you'll love it too.'

'Please,' she sobbed. 'Please don't. Please . . .'

He laughed, a soft, indulgent laugh. 'You'll thank me for this one day,' he said, spitting into his hand and caressing the end of his penis. Leila felt blood in her mouth where she'd bitten her cheek.

Visions of Rasa filled her head – his eyes, the way he'd told her that he'd look after her and defend her, teach her to fight. But where was he now?

'Rasa, help me,' Leila screamed, but even before she'd finished, Adam had grabbed her throat, choking her into silence.

'Shut up. Nobody is coming. It's just us,' he said, coming towards her now, looking down between her legs, wanting to guide himself inside her.

Finding her strength, Leila kicked away from him with a furious yell. In a second, she'd dived at the edge of the bed, determined to get through the mosquito net to the gun.

She was going to get the gun. She was damn well going to shoot him dead.

This could not happen.

But he was right behind her.

'You want it the hard way, huh?' His arms were tight round her waist, bending her over the bed like a rag doll.

And then he was kneeling in between her legs, holding her thighs in his vice-like grip and forcing himself inside her.

Outside, the crows broke from the trees into the sky.

PART THREE

CHAPTER THIRTY-SIX

Ibiza, present day

'I said I wanted three ice cubes,' Ivana snapped, her English heavy with a rough Russian accent, her pink, bejewelled talons holding the glass aloft. Jess watched the young stewardess on the mega-yacht flinch before taking back the glass.

'Sorry. I'll change it,' the girl said, spinning on her tanned bare feet, one arm behind her back in her smart navy uniform, and heading through the tinted sliding door to the salon.

Ivana didn't say anything, relaxing back on the grey squashy cushions on the deck before turning to her friend Tilly and laughing. 'Fucking idiot,' she added as an aside, although Jess knew that the stewardess had heard her clearly enough as she left.

Shocked, Jess looked away towards the harbour where they were moored in the swanky marina Ibiza Magna, wishing that Ivana would stop being so rude to her staff. Wishing that this whole thing didn't make her feel so uncomfortable and weird.

From where she was sitting, Jess could see both of the yachts next door, one of which Ivana said was owned by Jade Jagger. Roman Abramovich's yacht, *Eclipse*, was also moored, and he too had this view of the town, the strip of shops and the famous nightclub Pacha. Jess looked down at the reflection of the white yachts in oily water and for a minute was reminded of a caravan park she and Angel went to years ago near Whitby. The comparison made her smile. Not that she could ever say something like that to Ivana or her friends.

They'd flown out several days ago for their holiday in Ibiza, but Blaise had suddenly announced this morning that he was leaving her with 'the girls' on the yacht, telling her to have fun and that he'd be back in a few days. She had no idea where he'd gone, but he and Serge, Ivana's husband, had been laughing and joking together, slapping each other on the back like they were involved in some big conspiracy.

The girls staying on board included Becca and Tilly – also from London and both recently divorced, Tilly from husband number two, despite being only just thirty. They had a predatory air about them, scoping out everyone and anyone who passed the yacht, and Ivana had taken up the role of matchmaker for them both. Since Jess had arrived, there'd been people coming and going the whole time, Ivana delighting in hosting spur-of-the-moment long, raucous lunches and a huge party last night that had given Jess a terrible headache.

Tilly, dressed in a skimpy brown leopard-print bikini, her short blonde hair oiled back from her wrinkle-free forehead, had been studying her phone all morning hoping for a text from a DJ she'd kissed at the party last night. It seemed rather desperate to Jess. Girls like Tilly and her mate Becca, with her dusky, hawk-like looks and clanking gold jewellery, did nothing, as far as she could see, other than look perfect and spend other people's money. When they talked, Jess realized they had ridiculously high standards. She'd never even heard of the clothes brands they talked about, or the kitchen designers or cars they name-dropped constantly. Like their life would only ever be complete when they'd checked off every item on their long, long shopping list of desires.

And it seemed that the greater their material desires, the more respect Ivana had for her friends and her long, long list of acquaintances. It seemed to Jess as if everyone wanted to be Ivana's friend, or at least be seen with her, and Ivana knew it – insisting on the yacht being moored in the most exclusive part of the harbour and lounging on board in her spandex bikinis and stilettos for the world to see.

Jess knew Ivana wanted her to be impressed too, and grateful for having been propelled so effortlessly into Ivana's inner circle, but Jess had spent the last forty-eight hours in a state of jaw-dropping shock as she observed Ivana and her friends. And now that Blaise had gone, she felt proper panic setting in. Because at any moment, Ivana would discover the truth: that Jess had absolutely no idea how to exist in this world. She simply didn't know how to cope.

And the whole thing was making her feel more and more insecure about Blaise. How could he flit between this world and their time together so effortlessly? Because he obviously expected her to be able to do the same, and she wasn't sure she was up to the job. She would *never* fit in with Ivana and her friends.

It made her feel like she hardly knew Blaise at all. And now she wondered exactly what he and Serge were up to. Were they going somewhere like the seedy casino Blaise had taken her to? Jess wondered. She hoped not. She trusted Blaise, of course, but she hadn't been able to shake the meeting from the other week from her mind.

Blaise had been quick to dismiss it when she'd told him

afterwards how different the evening had been from her expec-
tations. Foreign investors were notoriously quirky and strange,
he'd told her – and this particular investor had a penchant for
women and casinos when he was in London. In his line of
work, he had to deal with oddballs all the time, but Jess had
passed with flying colours, he assured her.

But passed what? Jess couldn't work out why Blaise had
needed her there, or why the two men had paid her so much
attention. Because over dinner another man had joined them.
He'd been old too, with greasy hair, slicked back, and had told
Jess he liked jazz music, although his accented English had
been hard to understand. When they'd left, the man had kissed
Jess's hand.

'I'll be seeing you,' he'd told her. And the way he'd said it,
with an amused look in his eye, had made Jess shiver.

She hadn't told Blaise, but the whole evening had spooked
her out. She'd thought investors were rich and powerful.
She'd been prepared to put her best manners to the test and to
back up Blaise, but during dinner, they'd hardly discussed Lace
Island at all. In fact, since the conversation in the limo, Blaise
had been reluctant to talk about his new property investment
and she wondered whether it was because he didn't want to
jinx the deal.

She wanted so much to be involved, to support him, but he
always managed to rebuff her gently, or change the subject.
She'd already put a request in to have her routes changed so
she could get to India, just in case Blaise could be there at the
same time and show her Lace Island, but each time she tried to
discuss her plan, he seemed distracted.

Jess was determined to find out more. After all, she
couldn't deny that having a boyfriend who bought private
islands was *seriously* cool. And, of course, there was the little

voice in her head that kept thinking about the desert island poster she'd once cherished so much. What if the dream wasn't over? What if Blaise really was *the one*?

The stewardess dismissed, the conversation returned to Ivana's neighbour in Knightsbridge and her cruel husband, and Jess quietly excused herself to get some suncream from the cabin. But really she wanted to check her phone. Blaise must have texted her by now.

Inside the salon, the air conditioning sent Jess's skin into immediate goosebumps; her eyes adjusted to the darkness. The salon interior was the work of a famous designer, according to Ivana, but it reminded Jess of a gaudy nightclub, with its smoky mirrored walls and highly polished chrome. There were some shocking splodgy canvases by some famous modern artist that everyone seemed to coo over but looked to Jess like they'd been created by a heavy-handed infant in a nursery school.

Now Jess smiled at the stewardess, who was fixing Ivana's drink at the giant chrome bar in the corner, and walked towards her. She was probably the same age as Jess, Jess reckoned, with the kind of swishy blonde ponytail and high cheekbones that belied a posh English background.

'Hey. I'm sorry about that,' Jess said, feeling like she should apologize. 'It's Cathy, isn't it?' she added, seeing the sweet stewardess's wary face.

'It's OK. You don't have to say sorry. We're here to serve.'

We. The well-paid crew on board Serge's luxury yacht. Her look said it all. They put up and shut up, and Jess couldn't blame her. There were worse places to work.

'Yeah, well, I get people like her sometimes on board. I work for UKAir. Cabin crew,' she said. 'I've never been told off for ice cubes, though.'

Cathy smiled, a look of understanding crossing her face.

Jess pulled a face. 'What's the story with her, anyway? Don't worry,' she said, 'you can tell me. I'm very discreet. I just wondered, that's all. I've only just met her, you see.'

'Ivana?'

Jess nodded, seeing Cathy glancing around her. Even though the mega-yacht was huge, the walls were paper-thin.

'Well, I don't like to gossip, and you didn't hear this from me, but the rumour is that she used to be a prostitute in Russia before she married Serge. They have lots and lots of money. *Crazy amounts*.'

The implication in her knowing look was clear, and Jess felt herself shrinking for being associated with them, for so readily accepting their hospitality. For being seen on this yacht, for drinking their expensive champagne and eating the lobster and caviar the Michelin-starred chef served at nearly every meal. She wanted to explain herself. Tell Cathy that she had no choice. That she was with Blaise, who was different to these people. He was kind and gentle and well mannered. He didn't care about all the things they talked about.

But as she moved away towards the cabin, she couldn't help wondering again why Blaise *was* involved with Ivana and Serge, and why people as gaudy and money-orientated as them were his friends. They must be connected to his business deals. But which ones? There was still so much she didn't understand, or know, but it was difficult to ask him without sounding like she was being critical.

In the corridor below, near her guest bedroom, she saw another of the stewardesses coming out of one of the bath-rooms and she waved, but the stewardess looked embarrassed. Ivana insisted that every time anyone went to the bathroom, a stewardess went in and refolded the toilet roll into a point. It was the slavish attention to detail that continued to astonish Jess. It just seemed ridiculous. But more than that, she felt watched the whole time, as if her behaviour were being judged in the same way as Ivana's. She wanted to burst into the crew's mess to explain that she wasn't one of 'them'; she was normal, like the crew.

Except that she wasn't. Not anymore.

She went into her cabin and shut the door for a moment's solitude, sitting down on the mountainous soft beige bedding with a sigh and looking at her phone, but Blaise still hadn't texted. She lay back on the bed, staring at the polished chrome ceiling.

She knew she was lucky to be here in Ibiza on holiday. Most of the girls she worked with would bite her arm off for a holiday like this, and Blaise clearly assumed that she would be having a brilliant time with the girls, otherwise he wouldn't have left her. He'd just assumed that she'd fit in.

He had no idea that she was feeling like she was. If Blaise knew where she'd come from, perhaps he'd understand how uneasy this ostentatious wealth made her.

But that was the point. He didn't know where she came from. Not really. And in fairness, neither did she. She wondered now, though, why Blaise was so accepting of her situation. It felt to Jess as if her confession on Brooklyn Bridge had been enough and Blaise had decided that they wouldn't discuss the past anymore. That together they were making a fresh start and everything unpleasant or painful was over and gone.

In one way, it was comforting, but now, alone, Jess wondered whether he didn't want to share his past with her because he had stuff to hide. Or was it because he didn't want to know the truth about Jess? Did he have some kind of fantasy in his head that he thought Jess was?

Well, whatever the reason, there was no point in worrying about it. Right now, she was the luckiest girl on the planet, she reminded herself, staring at her reflection in the mirror. Blaise was a dream come true, and she'd do whatever it took to make him happy. Including getting on with his friends.

She got up and retied her hair in a ponytail, then gave herself a stern look in the mirror. She had to toughen up. Front it out. Do what it took to fit in.

Back on deck, Tilly was rubbing suncream into Becca's shoulders, and Jess grabbed her towel to spread it out on the sun cushion.

'I don't think she knows,' Jess heard Tilly say, and then there was a shocked silence and Jess knew immediately that they were talking about her. Ivana glanced at Tilly, who turned, caught out.

'Knows what?' Jess asked.

'Nothing,' Tilly said, but she looked embarrassed. She put on her mirrored shades.

'It's OK. You can tell me,' Jess said, trying to sound more confident than she felt, as she lay on her stomach.

Ivana twisted her lips, clearly enjoying this social impasse. 'You and Blaise seem pretty close,' she said. 'We were talking about that. That's all.'

Jess stared at Tilly.

'So you know, right?' Tilly asked sheepishly. 'About his past?'

'Yes, of course,' Jess lied, not wanting to lose face now that all the girls' eyes were upon her, but inside she was panicking. *What past? What were they talking about? What did they know about Blaise that she didn't?*

'That's a relief. We thought you didn't know,' Tilly said,

looking at Ivana over the top of her glasses. 'Because we're going round the coast and she'll be joining us for a few days.'

She. Who was she?

CHAPTER THIRTY-SEVEN

Lace Island, 1990

Parva stood in the doorway of Leila's bedroom and Leila didn't need to open her eyes to know the look on her face.

'Leila. Wake up. I told you half an hour ago. Timothy is waiting for your lessons. You can't cancel him again. It's been over a week now. A week you've been in here.'

Leila could hear the recrimination in her voice as she stomped across the wooden floor and flung open the shutters. She winced, still unable to open her eyes, turning her face away as sunlight flooded the room.

She wished Parva would leave her alone, but she sensed that this morning's new policy was tough love. She'd listened to the sounds of the house for a week and knew how busy everyone had been preparing for the monsoon, and how everyone, including Bibi and Chan, had been in the paddy fields collecting the harvest. At the busiest time of year, nobody had paid much attention to Leila, who had stayed resolutely in bed, refusing to get up. How could she? If Bibi saw her, then she'd see how bruised her arms were. It had taken some serious subterfuge to convince Parva to leave her alone and not call

Maliba or the doctor, but now Leila wondered if she'd ever heal. If she'd ever feel better.

'It's ten already,' Parva said. 'Everyone has been up for hours, and your mother is wondering what the situation is. You know, Leila, there's lots to be done. And you promised you'd collect all the candles, remember? You wouldn't think it on a day like today, but the rain is coming. We have to prepare for the power cuts while there's still time. Have you made your prediction with Anjum?'

Leila turned back, her head pounding. How could she pretend that life was normal and do something like predict the day the monsoon broke, like they did every year? How could everyone else be carrying on as normal, when it felt to Leila like her head was going to burst?

'Are you still sick?' Parva asked, suddenly appearing by the bed and putting her cool hand on Leila's forehead, her tone suggesting that she didn't believe Leila's stories of fever and stomach ache for a second. 'Because I'm serious. Your mother needs help. You should get up. This is not like you. You've been in bed now for long enough.'

Leila turned away, her nose prickling with tears. If she had the strength, she'd yell the fury she felt at Parva. She hugged her arms around herself beneath the covers, feeling cold and hot at the same time, feeling the tender flesh on her thighs. They were still slightly damp after her shower earlier. Crouching in the warm water was the only way she could get some relief on the torn, bruised flesh between her legs. Sobbing in the quiet dawn light, hoping that nobody would hear, she'd watched the blood trickle down the plughole, feeling all her hope drain with it.

'And what did you say to Rasa, hmm?' Parva probed. 'He's

moping around too. He won't go to lessons either. Did you two have a fight?'

Leila felt tears bulging from her swollen eyes. Who knew what Rasa thought of her? After she'd crawled out of Adam's beach bungalow, utterly wrecked, she knew there was no way she could go to him. She'd thought he would come looking for her, but when he hadn't, she'd known that Adam must have got to him first. She imagined the scene over and over in her head. How Adam would have implied what had happened. Only, he wouldn't have said it was rape, of course. He would have given Rasa the impression that Leila had given herself to him freely. And Rasa's continued silence could only mean one thing: he believed Adam.

'I don't know what we'll do with that boy,' Parva continued, fussing around Leila's room. 'He wants so badly to go to Cochin and get a job, but we need him here too much. What do you think he should do? Leila? Leila, come on.'

Leila pulled the sheet over her head, willing Parva to go away. She couldn't talk about Rasa. Not now. Not now she'd lost him for good. It didn't matter what Rasa did, because his future wouldn't include Leila.

She'd been awake all night thinking about it, coming to the same conclusion over and over. What would be the point of explaining herself and what had happened with Adam? What would Rasa be able to do? That's if he believed her. She'd already told him about one attack – the one at school. If she told him about Adam on the back of that, he'd just think she hadn't tried hard enough to defend herself. Or, even worse, that she was simply making excuses for who she really was.

And even if he *did* believe her, then what could he do? Use that gun and kill Adam? She knew he'd certainly want to.

Almost as much as she'd wanted to herself. And what good would that do, having Rasa become a murderer on her behalf?

Leila groaned, the horror of it all washing over her again. It should have been Rasa who had kissed her. It should have been Rasa who'd caressed her and taken her virginity. Not that disgusting man.

And now it was too late. If only she'd tried harder and had reached for the gun. If only she'd shot him dead. If only . . .

'Right. That's it, young lady. I'm going to get your mother,' Parva snapped. 'If you're really that ill, she can take you to the hospital in Cochin. But if I were you, I'd get up before that happens.'

Leila curled up onto her side as Parva left the room, and pictured Adam in his bungalow, blood pouring out of his head. She willed him to be dead in her mind, but it was no use. She couldn't stop the memory of him. The sheer size of him. It was as if she could still taste him, as if the very essence of him was inside her.

No matter how she tried, she couldn't get rid of him. The memory of what had happened was branded onto her brain and she could think of nothing else. She couldn't help remembering it all. And how afterwards, as she lay shaking and violated on the bed, he'd lain on top of her, his horrible stickiness on her leg.

'There,' he'd whispered, brushing her hair with his hand. 'You liked that. I know you did. You just needed breaking in. Next time, you will enjoy it more.'

Leila had only whimpered, unable to speak.

'One day, you'll see that your body will bring you great pleasure. Like it has to me,' he'd continued. 'Now I have made you a woman, you'll thank me for this.'

Leila had tried to pull away, but he'd pinned her down, grabbing her face and forcing her to look at him.

'Don't look like that. Like you regret it. You wanted this. I know you did – otherwise you wouldn't have watched me and Monique.'

Her eyes had bulged as she'd stared at him.

'And don't you go running out of here and telling tales to anyone, you hear me?' he said, his cold eyes blazing with triumph. 'Or otherwise next time, I won't be so gentlemanly.'

He shook her jaw, making her head nod.

He laughed, running his tongue over his teeth; then he looked down at her body. He ran his finger over her breast, pinching her nipple. 'You see,' he continued. 'You see how your body reacts . . . how much it likes this?'

Leila couldn't bear it. The pain in her nipple was intense as he squeezed harder.

'It's because you want sex. It's because you're just a dirty little slut,' he'd said, with a lascivious grin. 'Maybe now you can show your fisherboy your new tricks. I can tell him for you, if you like.'

Now, revolted by the memory, Leila sighed and turned to the window. She supposed that Parva was right. She would have to get up eventually, and she might as well try now. It was better to get up before Bibi came fussing around her. There was no way she was going to a doctor.

Slowly, painfully, she got out of bed and went to the dresser, selecting long blue trousers and a long-sleeved top. She felt weird getting dressed – as if her body was no longer her own. It was as if she was observing herself from the corner of the room. She couldn't look at herself in the mirror.

It felt weird, too, being outside her room. As if everything was different. She crept along the corridor, feeling light-headed and weak. It hurt to walk.

Downstairs in the hallway, the guests were preparing to leave and she could hear Adam laughing with Chan. She froze, pressing her back to the wall. She couldn't go down there. She couldn't face them. But suddenly Parva came out of Bibi's room.

'Finally, about time,' she said, with an annoying smirk of victory in her voice. 'Go on. They'll be wanting you downstairs.'

Leila forced herself away from the wall as Parva ushered her towards the stairs. She hugged her arms tightly around her, forcing herself to stay calm as she walked down the hallway, hoping she could slip past Chan and escape via the terrace.

'Ah. At last. Where have you been, Leila?' Chan said, seeing her on the stairs. 'There are chores to do, and Timothy has been waiting an hour or more for you.'

Leila didn't say anything. She stayed rooted to the spot.

'Come and say goodbye to Mr Lonegan,' Chan instructed, beckoning her down the stairs. 'He's leaving on the flight today.'

She watched as Adam took a wodge of notes out of his top pocket and handed them to Chan.

'A tip. For the staff,' he said.

'Most generous. Thank you, Adam. I'll run you down to the landing strip,' Chan said. 'I don't know where Rasa has got to today.'

Now Monique appeared in the hallway with Marc, who was carrying her heavy suitcase.

Leila stared at her, remembering how Monique had looked when Adam had had sex with her. How weird it was to now have an unspeakable bond with this glamorous woman.

Adam stood grinning at Monique, enjoying the moment, as if he was revelling in the unspoken secrets between them all circling like invisible bats. Then he turned his face up to Leila.

'Why the miserable face, Leila?' he asked.

Bibi appeared now from her room and came down the stairs behind Leila.

'Leila, don't be so rude to our guests. Come and say goodbye properly and thank them for coming.'

Guided by Bibi's hand, Leila walked the last few steps down to where the guests were standing.

'Bibi. Thank you as always,' Adam said, kissing her warmly on both cheeks.

'No, Adam. Thank you for coming.'

'The pleasure has been all mine,' he said, his teeth flashing at Leila.

Bang. She pulled the trigger in her head. Watched him fall to the floor. She'd do it in a heartbeat.

'You must sign the visitors book,' Bibi said, and Adam made a funny gesture, slapping his head as if he couldn't believe he'd forgotten to.

'Of course,' he said, going over and writing his name on the page with a flourish and adding a comment as an afterthought before signing it.

Clenching her fists, Leila looked down at the floor as more goodbyes were said; then Monique, Marc and Bibi drifted towards the door. Chan was behind them, right by the door. Adam put his finger under Leila's chin so she had to look at him.

'Are you sad to see me go?' he said, with a jokey laugh. 'You needn't worry, Leila. I'll be back.'

He put his hand on her bottom and squeezed it hard. Leila flinched, wanting to throw up. She was amazed that he had been so blatant, but Bibi hadn't seen, as she was already walking down the front steps with Monique and Marc.

But Chan had. He was standing by the door, and when Leila caught his eye, his look said it all. That he knew exactly what Adam had done to her and that he had done absolutely nothing to stop it.

CHAPTER THIRTY-EIGHT

Ibiza, present day

Jess had lost track of time. She groped along the corridor of the club to the loos, hoping for some respite – not only from the thumping house music but also from Ivana's inane chatter and her outrageous behaviour.

In the most vulgar show of wealth Jess had ever seen, Ivana had been ordering the club's most expensive magnums of champagne for several hours, in competition with some other Russians at another table. She'd also persuaded the waiter to strip off his shirt and had now been downing shots with the girls for the last hour with no let-up. Jess had clapped and whooped with the others, but she simply couldn't keep up.

Squeezing herself past a couple of girls who were giggling and chatting, Jess felt her head thumping and she let out an exhausted sigh. She knew she should be enjoying herself more, that she should feel psyched to be in the VIP area of the hottest club in Ibiza, but she couldn't relax. Today had been excruciating. She desperately wanted to know what the girls were talking about, but after the conversation on the yacht this morning, Jess had been left hanging.

As they'd sailed round the coast, Jess had been consumed

with worry. Were they meeting Blaise's ex-girlfriend? Was that what they'd meant about his past? And if so, why had Ivana invited her on board? To be mischievous? To upset Jess? Or Blaise? She'd tried calling and texting him, but she'd had no reception on her phone and she still hadn't spoken to him.

But whoever 'she' was had failed to meet the yacht, and now they were out at a nightclub. Was 'she' going to turn up here? Jess hoped not. She was in no fit state to face Blaise's ex. Not after the amount she'd drunk.

She pushed open the door to one of the loo cubicles. A girl with impossibly toned, long, tanned legs was leaning over in a tiny leather miniskirt.

'Oh, hey, come in,' the girl said. She leant up from the porcelain cistern and dabbed the side of her nose. 'Want some?' she asked, in a deep, husky Italian accent. She looked at Jess in the mirror, holding up a rolled-up bill. Jess didn't know where to look. She'd seen plenty of people taking drugs before, but never so brazenly.

The girl, who was very probably a model, or else *should* have been a model, was stunning, with a refined Amazonian stature that made Jess feel pathetic and cheap next to her. She flicked her mane of glossy brown hair over her shoulder and fixed Jess with an amused stare from beneath her choppy fringe. Her eyes were huge and heavily lined in glittery kohl, and now, as she smiled, Jess saw that she had a gap between her front teeth, which only seemed to enhance her natural beauty.

'Sorry. I didn't mean to interrupt,' Jess said, quickly backing out.

'Darling, it's fine. Have some. We're all friends here.' It was that voice. *Darr-ling*. It was so sexy and knowing.

'No, honestly. I should get back. I'm with people . . .' Jess said, but she still couldn't stop staring at the girl, who was now reaching for a packet of cigarettes from a small leather hand-bag. She watched as she lit one, blowing smoke from her deep red puckered lips.

'Stay and talk to me while I have this. You seem familiar . . . Have we met before?'

'No. No, I don't think so.'

'Who you with, darling?' She folded her arms across her washboard-flat stomach, her breasts bulging in her lace crop top.

Jess was taken aback by the direct question. Why was it even any of her business?

'Some people. Ivana and—'

The girl took a big gasp in, her eyes widening. She flapped the cigarette in Jess's direction. 'If you're with Ivana, then *you're* that girl. With Blaise, right?' The girl said it like it was a thing. Like Jess was known. Like everyone had been talking about her.

'You know Blaise?' Jess asked, feeling intimidated.

'Sure. Everyone knows Blaise.' She let out a low, knowing chuckle. 'Where did *you* meet him?'

'On a plane,' Jess said.

She blew out a rush of smoke in Jess's direction, then crushed the cigarette beneath the sole of her Jimmy Choo sandal. 'And you're English. Hmm. Figures,' she said, as if she knew something. 'He does spread himself around. Last two have been Latin American.'

The last two what? Girlfriends? Latin American? What did that mean? Tall, Brazilian beauties?

'You know, I've really got to go. I—' Jess began.

'Have a line. See you through. It's good shit,' the girl said.

'I can't really. I don't, anyway. My job. On the airline.'

'Oh. You *work*?' The girl sounded incredulous.

'Yeah.'

'Huh. That's funny.'

Jess bristled. 'I like my job.'

'You don't need to work, though. Blaise is rich, right? I heard he's getting his own island.' Her eyes glittered, probing for more details, but Jess felt defensive. How did this girl know about Lace Island, when it was all supposed to be confidential?

Her look was triumphant as she picked up the bag of coke and put it in the back pocket of her skirt. 'Come on. Let's go,' she said.

Then before Jess could say anything more, the girl linked arms with her, turning her round and back out into the corridor. She almost had to run to keep up with her long stride.

Back at the table, Ivana clapped her hands with delight.

'You found Porscha,' she bellowed to Jess, bumping everyone round the booth so that they could all sit down. Ivana whistled to their waiter.

Tilly and Becca kissed Porscha in a squeal of hugs. 'Finally you made it. We sailed all the way to the beach to pick you up today.'

Jess felt her heart hammering. *Porscha was the girl*. The girl they'd been talking about. *Blaise's past*. His ex-girlfriend. She felt winded by the revelation. Porscha was not only clearly loaded, but she was also compellingly beautiful, with that voluptuous Italian thing going on that Jess suspected drove men crazy. How could Jess ever compete with her?

She'd thought the whole relationship with Blaise was too good to be true right at the start, and now, as she watched Porscha and the girls, all those feelings came flooding back. Why would he love someone like Jess when he could have a girl like Porscha?

'Here we go, beautiful ladies,' the waiter said, setting down a tray of shots, to a cheer from the others.

Ivana thrust a shot glass into Jess's hand.

'I can't. No more,' Jess pleaded, but Ivana wouldn't hear of it, handing out the shots to the others. Porscha observed Jess from beneath her fringe, a knowing, catlike smile on her face.

'Drink, drink,' Porscha urged, throwing the contents of her shot glass down her throat with wild abandon. Jess's head throbbed, the ultraviolet light in the VIP booth making a small scar on Ivana's face glow. Had she had a face lift?

'She's so uptight, this little one,' Ivana said to Porscha, laughing at Jess. She pulled her in close. 'Take this, honey,' she said, and Jess looked down to a pill in her hand. Holding Jess in a tight grip, Ivana popped one in her own mouth, her face close to Jess's. 'Take it. Have fun with us. We're all together now.'

But as she swallowed the small pill with another shot, Jess knew she was slipping into new territory, where she didn't feel in control. And as she put the shot down on the table with a bang, all she could picture was Angel when she'd found her dead in that flat.

CHAPTER THIRTY-NINE

Lace Island, 1990

Leila squinted, pulling the shutters closed on the upstairs landing window, the furnace-like heat outside making everything in her vision swim. The chorus of cicadas was deafening in the blazing sunshine. It was always like this just before the monsoon started, but she could feel a change in the air, as if everything was charged with a certain kind of electricity. And she felt static too. Like she might spark if anyone touched her.

It didn't help that she had to wear her long trousers to cover up the bruises on her legs and her only long shirt to cover her upper arms. When she'd studied herself in the bathroom mirror, she couldn't believe how bruised she still was. It was nothing to how she felt on the inside.

In the grove, Leila could hear the horn of a tuk-tuk and bicycle bells, as people came and went. The ferry had arrived this morning, bearing fresh supplies, and it had been busy all morning. Now that the last of the guests had left on the plane before the rains, it was as if the whole island were breathing a sigh of relief. Except for Leila.

She felt strained and tired as she knocked quietly on Bibi's door and waited. It was early afternoon and she knew Bibi would probably be doing paperwork, but when she didn't answer, Leila tried the door and poked her head round. She saw that the room beyond was empty.

She walked inside, the familiar smell of Bibi's office making her feel sad and nostalgic. Trembling, she sat down at the wooden swivel chair next to Bibi's desk, twirling round on it, remembering how, as a child, her feet hadn't been able to touch the floor, how Bibi used to braid her hair and then spin her round in the chair, and her heart ached for those simple days.

She stood up and went to the cage with the little yellow birds in the corner, clucking to them and watching them flutter around. She stared out of the small window that was the birds' view too and saw over the trees that the sea was a searing blue, although dark clouds were gathering on the horizon. It wouldn't be long now until everything changed and the heavens discharged their downpour.

The door to Bibi's bedroom was open and she walked inside, picking up her mother's gown and inhaling the smell of her perfume. The bed was made and Leila ran her hand over the swathes of mosquito net, before drifting into the closet, where Bibi kept her saris and shoes.

This had always been Leila's place of sanctuary, where she'd played as a child, going through the box of photos and trying on the jewels that Bibi had worn when she married her beloved Ranjidan, Leila's father.

Leila had been expecting to wear them herself one day, but now that wouldn't happen, she realized with a jolt. There would be no lavish wedding for a girl who wasn't a virgin. The shame and sadness of it all made her want to curl up on the floor beneath the row of clothes and never wake up.

For one wild moment this morning, after the guests had left, Leila had decided that this afternoon, when they were alone, she would tell Bibi the truth about what had happened with Adam. But being here, in the heart of Bibi's room, Leila knew she couldn't.

How could she possibly break Bibi's heart? Which she would, if she confessed. No, she decided, she would have to keep her secret to herself. But now that it was so close to the surface, she felt the guilt settling inside her like a poisonous coiled snake.

She swallowed, forcing herself to be strong. It had been ridiculous to think Bibi might make her feel better. And what was the point in telling the truth, anyway? Nobody had believed her in school about Miss Sussman, and Leila hadn't had the nerve to tell Bibi about that. So what was the point of telling her about Adam now?

And what about Chan and how, from that awful look in the hallway, Leila had realized that he knew what Adam had done? Bibi would never believe that either, even though Leila knew it was true. No doubt Chan would find a way to deny the accusation. He'd blame Leila. He'd tell Bibi that Leila had been flirting with their prestigious guest. That she'd been spying on him because she wanted him.

The knowledge that she wouldn't be believed made Leila's heart flood with a bitter anger and she let out a frustrated moan. It wasn't only that Adam had robbed her of her virginity and innocence, he'd robbed her of so much more. She'd lost Rasa and now she'd lost all the trust she'd always shared with her mother too.

Miserably, she drifted back out of the closet towards Bibi's bed and ran her hand over the lace doily on the oak bedside table that Bibi's mother had crocheted long ago. Beneath it, the bedside drawer was partially open. Inside must be twenty or more bottles of pills. Leila opened the drawer now and took one of the brown bottles and studied the label. They were from a hospital in Cochin. What was Bibi doing with all these pills? She didn't believe in doctors. She took Maliba's herbs. And why so many bottles?

But she didn't have time to think more about it, because the door to Bibi's room was opening.

'Come in, come in,' she heard Bibi say.

Leila quickly replaced the pill bottle and ducked behind the bedroom door. Bibi was ushering into her office a man Leila had never seen. He was dressed in a smart suit and held an old-fashioned trilby hat in his hand.

'Please excuse the mess,' Bibi continued. 'Here. Have a seat,' she said, directing the man to the swivel chair Leila had been in only minutes ago. 'We can talk in private here,' Bibi said pointedly.

The man placed his hat on the desk and pulled his brief-case onto his knee. Silently, he handed Bibi a piece of paper, which she read slowly. Leila peered through the gap in the door, watching as Bibi pinched the bridge of her nose as if the pressure in her head could be dammed.

'It's really that bad?' Bibi said, her voice catching.

'You must have had some idea?' the man said.

'Not that he'd spent it *all*.'

Leila saw Bibi looking up at the ceiling fan and her eyes widened when she saw something she'd never seen. Her mother was crying.

'I'm sorry,' Bibi said, placing her hand on her chest and trying to compose herself.

The man stood and handed her a white handkerchief. Bibi briefly leant her head against the man's shoulder and he patted her back. Who was he that he could be so familiar with her?

'I know it is a shock, Bibi. That is why I came myself,' he said gently.

Bibi pulled away, wiping her eyes, then folding his handkerchief carefully. 'I don't know what to do. I haven't paid the staff for months. The whole place is falling apart. And I can't talk to Chan now his drinking has got so much worse.'

'What is it that Chan has done with the money?'

Bibi let out a bitter laugh. 'You name it. Cigarettes, alcohol, the girl he keeps in Cochin, his gambling habit.' Bibi was pacing now. 'I always used to overlook his behaviour in the past. I told myself that it didn't matter as long as he was here with me, helping me to bring up Leila. I told myself I was doing the right thing and I held it together for Leila's sake. You know Ranjidan would have wanted her to have a father. That's why I married Chan. But' – Bibi took a shuddering breath, as if unburdening herself – 'as soon as Leila went to England, the cracks were too big. We've broken apart and I'm too angry and weak to fight it.'

Leila quickly turned away as the man pulled out more papers from his leather briefcase and laid them on the desk. She shrank back in the shadows, worried that Bibi would discover her spying, the magnitude of Bibi's problems making her own fade for a moment. She could hardly take in everything she'd just heard.

'This is everything you've had to pay. All the cheques,' the man was saying.

'What's that one?' she heard Bibi ask.

'That's the insurance policy, remember?'

'Oh yes. That too.'

'You could stop paying for it. Or cash it in?'

'What are you suggesting? That I burn the whole place to the ground and start again?'

The man laughed sadly. 'If only it were that simple. Bibi, why don't you consider shutting up the place? Moving to the mainland?'

'This is my home. I won't desert it. Or the people here. Ranjidan loved it here. You know that. I can't leave.'

'But something is going to have to happen, Bibi. You know that, don't you? If this carries on, you will lose everything.'

Leila felt her heart hammering as she turned again and pressed her eye against the crack in the door. Bibi was pacing now, wringing the handkerchief in her fingers.

'Chan says he has plans. I'm not sure what they are, but he seems to think everything is going to work out.' Bibi sighed heavily. 'If only I could believe him.'

'And what of the will?' the man said gently. Leila could tell from his voice that he sympathized and was on Bibi's side. 'You mentioned it in your telex.'

Bibi stopped now. She covered her face. 'I told a lie.'

'What do you mean, a lie?'

'I shouldn't have done it, but I told Chan that I changed my will, that the island will be his after I die.'

'But you haven't?'

'No.'

'So Lace Island will pass to Leila?'

Bibi nodded.

'Are you sure? She's so young.'

'I know, but she's a good girl. She's everything to me. Everything,' Bibi said, gripping the fine gold chain she wore and pressing her fist against her chest. 'She always has been.'

Leila swallowed down tears, hearing the affection in Bibi's voice.

The man nodded. 'My wife rejoices in her sons, but I see in

you something she'll never have. Perhaps there is nothing stronger than the bond between a mother and a daughter.'

Bibi sighed. 'You're right. I don't think there is. We may clash, Leila and I, but she won't let me down, my girl. She'll do what's right for her family. I know that.'

My girl. Leila felt her heart swelling with an emotion she could barely comprehend. The way her mother had said it. With such power and love. With such *faith*.

She longed to rush into the room and throw herself into Bibi's arms, but she knew she couldn't. She would wait until Bibi and the man had gone and then leave the room.

But whatever she did next, she would save Bibi and Lace Island, before it was too late.

CHAPTER FORTY

Ibiza, present day

It was early – not even seven. Jess hadn't been able to sleep on the yacht. Blaise had woken at six and taken a call, and she hadn't been able to stop herself trying to decipher the low mumblings from the other side of the door. Who could he be talking to this early? Why was he being so secretive?

She'd lain in bed trying to fathom it out, telling herself that he was only being considerate and wanting her to sleep. But how could she sleep when she had so many unanswered questions? Frustrated, she'd got up and changed into her running shorts and headed out for a run.

This early in the morning, the only people around were the staff servicing the yachts in the harbour: vans delivering freshly baked loaves, crews furiously cleaning the decks before the guests got up. Jess nodded good morning to some of them, although she sensed an unspoken deference from them that made her uncomfortable. That 'them' and 'us' thing that had bothered her the entire time she'd been here.

She wondered what it would be like later when she went back to work herself and had to return to being in a subservient role. This week in Ibiza living the life of the super-rich had certainly been an eye-opener.

Now, a couple of days after the clubbing incident, she'd had time to clear her head. She hated herself for taking the pill in the first place, but when Blaise had arrived at the club later that night, he'd been sweet about it, telling her that Ivana was famously impossible to resist and that it was no big deal.

He'd taken her for a walk on the beach until she'd felt less high. Then he'd held her hand and taken her back inside the club, where he'd very deliberately snubbed Porscha, laughing off Jess's suggestion that they'd ever been an item. Since then, he'd hardly left Jess's side. She'd been so relieved to see him she'd been happy to cling on to him.

The others, seeing her and Blaise together and so clearly in love, had finally accepted Jess as one of their own, and so long as she was with Blaise, she could just about cope with them.

Yesterday, they'd sailed round the coast and dropped anchor in a secluded bay, and she and Blaise had spent hours jet-skiing and swimming in the sea. It had been so much fun. Only Porscha had been in a sulk and had stayed in her cabin.

Jess broke into a sweat as she headed up the cliff path now, her mind trying to process everything that had happened in the last week.

She just couldn't work out Porscha, or whether there had once been anything between her and Blaise. He'd laughed at Jess when she'd implied that they'd been together, but now, thinking about it, he hadn't exactly emphatically denied it either. But if they were exes, why had Porscha come on holiday? And why all the secrecy?

It didn't make sense.

But then perhaps it was nothing. Jess could have been reading hidden meanings into Porscha's provocative statements.

Or maybe she'd misinterpreted her. Jess hadn't exactly been sober when they'd met. In fact, maybe she'd invented the whole vibe between Blaise and Porscha because she was being paranoid. Porscha wasn't really watching her, waiting for her to trip up at all.

She stretched her arms now at the top of the cliff path, catching her breath, before stretching out her biceps. She should do some press-ups, but it was too hot already. She squinted at the view of the harbour below and the twinkling sea beyond the harbour wall, wishing she'd brought her shades.

It was only a few hours now before she had to leave and get her flight back to London. And Blaise was leaving later himself for Miami. But right now, Porscha was alone with him on the yacht, and Jess didn't trust her. Not one little bit.

Having decided to go through the old town on her route back to the yacht, she ran down the cobbled streets, putting in her earphones and enjoying an old-school blast of her disco playlist.

Jess smiled at the sights, the pigeons scattering ahead of her towards the pale, shuttered houses as she reached the *plaça*. She was running past the old church when she noticed a woman sitting on the stone steps, her head in her hands, a pair of high wedge sandals by her feet.

Jess approached, turning off the music, her head filling now with the sound of the clanking church bell, the birds chirruping in the trees and the woman's muffled sobs.

'Tilly?' Jess asked.

Tilly's eyes were bloodshot and swollen from tears as she looked up. Jess had only seen her looking manicured and perfect, but now she looked haggard and wrung out.

'It *is* you. What's the matter? What's happened?' Jess asked.

She hadn't seen Tilly since yesterday, since she'd told everyone she'd gone into town to meet friends. She hadn't come back at dinner time and Ivana had been triumphant that Tilly finally had a date.

Tilly sniffed loudly and wiped her nose on the back of her hand. 'I went to see Daryl. You know, the DJ?'

Jess nodded and sat down next to Tilly on the steps. 'What happened?'

'Everything was going fine. He slept with me, but then he told me to leave. Just like that. He said that he didn't date women like me. That I was too' – she took a great gulp of air, her voice shaking. Jess put her arm round Tilly's shoulders – 'too needy.'

Jess held her while she sobbed, then coaxed her back to her feet and walked with her through the old town and down to the yacht, listening to the whole story and Tilly's diatribe about her failed marriages and her lack of children. Jess was touched that Tilly had confided in her.

'You're so lucky,' Tilly said, when she could finally speak normally. 'You have Blaise and you're just so natural and sweet. You know, I used to be like you. Before all of this.' Tilly flung her arm out in the direction of the yachts. 'Money fucks everything up,' she said, staring at Jess. 'Believe me. People do very odd things for it.'

Was she talking about Ivana and Serge perhaps? Or even Blaise? Jess couldn't tell, but listening to Tilly had put a different perspective on things. Perhaps she didn't need to turn into a glamorous brand expert after all.

'You won't tell them?' Tilly said suddenly. 'About me. About all of this?'

'No, of course not.'

They were on the path leading down to the harbour now

and Tilly had started to cheer up. 'You know, when we get back to London, can we meet up?' she asked. 'Just you and me?'

'Sure.'

'I'd like us to be friends.'

'I'd like that too,' Jess said, meaning it.

Back on the yacht, Porscha was on the cushions on deck, her long brown legs stretched out in front of her. She was wearing a skimpy bikini beneath her open sarong. Jess wondered how long Blaise had been staring at her honed body.

There was an amused smile playing on her lips, which quickly faded when she saw Jess.

'There you are,' Blaise said, smiling and putting his arm round her.

'Hey,' Jess said to Porscha. 'Are you feeling better?'

'A bit, thank you. I'm as well as can be expected under the circumstances,' Porscha said, glancing at Blaise with a meaningful stare.

Under the circumstances. What did that mean? Jess wondered.

'I'm going to have a shower,' Jess said, folding up her earphones. She glanced at Blaise, with a 'what was all that about?' look and he took the hint.

Back in their cabin, Jess stripped out of her running gear.

'What is it with her?' Jess asked.

'Porscha?'

'What did she mean, "under the circumstances"?'

'I don't know,' he said, distracted and looking at his phone, but Jess had the feeling he knew perfectly well. She opened the door of the en-suite bathroom and stepped into the shower. Perhaps now that she and Tilly were friends, Tilly would be able to tell her the truth about Porscha. She suddenly felt powerful, knowing she had a new ally.

She'd started lathering up her hair when Blaise stepped into the shower behind her. She turned and gasped, shampoo suds getting in her eyes, but not before she saw how aroused he was.

'Come here,' he said, pressing up against her so that she fell back against the steamy glass. He kissed her deeply and she pressed against him. 'I missed you. You were gone for ages.'

The rest of the morning passed in a blur and Jess didn't have time to think about Porscha and Blaise, as they had to race to catch her flight. On the way to the airport in Blaise's hired jeep, Jess got a text.

'Oh my God,' she said. 'I just heard. My request has been accepted.'

'What do you mean?' he asked, signalling to turn into the airport lane.

'I'm on the flight to Cochin. Isn't that great?'

Blaise looked confused. 'Cochin, India? You're flying to India?'

'It looks like it.' She turned to Blaise in the car. 'Why are you looking like that? I've wanted to go there for ages. I thought you'd be excited for me. Besides, you're going to Miami and we'll still see each other at the weekend, right?'

Blaise didn't say anything. Why was he suddenly so annoyed that she was going to India? she wondered.

She was expecting him to drop her off, but he parked the jeep and came inside the terminal, all the way to passport control, insisting on wheeling her bag.

'I wish you weren't going,' he said, when they'd finally

stopped. He took her hand, watching his fingers twist round hers.

'But I've got to go,' she said, squeezing his fingers, before quickly glancing up at the departures board. They'd already cut it to the wire and she had to get the flight back to London or she'd miss her next shift. As it was, she'd have no time to go home and change. Thank God she had a spare uniform in her locker. 'It's my job.'

'Well, I wish you didn't have to work.'

'But I do and I can't just not turn up,' she said, surprised. 'I'd get sacked.' A second time, she thought, but didn't say.

Besides, she wanted this. She wanted to travel the world. This had always been her dream. She wished that Blaise could be more excited for her. In a few hours, she'd be on a flight to India. India! Didn't that make his heart race like hers did?

But at the same time, her heart was racing for a different reason too. Because she knew how badly she was going to miss him. If only he was coming with her.

'Why don't you just quit altogether?' he said.

'Quit? And do what?'

'I don't know. Hang out with me.'

His suggestion was serious, and as she stared into his eyes, she realized for the first time that he really meant it. She felt her mouth go dry. Her mind raced over the implications, but she couldn't fathom it out. What exactly would she do? Hang around while he made phone call after phone call?

But it was more than that. She'd worked so hard to get where she was. She couldn't give it all up now. Could she?

'I don't mean hang out,' he said, stepping closer and brushing the hair over her ear. 'I mean more than that.'

Jess felt her heart racing. She needed to look at the clock again, aware of the precious seconds ticking by, knowing that already she'd have to sprint to the gate. But she couldn't look away, not when Blaise seemed so intense. Why couldn't they have had this conversation this morning? Why were they having it now? What did he mean by 'more than that'?

She got jolted towards him as a large family bustled past her, the father shouting at the kids to get the wheelie bags in a line.

Blaise grabbed the tops of her arms. 'Marry me,' he said.

'What?'

'Oh my God! Jess, is that you? I thought it was.' Jess heard a voice blaring out behind her. It was Gina. The air hostess with whom Jess had worked during her first job, all that time ago. Jess closed her eyes in a long blink, astonished this was happening all at once.

'Hi,' she said, staring desperately at Blaise and then at Gina.

'You guys been on holiday?' Gina asked.

'Yes. This is Blaise,' Jess said. Gina shook hands with him and then gave Jess an impressed look. 'We're just saying goodbye. I'm on the flight to London.'

'Me too,' Gina said. 'We can fly together.'

'OK. Just . . . give me a minute. I'll see you at the gate,' Jess said, desperate to get rid of her. Gina waved flirtatiously to Blaise.

As soon as she'd gone, Jess turned back to Blaise, stepping with him out of the flow of people.

'Did you just say what I think you said? *Here*?'

He laughed and covered his eyes with his hands. 'I know. It's terrible timing. It was supposed to be romantic. I've been planning to say it all this week, but we haven't had a minute alone and—'

'Would the last remaining passengers for flight VE326 to

London please make their way to gate six,' the tannoy blasted above them.

'That's me. I've got to go,' Jess said, overwhelmed by his confession.

She leant up and kissed him, laughing at how crazy all this was.

He held her face. 'Jess, I mean it. This is the worst proposal of all time, and I will do better, I promise, but I love you. I want you to be my wife. Will you? Will you marry me?'

'Yes,' she laughed. 'Yes. Of course I will.'

He picked her up and twirled her round in a hug; then he kissed her deeply. 'Promise me you mean it.'

'I mean it,' she said, smiling at him. 'Now let me go. I have to catch this flight.'

'You're still going?' He sounded astonished.

'I've *got to go*,' she said, happy tears springing to her eyes.

'Then call me as soon as you land.'

'I love you,' she called out, then turned and shouted it out as loudly as she could, making the passengers around her stop and stare. '*I love you.*'

CHAPTER FORTY-ONE

Lace Island, 1990

It was Maliba's birthday and there was music coming from across the lagoon. From where she was standing behind the treeline in the forest, Leila could see candles flickering near the lagoon's edge, and fireflies danced. Parva and her friend were performing their traditional folk dances, their hands flicking against the fire, the bells on their ankles and wrists chiming. Looking at the scene, Leila couldn't believe that everyone was so happy.

Everyone except Leila. After everything she'd overheard in Bibi's room, she hadn't been able to think straight. Just when she'd thought her life couldn't get any worse, it had. Because Bibi was in serious trouble, and Chan was to blame.

It was so difficult to process: the thought that her whole childhood had been one long act. When Chan had come home each time from Cochin bearing gifts, had Bibi known all along he'd been with another woman?

The thought made Leila sick to her core.

Why had Bibi put up with it for so long? How could she even bear to look at him? What was worse was that she'd held it together for Leila's sake all this time. Leila would never have wanted her mother to compromise herself like that for her.

The whole thing was such a mess, and now Bibi was up to her neck in debt. Leila had been so worried about her own problems, so consumed by what had happened with Adam, but overhearing Bibi talking in her office had focused her mind. It was killing her mother to know how she was letting everyone on Lace Island down, and Leila knew that she had to park her own self-pity and find a way to help Bibi. She had to tell her that she knew the truth about Chan.

But first, she needed to get her facts straight. She needed to go to Bibi with proper evidence to show what Chan was up to. Because it was clear that whatever it was, Bibi had no idea. What's more, Leila was pretty sure it was something illegal. If she could only catch Chan, then Leila could get the police involved, have Chan arrested. There would be a scandal, of course, which Bibi would hate, but once it had died down, she would be free.

Which is why Leila crept determinedly now through the silver trees, placing her feet softly on the dry forest floor. The night was warm, the hot breeze blowing in off the ocean, the clouds scudding across the blue-black sky. All around her, the forest seemed alive with sound, including the party in the lagoon.

From up here by the lighthouse, she could see down to the coast. The tide was high and rolling breakers crashed on the shore, as if presaging the rough seas that would soon be here when the monsoon broke. She glanced across at the reef, a silver line of surf breaking in a streak across the dark water.

She froze for a moment, hearing voices up ahead coming out of the lighthouse. She crept closer now. Chan was standing talking to Shang.

'As soon as the next shipment from Laos gets here, I'll send word. Then one of the container ships will get near enough and we'll send out a boat to it. Adam says the route will take it into New Orleans.'

Adam. Leila's heart froze at the sound of his name coming so warmly from Chan's lips. It was just as she'd thought: Adam was involved with Chan and Shang. Whatever they were doing, Adam was involved and covering for them.

Leila waited until the tuk-tuk had disappeared with Chan and Shang down the rutted path and crept towards the lighthouse. She fumbled with the torch in her pocket.

She knew it was risky, but she didn't care. She was not going to let down Bibi. She was going to get in there, come what may. She stared up at the dirty window. If she could only smash it and force her way in, she'd get the proof of what Shang was storing in there and make a plan.

When Leila arrived breathlessly back down at the beach party, more people were round the fire and the music was louder, as sparks flew into the black night. Victor and his friends were drumming out beats, and people were singing. Maliba was in the middle of it all, clapping her hands. Leila went to her and kissed her, wishing her a happy birthday.

Maliba held her face in her very old, crinkled hands. 'Come and see me tomorrow. We must talk,' she whispered.

'I will,' Leila said, wanting to break away and look for Rasa, but Maliba held her close. She shut her eyes for a moment, breathing in, as if she were sucking in all of Leila's memories.

'Is something wrong?' Maliba said, her hooded eyes dark with concern.

Leila felt the words bubbling up. She longed to blurt out

everything to Maliba, to purge herself of all her worries, to tell her about Rasa and Adam and Bibi and Chan, but she couldn't. Not here. Not at her birthday party. She looked past Maliba to the crowd round the fire. There was only one person she needed now.

'Have you seen Rasa? I'm looking for him.'

'Ah, Rasa,' Maliba said, as if it were obvious Leila was thinking of him. 'Not tonight.'

'Hey,' one of the women from the village called out. She stumbled towards Maliba and Leila, still dancing. 'Come and join in.'

She grabbed Maliba and Leila watched, standing back from the crowd, wondering what to do. She'd been convinced Rasa would be here.

Now Vijay, Rasa's father, came over. He looked different off duty, out of his brown suit. His cheeks were rosy with good humour.

'I thought that was you,' he said, smiling. 'Maliba told me you have a problem and I should help fix it,' he said, nudging her in a jovial way. 'Is it true?'

Leila nodded.

'I will if I can, but if it's to do with my son . . .' He held up his hands and then smiled at Leila, and in that moment, Leila knew she could trust him. He was a policeman and Rasa's father. Someone she'd known all her life. Someone who was firmly on Bibi's side. If anyone could help, it would be Vijay. Without Rasa, he was the next best thing.

She pulled Vijay away from the noise of the party and sat down next to him on a log on the beach, away from the fire.

'I found something,' she began.

'Found something?' he asked. 'What did you find?'

'In the lighthouse,' she said. 'There's boxes.'

'Boxes?'

'There's a man. Lee Shang he's called. Rasa knows about him.'

'Well, I've never heard of him.'

Leila shifted, turning to Vijay, forcing him to take her seriously. 'He's storing drugs there. He and Chan are going to ship them to America.'

Vijay's happy expression faded. 'Miss Leila,' he said, fixing her with a stare, 'this is Lace Island. Nothing like that happens here.'

'I'm telling the truth. You've got to believe me.'

'Does Bibi know?'

'Of course not.'

'Are you sure it's drugs?'

'I'm not entirely sure, but it's so secretive. I . . . I went to check. Here . . .' She delved into her pocket and thrust her silk scarf at him.

He frowned and unwrapped it.

'It's white powder. Bags and bags of it. I managed to get some.'

Vijay tipped it towards the glow of the fire. Then he put his finger in his mouth and dabbed it in the powder. He licked it; then he put it on his tongue, recoiling at the taste. His face clouded.

'Do you know what it is?' Leila urged. 'Will you do something?'

Vijay took a deep breath in, as though the weight of the world were now on his shoulders. He looked up at the star-filled sky, as if asking for guidance. 'Yes. I will,' he said. 'But you must not worry your mother with this until I have discovered the truth. I mean it, Leila. Otherwise you could both be in a lot of danger.'

Leila nodded. She should feel relief that she'd told Vijay, but instead she felt her fear growing.

'You did the right thing to tell me,' he assured her. 'Does anyone else know about this?'

'Only Rasa. Where is he, anyway?'

'Didn't he tell you? He's gone to the mainland. He'll be back on the next ferry, I expect.'

Leila felt winded. What could Rasa be doing in Cochin apart from getting away from her?

'Come and dance,' Parva called, but Leila shook her head, refusing. She was in no mood to dance. Not now.

'Leave this with me,' Vijay told her, holding her arm. 'And promise me – don't tell anyone. Not a word.'

Leila nodded, watching him go until he was a silhouette against the fire. Secrets, she thought, so many secrets. When will this all stop?

CHAPTER FORTY-TWO

Kerala, present day

Jess leant her elbows on the edge of the open car window as the rickety white ambassador taxi climbed slowly up the pot-holed road. She breathed in the hot air, looking at the brown hillside, which was covered in terraces of green tea plants, the women and children dressed in colourful clothes as they picked the leaves, the sky above an azure blue. No wonder they called this place 'God's Own Country', she thought.

'Not far now,' her driver informed her. He was a funny guy and had entertained her all the way from Cochin Airport; she was looking forward to tipping him generously. He was certainly very proud of his taxi, which was bedecked inside with plastic flowers and hanging Hindu gods. He sang along now with the high-pitched singer on the radio, making Jess laugh.

Despite reading the guidebook and talking to the crew on the plane, nothing had prepared Jess for the assault to her senses as soon as they'd arrived in India. Just the noise, the people, the colours ... the sheer life on display ... it was magical. She watched now as an elephant lumbered along the side of the road, pulling what looked like newly cut telephone poles out of a grassy ditch.

If only Blaise were here to enjoy this too. She wished he could share this with her, especially as it was all so unexpected. It felt doubly cruel to be apart now, after what he'd said at the airport, especially as she'd assumed that she would be on a flight to India, stay the night at the airport and fly straight back to London. But then she'd been offered a stopover and now she had three whole days to soak up the glory of this place . . . alone.

On the flight to Cochin, a kind American lady had given her a tip-off and a voucher for an Ayurvedic spa in the foothills of the Western Ghats, just a few hours' drive from Cochin. The woman had insisted that Jess must take up her offer. She'd told her that the yoga overlooking the lake, the massages and the food were absolutely heavenly. With a three-day stopover and time to kill, Jess hadn't been able to refuse. And, boy, was she glad she hadn't. She needed to calm down. Catch her breath. To stop this giddy feeling that had been racing through her since Blaise had proposed.

There was something about this place. As if just the smell of the air filled her soul with happiness and a kind of wonder she'd never experienced before. As the car climbed through the tea plantation, she waved to the kids running through the trees.

The taxi crunched into a lower gear as they finally turned off the main road and along a bumpy, winding lane until a low stone building with a red tiled roof, almost entirely covered in bright pink bougainvillea, came into view.

The taxi stopped and Jess stepped out, butterflies dancing in the balmy air. An elderly bald man with a cloth dhoti greeted her with a low bow and put a wreath of fresh flowers round her neck and pressed a cup of delicious-smelling herbal tea into her hand.

Once she'd paid Varsi, her driver, promising him solemnly that he could drive her back to the airport in a few days' time, Jess went inside, through the low door to a courtyard with a fountain. A very pretty Indian lady in a red-and-gold sari greeted Jess like a long-lost friend, before showing her through the lush gardens to her teak bungalow overlooking the lake.

Left alone, Jess did a slow twirl and grinned, taking in the thick beams of the room and the very comfortable-looking four-poster bed. Hot and sweaty from her journey, she opened the door to the bathroom. But to her surprise, it was outdoors, the leaves of a banana tree hanging down from the bluest of skies above. She'd never been anywhere so exotic or sensual.

Stripping off and stepping under the water, she thought about the last shower she'd had, in the yacht with Blaise. It felt like ages ago, but it had only been yesterday.

Blaise, she thought. *Her fiancé.*

She wondered again what had happened after he'd left her at the airport. Had he gone back and told everyone at the yacht about their amazing news? She smiled to herself, thinking of their reactions. She already knew that Tilly was delighted. She'd texted her when she'd got to Heathrow and she'd replied straight away with a gushy text, begging Jess to let her be her bridesmaid. It felt to Jess as if the future she'd dreamt about really was rushing towards her, faster than she could comprehend. She longed for someone to share it all with.

After her long shower and wrapped in a huge, fluffy white towel, she sat on the bed and called Blaise, despite the fact that the time difference meant it was the middle of the night: she couldn't bear putting off calling him any longer.

'So how's India?' he said.

'Amazing. But it would be so much better if you were here.

I've got three days at a spa. For free. And it's *so* lovely here. You should see my outdoor bathroom.'

'Well, you've got to come back soon. We need to get a ring. We've been engaged for . . .' he paused, doing a calculation, 'thirty-one hours and you still don't have a ring.'

Jess hadn't even thought about a ring.

'You've still got time to hop on a plane and join me,' she said, trying to sound as enticing as she could. 'We could get one here. And I looked on the map. We're quite near Lace Island. We could go check it out.'

'No,' Blaise said harshly. 'I mean, I want to take you there,' he said, though he sounded uncertain. 'But when we have a decent amount of time. Just you and me. Don't even dare think about going there alone. It's undeveloped and dangerous and—'

'OK.'

'Promise me you won't.'

'I promise.'

There was a moment's silence. She picked at the edge of the towel, disappointed that he didn't want to join her. She knew it had been a crazy idea, but if he could only see this place, he'd be as entranced as she was, wouldn't he?

'So . . . how's Miami?' she asked, changing the subject.

'I'm a bit tied up at work,' he said, with a sigh. 'I've got lots on. After our holiday, I'm so behind.'

She bit her lip, hearing the slight rebuke in his tone. She knew it would sound petulant to demand more of him when they'd just had a week together in Ibiza. What was so important, though? The Lace Island deal? She longed to know more. She thought of how close she'd felt to him in Ibiza and how distant he seemed now.

'You sound tired.'

'It's two in the morning.'

Jess heard a muffled laugh. It sounded like a woman.

'What was that?'

'Nothing. Just the TV. I'll turn it off,' Blaise said. She heard something shutting and then there was silence.

'I shouldn't have called so late.'

'You can always call me. Whenever you like. I like hearing your voice.'

'You know what I did today before we left Heathrow?' she said, turning round on the bed, glancing at her new purchases. 'I know it's girlie, and I've never even thought about doing this before, but I was so excited I couldn't help myself. I bought three bridal magazines.'

She stared at their covers and the picture-perfect brides. She couldn't actually believe now that she'd bought them. She'd thought they'd be exciting, but she couldn't relate to a 'perfect' wedding in an English stately home. In fact, having flicked through them, she was more confused than ever about what she really wanted. Certainly nothing that was contained in the glossy pages. Doing it all properly – as the magazines implied she should – seemed so formal and so stressful. Not to mention expensive. But it was all the decisions that seemed so overwhelming to Jess. Choosing cutlery and china for her wedding list. Where on earth would she start? How could she possibly work out what she and Blaise needed for their married life together?

'Oh?' Blaise sounded surprised.

'Well, I guess we should start discussing it, right? When, where, all that stuff.'

'What did you have in mind?' Blaise asked, before going on quickly, 'And don't say on a beach. I can't stand those beachy weddings. I've been to too many where the weather ruins everything.'

Jess forced down her disappointment. Not only that he'd been to so many weddings already, when she hadn't been to any, but that she was going to have to persuade him into her dream wedding. Having a simple ceremony on a beach felt like the only way to bypass all the fuss.

'What about on Lace Island?' she suggested. 'You said it was like paradise. We could get married there.'

Blaise seemed to consider this for a moment. 'It'll be ages before it's even halfway ready.'

'So? We're not in a rush, are we?'

'Well . . . I thought we should do it sooner rather than later. I mean, why wait?'

Jess was taken aback. 'When did you have in mind?'

'I don't know. Next month.'

'Next month!' Jess spluttered. 'We can't, can we? That soon?'

'What do you want to wait for?' he said. 'You said yourself you don't have a big guest list. I know a place here in Miami. A nice hotel. We could have the ceremony there.'

Jess was scrambling over the implications of what he was saying. If they got married in Miami in a month, then that would rule out Tony and Maeve coming. But it wasn't just that. A month was so soon.

'You know I love you, right?' Blaise said.

'I love you too,' she said.

'I just want to be married to you. For you to be my wife. Because when you know, you just know. That's what I think. Jess, let's not get tied down with all that wedding stuff. Let's just do it.'

Jess lay back on the bed and chucked the bridal magazines

on the floor. He didn't want a fuss either. She didn't have to worry about wedding lists or crockery after all. What had she done to deserve this wonderful man?

A few hours later, Jess went for her treatment in the wooden spa room, her jet lag kicking in. She yawned as she listened to the soft, tinkling sitar music, the candles floating in the lotus flowers on the water making for a soporific atmosphere. The beautiful Indian girl with glossy hair and a red bindi helped Jess lie on a bed of towels, then positioned a brass bowl above her head.

'This is wonderful for relieving stress,' she said, as the hot oil started dripping onto Jess's forehead. Jess sighed as the girl massaged her temples, before letting the oil drip through her hair onto the wooden tray under her pillow. She wanted to tell her she'd never been less stressed in her life. Everything was amazing. She was in love and Blaise had just proposed.

But married in a month? Now that was a tiny bit stressful, Jess thought, feeling the steady drip of the oil massaging her head. Soon, her whirlwind romance would end in a fairy-tale wedding. But what then? she wondered.

Well, then she'd live happily ever after, right? But where? They hadn't discussed that fully yet, or how where they lived would affect Jess's job. There were so many things she needed to pin down, but Blaise seemed so sure of everything.

He had people, he'd assured her on the phone, when she'd questioned whether getting married in a month were even possible. People to sort out the paperwork and the necessary documents to make the wedding happen. It seemed to Jess as if he was used to just waving his hand and everything falling into place. Was this going to be her life from now on? she wondered. No queues, no bureaucracy. All her desires dealt with, just like that? Because according to her fiancé, life as Mrs Blaise Blackmore would just be one smooth ride. But still a tiny part of her nagged at her conscience. It all seemed too good to be true. Life didn't get to be this simple, did it?

Maybe it did. Maybe she should just let go and enjoy it.

After her massage, as Jess wandered from her bungalow down to the communal dining room, rather than feeling relaxed, she was still trying to get her head around the practicalities of being Blaise's wife.

She play-acted introducing herself to his business associates. 'Hi, I'm Jess Blackmore,' she muttered, imagining her embossed at-home cards, the 'J.B.' of her new initials in gold. But it didn't seem real. Even thinking about these things made her feel like she was going to have to turn into someone else entirely. Did Blaise really think she was up to the job?

Her stomach brought her back down to reality, rumbling with the delicious aromas drifting towards her from the kitchen.

She walked towards the dining room and was shown to a low table. The sides of the dining room were open and she stared out at the sun setting over the milky blue water of the lake. She wished again that Blaise was with her so he could put her mind at ease. He'd love it here.

Or would he? She wondered now if Blaise would consider coming to a place like this with her. Or whether their holidays from now on would involve mega-yachts and city breaks. Not that she was complaining, but she wondered if he'd understand that to her, this was far more luxurious than any of the places he'd taken her to.

She took a sip of her jasmine tea, her attention caught by a guy and a beautiful girl by the buffet table. She was wearing a coral-coloured silk chemise, her long black hair tied in a glossy up-do. Jess felt embarrassed that she hadn't made more of an effort for dinner, flinging on some baggy pants and a T-shirt, her hair still oily and straggly from the treatment.

The man next to her had bare feet and was wearing baggy linen pants, but Jess saw straight away that he had a good figure. Maybe he did the yoga classes, she thought. She was about to look away when he turned round and looked over to where Jess was sitting.

And then something extraordinary happened. As his eyes connected with hers across the sun-filled dining room, Jess felt something she'd never felt. As if she'd just erupted into all-over goosebumps.

Startled, she put her cup back down on the table with a clatter, but her mouth was dry. She reached for a glass and took a gulp of water.

The guy was still staring at her, and he looked as jangled as she felt. He couldn't have felt it too, could he?

She watched the girl with her huge almond eyes glance over in Jess's direction, looking her up and down before tugging at the sleeve of the man to get his attention. Who was he? Her boyfriend? Husband?

And why did it even matter?

Quickly, Jess finished her tea and headed back to her room. It was completely unthinkable to be attracted to another man. Not when she was in love. Not when she was *engaged*.

CHAPTER FORTY-THREE

Lace Island, 1990

'Parva won the sweepstake,' Anjum yelled to Leila, over the din outside. 'I said it would be tomorrow, but it's today.'

Leila grinned at him as he stood by the kitchen door, waiting to open it for her. She'd been so caught up in everything going on that for the first time ever she hadn't placed a bet on when the monsoon would come, but there was no doubt about it now. Ten minutes ago, the heavens had opened, with a boom of thunder announcing the deluge. Rain hammered on the corrugated-iron roof of the kitchen above them.

'Here we go,' Anjum said, grinning at her before flinging open the kitchen door and twirling into the backyard, his face shiny with rain as he turned it up to the heavens. And for one second, despite herself, Leila laughed, remembering how happy everyone was on this particular day of the year, when the weather finally broke. It was as if Lace Island were suddenly free from the grip of the heat that had crushed them for the past months.

Leila followed Anjum out, pushing up her black umbrella, the raindrops drumming on the worn cloth. She cursed, seeing the rip in the fabric and feeling the trickle of water down her neck. She put it down, leaving it near the kitchen step, the rain making the tin bin lids ring out. Scrunching up her face as the warm rain soaked her, she ran towards Anjum, who laughed with glee, stretching out his arms and turning his face up to catch the drops on his tongue, like they always had done when Leila had been little, but today her heart wasn't in it.

Wrapping her cardigan around her, she ran down the steps to the garden, the fat splashes of rain making the pool surface dance. Almost before her eyes, she saw the dried-out vine on the cracked pool wall start to unfurl its crinkled leaves.

In the grove, the air was pungent with the tangy smell of rain on the hot ground that she'd always loved so much, but Leila didn't stop to take it in, ignoring the shouts of the little kids who were sliding joyfully in the mud. Instead, she rushed along the path, sidestepping the rivulets of water cascading down the ruts.

She ducked as a sudden boom of thunder clapped right overhead. The children squealed with delight. Lightning flashed and Leila pressed on. The ferry had come this morning and would be leaving again at lunchtime. She prayed that Rasa had been on it. She had to tell him what she'd heard Bibi say.

But Rasa wasn't in any of the usual places, and it wasn't until she went to Maliba's house that she saw him stepping out onto the wooden porch.

'Rasa,' Leila called, splashing through the backyard towards him. 'Where have you been?' She couldn't keep the accusation from her voice. She stood before him, rain streaking down her face. She pulled the edges of her cardigan over her chest, but she knew her dress was practically see-through. 'Your father said you'd been to the mainland?'

Rasa stood under a black umbrella, his sneakers drenched in mud. He looked different. Like he was resigned to something.

Resigned to her, perhaps, Leila thought. She longed for him to be the old Rasa. Her friend.

'What of it?' he said, as if it were none of her business. 'I would have told you, but you've clearly been busy.'

He was talking about Adam. That's what he meant. As if she'd been 'busy' by her own choice. Leila felt sick.

'Please, Rasa. You've got to listen,' she implored, as he strode past her and through Maliba's gate. Leila grabbed Rasa's arm and forced him to turn round.

'What do you want, Leila?' He was cold. Already detached from her, but she couldn't blame him.

'I'm sorry about that day. I was coming to meet you and . . .' she began, bracing herself, knowing that she was going to have to tell him what Adam had done. Even if it meant he never spoke to her again. He had to know the truth.

'Don't,' he said quickly. 'Chan explained that you had other, more important commitments.'

Chan? She dreaded to think what he'd told Rasa.

'Honestly, Leila, it's quite all right,' Rasa added.

But it wasn't all right and they both knew it. She could see then that he'd churned over that day in his head and come to all the wrong conclusions. Conclusions he believed were the truth.

'Whatever you think about why I was there . . . you've got it all wrong,' Leila persisted. 'Adam, he—' But Rasa held up his hand to stop her.

She saw him take a deep breath. 'Leila, I'm going away,' he said.

'Going away?'

'I've got an apprenticeship on the mainland.'

'What?'

Leila felt her heart shattering into little pieces. Any hope that she had of mending things between them was gone forever.

'It's good,' Rasa said, with false bravado. 'It's what I want. I can learn a trade. Make something of myself. I could never have become a lawyer you know. Too long at law school.'

Leila dared to glance up at him now, her eyes swimming with tears, lost in the fat raindrops on her face.

He stared into her eyes now and she saw that he'd made up his mind.

'Please don't go,' she implored him. 'You don't understand. I need you.'

'You don't—'

'Bibi is in trouble,' she said. 'I know things.'

'What things?'

Leila took in a deep, shuddering breath. Then she told him everything. About how Chan had bankrupted Bibi. And how she'd broken into the lighthouse and found drugs, and how Adam was helping Chan to ship them abroad.

Rasa's gaze was dark. He shook his head. 'Who have you told?' he asked.

'Just you. And I told your father last night at Maliba's party,' she spluttered.

'You did what?'

'I told Vijay. I didn't know what else to do. You weren't here.'

Rasa was clearly furious that she hadn't come to him first. That she'd got his father involved.

He ran his hand over his hair. 'Do you realize how serious this is?' he said.

'Yes,' she exclaimed. 'Of course I do. That's why I told him. He said he'd investigate and help.'

'No, that's not what I mean,' Rasa said, through his teeth,

as if Leila were the dumbest person in the world. 'If he tells the authorities and they come here and find drugs anywhere on the island, then Bibi will be held responsible.'

'Bibi?'

'It's her island. If they find anything illegal, then she'll be the one in trouble. I mean, have you thought of that? What if she ended up in jail?'

Jail? *Jail?* Leila's mind was reeling.

'Then you've got to do something. You've got to help,' she said.

Rasa shook his head, his expression pained as he looked at her. 'I can't. It's too late. I just came to say goodbye to my family. The ferry leaves at two.'

It was already gone one. He couldn't mean it, surely? He couldn't just leave. Not now, after everything she'd told him?

'I'm sorry that it's bad timing, but I'm sure now you've trusted my father with all of this, he'll help sort it out,' Rasa said. 'I can't get involved, because this really isn't my problem. Not anymore.'

Not his problem? What did that mean?

That *she* wasn't his problem. That's what he meant. It was clear in his face.

'I've got to go. Goodbye, Leila.'

And then he turned his back on her and walked away.

The start of the monsoon had always called for a celebratory supper, but tonight the mood was sombre. In the dining room, Bibi, Chan and Leila sat at the long table, the rain drumming relentlessly on the tiles above. As predicted by Bibi, the roof was leaking even more than it had last year and there was a steady drip of water in the buckets and empty plastic ghee tubs that were placed all around the room.

'There's so much to be done. This roof is like a sieve, for a start. Did you know he was leaving, Leila?' Parva asked, as she served the spongy bread that Leila usually loved. But tonight she couldn't stomach it. She felt queasy, and not just because Parva was talking about Rasa.

Leila shrugged. 'He told me today.'

She couldn't look at Parva. If she did, then Parva would see the truth: that since she'd come back from seeing Rasa, she'd cried non-stop for an hour. She pushed the okra curry round her plate with her fork.

She simply couldn't process the fact that Rasa had gone. Just like that. Just when she needed him the most. If he'd cared at all about her, he wouldn't have gone. He would have stayed. But now it was too late, and his parting words – that Bibi would go to jail – still rang in Leila's ears. She glanced up at her mother and Chan at the other end of the table, feeling wretched. Should she confess everything to Bibi, tell her what she'd told Vijay?

'I think it will do the boy good, don't you, Bibi?' Chan said.

Bibi raised her tired eyes towards him. 'What?' she asked, and Leila realized that she hadn't listened to a word Parva had been saying. Parva glanced at Leila, her look making it perfectly clear that she was not to say anything about her mother's absent-mindedness.

But what exactly *was* wrong with Bibi? She was usually so on top of everything – especially when it came to the affairs of everyone on Lace Island – but she seemed more distant than ever tonight.

Chan put his hand over hers. 'You've still got that headache? Why don't you lie down?'

His voice was placatory and kind, as it always had been,

but now that Leila knew it was all a sham, she felt bile rising in her throat. How could Bibi even let him touch her, after everything he'd done to her?

Chan, who had betrayed her over and over again. And he'd betrayed Leila too, in the most hideous way possible. She tried not to think about it, forcing her mind away from the memory, but there was Adam, like he always was, right above her, forcing his way into her, violating her with that unforgettable grin on his face.

Had he laughed with Chan about it afterwards? Had Chan delighted in giving her up to him, like some sort of prize? Is that what had happened?

And the worst part? He'd got away with it. Because Chan knew that Leila would never have the guts to admit to Bibi what Adam had done. She looked down now, her eyes filling with furious, impotent tears. Her knuckles were white where she was gripping her fork in her hand.

Bibi scraped her chair back and stood unsteadily with a sigh. Leila couldn't bear to look up at her. But suddenly, the door banged open and Bamu rushed in.

'What is it?' Parva asked, clearly horrified that he was dripping all over the dining-room floor.

'I'm sorry, Bibi,' Bamu said, 'but something terrible has happened.'

Leila sat up in her seat. She saw how agitated Bamu was as his eyes flicked to hers; she looked at Chan, who placed his napkin down carefully next to his plate.

'What is it, boy?' Chan asked.

'They've found Vijay,' Bamu said, his voice urgent.

Suddenly, there was a huge clap of thunder right overhead that made them all jump. Leila jumped up.

'What do you mean, found him?' Bibi said.

'He's dead,' Bamu said, his voice cracking. 'They're saying he's been murdered.'

CHAPTER FORTY-FOUR

Kerala, present day

Jess stretched in the downward-dog position on her yoga mat, looking through her legs at the other people in the dawn class, amazed at how supple they were. She'd thought she was fit from all the kick-boxing she'd done, but this was the second yoga class she'd taken in the spa and it had already pulled her body in directions that she'd never thought possible.

'And breathe deeply,' the lithe male teacher at the front instructed, gracefully walking around the class, making adjustments.

Jess's hamstrings were killing her as the teacher touched her lower back, stretching her even further.

'Relax,' the teacher said in a slow, breathy voice, but Jess's mind was buzzing.

This place was supposed to be chilling her out, but last night she'd hardly slept. This morning, she had hoped the yoga class would set her mind at ease, but she was still reeling from the email that had pinged into her in-box late last night from Blaise.

The content of the email had been short. He'd been in a rush, he'd explained, but he'd just had a meeting with his lawyer in Miami, who'd asked if Jess would sign a prenuptial agreement. The attached document had been thick with legal-speak and Jess had only scanned the first paragraph before giving up.

'It's just a precaution the lawyer wants,' Blaise had ex-plained on the phone, when she'd called him, after trying to make sense of the email. 'Nothing to worry about. It's no biggie. Everyone has them these days.'

But lying alone in bed, it had felt like a big deal. She didn't even have an engagement ring and already he was thinking about what happened when their relationship ended. Like he just assumed it would.

Or was she overreacting? Maybe he was right. Maybe this *was* just normal these days. Jess couldn't fathom it out, but she couldn't help feeling that Blaise's email had somehow punc-tured the romance of their whirlwind engagement with a sharp dose of reality.

As she came up to a standing position for a tree balance, Jess wished she had a girlfriend to talk it through with. She didn't trust Tilly enough to call her with something so per-sonal. And besides, Tilly would be very matter-of-fact about such things, having gone through two divorces herself.

She longed to chat to Angel, to the Angel of old, before the drugs had taken her. But she knew it was a ridiculous thought. This life Jess was living would be unrecognizable to her old friend. Angel wouldn't believe that Jess was here in this gor-geous spa in India, let alone that she was planning to marry a multimillionaire. It made Angel feel further away than she ever had. Like Jess had separated herself from her old life entirely.

Everything would be OK, she told herself, staring out at the horizon. Blaise was just protecting his business interests.

Who could blame his lawyer for making her sign a prenuptial agreement? After all, she was just an air hostess, with nothing to her name, while Blaise was worth a fortune. And according to Blaise, they were getting married in a month. No wonder he was getting all the legal paperwork in place already.

And then there was the other thing. The thing Jess didn't want to think about but couldn't help it. *That guy*. The guy she'd seen in the dining room with the beautiful girl. And, more specifically, how she'd felt when she'd seen him. Because standing here, looking out at the sun coming up, feeling her balance, her arms above her head, one leg bent onto the other, once again she couldn't get his eyes out of her head.

And it was weird, because he so wasn't her type. Not that she actually had a type. She never looked at men and fancied them, but there had been a very tangible rush of . . . well, of *something*. Was it desire? Surely not, she thought. Why would she be attracted to a complete stranger across a room?

Perhaps it was just some weird psychological phenomenon, she told herself. A kickback reaction because she was getting married. Her subconscious trying to sabotage her relationship. Well, she wouldn't let it. She loved Blaise and they were getting married. End of.

The guy was probably awful, anyway.

After the class, Jess was getting a drink of water from the copper jug in the foyer and planning the day ahead when she saw him. She busied herself with the water, accidentally spilling it as he walked towards her. He was wearing a light shirt and linen trousers, and his hair was slicked back. He looked thoroughly comfortable in his own skin.

'Hello,' he said, smiling. He had a soft, friendly voice. Slightly Indian-sounding.

'Hi,' she said, pushing her hair behind her ear. She was aware of how awful she looked. No make-up and her face flushed. There was a beat as they looked at each other.

'I'm Suresh,' he said, but he said it in a funny way, like she must have already known that and he was reminding her.

Maybe it was the yoga, Jess thought, or the sun glinting on the lake, but she suddenly felt intensely present in this moment.

'Have we met before?' he asked.

'No, I don't think so,' she said, wondering why her throat felt dry.

'When I saw you yesterday, I thought . . .' He fizzled out and Jess looked down at the cup in her hand, feeling her cheeks reddening.

'Suresh, come on – I want to have a shower.'

Jess looked up to see the woman Suresh had been with yesterday coming down the hall towards them. She was wearing a dazzling blue-and-gold embroidered salwar kameez, the beautifully tailored trousers and tunic top showing off her perfect figure, and her long black hair fell in glossy curls over her shoulders. She stopped, looking Jess up and down, and Jess breathed in the heavy, musky perfume she was wearing.

'This is my fiancée, Kareena,' Suresh said.

So he was engaged, then, Jess thought, wondering why she felt such a stab of disappointment. The girl, Kareena, had the most beautiful skin, Jess noticed. She stepped forwards and shook Kareena's hand, introducing herself, and there was an awkward moment, as if Kareena was expecting Jess to say something.

'I don't want breakfast, so I'll see you back at the bunga-low,' Kareena said, throwing Jess a filthy look and sweeping away through the door onto the terrace, the peacock-blue silk of her scarf trailing behind her.

'I'm sorry,' Suresh said, stifling a smile. 'She's not usually that rude.'

'Did I do something?'

'She's a news anchorwoman,' Suresh explained. 'People around here know her face. She expected you to recognize her, that's all.'

'Oh, sorry.'

'Don't be sorry,' Suresh assured her. 'It does her good to realize that she is not the centre of everyone's universe.'

Jess smiled, astonished that he'd said something like that about her, even though he'd said it in a jokey kind of way. Perhaps realizing, he looked after Kareena. 'I'm being mean. She's just a little overwrought, shall we say. Wedding planning, you know. This place was supposed to relax her, but I think it's having the opposite effect.'

'Oh? How long have you been engaged?'

'Two years.' Suresh rolled his eyes. 'It's a long time, right? But there's a lot of logistics involved. Family and more family. Oh, and let's not forget the media, who want to photograph the whole thing, like we're performing monkeys.'

'Oh,' she said, hoping that she sounded sympathetic. 'I'm sorry.'

'Don't be. It's a mess of our own making. Anyway, I'm not even sure why I'm telling you any of this.'

There was a long moment when Jess felt it was almost impossible to tear her eyes away from his.

'Well, I should . . .' he began, nodding in the direction of the dining room.

'I'm going for breakfast too. Will you join me?' she asked, suddenly desperate to fill the gaping silence.

'Yes, I'd like that very much. I'm starving,' he said, with a laugh.

They walked together from the hallway to the open dining room, and Jess self-consciously tried to tidy her hair. If only she'd had a shower and looked a bit more presentable. But then, why did it matter? Why was she behaving like this? Suresh was engaged. *She* was engaged. So why had she just invited a stranger to join her for breakfast?

'I love cooking,' Suresh said, as they arrived at the buffet, 'but I can never make dosas like this. They're so difficult to get this thin and crispy.'

'They're delicious,' Jess agreed, taking one of the large, folded white pancakes filled with potato curry from the buffet.

'You must try this pickle with it,' Suresh said, loading some coconut chutney and a chunky-looking pickle onto her metal plate. 'It's wonderful.'

It was such an intimate gesture – something Jess would expect a lover or a friend to do, not a stranger – but she realized she didn't mind. In fact, it felt fun to be with him, choosing food and enjoying it together. Suresh was clearly a man in touch with his senses. Blaise had never cooked anything for her, she realized. They'd only eaten out in restaurants. She wondered now if he even could cook.

'Kareena won't eat anything like this at all in the mornings,' he said. 'But breakfast is my favourite meal.'

'Me too,' Jess said, glad that she was sharing this small pleasure with him.

They both took a bowl of vegetable curry, then carried their trays to a table and sat together, the cheerful bustle of the morning diners around them, but Jess hardly noticed the other people. She couldn't work out what it was about Suresh that made him so easy to be with.

Soon, without even trying, the conversation flipped back

and forth as if they'd known each other for years and were catching up. It was as if they just *clicked*, Jess thought.

And he was funny, too. He told her about the law practice he worked for in Cochin, making her laugh about his senior partner. He told her too about his overbearing mother and sisters, doing funny impersonations of them.

And in turn Jess found herself being effortlessly open and honest. She told him about growing up in care homes and trying to make something of herself by becoming cabin crew, feeling a flush of pride that he was so impressed she worked in first class. She explained how the rich and famous hardly fazed her anymore, but even so, when she mentioned some of the celebrities she'd served, Suresh hadn't heard of any of them. In fact, the kind of things that would have impressed Ivana and her friends were completely lost on him.

'So,' she said, smiling shyly at him as they sipped the last of their tea. 'You must be excited about getting married?'

'Kareena hates me telling people this, but ours is an arranged marriage.'

Jess was intrigued. 'How does that work?'

He sighed. 'My family chose a shortlist of suitable candidates. To be honest, it was like choosing a bride from a magazine,' he said. 'I tried to object, saying I wanted to actually meet and get to know the person first, but it was a done deal from the start . . .'

'Come on. You didn't do so badly,' Leila laughed.

He smiled sadly. 'But it's strange for Kareena too. She was hoping for someone . . . I don't know . . . different. Maybe a high-flyer at the TV station where she works. Not someone boring. Like me.'

He wasn't boring, Jess wanted to blurt, as his eyes met hers. She liked his kind smile. She wouldn't mind betting that it was Suresh who supported Kareena in her career and kept her feet on the ground.

'I don't even know why I told you that,' he said. 'I'm sorry. That was very indiscreet.'

'It's OK. I understand. I'm engaged too. *Just*,' she confided. 'Mine has been a lot quicker. Much more of a whirlwind romance you could say.' She looked down at her empty ring finger, wondering what it would feel like to be wearing the ring Blaise had promised her on her return.

'My fiancée watches lots of movies. I think she believes that love is better that way. And so . . . tell me, Jess, just for the record, is it?'

Jess smiled, liking the self-deprecating way he had about him. 'I'm not sure. I mean, sure, at first, I was dazzled.'

A big 'but now' hung in the air between them, and she couldn't bring herself to finish the sentence. She couldn't bring herself to say anything against Blaise, but this was the most honest emotional conversation she'd had in months, and now she realized that there was a 'but'. The feeling made her scared.

She thought about how often she'd gushed to the girls on her flights. How she'd bigged up Blaise, embellished him, bragged about him. And how each time she'd seen him, it had been as if she were ticking boxes against the claims she'd made, as he rose to each standard. Good-looking. Thoughtful. Caring. Generous. She couldn't fault him, except right now, chatting with Suresh, she felt more herself than she ever had with Blaise. She felt rocked that she'd even started to voice her fears.

'I think love grows over time,' Suresh said, saving her. 'Proper love, that is. And maybe love can grow from a friendship.' He didn't seem so convinced.

'I think we're in the same boat. Being engaged is stressful,'

Jess said. 'I already know that my fiancé wants a very different wedding to the one I want. And he wants it to happen soon. And . . .' she sighed heavily, 'I can't tell him, but it feels too rushed to me.'

She almost started talking about the prenuptial agreement Blaise wanted, but she managed to stop herself in time. Why was she confiding all of this in a stranger?

They smiled at each other, perhaps both acknowledging that neither of their situations was perfect.

'I should get going back to my bungalow,' Jess said. She felt embarrassed now that she'd shared so much, and her usual boastfulness about Blaise hadn't tripped off her tongue. It felt disloyal.

'Me too. I should go and check on Kareena. Let's walk together,' he suggested.

They strolled down the tiled steps to the path between the grass lawns, and Jess was suddenly aware of all the colours around her and the hummingbird moths kissing the stamens of the orange lilies on either side of the path. Ahead, the sun stretched towards them over the rippling water, and a wooden boat glided gently between the lily pads. She wished she had a camera to capture the moment.

'So, where are you getting married?' Suresh asked, his slow step falling in with hers.

'In a hotel in Miami, I think,' she said. 'We haven't discussed it much, but I think that's what he wants. I always wanted it to be simple. On a beach.'

She smiled, thinking of the poster Angel had given her. How alive that image still was in her head.

'Ah! Me too,' Suresh said, with a chuckle. 'However, mine is going to take place over three days. There'll be dancing, elephants, feasts.'

'It sounds wonderful,' Jess said.

'Does it? Perhaps if you are a guest, maybe. Not if you're in the centre of it on show. You might as well come,' he added. 'I already know you ten times better than I know most of the guests.'

He stopped and stared into her eyes, and for a second she felt something connect with her deep down. As if he recognized her. As if he really did know her ten times better than anyone else did.

'What are you doing now, for the rest of today?' he asked suddenly, as if on a whim.

'I don't know. I hadn't planned it.'

'Kareena has a massage this afternoon.' His voice was urgent. 'I heard there was a temple, up on the hill behind here. They say the view is amazing. Would you like to come and find it with me?'

'Sure,' Jess said.

'Good. I'd like that,' he said.

As they parted, he gave her a shy wave and she felt as if they'd made some sort of secret promise.

CHAPTER FORTY-FIVE

Lace Island, 1990

The light had faded and all the villagers were out with oil lanterns, candles and torches in the grove, as Chan pushed through the crowd that had gathered, holding his torch, Leila and Bibi following closely behind. Bamu shouted to the villagers to let them pass. The rain had stopped, but the trees dripped, and the air was cool and damp.

At the foot of the tree, not far from the lighthouse, Vijay lay slumped on the ground, his hands tied behind his back. Leila felt her heart pounding, her mouth filling with saliva as more people arrived and tried to see what had happened.

She gasped, stepping back. She'd never seen a dead body before, let alone someone she'd known all her life. She felt as if she'd been punched very hard in the chest.

But there he was. Vijay. Unbidden images of him flicked through her mind: Vijay swatting away flies, chewing betel nut, his smile, the pride on his face when he looked at Rasa. Vijay throwing a cricket ball to her when she'd been a tiny child, his laughing face in the firelight at Maliba's party. And the look on his face when he'd tasted that white powder Leila had given him.

Maliba was weeping loudly, cradling Vijay's head on her lap, rocking back and forth, the congealed blood from the wound on his neck smearing over her tunic.

Chan knelt by Vijay's body, extending a comforting hand to Maliba. Parva pushed through past Leila, screaming suddenly at the sight of her dead brother, as if she hadn't believed it until she'd seen it with her own eyes. Bibi's arms went around Parva.

Leila watched the crowd close in around her, but she couldn't move, jostling backwards, numb with terror.

Bibi called for quiet and the crowd settled down, apart from the anguished sobs of Parva and Maliba. Even at a time like this, it amazed Leila that Bibi could command such immediate respect.

She turned to one of Rasa's cousins, Dev, who stared, wide-eyed, at the body. 'When did this happen? When did you last see him?' she demanded.

'He went to Maliba's party and then came home and left early the next morning. I thought he was delayed because of the rain,' Dev said.

'Nobody must panic,' Chan said, untying Vijay's hands. He checked for a pulse, but it was clear from his stiff limbs that Vijay had been dead for many hours. Chan squeezed Maliba's hand. 'Take his body home.'

Chan gestured to Bamu and some of the other young men, gathering them together to carry the body. He was being professional – like a detective or a policeman himself, Leila thought, as he comforted Parva and Bibi. But Leila saw through it. It was all an act.

'We will find out who did this terrible thing,' he said to the crowd. 'I promise. We will have to talk to everyone. Everyone who is here on the island. But if anyone knows anything, then they have to tell me now.'

'It can't be anyone here, Chan,' Bibi said. 'Nobody here would do such a thing.'

There were murmurs of agreement from the crowd, everyone looking at each other in bafflement.

'I can't believe it,' Parva said, tearfully wiping her eyes. 'Vijay never hurt anyone in his life.'

'What about Rasa?' Chan said, looking around the crowd. There was an icy glint in his eyes. 'He's not here, is he?'

'What about him?' Parva asked.

'They argued,' Bamu said.

'Argued?' Chan pressed.

Bamu looked down at the ground, suddenly unsure of himself. 'So I heard. Vijay was unhappy about him going to Cochin. He wanted Rasa to stay here and complete his education with Timothy. He thought Rasa was throwing himself away on an apprenticeship in a car shop.'

'And now he's gone and his father is found dead,' Chan said, his insinuation hanging in the air.

'You can't honestly believe that,' Bibi said. 'Rasa loves Vijay. He would never do something like this.'

'Well, sometimes you never know what people secretly feel,' Chan said, his gaze suddenly turning and focusing on Leila. 'Isn't that so, Leila?'

She turned and pushed her way through the crowd, desperate to get away, panic threatening to choke her. Because this was all her fault. If she hadn't told Vijay about what she'd found in the lighthouse, then he would still be alive.

'Leila,' Bibi called.

'Leave her,' Leila heard Chan say. 'She's upset. We'll get to the bottom of this, I promise.'

She ran away fast then, her feet pounding with her heart-beat, panic fluttering inside her like a trapped bird.

Chan's face filled her vision.

He knew.

He knew exactly who had murdered Vijay. Maybe he'd even done it himself. With his own hands. Leila certainly wouldn't put it past him. If he'd known Vijay was on to him. And on to what was going on in the lighthouse.

And now Chan was going to frame Rasa for it.

She stopped at the top of the hill, leaning on a tree, gasping for breath, trying to think, a choked, horrified sob escaping her.

She had to leave. She had to leave and find Rasa. And she had to get Bibi to safety. Tonight.

No matter what it took, she would force Bibi to face the truth about Chan.

CHAPTER FORTY-SIX

Kerala, present day

'You didn't tell her, did you? Kareena, I mean?' Jess asked, as she and Suresh walked up the path behind the spa buildings at the far end of the resort's complex and the gate that led out towards the main road. It was later on in the afternoon and Jess had been looking forward to this walk to the temple ever since she'd left Suresh this morning. She wondered if he could tell that she'd already changed three times, furious at herself for even caring what she looked like.

He was wearing khaki shorts and hiking boots and a canvas hat, which made him look like an intrepid Boy Scout. She had opted for shorts too and trainers, but she shouldn't have bothered with make-up, which now felt slick on her face in the afternoon heat. She took a swig from the water bottle she'd brought, then offered it to Suresh, who accepted it gratefully.

'No,' Suresh admitted. 'But she would never do something like this. Go on a trek, I mean. Or have an adventure that might involve getting dusty or dirty.'

He grinned at her and swallowed some water, before handing back the bottle. Jess felt butterflies dance in her stomach as they stepped onto the road. Because he was right. This did feel like an adventure.

She knew she was telling herself that it wasn't a big deal that she'd so readily agreed to spend time alone with Suresh, but the truth was that she didn't want to miss out on an opportunity to take in some sights. As much as Kareena wasn't up for this, Jess certainly was.

She thought momentarily of Blaise and felt a pang of guilt. What would he say, she wondered, if he could see her now, walking beside this stranger? But it was safe, she reminded herself. They were new acquaintances and both engaged. What was wrong with them wanting to explore? It was safer than Jess exploring on her own.

At this time of day, the road was busier than Jess had expected, rickshaws and mopeds – some of them with whole families on board – competing with lorries and buses.

'Come on. The turning up the hill is just over here,' Suresh shouted, grabbing Jess's hand and darting across the road.

They walked on past a lumbering elephant and a huge hoarding advertising a brick company, the picture showing a beautiful girl in a sari next to a very new wall.

'She looks a bit like you,' Suresh said.

'Thank you very much,' Jess laughed.

'Seriously. Maybe one of your relatives is from India?'

Jess stopped in the street and Suresh had to grab her to pull her out of the path of a bus that suddenly overtook a tuk-tuk on the other side of the dusty road, narrowly missing a lorry going the other way. Jess fell a little way into the ditch on the roadside, the smell of the rubbish making her eyes water.

'Oh my God,' she laughed, clutching on to Suresh. 'You weren't kidding that this was going to be an adventure.'

'Don't worry. Look. There it is,' he said, pulling her upright and pointing to a small gate and a tree-lined path disappearing between the fields at the side of the road, towards the mountains.

Soon, they were safely on the small lane, the insanity of the road forgotten as they became surrounded by trees and lush vegetation. Jess picked the head off a tall piece of grass, marvelling at the intense bright green of the paddy fields through the trees.

'You know, maybe you're right,' she said to Suresh, walking beside him. They climbed over a gate, following the makeshift wooden sign pointing up through the trees to the hill. 'What you said back then. Maybe I do have Indian heritage. I'd never thought of it before, but I could have. I certainly feel connected to this place in a way I never have to anywhere.'

'Don't you know?' Suresh asked. 'What about your parents?'

Jess filled him in on what little she knew, even about the crucifix that had gone missing from her apartment.

'I've thought about looking for my parents for so many years,' she said.

'Why haven't you?'

'The time, the expense. And to be honest, I'm a bit scared of what I'll find out.'

'How so?'

'I just don't want to discover that my mother didn't want me,' she said, feeling more emotional than she expected to.

'Well, I understand that.'

'It's never really bothered me that much, but when I think about it – as I have done since I've been here – I can't help feeling weird that I'm committing myself to another person when I'm not really sure where I come from,' Jess said.

'Can't Blaise help you? You gave me the impression he's wealthy. Maybe he could pay someone to find out.'

Jess sighed. 'I don't think he's that interested. He's happy for things to be as they are. And I guess it's convenient not to have much family hanging around. He's keen for us to get married. He wouldn't welcome any distractions now.'

'Well, I can't blame him. Kareena's family are a *nightmare*,' he joked. 'Well, all families are, to be honest.'

As they walked on, she listened as Suresh opened up about how his and Kareena's families tried to control them both and wanted a say in every decision to do with the wedding. No wonder the engagement had already lasted for two years.

They climbed higher and soon Jess was out of breath as the path rose steeply upwards through the trees, but with the birds singing all around and the sunshine glinting through the thick trees, it felt magical.

But it wasn't just the walk that was magical. It was being with Suresh. As they walked and talked, Jess found herself opening up to him about so many things. She told him about what had happened with Angel and how much she missed her.

'That is a very sad story, Jess. I'm so sorry. There is nothing worse than losing a friend. I lost my best friend in a car crash when I was twelve. It still hurts to this day. I really am sorry for your loss.'

'Thank you,' she said, feeling so touched that he understood.

'She'll always be with you, though,' he said. 'I believe that, anyway. I bet she's looking out for you right now.'

'I hope so. It's such a relief to talk about her,' she admitted. 'I don't chat like this to Blaise.'

It felt like a big admission and she looked away.

'You can't talk to him?'

It was a direct question, but the answer that should trip off her tongue stalled.

'It's just . . .' She blew out a breath, her eyes filling with sudden, unexpected tears. 'It's just all gone so fast. I don't think I really know him well enough.'

'Maybe it's good to find out his faults over time. Then you can change them one by one.'

'I don't want to change him. Not really. I don't think that's fair.'

'Kareena wants to change everything about me.'

'Why? You're lovely as you are.'

Suresh looked down at the ground, not meeting her eyes. 'You're the first person to say so in a long while.'

They walked on, the cool damp green of the thick trees suddenly giving way to intense sun as the path climbed from the treeline upwards towards the rocks. Jess tried to figure out exactly what it was that had passed between them as she walked around the large boulders. Because it felt as if her opening up had formed some kind of unspoken bond. Why did it feel so easy to trust him? she wondered.

'Tell me more about this Blaise of yours,' Suresh asked, as the path widened out so that they could climb upwards side by side. Wild cacti, with their purple flowers, sprouted between the rocks. Above them, a bird of prey circled. 'What does he do for a living?'

'He's in property. Actually, he's investing in an island not far from here,' Jess said. 'It's called Lace Island.'

Suresh stopped on the path. His eyebrows shot up. 'Lace Island?'

'You know it?' Jess asked.

'Of course I do. There's lots of stories about that place. About what happened before the fire.'

'What fire?'

'The whole place burnt to the ground, must be twenty years ago, no, longer than that. Before then, a family lived there. It was this exclusive resort. They said it was paradise. Kareena worked with a guy once who told her all about it. She was trying to get a news crew there, but everything was blocked. In the end, her boss dropped it.'

Jess was astonished. Why hadn't Blaise mentioned any of this to her?

'What else do you know?'

Suresh shrugged. 'Not much. That's about it.'

'Can people go there?'

'No. Not according to Kareena. Anyway, it's a wilderness now. The ferry used to go there many years ago, apparently, but it's not on the route anymore.'

'Blaise says they're going to develop it into a luxury resort.'

'It's about time, I suppose. I'm sure he'll make a fortune,' Suresh said, but he sounded uncertain. 'It's a fantastic location. Once, there was a landing strip there for planes, so I'm told. And I think there's some coral reef nearby, so there could be diving.'

Jess climbed up the steep slope behind him, her mind going over and over what he'd told her about Lace Island. She tried to imagine the overgrown wilderness that Suresh had described and the vision Blaise had for the island's future. She couldn't wait to go there with Blaise, but she wondered why Kareena's efforts to investigate had been stopped. By whom?

As soon as she got home, Jess decided she'd Google it properly and see what she could find out about what Lace Island had once been like.

They climbed up and up, over the steep rocks, crude yellow arrows painted on the path to show them the way. Jess couldn't believe how steep the path became in places and she had to press herself against the rock face and steel herself not to look down, over the thin ledge and the cliffs below. A goat bleated at them, scurrying up and away towards the deep blue sky.

'Last bit of the path,' Suresh called back down to her.

She scrambled up the rock to the flat summit where the monks' temple looked out over the Western Ghats. Suresh pulled her the last of the way and she laughed, out of breath.

'Wow,' she said, breathless but happy as she absorbed the astonishing view. 'It's like we're on top of the world.'

'No wonder the monks thought they were closer to God here. It feels amazing, the energy. Don't you think?' he said. 'Although, I have no idea how they brought up all the materials to make the temple.'

She shared her bottle of water with Suresh again, and they sat on the temple steps together in quiet contemplation of the view, the odd, distant buzz of a moped drifting up to them over the tops of the trees. But up here, it was as if they'd entered another dimension. Another world. Where nothing else mattered, and everything that did was far, far below.

Jess felt a quiet sense of peace descending on her as she sat side by side with Suresh, looking out at the view, which stretched on for hundreds of miles. Maybe she'd answered her own question. Maybe her sense of unease was nothing to do with marrying Blaise. Maybe it was to do with *her*. About finding out who she was. That was the answer. Up here, her eyes stretching towards the distant, hazy horizon, she felt sure of it. She had to know the truth. And then she would be free.

CHAPTER FORTY-SEVEN

Lace Island, 1990

It was gone midnight as Leila paced in Bibi's office, waiting for her mother to come back from Maliba's house. She'd been gone for hours, comforting Vijay's family and calming everyone down. But where was she? She must be home soon. Then Leila could tell her what she suspected about Chan. And Bibi would help her get a message to Rasa. Her heart ached for Rasa, for the dreadful knowledge of what she knew and he didn't.

Was it really true, as Bamu had said, that Rasa and Vijay had argued? She could imagine that they would have. Vijay must have been furious that Rasa was giving up on his studies when he was so bright. Or had Rasa told his father that he was leaving because of Leila, because he could no longer bear to look at her?

The thought of it clutched her heart and made it hurt.

Had Rasa found Vijay to say goodbye before he went to the ferry? And if he had, what had passed between them? Had Vijay said anything that might have indicated that he was in danger? Did Rasa know anything that might shed light on who would do such an appalling thing to his father? If only he was here and hadn't left. She couldn't blame Bamu for speaking up earlier and she knew how readily people on the island jumped to conclusions but, even so, she was horrified that anyone could possibly think that Rasa was in any way to blame for Vijay's death.

Chan was.

Her own stepfather.

Leila stifled a shuddering sob. If only she knew how to get the telex machine to work herself, but only Bibi knew how to connect the ancient apparatus. But even if she could work it, she had no idea where Rasa was staying in Cochin. There must be hundreds of car shops.

She kept thinking of Rasa's face when he found out that Vijay had been murdered. Would he blame Leila after what she'd told him? He would certainly believe her then about bad things going on at Lace Island. Bad things that Leila no longer had any idea how to control. Because what if Vijay *had* got word out to the police? What if the authorities were already on their way?

'Leila, what are you doing here? Why aren't you in bed?' Bibi said, making Leila jump as she came into the room, uncovering her head, shaking out the raindrops on her yellow headscarf.

'How can I sleep after seeing that?' Leila said, and Bibi took her into an embrace.

'I know. I know. It's a terrible business,' she said, kissing Leila's cheek.

Leila pulled away and paced for a moment.

Bibi watched her. 'What is it?' she asked.

'It's my fault.'

'What is?' Bibi asked.

Leila's voice was shuddering as she spoke. 'It's my fault that Vijay is dead.'

'Leila, calm yourself,' Bibi said, with a sigh. 'We're all upset, but pull yourself together.'

'No, Mummy,' she said, raising her voice. 'No. This time, you have to listen.'

Leila grabbed Bibi's arm and forced her into sitting down on the swivel chair. Then she rushed to the door, looking out for Chan before shutting it firmly and turning the key.

'What is all this?' Bibi asked, clearly picking up on Leila's terror.

'I know you don't believe me sometimes, or the things I say, but you have to know that everything I'm going to tell you is the truth. Promise you'll believe me.'

Bibi was listening intently, her hands in her lap. 'Go on.'

Still standing, Leila took a deep breath and told Bibi all about her discovery of the drugs in the lighthouse. How Chan and Shang were planning on shipping them to America with Adam's help.

Bibi stared at her, her eyes dark with fear. 'It can't be true.'

'That's what Vijay said when I told him what I'd found.'

'You told Vijay? When?'

'At Maliba's party. He said he'd investigate and now he's dead.' Leila's hands were shaking, and she saw now that Bibi had gone pale.

'And you think Chan did it?'

'Yes.'

Her mother was silent for a long while, then shook her head and sighed. 'He's capable of many things, Leila, but not murder.'

'Well, if it wasn't him, it was Shang, or one of those other men Chan is involved with. Vijay must have found out what they were planning. The point is that Chan knows what happened. And now he wants to pin the blame on Rasa. When Rasa could never, never . . .' Leila covered her face with her hands, her tears overcoming her now.

She felt Bibi's arms going around her then. 'Oh, Leila,' she said. 'Oh, my girl.'

She stroked Leila's hair, but Leila could tell Bibi was already trying to rationalize everything she'd heard. Already trying to find a plausible explanation. She pulled away and stared at her mother, clutching her arms.

'We can leave,' Leila said. 'On Rasa's boat. We don't have to tell Chan. We can make a fire happen in the lighthouse. Make all the drugs disappear so that the island's reputation isn't destroyed. And then we can claim on your insurance and start again.'

Bibi laughed a strained, horrified laugh, the realization that Leila knew about the insurance dawning on her face. 'The insurance . . . ?'

'I heard you talking about it. And what you said about Chan.'

Bibi stared her in the eyes. Woman to woman. 'Is that really your plan?' Bibi said, her voice low.

'It's the only way.'

'Leila, listen. Even if what you're saying is true, I will not leave. I owe it to Vijay's family to stay until the police come.'

'It'll be too late. Bibi, please. They'll find the drugs and you'll be in trouble. Rasa said you could go to jail even. You have to leave with me. It's not safe for us here. You can't trust Chan. You know you can't.'

Bibi closed her eyes for a long moment and Leila braced herself. This was it. She was going to tell Bibi about what had happened with Adam. How she was convinced that Chan knew about it. If her confession was the final piece of evidence to convince Bibi of the truth about Chan, then so be it.

'Mummy,' she began, 'there's something else I have to tell you.'

Slowly, Bibi placed her soft hand on Leila's cheek. 'Save it.'

'But—'

'Whatever it is that you want to say to persuade me to go, you have to understand, Leila, I can't. I can't leave.'

She sank slowly into the chair as if she'd suddenly deflated. Leila's confession stalled now as she saw the look of defeat on her mother's face.

'Yes, you can. We have each other. We can escape.' Leila knelt next to Bibi's chair, holding her hand. 'We can go to Cochin and find Rasa. Get help—'

'Stop,' Bibi said. 'Please stop.'

'But—'

'I should have told you this before. I should have warned you, but I have no other choice because of what you're saying. So I will tell you now.'

'Tell me what?'

Bibi stared into Leila's eyes and she held her arms as if she were trying to hold on to her.

'I'm dying, Leila.' It was no more than a whisper, but Leila saw the truth as Bibi's eyes welled with tears.

The pill bottles, Maliba's potions, Chan's sympathy about her headache, her mother stumbling near the terrace door – all of these images suddenly rattled through Leila's mind and she gasped as she finally realized what they meant. She saw it all now in her mother's face. In the grief-stricken expression in her eyes.

'I'm sorry,' Bibi whispered.

Tears fell from Leila's eyes. 'What do you mean?'

'It's cancer, Leila. And it's got me,' Bibi sighed. 'They can't treat it. And now it's the end. I can feel it. It's too late.'

'It's not too late,' Leila implored her, trying to breathe through her tears. 'It can't be. I'll take you to the hospital. I'll—'

'They can't cure me. I know that. They've tried, but . . .' Bibi's voice was different now. Resigned. Like saying these words had already made her die a little. 'Darling, if what you're saying about Chan is true and the people he's mixed up with killed Vijay, then it's not safe here for you,' Bibi said urgently, pulling Leila up from the floor. 'Listen to me. You must go on without me. I will work this out with Chan and find out what he is planning, and I will stop him. But you must take the boat and stay away until all this has blown over. You can find Rasa. Make sure he clears his name. He's a good boy.'

'I'm not going to leave you, Mummy. Not now.'

Bibi stood up out of the chair with difficulty, as if she was fighting the pain. 'You must. I insist. It's too dangerous. You must go.'

'I don't want to leave you. I won't leave you,' Leila protested, but as she stared into her mother's face, she knew that Bibi would not take no for an answer.

'Here.' Bibi took off the gold crucifix she always wore and placed it round Leila's neck. 'I've tried to protect you, my darling, but I can't any longer. It's up to the will of God now.'

CHAPTER FORTY-EIGHT

London, present day

Maeve and Tony sat opposite Jess in the Golden Lion, their local South London pub, admiring the huge diamond Blaise had presented her with when she'd got back from India. He'd taken her straight from the airport to a candlelit restaurant in Knightsbridge and had made a great show of proposing properly, getting down on one knee. There'd even been a violinist.

Jess had been blown away by the ring – not only by its size and obvious value, but by everything it symbolized. After the simplicity of India, it had all felt like too much. The modern, chunky diamond in its square setting was so far away from anything that she would have chosen for herself, she'd been speechless when Blaise had put it on her finger. And when he'd kissed her, telling her that her ring would make all the girls jealous, she'd swallowed her misgivings and had told him that it had been perfect, telling herself that she'd get used to it. That she'd even love it in time.

Now, after three weeks, she was just about getting used to how it felt on her finger, but when she looked at her hand, she still did a double-take. And since the ring had been placed there, it felt like time had accelerated and she was hurtling head first towards the future. All the stillness and peace she'd felt in India had gone. She'd felt so clear-headed being on the top of the hill with Suresh, but her resolve to find out about her past had vanished as soon as she'd come home. She wished she could talk to Blaise about it, the way she'd talked to Suresh, but he was always on his phone or typing emails and she hadn't had the chance to talk to him about how she felt.

Which is why it was so nice that she was still in touch with Suresh. She'd already emailed him a couple of times, but she guessed that over time, their communication would stop. After all, they lived on opposite sides of the world. Nevertheless, it felt fun to have an ally in the 'being engaged' phase of her life. And being in touch with him meant that she didn't have to let the whole wonderful experience of India go. Not quite yet.

Actually, meeting Suresh had done her a favour, she told herself. Not only had she found a new friend, but it had shown her how easy it would be to ruin things with Blaise. And she wouldn't do that. Blaise was everything she'd ever dreamt of. He loved her. He told her again and again. And she loved him too, right? What more could she want?

But this evening, the jangled feeling she'd managed to dampen down over the last three weeks was back. Because here in the scruffy pub, with its scuffed bar and sticky carpet, the ring felt too flashy. Way too flashy. And they all knew it. Jess pulled her hand away and smiled.

'Married. Well, well,' Tony said, taking a sip of his pint. He rarely drank, but he'd declared tonight a special occasion, after Jess had told him the news at the gym.

'I wish you were coming,' Jess said, smiling sadly at Tony.

'Even if I could afford to come to Miami, I couldn't get our passports arranged in time.'

'I could pay?'

'No way,' Tony snapped, with a frown.

'It's so sudden,' Maeve said. 'Are you sure it's what you want, Jess?'

Jess gave them a 'what can I do?' shrug. 'Why wait? Why not just seize the moment?'

She sounded falsely optimistic, even to herself, and she saw Tony and Maeve exchange a look.

'So long as you know what you're doing,' Tony said. 'I wish I'd met the guy.'

'And what about his family? What are they like?' Maeve asked.

'I'm meeting them later. Blaise is in town and they're coming to his suite at the Dorchester.'

'His suite at the Dorchester,' Tony mimicked. 'Listen to you, Jess.'

'Well, I could hardly have them round to my place,' she countered.

'Why not? There's nothing wrong with the estate. It's where you're from.'

Not anymore, she wanted to say, but she didn't.

But back on the estate, an hour later, Jess was more sure than ever that her decision to keep Blaise away from here had been the right one. She shivered as she walked into her empty flat, the letters and pizza flyers concertinaing in a pile on the carpet behind the door. It was as if she'd walked through a time warp to a past life, she thought, running her fingers over her dusty bike. The faint stale smell of cigarette smoke made her think of Angel and her breath caught, sudden tears threatening to overwhelm her. Because this was her home, and after tonight, she'd be leaving it forever.

Her email pinged, making her jump, and she picked up her

phone. It was probably Blaise, wondering where she was. She hadn't told him she'd be stopping by the flat.

Instead, she saw an email from Suresh – a reply to hers, taking him up on his offer to look over the prenuptial agreement that Blaise had sent her.

She read his polite email now and his points about the agreement, her eyebrows crinkling together as she read his analysis. There was nothing to worry about, he said. The agreement was, in fact, the reverse of most prenuptials, Blaise setting out that every asset was to be shared. In short, what was his was hers and what was hers was his.

But that didn't make sense, surely. Surely Blaise wanted to protect his assets and his wealth.

He obviously loves you very much, Suresh had written. *And I can see why he does. I wish you lots of luck with your wedding. Take care, Jess. x*

One kiss. He'd signed off with one kiss. Jess bit her lip, thinking about the hilltop and how comfortable she'd been with him.

Suddenly, she knew she had to talk to him. Standing up, she dialled the number on his email, pacing as she waited for the expensive long-distance call to connect, but the phone went straight to his voicemail. She cursed silently, annoyed at how impulsive she'd been to ring. It was probably the middle of the night in India. He was probably cuddled up in bed with Kareena. Why was she even calling?

She bit her lip, unable to back out now. If he saw that she'd called and hadn't left a message, then he'd be worried. She stared at the stained wall and the sofa, and took a deep breath, trying to keep her voice cheerful as she spoke after the beep.

'It's me. Jess. I got your email and I wanted to say thank you.'

And to hear your voice. I wanted to hear your voice.

She rang off and deleted Suresh's message from her phone. She couldn't risk Blaise finding it.

Half an hour later, Jess hurried into the lift at the Dorchester, feeling like she'd stepped through a mirror back into a different world to the one she'd left in South London. And now that she was here, she was desperate to see Blaise. All the sentimentality she'd felt about Suresh in the flat had jangled her. *He* couldn't give her any answers. It had been pointless to call him. Besides, her life was here with Blaise, and as soon as she was back in his arms, everything would be OK. With a bit of luck, they'd have time to have sex before his family arrived.

But when she got to the hotel suite, Jess was surprised to find that Lance Blackmore, Blaise's brother, was already in the sitting room of the giant suite, staring out at the view over Hyde Park. It could only be Lance, as even from his reflection in the floor-to-ceiling glass, he looked so much like Blaise. Except that Lance had thinning blond hair and a jowly chin, and when he turned to look at Jess, she saw that there was a paunch underneath his blue blazer, and one of the gold buttons was falling off.

Jess apologized for not getting here sooner as she rushed across the thick beige carpet and shook his hand, giving Blaise, who was standing near the kitchenette, a worried look. If his family were already arriving, then she had no time to shower and change. It was her fault for stopping by the flat.

'So you're the one who's gonna save my little bro,' Lance said to Jess, pulling her roughly towards him and kissing her cheek.

There was something wolf-like about Lance – a hungry look in his beady eyes that took Jess by surprise. He put his hand in the pocket of his chinos and swilled the ice round his whisky glass before draining the amber liquid.

'I'll have the other half of this, Blaisey-Boy,' he said loudly.

Blaise came over and put his arm proprietorially round Jess's shoulder as he took Lance's glass.

'She's quite a looker, eh?' Lance said, his gaze darting between Jess and Blaise, as if Blaise had won some sort of bet.

'He's always been a charmer,' Blaise said stiffly in Jess's ear. Jess had never heard him speak like he was now, his refined accent slipping for a minute into an Australian twang she hadn't heard before.

'He drinks,' he explained. 'Don't take any notice of him. Or anything he says. Absolutely promise me,' he added, loud enough for Lance to hear.

Jess followed him to the kitchen and grabbed him and pulled him to one side, by the drinks cabinet. 'Why is everyone here so soon?' she said. 'I haven't showered or anything.'

'You went dashing off. I tried to call,' he said, but Jess knew he hadn't. 'It doesn't matter. It's only a casual hello. Come and meet Wes,' he continued, introducing a man in a beige suit, who now appeared from the kitchen with a mug in his hand.

'We meet at last,' Wes said, in a thick Texan accent. 'I don't know if Blaise explained, but there's just some paperwork to sign.'

'You know, the prenup,' Blaise said. She now saw that there were several sets of paperwork laid out on the glass dining table.

'Oh,' said Jess, suddenly feeling wrong-footed, after reading Suresh's email. 'Sure. Of course.'

Jess went with him to the table, and he unscrewed a heavy fountain pen and showed her where to sign. Not wanting to cause a scene, Jess briefly scanned the document, hardly reading a word. She was more aware that Wes was looking meaningfully at Blaise. She heard him flicking his tongue in his mouth. Why did he remind her so much of a lizard?

'Tremendous,' Wes said, smiling at Blaise, who now kissed Jess on the forehead and put his hand round her waist.

'Are you staying? Would you like a drink?' Jess asked, surprised that Wes had been so perfunctory and that he was now quickly shuffling the papers into a pile and then into his brief-case.

'I'd love to, but I must get back to the office.' He patted his briefcase. 'No rest for the wicked.'

Jess smoothed down the front of her hoody, wishing again that she'd had time to change into the black cocktail dress she'd planned to wear, before Blaise's mother arrived. But it was too late. As Blaise was escorting Wes across the carpet, there was a knock on the door and Blaise answered it.

A tall, strict-looking woman with angular features was on the threshold, clutching a dark green crocodile-skin designer handbag against her chest, as if it were a shield. She stared into the room, her face stern, her jawline accentuated by her razor-sharp grey bob. Jess had expected someone warm and posh, but her future mother-in-law looked steely and hard.

'You're early,' Blaise said, kissing his mother, but she didn't return his affection, offering her cheek.

'I don't have long.'

'That's a shame. Jess and I—'

'Where is she?' Mrs Blackmore demanded, and Jess stepped forwards shyly. 'Let's get this over with.'

'You must be Blaise's mum. I'm so looking forward to us getting to know each other,' Jess said, wrong-footed once again, shaking Blaise's mother's hand. A kiss was clearly out of the question.

Blaise's mother seemed to look down her nose at her. 'Yes,' she said, her eyes and her answer giving nothing away.

Jess busied herself fixing her future mother-in-law a Martini, constantly glancing towards where she was standing with Lance by the window. She was wearing a simple black shift dress and high heels, an outfit that suited her so entirely Jess wondered if she ever wore anything else. She watched as Mrs Blackmore rocked her head back and laughed at something Lance was saying. She was clearly a woman who only liked the company of men. Or maybe just one of her sons. Jess could see that Blaise looked put out.

'I hope it's OK,' Jess said, with a smile, handing over the drink.

Mrs Blackmore took a sip and nodded. 'Not bad,' she said, and Jess felt a shimmer of satisfaction. She sensed that any praise from this woman would be hard won.

'So . . . Jessica,' she said, twisting the olive round in her glass. 'Tell me about your family.'

Jess took a breath. 'I'm sure Blaise has told you, but I've never had a mother of my own,' Jess confided, smiling at Blaise's mother and then at him, knowing she'd jumped over twenty of the things she'd meant to say before this. 'Which is why it's so nice to meet you. Perhaps we can go shopping and—'

'I don't think so,' Blaise's mother said, fixing her with a stare. 'I don't like shopping.'

'Oh, well, perhaps we could do something else?'

But Jess knew she was clutching at straws. There was a tiny beat of silence that her future mother-in-law failed to fill. Almost as if she was enjoying leaving her to dangle.

'Blaise, we have dinner booked for seven,' Mrs Blackmore announced, raising her gaze away from Jess's with a kind of stiff-jawed triumph that made Jess shrivel inside. 'But I think I'll eat in my room.'

'Whatever you want, Mother,' Blaise said. His tone was flat and cold.

Jess's overtures at friendliness stalled. Perhaps she'd overdone it. She looked at Blaise, completely baffled, but he didn't look at her. What had just happened? What had she said? How could this have gone so wrong?

She shuffled backwards, extricating herself from the conversation to get her own drink. She heard the trill of laughter as Blaise and his brother crowded round their mother. She felt more excluded than she'd ever felt. Like she'd already failed some vital test she hadn't realized was a test until it was too late. She felt her eyes fill with tears as she downed a glass of wine in the kitchen.

She could barely speak when, a few minutes later, Lance and their mother swept out of the room. They didn't even look in her direction, or say goodbye.

'I'll go and get changed, shall I?' she said to Blaise, once the door had closed, her voice shaking.

'I'm sorry. I'm so embarrassed,' he said with a groan. 'They're awful, aren't they?'

Jess put her hands on her waist, staring at the closed door, trying to work out what the hell had just happened. She could see Blaise was upset, though, which punctured her fury. Perhaps he was on her side, after all. She took a breath, choosing her words carefully.

'They're your family. Of course they're not *awful*,' she said. 'But I was expecting them to stay for a little bit longer.'

'I know. It's all such a mess,' Blaise said.

He took a deep, shuddering breath and Jess moved towards him and flopped down heavily on the sofa next to him. She'd never seen him like this before. He closed his eyes as if his head were bursting with unspoken anger.

'Fuck,' he said, through clenched teeth. 'I should never have invited them.'

Jess put her hand over his. 'What's the matter? Please tell me. Is it me? Have I done something wrong? Didn't they like me? What did I say?'

'No. No, it's not you. Of course it's not you. But my family,' he said, 'they sometimes make me want to run away. You know?'

'Not really. My family ran away from me,' Jess said, shrugging. 'I don't understand what just happened, but I'm sure they love you. And they gave you everything. A happy childhood. I mean, all that stuff you told me in Miami . . .'

'Maybe I embellished a bit,' he said. 'I just wanted you to see the best side of me.'

Jess bit her bottom lip. This was news to her, but she couldn't blame him. On that day, she'd lied about her mother being a travelling singer. It seemed ridiculous now that she'd ever lied to him, but even so, she'd always assumed that Blaise had been a hundred per cent honest with her. What else had he 'embellished'? she wondered.

'You are so nice, Jess. I didn't expect you to be—' He stopped suddenly.

'What? What didn't you expect me to be? When?'

'I mean, after everything you went through as a kid. You've turned out so . . . so . . . well, normal,' he said.

She laughed, surprised. 'I'm not so sure about that. I'm not so sure that anything about this is normal,' she said.

'All I mean is that you're a good person.'

She snuggled into him, kissing him, but she was confused by his mood. She couldn't figure out what was going on.

'So you reckon we'll have cosy family Christmases together, then?'

Blaise let out a laugh at the thought. 'No. But all that matters is that we're together,' he said, taking her hand. 'You know that, don't you?'

She nodded.

'You don't have doubts, do you?' he asked. 'About us.'

'Of course not,' she lied. 'What about you?'

'Marrying you is all I need,' he said.

CHAPTER FORTY-NINE

Lace Island, 1990

Leila tried to keep her breathing calm as she hurriedly packed a T-shirt and shorts into her rucksack, treading carefully over the creaking floorboard in the middle of her bedroom, feeling her way in the dark.

She was leaving. Tonight. With Bibi. Whether she liked it or not. Before it was too late.

Bibi might not think it, of course. In fact, as Leila had helped Bibi lie down in her bed earlier after their talk and she'd kissed her mother's forehead, it had seemed to Leila that Bibi's wonderful aquamarine eyes had lost all their fight.

But Leila would fight for them both. She had to.

'I need to sleep, Leila,' Bibi had whispered. 'Don't do anything tonight. We'll discuss it in the morning. Everything will be better in the morning,' she'd said, as she'd drifted off.

But the morning would be too late.

Bibi. Her darling mother . . . *dying*. The word sounded like a deafening alarm in Leila's head. The only way she could cope was by telling herself that she wouldn't allow it to be true. Leila forced away the memory of the words Bibi had told her earlier, in case they would derail her from her plan.

She froze now, listening, worried in case Chan had returned. She had to escape before he came back to the house.

The wind had come up, making the palms chatter outside. A loose shutter on the house banged.

Dressed now and carrying her bag, Leila tiptoed down the staircase to the main hallway. The draught of the wind made the muslin curtains billow like ghosts in the dark. She shuddered, scooting quickly behind the lectern to the cupboard where she knew the fireworks were.

The memory chimed in her head of a day that felt so long ago, when she'd believed everything was good and true in Lace Island, when Chan had returned laden with presents. She heard his words across time: *Leila, don't you ever think of playing with these. They are highly flammable. You know how paranoid your mother is about fire.*

Well, he'd eat his words now, she thought, sliding open the door and reaching inside. She felt inside the cardboard box and pulled out the cylinders and stuffed them in her pockets.

Then, standing, she stared around her at the hall, feeling the enormity of the moment. Because once she'd started the fire in the lighthouse, Bibi would have no choice but to get up. And Leila would take her straight to the lagoon and Bamu's good powerboat and by morning, they'd be on their way to Cochin. And Chan could face the authorities alone when they came and make up any lies he wanted. Because by then, Leila would be helping to nurse Bibi back to health in the hospital.

She blew out a pent-up breath, forcing down her panic, and then her eyes rested on the visitors book.

She went to it on the lectern, thinking of the sweet letter to the guests in the front that Bibi had written, full of her warmth and humour, full of her faith that everyone who came here was lovely and kind.

Well, they would come again, Leila thought. Once the drugs had gone, Leila would help Bibi run this place properly – as Bibi had always intended. The visitors book would remind them, Leila thought, of all the people who loved it here, before Chan had allowed his corruption and vice to turn their paradise sour.

She lifted the heavy book off the lectern and slid it into her bag. She might as well take it now, while she remembered. She didn't know how much time she'd have later on.

She tiptoed silently along the corridor now, cursing the creaking screen door that led to the terrace. More determined than ever, she gripped the strap of her bag and made for the far steps down to the pool. She would sneak through the kitchen garden and find Anjum's matches and paraffin.

Half an hour later, Leila crept through the dark trees in the grove, avoiding the path to the lighthouse. She had worried that Chan or the dreadful Shang might be here to hide the evidence themselves, or that they might have a man with a gun on guard, but the lighthouse was dark, the chain across the doors.

Leila felt her hair whipping around her face, blown by the wind, and she spat it out of her mouth as she pulled the fireworks from her pockets, empting the gunpowder on the earth in the small gap under the cracked brown door of the lighthouse. She looked behind her, still terrified of getting caught, knowing she had to get this done and fast.

Behind her, the tops of the palm trees thrashed and still the matches wouldn't stay lit long enough to light the gunpowder.

She wished now that she'd thought this through better. It would have helped if she'd been able to find Anjum's paraffin, but there hadn't been any. If only she was able to throw a lit bottle through the hole in the window she'd made the other day.

Now, kneeling in the dirt, her heart pounding, Leila scraped together a pile of tiny twigs and leaves, hoping to start the fire. She knelt over it, shielding it from the wind with her body, and lit the kindling, blowing on the pile of leaves until there was a familiar, satisfying crackle.

She gasped, sure she'd heard something. Was it a person? Was someone on the other side of the lighthouse?

Quickly, she stumbled to her feet, tripping backwards and running into the cover of the trees. She crouched in the darkness, waiting, seeing smoke start to billow up from her pile of leaves. She held her breath, counting to five, then looked again, seeing the wind had now ignited the leaves. A strong yellow flame burst up from the twigs, licking the bottom of the lighthouse door.

She turned, pressed herself against the tree trunk, waiting a moment; then looking round again, misgivings filling her. She felt her knees shaking, her instinct telling her to put out the fire. It wasn't too late. But the fire, whipped now by the wind, was spreading.

This was good, she told herself. This was what she wanted. To get rid of the drugs. As soon as there was a strong fire, she had reason enough to go back to the house and wake Bibi. Chan couldn't stop her.

There was more smoke now, coming out from inside the lighthouse doors. The fire was on its way. She crept forward again, just to check, surprised that it had taken so quickly. She saw the yellow shadow of jumping light from under the lighthouse door.

The wind made the branches above her thrash. A waft of acrid smoke filled her nostrils.

She said a silent prayer of thanks, then set off back through the trees towards the house. It was time to rouse Bibi and get her to the boat.

But she hadn't gone twenty paces before it happened.

The explosion was so loud and so forceful it threw Leila ten feet forward. She landed on the forest floor in damp undergrowth, completely winded, her ears ringing, and for a few seconds everything went black.

Gulping, gasping, her eyes stinging, she turned to see that the whole of the lighthouse was a towering inferno of flames. She cried out, covering her head, as parts of burning masonry started falling through the trees, raining down on her.

There was a terrible roar now, like nothing Leila had ever heard, and she looked through her arms over her face and saw that the tops of the trees were on fire and the wind was whipping them in all directions.

'No,' she cried, scrambling to her feet, coughing with the smoke, but around her, the trunks of the palms started burning, the fire fizzing and crackling down the trunks.

She staggered backwards, hoping to find another way, horrified at what had happened, but suddenly the fire was all around her. And now the path back up to the house was impassable.

For a second, Leila froze, panic engulfing her. No wonder Bibi had always been so terrified of fire. Leila couldn't believe how quickly the fire was spreading . . . rushing, dancing, gleefully gobbling up trees in every direction.

And it wasn't going to stop. She had to get to the lagoon and warn everyone.

Spluttering, covering her face, she slid through the undergrowth down the slope, to where she could see down to the lagoon, but behind her, there was another explosion. A roar now in her ringing ears as Leila raced to the treeline. She couldn't believe this was happening so fast; not after the rain had drenched everything in the past few days, but the trees and plants had obviously dried out again in the hot wind.

She stopped short as she looked down, seeing something she hadn't even considered. The tops of the trees in the grove were all ablaze now, the wind like a blow torch, fanning the fire along the forest towards the huts.

'No. No!' she screamed. If the fire reached the huts, then everyone would be trapped.

Sprinting, Leila raced forward, towards the lagoon and the other pathway, but the heat of the fire threw her backwards. She looked desperately through the trees, watching each trunk crackle into life, showers of sparks flying upwards to the black sky.

What about the house? What about Bibi? If the fire was spreading this quickly towards the lagoon, it would almost have reached the house by now. Would Parva have woken Bibi? She must have done. But how would they get to the lagoon now?

She ran, hot sparks of air chasing her, but when she got nearer to the path to get down to the lagoon, she could hear screams and saw that several of the roofs of the huts were already on fire. Where was everyone? Maliba, Bamu and the children?

'No!' she screamed. 'No!'

The fire rushed along the huts. She saw people running, heard screams above the roar. She saw the top of the hut where all the rice was stored whooshing into flame.

How had this happened?

This was not meant to have happened.

Another explosion now, the whole of the lighthouse, a huge wall of fire. She ran forwards, coughing as the smoke choked her. The noise was deafening as the trees crackled and sparked all around her. A tree crashed in front of her, blocking her way down to the lagoon. Coughing and spluttering, she patted the scorching singe-holes on her tunic, her hands burning. There was no way to get down. No way to help.

She covered her elbows over her eyes, the smoke blinding her. Another palm tree toppled, crashing sparks into the night.

Leila screamed and ran for her life, down in the other direction, towards the guest huts, where she'd seen Adam and Monique, running ahead through the mangrove flowers. Tripping, spluttering.

She ran to the beach, up the jetty to where Rasa's old blue boat was moored. It slapped against the wooden posts on the swell of the tide.

Shaking, her clothes singed, Leila cast off from the jetty, determined to get round and save people from the lagoon. She coughed, exhausted, yanking at the string of the outboard motor.

'Come on, come on,' she sobbed, but the engine wouldn't start. Only Rasa had the knack.

'Please, please, please,' she yelled, realizing how quickly she was floating away from the jetty. The fire had followed her down to the beach, the guest bungalows in flames. She could see the tiny flecks of fire reaching the sea now, where they fizzled in the surf.

Giving up on the motor, wiping her dripping nose, she grabbed for the oars, clumsily manhandling them, but she was in such a panic she dropped one. She heard it splash in the water and lunged, too late, almost toppling the boat. The oar floated away from her, out of reach, then sank into the black water.

The current was pulling her away, further and further out. She knelt on the hard boards, sobbing as she plunged her hands into the water, trying desperately to manoeuvre herself back round towards the lagoon, but it was hopeless. Hyperventilating, she fell back in the boat.

And that's when she looked up and saw that everything was on fire.

Everything.

She could see the house now, flames licking across the red roof tiles. Over the roar of the wind and fire, she heard glass smashing, screams of people.

She stared, transfixed, as she bobbed further and further away towards the reef, as the island burnt orange and red into the black sky, huge shards of yellow sparks flaming up occasionally. And the roar of it, the unforgettable sound of the ferocious fire she'd started, razing everything in its path.

CHAPTER FIFTY

Miami, present day

The sound of Etta James singing 'At Last' played softly through the speakers in the plush hotel room in Miami, adding the final touch of romance to the moment. Jess twirled round on the thick yellow carpet in front of the long gold mirror, still not able to believe it was really her own reflection she was seeing. With her hair all curled and styled as it was and her eyes so heavily made up, she looked almost unrecognizable. Tilly, who was wearing a champagne-coloured satin bridesmaid's dress with a huge bow on the front, stood back and watched her.

'You know, it is worth it. A designer dress, I mean. And you know you can sell it after, right? I had one like that for my first wedding and I sold it on eBay for two grand.'

Jess stopped and stared at Tilly in the mirror. She couldn't believe she'd been so insensitive on this, Jess's big day.

'What?' Tilly said defensively. 'I'm just saying.'

Jess had yet to get used to quite how outspoken Tilly liked to be. It was as if since they'd shared that moment of intimacy in Ibiza, Tilly was on a mission to prove to Jess that she was *just fine*. It helped that she had a new boyfriend and had spent the entire time since they'd been in Miami either talking about him or texting him.

It had been Tilly who'd insisted on shopping for the dress with Jess, who had been rather strong-armed into the strapless designer number, which had cost a fortune. It had all been pre-arranged between the shop and Blaise, who had instructed Tilly to let Jess choose whichever dress she liked. Tilly had made no secret of her joy at spending Blaise's money, bagging a designer dress and shoes for herself into the bargain.

The whole thing had been so brash and intimidating and not how Jess had imagined choosing a wedding dress might be at all. And yes, Jess could sell it, but the idea rather ruined the romance. She wanted to tell Tilly that she intended to have her dress properly cleaned and carefully wrapped in tissue paper so that one day her daughter could wear it, but she doubted Tilly would understand.

Jess thought about that future day, imagining herself going into the loft in the grand Miami mansion Blaise had told her they were moving into and finding the box with this dress in it. She couldn't work out which was more fantastical – the designer dress she was wearing or that shortly she'd be living in her own house. One that had a loft. And a carport. And a pool. Oh, and some stables. Blaise was insisting they have a horse. A horse!

Tilly turned and looked out of the window of the hotel suite and the French doors that should have been open onto the golf course but were resolutely closed against the rain. Jess hated to admit it, but Blaise had been right about the beach wedding. It would have been a disaster if they'd been getting married outdoors today.

'Shame about the bloody rain,' Tilly said. 'I was hoping to top up my tan. I thought it was always supposed to be hot in

Miami. Hang on.' Tilly's phone was trilling. She walked away to answer it, a squeal of joy escaping her. It was her boyfriend, Marco, Jess thought, feeling irrationally annoyed. Couldn't Tilly just commit herself to paying Jess attention for one moment? Wasn't that what bridesmaids were supposed to do just before the bride went in for the ceremony?

'What do you reckon, Angel?' Jess whispered to her reflection, her heart aching for her friend. Waking up today, alone, knowing Angel wasn't here to hold her hand, had hurt like hell. And it felt strange, too, that Tony and Maeve weren't here. Apart from Tilly and Ivana, Jess barely knew any of the guests at her own wedding. She wondered what kind of dress Blaise's mother would be wearing and whether she would thaw any more when Jess was married to her son. She hoped so.

She smoothed her hands over the silk of her wedding dress, the enormous diamond ring on her finger glittering. She took a deep breath, but still she felt nerves slicing through her, making her knees weak.

Imagine how she'd feel if there were hundreds of guests, she told herself. Or even thousands, like Suresh's wedding. A brief flash of an image flitted across her mind: his face across that dining room the first time she'd seen him. How he'd filled her up with sunshine.

She thought about how their friendship would be affected now that she was about to be married. She'd kept Suresh a secret from Blaise, deleting his texts and hiding the letter he'd sent her last week, not that she really had anything to hide. Suresh was her friend and confidant and nothing more. He'd only ever been entirely respectful about Blaise, but something about their secret relationship brought Jess more comfort than she could express. Sometimes it felt like Suresh was the only person on her side, even though he was thousands of miles away.

She turned and picked up the bouquet of cream roses she'd carry into the ceremony room in a moment. If Suresh were here now, he'd be telling her to be brave. That nerves were normal. She could almost hear him saying the words.

She took another deep breath, preparing herself. Any moment now, she would go through that door and she would commit to Blaise and their life together. And she would be happy. She would want for nothing. He'd told her that. And in return, she would make a perfect home for him. It was every dream she'd ever had come true.

So why didn't she feel more elated?

Was it just the job thing? The certainty that Blaise would want her to give up her career to fit in with his life? Is that what was bothering her the most? Or were these normal pre-wedding nerves?

She was about to say something to Tilly when Tilly let out a shriek of laughter. 'You didn't,' she gasped. 'Back in a moment,' she said to Jess, still chatting on the phone. She went out into the corridor and Jess was left alone in the room.

Jess took a deep breath in and let it out slowly, but she still couldn't stop the nerves from making her feel breathless. She walked across the cream carpet and opened the door a crack, breathing in some fresh air.

But as she leant her head out of the door, all she got was a waft of cigarette smoke.

She ducked her head round the door. Blaise had his back to her and was with Lance, standing further along the terrace, outside the main room. Was Blaise *smoking*? She shrank back, astonished that she'd seen him. Maybe he was as nervous as her. Was this just a one-off before the wedding?

She told herself to close the door. It was bad luck for him to see her. Besides, as much as she needed a reassuring hug from him right now, she couldn't exactly go out there – especially if she was going to catch him smoking. Maybe he was having a last-minute wobble too.

Well, soon enough it would be over. They would be married and they could get on with enjoying their day and then their honeymoon. She couldn't wait to fly to Venice and stay in the hotel Blaise had chosen. She was about to shut the door, as quietly as she could, when she heard them talking.

'It's a fairy tale as far as she's concerned,' Blaise was saying. 'She thinks she's nothing. A nobody.'

'That's good, right?'

'Yeah, thank God. She has no idea.'

Jess froze. *No idea about what?*

'Don't look so stressed, man,' Lance said. 'You've done the hard work. She's signed the paperwork.'

'I know. I just have to get through the ceremony.'

Get through it? *Get through it?*

'You can do it. It's just words. After all the bull you've spouted, just a few more can't hurt.'

Jess gripped the door, listening intently now, her heart hammering.

'But she believes me.'

'So? This is what you were paid all that money for. To find her and marry her. It's what you agreed to. Remember the deal.' Jess felt her heart constricting. She couldn't breathe. 'It's not exactly been a tough gig. You hooked her in so fast. I mean, what did you do? Let me know your secret, man.'

'Nothing really. It was easy,' Blaise said, with a callous-sounding laugh. 'I bombarded her with flowers, gifts, clothes. Stuff she could brag about with the cabin crew. Threw budget at it. The hired apartment in New York got her into bed. Porscha wasn't happy about that.'

Porscha?

'She looks like a gold-digger. I could see it straight away.'

'I don't think she is. Not really. As soon as I gave her all the "I love you" spiel, she was putty in my hands, but I don't know . . .'

'Stay strong, man. Don't get sloppy now. Think of Porscha. She's stood by you through all of this. It's tougher for her, knowing what's going on today.'

'You're right.'

'This is no time for a crisis of confidence. Think of Lace Island. It's so close.'

'I know.'

Jess heard the sound of cigarettes being ground out and Blaise and Lance walking away.

'And what will happen to Jess? After, I mean?' Lance said.

'I expect the others will take care of that. She'll be . . . well . . . disposed of, I guess. To be honest, I'd rather not know.'

Outside, Jess heard the function-room door open and close, and then the roses in her hand dropped to the floor with a thud, right before her knees buckled.

PART FOUR

PART FOUR

CHAPTER FIFTY-ONE

Lace Island, present day

Leila woke suddenly in the darkness with a terrified gasp. She stared up from her narrow bed through the thick metal bars on her window at the impossible number of stars streaking across the black expanse of sky. The moon was full tonight and the dirty, bare walls of her small room were bathed in silvery light. She swatted at a mosquito that buzzed against her face and dabbed her sweating brow with the sleeve of her filthy jacket.

Lying back exhausted, Leila tried to breathe normally to get her heart rate down as the dream faded. But even when she was awake, it was still there, the truth of it tethering her and trapping her with no respite.

It amazed her that she could still dream the full dream. That every tiny detail was intact, everything as sharp as if it were happening all over again. When every day it felt like her brain had turned to mush, it was a small comfort to know that the old Leila must still be inside her, if only in her subconscious dreamworld. But now, over a quarter of a century after the events of her dream, she wondered where that brave girl she'd once been had gone.

She groaned, rubbing her face, knowing that with the

dawn, her living nightmare would start all over again for another day. She'd do her duties, like the zombie she was, and if she was lucky, she wouldn't dream the terror that still haunted her. She didn't know which was worse, being awake or asleep.

Perhaps the dream had started with the stars, before she'd gone to sleep. Or maybe it was because she was so dog-tired when she'd fallen down on the bed it had been like she'd still been rocking on that boat. She remembered thinking earlier of that first night – not far off thirty years ago now – as she'd stared at Lace Island becoming just a red dot on the horizon, until her eyes had felt as if they'd been bleeding. The image of the fire permanently burnt onto her retinas. And how she'd settled down into the bottom of the boat and wished that the stars would take her and swallow her up. How she'd drifted off on the waves, not caring about her future, only floating in the vastness of her grief and misery.

She hadn't cared at all if she ever saw the morning, and it wasn't until the booming horn from a cargo ship had woken her – and she'd squinted into the bright morning light and seen the huge bulk of red-and-grey steel bearing down on her – that she'd considered it even possible for life to go on.

She'd been certain that the ship would mow her down and she'd cowered in the boat, waiting for certain death, but then she'd heard a voice and had seen that a small inflatable craft had been launched from the huge vessel. A man in a yellow life jacket had been rowing towards her.

He'd been Dutch and had shouted instructions to her as the ship towered over them. Leila hadn't understood a word he'd said, but eventually, he'd gently coaxed her into the life craft with him. Her exhausted legs had hardly been able to carry her up the metal steps onto the ship. Her rucksack had felt like it weighed a ton.

She'd been pulled on board by the ship's workers, one of whom had taken her down to the galley kitchen, where the cook – a Dutchman with a huge ginger beard and kind green eyes – had given her a bowl of lentil soup. She'd eaten it greedily, shivering violently in the corner, as the men had talked around her, clearly flummoxed by this soot-covered lone girl adrift in the ocean. She hadn't been able to explain to them what had happened to her. She hadn't known where to start.

When they'd eventually arrived in Cochin, the cook, Matteau, had escorted her onto the dock. He'd given her sympathetic looks as they'd driven into town, the rickshaw splashing through the muddy streets in the rain, and he'd asked the driver to wait outside the Portuguese church.

Leila had stared up at the pale building, rain lashing the facade, the statue of the Virgin Mary on the roof looking as forlorn as she'd felt. With a little coaxing, she'd followed Matteau up the steps, her teeth chattering with cold and fear.

Inside, the air had smelt of incense and dust, and a priest had been whistling, his voice echoing around the cavernous church. He'd been friendly as the cook had explained in broken English that they'd found Leila floating alone on a boat. Leila had listened to them debating what to do with her as she'd sat on the pew, terrified that God must know her tremendous sin.

The priest had taken her to the back of the church and wrapped her in a musty-smelling robe. Then he'd called a boy and had given him a note.

Leila had been asleep on a pile of prayer cushions when the nun had arrived, drifting towards Leila in her long blue habit with such a kind smile on her face that for a second, Leila wondered if she'd died and gone to heaven by accident.

'I am Sister Mary,' the nun had told her, her English heavy with a Portuguese accent. 'Come with me, child.'

For the next few days, Leila had hardly been able to speak, her grief had been so huge. But slowly, over the next few months in the peaceful mission, Sister Mary had skilfully extracted nearly the whole story out of Leila. She'd been cautious to edit the truth, of course. She hadn't told Sister Mary about the drugs she'd found in the lighthouse or about Adam and what he'd done to her.

But she'd sobbed uncontrollably when she'd admitted to Sister Mary that Bibi was dead and that she herself alone was responsible for the fire, although the nun had repeatedly told her that this couldn't be the case. But Leila wouldn't be comforted. The facts were true and insurmountable. It was because of her that everyone and everything on Lace Island had been destroyed. It had all been her fault. She alone had been responsible for burning paradise.

For hours each day, she had vigorously scrubbed the missionary chapel's floor in silent penance, waiting for God to find some appropriate way to punish her, the vision of Bibi's room in an inferno of flames etched on her mind.

But the monotonous routine had stayed the same, and over time, Leila had come to find solace in being left in silence. She'd liked the quiet, high chanting in the early mornings, the calm of the nuns' services, the gentle balm of prayer, the cool cloistered garden with the view of the hills and the beehives Sister Vimla was so proud of. Surrounded by such tranquil beauty, Leila had put her wholehearted effort into asking for God's forgiveness.

Deciding not to torture herself with what had been lost,

she'd taken the visitors book, which had survived in her back-pack throughout the ordeal, and wrapped it in a plastic bag before lifting one of the loose grilles in the flagstone floor of the chapel and placing it carefully beneath. Each time she'd thought of a sad memory, or of what she'd lost, she'd tried to bury it too, deep within herself. She'd tried to ignore all the pain and had concentrated on prayer and living in the moment.

For a long time, she'd even managed to ignore what had been happening to her body, but soon she hadn't been able to hide it any longer from the nuns. When the kicks inside her had made her gasp out loud, Sister Mary had banned Leila from scrubbing the floor and had summoned her to the office to explain herself.

Leila had shamefully relived that horrendous day with Adam and how he'd brutally taken her virginity, and as she'd tearfully spoken, she'd finally admitted to herself what she'd known for several months: she was carrying Adam's baby. She hadn't told the sister her plan – that as soon as the child was born, she was going to take it outside the mission walls and leave it on the steps of the British Consulate. There were bound to be people out there like the Everdenes – kind people, good people, who would cherish a baby and bring it up as their own.

But as far as Leila had been concerned, she'd just wanted it out of her and gone forever. She didn't even want to so much as look at it.

Sister Mary could sense Leila's reticence towards her unborn child without having to hear any of her inner thoughts and had pleaded with her. She must have someone – some relative, somewhere – who could assist Leila now, in her hour of need? This wasn't a maternity hospital, she'd explained. The sisters might not be able to help her when her time came, but Leila had begged her to let her stay and to keep her whereabouts a secret. She'd seen that the old nun was torn, but in the end, Sister Mary had agreed to give Leila more time to work out what she was going to do.

And so Leila had carried on, pretending nothing was happening. That was until the searing, stabbing pain of her first contraction had brought her straight back to reality. In the dead of night in the small cell that was her bedroom, she'd grabbed on to the iron bed for support, gasping with terror, before the scream with her next contraction had brought the nuns running.

The next few hours had been terrifying. But eventually, Mother Nature had taken over, and with Sister Mary's help, Leila had pushed out a baby into the world. She saw the nuns gasp, and one of them, Sister Agnes, had crossed herself before kissing Sister Vimla, tears streaming down her face.

'God bless you and your baby,' Sister Mary had said, her eyes shining as she'd carefully lifted a bloodied bundle of flesh towards Leila.

Leila had recoiled, squeezing her eyes shut. She hadn't wanted even to look at the baby, but Sister Mary had simply placed the baby on Leila's chest. And curiosity had made Leila open her eyes.

And that had been that.

Leila sighed now, trying to remember that first, heady scent of her baby's head. How she'd looked at that small face, those huge eyes staring up at her, her little limbs flailing.

'She's yours,' Sister Mary had said, wrapping a towel round the baby, over Leila. 'And she needs you.'

And right there and then, as Leila had felt the smallest of fingers reaching out to grip her own little finger with surprising force, she'd fallen in love.

A love so powerful it had been like falling off a cliff. And

Bibi had been there too, right there in that little girl's angelic face, and despite everything she'd planned, Leila had known with absolute conviction that she would do everything in her power to look after this precious gift from God. That she was her girl. And that she would love her no matter what.

Leila smiled now, a rare smile, picked up her worn Bible from the scuffed cabinet beside her bed and held it to her chest, knowing she would open it and go through the precious cargo hidden between its pages, torturing herself with longing in the yawning hours till dawn.

CHAPTER FIFTY-TWO

Miami, present day

'You don't understand,' Jess said to the nonchalant woman at the airline desk at Miami Airport. 'I have to leave *right now*.'

'Let me see,' the woman said, rattling the keys of the computer. She was wearing heavy make-up, with painted-on fawn eyebrows and the unflattering red uniform of Jess's rival airline, but Jess wasn't going to let on that she was industry herself. Not unless she had to.

Above her, a colourful hoarding advertised the joys of Miami Beach, and pop music blasted out. The tannoy announced a flight, adding to the din, and everywhere there were people – all sorts of people, travelling on escalators, meeting family, pulling luggage, talking, eating, living normally. None of them as desperate as Jess.

'I can get you on a flight to Paris?' the woman said, checking her watch.

'Fine. I'll take it.'

'You'll have to go to the gate almost straight away,' she said, printing a boarding pass as Jess pulled out her credit card from her purse with shaking fingers. 'Do you have any luggage?'

'No. I'm just . . . This is everything I have.'

Jess saw the woman give her colleague on the next desk a wide-eyed look. She must look a total sight, Jess realized: a desperate-looking woman in a white wedding dress and trainers, with a leather handbag, a hoody falling out of it.

Grabbing her boarding pass, Jess hurried to the ladies' toilets, her dress making a rustling sound as she moved. As she walked through the doorway, her phone rang again, and when she took it out of her bag and saw Blaise's number, she let out a small yelp. She threw the phone in the sink as if it were burning her. When it stopped ringing, she ripped it open and took out the battery, broke the SIM card and put the whole lot in a sanitary disposal unit.

At the sink, she cupped cold water and washed the sweat from her face; then she stared at herself in the mirror. Her make-up, which had been so beautiful just an hour ago, was smudged now, and mascara ran underneath her eyes. She pulled at a tissue in the dispenser and wiped her face, forcing the hysterical tears inside her down. She panted out a pent-up breath.

'Don't panic,' she said aloud to herself, but it was hard not to, as she gripped the sink for support.

Blaise would have been waiting for her with the registrar in the hotel function room, the rain pounding on the windows. She thought of the dark look that must have crossed his face when he'd realized that Jess wasn't going to show up. She thought of Tilly and how, by now, she'd be loving all the drama, as they searched the hotel for Jess.

And then they would come here, Jess thought. Soon. They'd realize she'd got a cab from the hotel to the airport and they'd come here looking for her. And it wouldn't be hard to find her. She couldn't be more conspicuous in her wedding dress.

She'll be disposed of.

She was putty in my hands.

This is what you were paid all that money for.

Blaise and Lance's cruel words tolled inside her head like a bell. She stared at her reflection and removed the diamanté tiara from her head. It clattered into the sink.

A woman came into the toilets now with a red wheelie case. She was a large lady in her fifties, with bouffy strawberry-blonde hair curled like it had been set at a hairdresser's, and she had lots of blue eyeshadow on and bright pink lipstick.

Jess blew out a breath, forcing herself not to cry. Not yet. She couldn't break down yet.

'Hey, hon – are you OK?' the woman asked, concerned. She looked around, as if she were wondering if she'd stumbled inadvertently onto a film set and there were hidden cameras.

'No, not really,' Jess said, grateful for the lady's smile in the mirror. She dabbed at her eyes with the tissue. 'To be honest, I'm having a very bad day.'

'Oh,' the woman said. 'Well, I'm sorry to hear that, honey.'

Jess nodded, swallowing down tears.

'That's a very fancy dress,' the woman said, nodding at Jess's attire. 'Lovely, in fact,' she said, stepping closer and taking in the detail. 'My daughter is getting married. As a matter of fact, I'm flying to Minneapolis to go shopping with her for dresses. She'd love this one.'

Next to her now, Jess saw the woman eyeing up the dress, with its lace overlay and diamanté and pearl detail.

The woman came closer now and touched the fabric. 'Look at that,' she said in an awed voice.

Jess suddenly felt a glimmer of hope.

'You want it?' she said. 'The dress, I mean. It's brand new. I didn't even get married in it.' Jess struggled to keep her voice from sounding too crazy.

The woman's eyebrows shot up.

'It cost thirty thousand dollars, but I'll swap it for a pair of jeans and a shirt . . . anything I can wear instead,' Jess hurried on. 'I bet your daughter would love it.' She fished out the tiara from the sink. 'There's this too,' she added.

The woman shook her head suddenly, as if coming to her senses. 'I couldn't possibly. No. I want to go shopping with her.'

'It's a *free* designer dress. I mean it,' Jess urged her. 'I'm desperate. I'm running away and I can't run away in this dress. So if you'll help me get it off . . .' she said, turning round and pointing at the row of tiny silk buttons, which she couldn't reach herself. It had taken Tilly half an hour to do them up earlier.

'I don't know,' the woman said, backing off.

'I know this sounds crazy, but please. You've got to help me,' Jess implored, grabbing the woman's arm. 'My fiancé, he, he . . .' she began, but then the tears came, making it difficult to carry on. 'I was going to marry him and then I found out . . .'

The woman, seeing Jess's tears, took pity on her and softened. 'There. There,' she comforted. 'What did he do,' she said, 'if you don't mind me asking?'

'You don't want to know,' Jess said. 'But' – she took a deep, shuddering breath, pulling out more paper towels from the dispenser and wiping her face – 'all I know is that everything he ever told me was a lie.'

'Oh, honey, that's tough,' the woman said. She patted Jess's shoulder.

'He had another girlfriend all along and—' Jess stopped, too overwhelmed by the truth to carry on. The woman wouldn't believe her if she told her that she'd been set up from the beginning and that Blaise was bargaining with her life. That she was part of some other purpose she couldn't possibly begin to understand.

'I can't believe he'd do something so terrible to someone as pretty as you,' she said.

'Have you got any clothes? Anything at all I can change into?' Jess asked.

'Well, look here. I've got these things I've picked up for my daughter,' the woman said, looking in a carrier bag that was balanced on top of the wheelie case. She pulled out some leggings, a T-shirt and a baseball hat.

'Those are perfect. I'll swap for the dress,' Jess said, turning round again for the woman to unfasten her buttons.

'No, no, I couldn't,' the woman said, but Jess could see she was tempted.

'I insist. But please. Hurry.'

Soon, Jess was out of the dress, and she quickly changed into the leggings and T-shirt. She helped the woman bundle up the dress, squashing it down inside her case.

'What will you do now?' the woman asked. 'Will you be OK?'

Jess swallowed hard, putting the baseball cap on in the mirror. If she went home to London, then Blaise could find her easily. If she went back to work, then he would find her too.

The only person who could possibly help her find out her connection to Lace Island was Suresh. But Suresh was on the other side of the world. How could she possibly ask him to help her? Would she help him out, if their situations were reversed? she wondered.

She looked at her reflection.
She had no choice.
'I'm going to find out the truth,' she said.

CHAPTER FIFTY-THREE

Lace Island, present day

In the night, the baby woke up and cried. Quietly at first, then a rasping 'Wah, wah, wah.' Leila was immediately alert. She reached down into the Moses basket next to her bed and pulled up the baby into her embrace.

'There, there,' she said, soothing her baby girl, kissing the tiny red cheeks and trying to unfurl the angry clenched fists. She was a fighter all right, Leila thought.

She felt her breasts tingling and she pulled aside her night-gown, the baby's mouth open, wobbling its head from side to side as if it could find its way by scent alone.

'Here you go, darling,' Leila said, feeling the sharp, sweet pinch as the baby's mouth latched onto her nipple.

She leant backwards, carefully adjusting the pillow behind her as the baby suckled, amazed that her body could do this so naturally. She smiled down, her palm stroking the fine, downy hair on her baby's perfect head.

'I'll look after you, baby girl,' she whispered. 'I won't let you go.'

The baby relaxed as she fed, her little fist unclenching, until finally, she was done. Then Leila lifted her into a hug, resting her on her shoulder, feeling the weight of her precious baby in her arms. She stood and paced over the cold flagstones and hummed the lullaby that Bibi used to sing to her, conjuring in her mind her sun-filled bedroom and Bibi's calm hands. She rubbed her baby's back as Bibi had rubbed hers, and in giving comfort found it too.

This little being had brought the only peace Leila had found since leaving Lace Island. She was like a ray of sunshine in an otherwise bleak, ashen desert. In the quiet sanctuary of the nun's cell, Leila breathed in the milky scent, kissing her baby's head over and over, feeling love flowing out of her, hoping she could fill up her child, hoping that she'd never have to experience anything like Leila had. That whatever happened, Leila would protect and shield her.

But where? Leila was starting to worry. She knew she couldn't stay here at the nuns' mission forever. It was no place to bring up a child. Sister Mary had even said as much herself last week, when the baby had been twelve weeks old. It wasn't healthy, the sister said, for the other nuns to bond so much with the baby. Already Sister Agnes had had a crisis of conscience over the life of piety she'd chosen. Leila could see why. The baby had filled the cool nunnery walls with a giggling reminder of life, bringing joy to everyone who looked at her.

Leila gently bounced the baby on her shoulder, listening to her contented gurgling sounds. It wouldn't be long until she fell asleep again, but she loved holding her like this, feeling the warmth of her small body against her shoulder, her face burrowed into Leila's neck, her small hand gripping Bibi's chain, which Leila always wore. She whispered stories to get her to sleep about Tusker the elephant down by the lagoon, and Parva hanging out the colourful silk saris on the line to dry, and the cricket matches in the grove and Rasa.

Dear Rasa. Leila's heart longed for him so often. She'd thought many times of asking Sister Mary to try and find him, but each time, she remembered what had happened and her nerve deserted her. After his father's death, Leila was the last person in the world Rasa would want to hear from, not to mention what had happened to his friends and family on Lace Island. She dreaded to think how many people had died. Each time she thought of everyone – Parva, Maliba, little Mina – her heart contracted with a pain she couldn't shake, followed closely by an intense fear. What if the police found her? She'd be thrown in prison for the rest of her life for starting the fire.

But still a thought nagged. Surely Rasa would be glad to hear from her, glad to know that at least she'd made it out?

No. No. It was impossible, Leila decided. Rasa wouldn't want to know her now that she had a baby, and Leila couldn't show him her daughter. She didn't want Rasa to think of Adam every time he looked at the child. She wouldn't have that horrible man's name mentioned. She barely could admit it to herself: that Adam was the father of this precious, darling girl. As far as she was concerned, the baby was hers and hers alone.

The baby's breathing had fallen into a gentle rhythm and Leila tiptoed over to the Moses basket and laid down her daughter. She stared down at her in the soft light, drinking in the features of her perfect face and her little rosebud mouth.

'I love you,' she whispered, stroking her head before gently tucking in around her the soft yellow blanket she'd knitted. Then she got into the bed next to the basket, pulling the pillow under her head so that she could stare down at her daughter.

Her little Jessica. It felt weird to say her name, and it had taken months to find the right one, but Leila was glad that she'd found it. She wanted her girl to have a Western name, and Jessica was a sweet name, meaning 'Precious Gift from

God'. Which everyone in the mission agreed she most certainly was.

Leila had nearly drifted back into a contented sleep herself when the silence of the mission was broken by a distant clanking of the doorbell and she sat bolt upright in bed. It was always silent at this time of night, but now there were hurried footsteps in the corridor and raised voices.

A sudden commotion outside the room made Leila's heart pound. She heard Sister Mary's protests as the door was punched open. And then the doorway was filled with the unmistakable silhouette of her stepfather and Leila felt the bottom dropping out of her world.

'So this is where you've been hiding,' Chan said, running his hand over his slicked-back hair.

Leila stared desperately at Sister Mary, seeing the truth in her terrified face. Despite all of Leila's protests, she must have sent word to Lace Island that Leila was here with her baby.

Leila's brain was scrabbling over the facts, but all the time, she felt as if the ground were disappearing beneath her like quicksand. How was it possible he was here? And if Chan was still alive, did that mean that others survived the fire? Had Bibi and Parva got out too?

She took in the cold glint of triumph in Chan's eyes as he saw her shock. Any pretence that there was real affection between them was long gone.

'Oh? And what have we here?' Chan said, his eyes wide as he registered the baby. 'Is this *the* baby?'

Leila had no time to contemplate what he meant. Instead, she felt bile rising in her throat as she saw Shang stroll through the doorway. She cowered, shielding her baby in the Moses basket and grabbing at the neck of her robe.

Shang strode towards her and pushed her roughly aside and she cried out. Quickly, he yanked the baby out of the Moses basket, the yellow blanket falling to the floor.

'Don't take her. Don't,' Leila screamed, lunging towards him.

The baby woke now, crying out. Shang held little Jessica away from Leila in his huge hand, like she was a ball he was about to throw. Sister Mary tried now to jump up and take the baby, but Shang punched her hard with his other hand. Leila cried out as Sister Mary fell to the floor with a thud, pulling the water jug on the sideboard down with her. It smashed on the flagstones. The baby wailed even louder.

'No,' Leila screamed, launching herself at Shang, but Chan strode towards her, slapping her hard in the face.

'Stop it right now and listen,' he said, his voice laden with menace.

Terrified tears spilt down Leila's face as Shang backed away with the baby.

'Please, Chan, please,' she begged. 'Leave me alone.'

'After finding you? Not a chance,' he said. 'Do you know how much damage you've done? How much mayhem you've caused? With that fire you started?'

'Don't harm her,' Leila whimpered, her eyes not leaving her baby.

'Because now you're going to have to put it right.'

'Please don't harm her.'

Chan held her face, forcing her to stare at him. 'If you want her to live, then you will do exactly as I say.'

Leila wept, her eyes darting to Shang, who was now at the door. 'Please,' she sobbed.

'Well, that is all down to you. Because from now on, her life will depend on how well you behave,' Chan said.

'What do you mean? No. You're not taking her from me. You can't,' Leila sobbed.

'Oh, I can. She's going far away. But we will know where she is. And if you want her to stay alive, then you will come back to Lace Island and do as I say.'

'Don't take her. I beg you.'

'Pack her things now,' Chan demanded. 'Put them in here,' he said, nodding to Shang, who reached behind the door. He threw Chan a leather bag.

'Do as they say, Leila,' Sister Mary whimpered, sitting up on the floor. She could see the other nuns now in the corridor. She couldn't put them in danger too.

Leila's hands were trembling as she pulled the small collection of baby clothes from the drawers in her room. She could hardly see, her eyes were so full of tears, and her hands were shaking violently. But she knew she had to do what Chan said. Even so, her mind was racing, desperate to find a way out. Desperate for them not to take her baby.

'Why are you doing this?' she said, her voice choking.

'Because that stupid mother of yours should have left Lace Island to me, but she left it to you,' Chan hissed. 'Now I have found you, you will do as I say. Hurry.'

The baby's cry was hysterical and Leila whimpered, the noise cutting her heart like razor blades. Quickly, she pulled off the chain that Bibi had given her from round her neck and put it in the bag. Then Chan snatched the bag and threw it to Shang in the doorway. Without a backwards glance, Shang left, the baby's screams echoing through the mission corridors.

Leila woke in a full body sweat. The dream again. The same dream.

She always woke at the same point. With the sound of

Shang's heavy footsteps and her baby's desperate crying making her heart shatter.

Sitting up in bed, she picked up the Bible from her bedside, leafing between the pages for the precious photographs.

One photograph for every year. That's the deal she'd made with Chan. And that's what she'd been given. One photograph of her darling daughter to prove that she was alive. In return for Leila doing Chan's bidding.

The photographs were everything to Leila. With them, she had just about been able to bear the fact that her paradise had become a prison, knowing that her baby was growing up in the real world, a free woman.

And she *was* free. Of that Leila was sure. Jessica was living free of any knowledge of where she came from. And she would never know, according to Chan.

But she must be curious, surely? Leila thought, flicking through the pictures. Didn't she ever think of her mother? Couldn't she sense how often Leila prayed so desperately for her safety and happiness? How every fibre of Leila's being longed for her, like a physical ache she could never cure? Could she not sense her mother's longing – even though she was on the other side of the world? Surely this love, this secret love Leila had inside her, must have some kind of power? Because if it had the power to keep Leila alive, it must have the power to reach her daughter.

Or maybe it didn't. Maybe she was just kidding herself. Keeping herself alive with a hope that was simply foolish.

Now Leila tortured herself, staring at the photograph Chan had given her last month. The one she'd been holding out for. It showed her baby – a young woman now – standing on the steps of a grey building, dressed in black. Her face was pale and drawn, and Leila ran her finger down the image of her cheek as if she could smudge the tears away. Why was she crying? What had happened to make her darling girl so sad? Leila ached to comfort her, to know what was going on in her life.

She heard the footsteps coming up the concrete steps from the yard outside and quickly replaced the photographs in the Bible, tying it with its ribbon before placing it back in the bedside drawer and wedging it shut.

'Get up,' she heard Hakem's rough voice, before her door was unlocked from the outside. 'The boys are hungry for breakfast.'

Quickly, Leila got up, not bothering to change from the clothes she slept in. She walked out of her cell at the back of the kitchen and looked out, a glimmer of a new dawn lighting the sky in the east.

As usual, she pretended to herself that this wasn't Lace Island. The Lace Island in her heart had gone forever. Because where there had once been those endless lush green paddy fields were fields of ugly dull green poppy heads.

She could hear the gruff voices of the workers as they woke up in the makeshift barracks where they slept. Soon they would demand their morning chai and the sticky rice Leila made. Then the day's heroin harvest would begin.

CHAPTER FIFTY-FOUR

Cochin, present day

All the bravado Jess had felt in Miami Airport had deserted her by the time she arrived, nearly twenty-four stress-filled hours later, into the suffocating heat of Cochin. She felt wrung out and exhausted, her terror that she might be being followed having made any kind of sleep impossible. Not that she could possibly imagine sleeping with all the questions churning round and round in her head.

And now, the most relevant question of all made her almost ask the cab driver to turn round and take her back to the airport. What the hell was Suresh going to say when she turned up unannounced?

The driver was talking loudly on a mobile phone, waving at her to get out. Gripping the business card Suresh had given her, Jess stepped out of the air-conditioned cab into the wall of heat on the Cochin street. The noise of the honking horns and the bicycle bells made her jump as the traffic swerved round the cab. Fumbling, she paid the driver, and still talking on his phone, he sped off, completely oblivious to the turmoil she was feeling.

Disorientated, Jess stood staring across the wide pavement

to the white building in front of her with its wrought-iron balconies. She looked again at the card in her hand. This must be it: Suresh's office.

People bustled past her, mopeds zooming, lorries honking, a waft of cinnamon coming on the hot breeze, someone chanting prayers, the high-pitched voice of a woman singing loudly blaring from the speaker on the front of a multicoloured bus. She watched it, full of passengers holding on, the sound distorting as it passed her.

Jess had never felt culture shock so profound as she felt now. And after all the anguish she'd gone through since she'd left Miami, she felt her nerve deserting her. If someone so much as pushed her, she might crumble into dust.

Suresh would think she was mad, surely? She couldn't just turn up like this without warning him first. But without her phone, it had been impossible to call ahead.

Maybe she should find a hotel, she thought, trying to stop the trembling feeling inside her. Maybe she should settle in, clean up and then call Suresh and arrange a meeting at his office. He might not even be in Cochin, she thought, amazed at the kind of assumptions her panic had inspired. He might be away on business. Or with Kareena. It was the weekend, after all.

'Think, Jess,' she said out loud, but getting here had taken all her strength and it was as if her feet couldn't move.

And that's when she saw a man coming down the pavement towards her. He was wearing a cream linen suit and carrying a leather satchel, and was talking on a mobile phone. She watched him pause in the street, ending the call. And at that moment, everything stopped.

Because it was him. Suresh. Her dear Suresh. And the sight of him made Jess gasp.

She watched him glance in her direction and do a double-take. Then he slowly took off his sunglasses as if he couldn't believe his eyes. A moment later, he was running towards her.

'Jess?' he said, gripping her arm. 'Is it really you?'

She nodded mutely, too overwhelmed to speak.

'What is it? What's happened?' he asked. 'Aren't you getting married?'

It was only now, seeing Suresh's friendly face, that she felt the magnitude of what had happened. She felt her knees trembling and Suresh frowned and put his arms round her, pulling her into a hug that was so exactly what she needed she cried out a great sob of anguish.

'Come,' Suresh said. 'I have my car down here. I was going home anyway. You must come.'

She nodded, trying to pull herself together. With his arm still round her shoulder, he escorted her along the road and down an alleyway between the buildings. At the back was a car park, and she heard an electronic beep as he unlocked a smart navy-blue BMW. She climbed into the passenger seat and he turned on the engine.

'I'm sorry,' she said, her voice cracking. 'I'm so sorry to turn up like this. I can explain.'

Suresh put his arm round the headrest of her seat and reversed, looking at her with concern, until he'd pulled out of the car park.

'There will be cooler air in a moment,' he said, fiddling with the dials on the dashboard. Jess nodded and sat with her handbag in her lap, her chin wobbling, fat tears rolling unbidden down her face. She could sense Suresh's confusion. He reached past her and opened the glove compartment as he drove, pulling out a box of tissues. 'Here,' he said.

'Thanks,' she said, wiping her eyes. 'I'm so sorry. I didn't know what else to do. Where else to go.'

'What has happened, Jess?' Suresh said, looking at her, then in the rear-view mirror and swerving onto the highway. He expertly weaved into a faster lane and soon they were travelling at some speed, the city flashing below them.

Jess tried to compose herself. Then, in a tumbling jumble of words, she told him the main facts. About the wedding and what she'd overheard Blaise saying.

'Wait,' Suresh said, holding up his hand, his eyes wide as they met hers. 'You heard him say that he'd deliberately found you? And the whole thing was a set-up?'

Jess nodded, relieved that Suresh was almost as shocked as she had been. 'And the thing is, I've been going over and over it and I can only assume that I must have some kind of connection to Lace Island,' she said. '*That's* why Blaise found me. That's why he made me sign that prenuptial agreement saying what was mine was his. And I'm so confused, and I'm sorry. I'm sorry to barge in on you like this.'

'Stop apologizing,' Suresh said, shaking his head, trying to take in everything she'd said. 'It's fine. My apartment is close now. Here we are,' he added, indicating off the highway.

They drove past several large hoardings and then into a modern-looking residential area. Jess looked at the patch of grass under the steel legs of the hoardings, a mangy dog staring back at her. A man selling tea from a cart watched their car speed past.

'What about Kareena?' Jess asked.

'She's at the network this weekend.'

Jess nodded, not sure what to make of the way he'd said it. Or how easily he'd agreed to let her come to his apartment. All she knew was how glad she was that she didn't have to deal with Kareena right now, or explain herself.

Instead, she told Suresh about swapping her wedding dress in Miami Airport for the clothes she was wearing.

'That will be some story for the bride's mother to tell,' Suresh said, with a friendly laugh. 'She certainly got a bargain.'

It was only now that she realized how little she had in the whole world. Not that she really needed anything, but all her clothes, her make-up, everything was in the hotel room in Miami. She didn't care, though, she realized. None of it mattered.

She looks like a gold-digger. I could see it straight away.

I bombarded her with flowers, gifts, clothes. Stuff she could brag about with the cabin crew. Threw budget at it.

Jess felt another shiver of fury run through her as Suresh indicated and turned off the road by a block of high-rise apartments into an underground car park. How wrong Blaise had been. It had never been about the money. Hadn't he known her at all?

Jess thought back to that awful meeting a few weeks ago with his family at the Dorchester. How on earth had he explained to his mother what he was doing? Were they all in on it? They must have been. Or had they even been his real family? Maybe they'd been actors, Jess realized now.

Because now she thought back to Blaise after they'd gone, the way he'd been – as if he was having a crisis of confidence. *You're a good person.* That's what he'd said. Maybe that was the only honest thing he ever had said to her.

Because she was a good person, and he . . . he . . . he was a lousy, manipulative, cheating—

'It's not much,' Suresh apologized as he parked in a space, interrupting her internal rant. He got out of the car, and Jess did too, the doors echoing in the gloomy concrete space as they shut them. She walked with Suresh to a stairwell, and he nodded to the guard, who was reading a newspaper.

'This will set tongues wagging,' Suresh said in a whisper as he pressed the button for the lift. 'Everyone knows everyone's business in this building.'

'I don't want to cause any problems for you,' Jess said. 'Or Kareena.'

'It's fine,' he said with a reassuring smile, but Jess wondered whether it really was fine as they stepped inside the lift. She could see the curious face of the guard staring at her and Suresh.

'Please prepare yourself. My apartment isn't very grand. And this damned lift . . .' he said, jabbing the button on the control panel. Slowly, the doors closed.

'You have no idea how grateful I am. I had nowhere else to turn.'

Suresh gave her arm an awkward squeeze.

His apartment was simple but elegant, with bright purple-and-green flowery wallpaper in each room and black modern furniture. The effect was rather stylish, and she saw how house-proud he was, falling over himself to clear things away.

In the small bathroom, Suresh explained the complexities of the water system, but Jess didn't care. It was a shower. She felt awful borrowing what was almost certainly Kareena's shampoo and body wash, and her clean cotton robe, but Suresh was insistent that she treat this as her home.

As she stood in the shower, feeling safe for the first time since being in Miami, Jess tried to make sense of everything that had happened, but it was as if months', years' worth of emotions had been crammed into just a few days. In another, parallel universe, right now she would have been on her honeymoon with Blaise. He'd suggested Venice and she'd accepted willingly, awed by his romantic gesture. Now she wondered if that had been one big lie too. Maybe once they'd been legally married, he'd have turned on her straight away. Would he really have gone through the charade and expense of a honeymoon? Was he even who he said he was at all? If the apartment in New York had been hired, what else had been fake? She thought of the engagement ring she had put in the pocket of her rucksack on the flight to Paris. Was that a real diamond? Probably not. Blaise had saved the real diamonds for Porscha.

She shook her head, still reeling from the level of his deception. Had they been laughing at her behind her back the whole time when she'd been in Ibiza? The thought made her furious. Perhaps Tilly's offer of friendship had been a set-up too?

In one sense, she felt relieved, she realized. Because a little voice inside her all along had told her that Blaise was too good to be true. That a dream man like him wasn't possible for a girl like her, but it hurt. Man, it hurt to be *so* wrong.

She should have listened to her gut instinct. Because when she didn't, that's when things had always gone wrong, and *now* where did she stand?

She growled, her impotent rage growing. If only she had more answers.

Should she have stayed? she wondered, as she dried herself. Had she left too soon? Perhaps she should have challenged Blaise and demanded to know the truth. But a liar like him would never have told her the truth, she reminded herself. No, it was much better that she'd got away.

She'll be disposed of.

She shuddered, terrified by how much danger she'd been in. How much she might still be in. She had to work out *why*

384

Blaise had done what he'd done and why she'd been chosen before they found her.

Suresh was cooking when she found him in the kitchen, and he'd changed out of his suit into some long cotton trousers and a loose cotton shirt. He was chopping up ginger on a wooden board, a large pestle and mortar on the worktop in front of him, filled with spices.

'That smells good,' she said, peering into the bubbling curry in the saucepan on the stove. A rice steamer was chugging, and there was a bowl of freshly chopped salad and chapattis on the table. She was touched that he'd already rustled up all of this for her.

'I thought you must be hungry. When was the last time you ate anything?' he asked.

'I can't remember,' she said, with a small smile.

It was like her life was split into two. Then and now.

'You want a beer?' he asked, opening the fridge, and she nodded.

She watched as Suresh poured her beer into a glass, and then she chinked glasses with him.

'Thank you,' she said, staring into his eyes.

'What are friends for,' he said, turning away quickly. 'Ah. It's almost time.'

'Time for what?'

'Pass me the remote.'

He flapped his hand at the table and Jess passed him the black remote control. He pressed it at the TV on a bracket on the wall in the top corner and with some loud intro music it flickered onto the news.

'There she is,' Suresh said, smiling over at Jess.

She watched the screen and saw Kareena on it, talking

direct to camera. She looked amazing, Jess thought, her make-up heavy but perfect, her hair perfect too. She was wearing a light blue suit and looked like a woman who was very definitely in control.

'Wow,' Jess said, feeling more deflated than she could cope with. She looked at Suresh, his eyes shining with pride.

'She'd kill me if I missed it,' he explained. 'She's just been promoted.'

'Good for her. She looks incredible.'

'I tell her that, but she doesn't believe it.' He glanced across at Jess. 'But between you and me, this is absolutely the best bit,' he said, pressing the mute button at the TV.

Jess laughed, but she felt guilty. She couldn't tell if he was joking or not.

'It's good to see that smile at last,' he said.

'I feel like I've been run over.'

'Well, emotionally, you have. Some food will make you feel better, though. I promise. It's Mummy's recipe. She always gave me this when I was feeling sad.'

She smiled, liking the way he said 'Mummy'. As if his mum was part of him. Someone who had the power to make him feel happy, no matter what.

He now served up two plates of delicious-smelling vegetable dhal and turmeric rice, and brought them over to the table, carefully placing a plate in front of Jess, whose mouth started watering instantly.

'Eat, eat,' he urged, and Jess wanted to cry with gratitude.

After she'd complimented Suresh profusely on his home cooking, he started talking urgently.

'So, while you were in the shower, I got busy. My assistant just called from the office. I hope you don't mind, but I had to explain what had happened.'

She wondered what else she'd disrupted by suddenly turning up in Suresh's life.

'Anyway, she's done some digging around. One of our partners, many years ago, was vaguely involved with the affairs of Lace Island, so she'd heard of it.'

'Oh?'

'Lace Island is privately owned. Or was. Bibi, as everyone called her, died in the fire, but if her descendants are alive, then they will have inherited Lace Island.'

'Descendants?'

'She had a daughter, Leila. And if she's alive, then Lace Island would belong to her, and then – according to the land laws – to her daughter.'

Jess remembered Blaise's face now when she'd asked him in London if he was buying Lace Island and he'd said, 'It's complicated.'

Leila stared at Suresh, this information sinking in. 'Do you think . . . ?' she began, feeling her mouth go dry at the possibility. 'Do you think that means I'm . . .'

'. . . related to Leila or Bibi?' Suresh said, finishing the sentence for her. He shrugged. 'Maybe. Maybe that's the answer. Maybe that's what all this means. Maybe that's why they found you. Whoever "they" are.'

Leila blew out a breath, something trembling deep inside her. Fear? Anticipation? Hope? She couldn't tell. She only knew she'd never felt anything like this in her life. As if a door to the truth that she'd been banging on for so long was finally creaking open.

'Do you think she's still alive? Leila, I mean?'

'Who knows? What I do know is that Lace Island pays above and beyond its revenues in tax, so there must be people on it. But strangely, my assistant says that the files on it are blocked. I called my friend in the police department. He says there are no accessible files on the computers in the police department either. Someone, somewhere is making sure it stays completely off the radar.'

Jess pushed her hair back from her face, too overwhelmed to eat for a moment.

'I think I need to go to Lace Island,' she said. 'See what is there. *Who* is there. That's the only way I can start to put this puzzle together.'

'I agree,' Suresh said, shovelling rice into his chapatti with his fingers. 'We'll leave in the morning.'

'You'll come with me?'

'You think I'd let you go alone? We'll take my friend's boat. It's a good day's sailing, but I've looked at the weather. If we leave first thing, we can make it there by nightfall.'

CHAPTER FIFTY-FIVE

Lace Island, present day

It was late, and after a grubby day in the fields, the workers sat in the makeshift canteen, with its wooden benches and corrugated-iron roof, passing the opium pipe round, one of them leering at Leila as she cleared away their dirty metal supper plates. She knew if they could, they'd touch her, but she kept her eyes downcast, like the slave she was. Instead, she clanked their plates to show her displeasure, before taking them up the concrete steps to the kitchen.

Chan had told her once to smoke with the workers, that it would dull her memories, but Leila used her denial as a small means of defiance. It was only tiny acts of rebellion like this that had kept her going all these years.

On her way back to the table for the next lot of plates, she picked up a nushtar from the ground outside the kitchen door. It was one of the small knives used for slicing the poppy heads, its tiny sharp blades just millimetres apart. Leila chucked it in the rough wooden box with the others.

Now, she felt the hairs on the back of her neck rising when she saw that Hakem was standing blocking her path. He was tall, with a shaved head, and he stared down at her, that cruel, sly smile on his lips as he sucked on a toothpick. Leila fought not to show any emotion on her face.

It was Hakem who was the foreman on Lace Island and ruled the workers with a grip of terror. When Shang was away, it was Hakem who did his bidding and made sure that everything ran smoothly. And it was Hakem who locked her into her room every night, like a dog.

He got a perverse kind of thrill out of it, Leila knew. She'd heard one of the guards say that he'd been a torturer in Burma when he'd been younger and Leila could believe it. He was a psychopath, as far she was concerned. Left to his own devices, he'd torture and rape her without any mercy, but because of Chan, he couldn't touch her.

She saw him sneering down at her now and she longed to take one of the nushtars and slit his throat. She imagined how sticky and satisfying his blood would feel on her hands.

'Clear all this up,' he said, 'and make breakfast earlier tomorrow. The shipment is going out. The workers are needed at the dock.'

Leila nodded, not making eye contact with him.

'And don't think I'm not watching you,' he added.

She said nothing, hating the way he always reminded her of the one time she'd tried to escape on the boat. How a momentary lapse in Hakem's concentration had given her the opportunity to get on board with the heroin shipment bound for the States. It had been such a spur-of-the-moment impulse, but in that moment, she'd imagined getting away from Lace Island forever. How she'd go to the authorities in whichever port she arrived at and confess everything.

But Hakem had found her, and Chan had ordered him to whip Leila. She still had the scars on her back, and she knew that she wouldn't have the strength or nerve to attempt such a rash escape again.

Leila ducked under his arm and into the kitchen with the plates she was carrying. When she saw that Hakem had got bored of taunting her and had gone to pick on the workers, she leant on the sink and exhaled. She could hear the workers singing now, the leery, out-of-tune chorus they favoured.

When would this hell end? Leila wondered, setting to and washing the dishes in the hot, mosquito-infested kitchen, slinging the plates with careless abandon on the side. When would the monotony ever end? Her life was whizzing past her, and each year made her feel less and less like a real human being and more like the slave she was. How old was she now? Forty? Forty-one? She couldn't be sure. She hadn't celebrated or marked her birthday since she'd been a child. No one had. Would Chan make her carry on like this until she was an old woman?

The dishes finally done, Leila sneaked round the front of the kitchen and onto the roof of her prison room, relishing the moment of solitude and the cooler night air. From inside her grubby apron, she took the cigarette she'd saved from the lot Tapi had given her and lit it, inhaling the smoke, relishing the one small pleasure she had in life. She remembered smoking on the roof in school with Judith all those years ago. Whatever happened to her? she wondered.

She was probably a mother herself, Leila thought. Or maybe she'd made it as a singer. She laughed mournfully to herself, thinking of those long-distant days at school and how much she'd hated it. She let herself enjoy a wry smile.

She hadn't known she was born.

She listened now to the sounds around her, but Lace Island was unrecognizable from the place of her childhood. It was a brutal place, designed for producing heroin in secret, and the air was filled with the crackle of electric fences, the distant noise of the machines in the factory.

As usual, a feeling of hopelessness washed over her. Hopelessness and guilt and anger. The truth was that Chan had kept her prisoner here all these years, but she might as well have been dead. What was the point of torturing herself with the photographs of Jessica that Chan gave her each year? She would never see her daughter again. She knew that. She would never know her. But the thought of her poor Jessica being kept under surveillance year in, year out by those scum so they could use the threat of killing her to make Leila do what they needed her to do had made her furious enough all these years not to give up.

Using Leila as a slave was just the tip of the iceberg. The real reason she'd been kept alive all this time was because Chan needed her to sign paperwork. She had no idea what half the documents were, only that Lace Island operated in her name, which meant that everything that went on here was her responsibility. She'd refused to sign her name once – right at the beginning – and Shang had beaten her so badly he'd broken her nose and ribs.

It turned out that it was Shang who had masterminded the whole plan for Lace Island, with his links to gang chiefs in Laos and Vietnam. Chan had gone along with all his plans in return for a free and plentiful supply of opium, to which he was still addicted. Leila remembered seeing Shang delivering something to him in the middle of the night when she'd been a child. How Chan had managed to keep his addiction from Bibi for so long was amazing. Or maybe Bibi had known. She often thought of how conflicted Bibi must have been in her last, dying days and how she'd been unable to leave Chan.

And now Leila couldn't either. She had no choice but to comply with Chan's wishes, who delighted in telling her that if there was ever a police raid, it would be Leila who went to jail for the rest of her life and that an Indian prison would be even worse than her incarceration here.

She had no doubt that he was telling the truth. Leila knew that Chan had spent years cultivating his contacts with everyone from the coastguards to the customs officials. From the fortune he made from the produce of his poppy plants, she knew a sizeable chunk of the profit went on bribing the necessary officials. She knew because she signed the cheques and the paperwork.

Even taking the huge bribes into consideration, Chan's arrangement had worked so well that he'd become fat and gluttonous on his wealth. And, as Adam Lonegan had predicted long ago on that Bali bed with Monique, he'd also become monstrously rich from Lace Island, being the vital link in the supply chain. Leila had even heard a rumour that he was now in politics in the States.

But what if she stopped playing ball? Leila thought. What if she was out of the picture? Because if she was, she could bring the whole operation at Lace Island crashing to the ground. She'd burnt this place down once before, but it hadn't been enough. Now she needed to remove herself entirely. That was the only way to stop the evil here. And if she was out of the picture, they'd have no reason to hurt her daughter.

'Hey, Leila, Tapi was asking for you,' she heard someone call to her from below.

Groaning, Leila dragged herself away from the roof and walked down the path to the makeshift concrete bunker that served as Chan's security centre on this side of the island. He'd upgraded it recently, installing new cameras and new monitors, ever more paranoid about people coming to Lace Island.

There'd been a few chancers over the years – a few holiday-makers on a boat that had lost its course. The patrol boat had blown them all up. And now, for the most part, they were left alone. That didn't stop Chan being ultra-paranoid, though, and she grinned now at the CCTV camera and stuck her middle finger up. She knew Tapi would be watching inside.

She supposed it was Tapi who was the closest thing she had to a friend, even though the sight of him repelled her. He was fat, his teeth red with betel-nut juice, and he stank.

'You look pretty tonight,' Tapi said to her now, pressing his tongue through the gap in his teeth.

Leila turned away, revolted by his compliment, but even more revolted by herself. She wouldn't know if she was good-looking. She hadn't looked in a mirror for years.

'Someone said you wanted me?' she said, and he nodded, furtively looking outside and ushering her inside. She rolled her eyes at his paranoia.

'Will you stay here for me? Just for a moment?' he asked.

'Why?'

'I won a bet from Taj and I need to see him,' Tapi said, and Leila pulled a face. Tapi was a terrible gambler. 'I will be two minutes. You shout if anything happens.'

Leila nodded, slumping into his chair. What did he think might happen? And what's more, why did he think he could trust her? If Chan found her in here, or Hakem, he'd be in very serious trouble.

In the dark, Leila stared at the grainy CCTV cameras and the fields of poppies. She yawned, staring out at the images, thinking of those harmless plants and what they produced and how much misery they must cause all over the world. She tried not to think of it, but sometimes, like now, the horror of it made her feel sick to her stomach.

She took a cigarette from the packet on Tapi's desk, trying to catch it in her mouth, as he always tried to do, but it fell on the floor.

Cursing, she knelt down on the dirty concrete floor to retrieve it, which is when she looked up and saw that the wires from the computer went out through a hole in the wall outside. That must be where the mosquitos were coming in, she thought. And then she saw something else. There was a metal box attached to the underside of the desk.

She crawled over to it and fiddled with the catch and the flap fell open. Inside was a gun.

Leila gasped and took it out, holding it in her hand, feeling the weight of the small weapon. She scrambled back out to the chair with it, her heart racing with excitement.

A gun. A real gun. Which meant power.

She felt herself trembling at the thought of it. Because this meant that tonight she could do it. The thing she'd only dared dream about. She could take the gun and slip the tip of it into her mouth. And then she could pull the trigger. And this hell she was living in would be over. And she'd have finally won.

As she stuffed the gun into her jacket, she didn't notice the grainy picture on screen three of Chan in his office on the phone, angrily putting his hand to his head in frustration.

CHAPTER FIFTY-SIX

Lace Island, present day

Jess held on to the wheel of the twenty-metre yacht and watched the wind billowing in the white sails. So far, the crossing from Cochin on the boat had been fairly smooth, but with blue sea and horizon in every direction, she was starting to feel like they really were in the middle of nowhere.

The sunshine and fresh air were doing wonders for clearing her head, but despite the baseball hat she was wearing, her cheeks had caught the sun. She patted them and they felt tight.

'Here you go,' Suresh said, coming up from below deck. He handed Jess a bottle of water. 'We're making good progress,' he said. 'I just checked the GPS. A few more hours and we'll be closer.'

'You're a good skipper,' she said, meaning it. And he was an even better shrink, she nearly added. Talking to him had made her feel normal for the first time in months.

'I love sailing. I wish I could go more.'

'Why don't you, then?'

'Kareena wouldn't come on a yacht. Maybe a big one, but nothing like this.'

Jess told Suresh the next part of her history with Blaise and about being in Ibiza with Ivana and Serge on the mega-yacht.

'Kareena would have loved that,' Suresh said.

'Yeah, well, I couldn't stand it,' Jess said, glad to admit what she'd truly felt. 'They were awful. And I bet Serge knew about Blaise and me. *And* what was going on between Porscha and Blaise.' She shouted with pent-up fury. 'I'm such an idiot.'

'Stop blaming yourself, Jess. You weren't to know. It sounds like Blaise was pretty clever.'

'You know, the truth is that I didn't really care about how rich he was. It always felt wrong. I was always uncomfortable with him flashing his wealth. You know, we had a row in Cartier in Dubai and he said, "I'm just the guy who is buying you diamonds,"' she said, doing a mean impersonation of Blaise. 'I mean, *come on*. How could I have been so stupid?'

'So why did you fall for him?' Suresh asked, laughing.

'Honestly? Because I've always believed in fate. Call me an idiot, but I always thought that fate would bring me together with the man I loved, and when I fell into Blaise's arms on the plane, I convinced myself that it was him.'

The sentence hung between them for a moment.

'Does that make me sound like an idiot?'

'No,' Suresh said. 'Not at all.'

She sighed and stared out at the sinking sun.

'I just wanted it to be perfect, you know? All my life I've been waiting for someone to care about me. And to be honest, I couldn't believe it at first, but then he just seemed to say all the right things. I told myself – and everyone else who would listen – that he was my fantasy man.'

'Oh? And what is your fantasy man?' Suresh asked.

Jess laughed now at how absurd the question seemed coming out of his mouth. 'Well, I certainly don't have one anymore. I don't know . . . When I met Blaise, he just ticked all the boxes. He was rich and handsome. Someone I could boast about.' She sighed heavily.

'I mean, thinking about it now, I got so swept up in how impulsive it all was, but it could never have really worked out with someone like him. Even if it wasn't all bullshit.'

'Why?'

'Because he would have wanted me to give up work. And I've worked too hard to do that. He would have wanted me to become someone I couldn't be. One of those . . . women . . . who spend all their time trying to look perfect and spending all their husband's money on things they pretend they need. I think you're much more sensible – getting to know someone properly before you commit. And you support Kareena in her career.'

Suresh laughed.

'What?' Jess asked.

'I might not be married, but I'm already committed way over my head. With everything Kareena has planned, there's no way I could back out, even if I wanted to.'

Jess wondered why his words hurt so much.

'And *do* you want to?'

Suresh looked down, not meeting her eyes.

'I'm sorry. It's none of my business. I shouldn't have asked that,' she hurried on. 'It's just . . . after everything I've been through . . .'

'What?'

'Since we're being so honest, I just wondered . . . do you love her?'

Suresh paused for a long moment; then he sighed. 'I love her enough,' he said. 'Now here, put on a jacket. Once the sun goes down, it gets cold.' She nodded and took it. 'And, Jess?'

'Yes.'

'This time, I did tell her that I was going on an adventure with you. I emailed her before we left. I told her what was going on.'

Jess nodded. 'That was probably for the best,' she said.

Suresh smiled and cocked his head. 'You hear that?'

Jess drew her eyebrows together, confused. 'What?'

'That's the sound of her exploding, like a firework.'

Jess bit her lip and stifled an embarrassed smile. 'She won't be happy, will she?'

'No.'

'I'm sorry.'

'Don't be. You're a risk worth taking. And this is the first thing I've done without Kareena's say-so since the last time we met.'

It was gone eleven at night and a full moon had come out by the time Jess spotted land through the night-vision binoculars on the horizon.

'I think it's there,' she said, suddenly sitting up.

Suresh took the binoculars from her. 'It's definitely land. And I think the coordinates are right.'

Once they'd reeled in the sails and tied them off, Jess stood at the prow of the boat, staring down into the moonlit water, wondering how deep it was below the surface and whether they'd hit a reef.

'Over there,' she called, pointing to the right. 'I can see a jetty.'

Suresh slowed the yacht, then killed the motor. They drifted towards the jetty, the moonlight making the cracked boards silver. Jess jumped off the yacht and Suresh threw her a rope.

Once they'd secured the yacht, they walked down the jetty onto the beach. 'I feel weird walking on land, don't you?' she said. Suresh held her hand for a moment and she laughed, trying to get her balance.

The sand glowed white in the moonlight. Small crabs scuttled between the dried coconut husks that had fallen from the overhanging trees. Together, they walked a small way down the beach, the silver surf lapping against the sand.

'It feels like a desert island, doesn't it?' Suresh said, smiling. 'I mean, it's stunning. You can imagine this being an incredible resort, right?'

The beach curved round and Jess laughed and pointed to a rock. 'Look. It's like a frog,' she said.

'Shhh,' Suresh said. 'Do you hear something?'

Jess stopped still. All she could hear was the waves lapping gently against the beach and the rustle of palm leaves. Then she heard a noise and realized it was the sound of an engine.

They ducked off the beach under cover of the trees. On the other side of the trees was a road. A jeep sped down it.

'So much for it being a deserted island,' Jess said. 'It's a new road.'

When the jeep was out of sight, they crossed the road and climbed a short way up a bank. The interior of the island, away from the beach, was spread out before them. It had all been landscaped into field upon field of some kind of crop. Suresh ran quickly to inspect the plants.

Jess felt her heart hammering. 'Oh my God. Are these what I think they are?' she asked Suresh.

'They're opium poppies,' Suresh said, his voice lowered to a whisper. 'See the cuts in them?'

Jess stared closely at one of the poppy heads. She could see the skin of the pod had been scored several times and a white substance had leaked out. On some of the plants, it had dried to a hard brown resin.

'That's what they make opium out of,' Suresh said. His face was ashen. 'My guess is that they turn it into heroin.'

'Fuck,' Jess said slowly, swallowing hard, the implications of their discovery tumbling over in her head.

Because Blaise must have known about this. This is what the big deal with Lace Island was all about. It was nothing to do with a luxury resort. How naive that sounded now. She felt dread make her tremble. Because her curiosity about Lace Island had put them both in serious trouble. Because if anyone found out they were here . . . With all the surveillance, someone must have spotted their yacht. She'd brought them straight into a trap, she realized.

Suresh was thinking the same thing. His eyes were wide as they met hers.

'What do we do? Should we call the police?' she whispered. 'Or shall we just get the fuck out of here? Like *now*.'

He pulled out his phone. 'I've got no signal.'

'Take some pictures anyway,' Jess said.

Another engine. They ducked down as the vehicle sent an arc of light into the trees.

'Where are they going?' Jess asked.

Running crouched alongside Suresh, they made their way along the tarmac road until the land curved up and away. Jess was out of breath as she reached the top of the hill to join Suresh, who was standing motionless.

'What?' she asked, standing by his side.

And then she saw what had made him stop.

Down below them were mile upon mile of poppy fields. And beyond them, in the distance, on the other side of the island, a ship was docked in a floodlit port. He took another photo and then another.

'I'm sending these to Kareena,' he said, but he sounded scared. 'If they'll go through . . .'

Suresh grabbed her hand and ducked down and pointed. Round the bend from where they were was a heavily guarded compound with a huge wire fence. Guards with weapons slung across their shoulders laughed and played dice in the dust.

'What the hell is this—' Suresh didn't have a chance to finish his sentence, his phone dropping into the dirt.

She saw his eyes widen, and that's when Jess felt something metallic and cold press against the back of her head and the unmistakable click of a gun being cocked.

CHAPTER FIFTY-SEVEN

Lace Island, present day

Do it. Do it, Leila urged herself, squeezing her eyes shut in the heat of her cramped room. She had to be fast. She'd left Tapi's hut five minutes ago, but he might discover the missing gun any second. She had to grab this opportunity.

Now.

In all the years that Chan had kept her captive, she'd never had the chance to end it all. And now it was here. She felt the bundle of photographs pressing against her heart.

I love you, she said in her head, beaming the message to her daughter. She wanted it to be the last thought she had.

But even as she did, she knew it was useless. Jessica would never know that Leila had even existed. Her longing all these years had been utterly futile. It was time to let the past go and move on for good. Even so, she said it one more time to herself. *I love you . . .*

Leila felt every fibre of her being tense, waiting for the inevitable, as she counted down in her head.

Three . . .

Two . . .

One . . .

She squeezed the trigger with all her strength.

Click.

It took her a moment to realize what had happened. She took the barrel of the gun out of her mouth, gasping, realizing her lips were so dry they'd stuck to the cold metal.

It hadn't worked. She retched, not just shocked that the attempt at taking her own life had failed but that she had finally been brave enough to attempt it in the first place. She was shaking violently now as she cocked the gun, staring into the barrel, seeing five bullets, the empty hole for the sixth. The bullet that should have just blown off her head.

She could still do it. There was still time to end it all. But something stopped her. What kind of sick joke was it that had made the empty barrel the one for her? She felt tears bubbling up and she patted her chest, scared by the emotions flying around inside her. Relief? Shame? Disappointment? It was hard to name them all.

The sound of the siren made her cry out and drop the gun in shock. She twirled round to face the door, convinced the siren must be something to do with her.

She raced out of her room to the steps outside, amazed that Hakem hadn't been yet to lock her in. She'd been hoping that he'd find her with her head blown off. She'd hoped he'd be the first to slide in the mess of her blood and brains, and have to be the one to tell Chan that he'd failed in his duty.

Instead, the sound of the alarm siren shrieked through the night.

She ran over to the bunker, knocking on the door.

'Who is it?' she heard Tapi call, but he must know it was her from the knock.

'It's me.'

The door opened and Tapi stood in the doorway, looking worried. He pulled her inside, quickly looking around him.

'What's happened?' she asked.

She still felt shaky and frightened. Could he tell that moments ago she'd nearly taken her own life?

It felt weird even talking. As if this was all new. Borrowed somehow.

'A break-in. A couple on a yacht. Hakem has them now in the jeep and is taking them up to the house.'

Intrigued, Leila followed him over to the screens and stared at the grainy images.

'There. See,' he said.

On one of the screens, Leila saw a view of the beach, the old jetty in the distance, a white sailing yacht bobbing on the black water. On the screen, it was almost possible to believe that Lace Island was once as it had been. Back in the old days. Back when Rasa used to fix the blue boat.

But that Lace Island was long gone. As soon as the people from the yacht had stepped on shore, they'd have found out the truth. They would have been marked long before they'd even tied their boat up at the jetty. And now there would be no escape.

But who the hell had sailed here? she wondered. And what would Hakem do to them now? Why hadn't he killed them straight out? That was his usual style. Or maybe he fancied a bit of torture with these newcomers.

She watched another two screens as the jeep sped up the tarmac road and then bumped onto the dusty track up towards the house. It stopped by what was left of Bibi's house. A close-up now of the front of the house, lit by floodlights. There was still the well there and the stone steps, but the building behind was only one storey and ugly.

She watched on the screen as Chan waddled down the front steps. The jeep had stopped now and a couple were getting out of the back. An Indian guy and a girl.

The girl looked upset, a guard pushing her roughly.

Who were they?

Leila felt something shaking inside her as she leant in towards the screen.

'Boy, they're in trouble,' Tapi said.

Leila was silent, her eyes glued to the screen and the back view of the slim girl with her long, dark hair in a ponytail. The guard pushed the couple towards the steps, and that's when the girl looked up. For one split second, her face was caught in close-up and Leila felt saliva rush into her mouth.

She felt her heart contracting.

It couldn't be. It wasn't possible . . .

That face . . . *that face* . . . she knew that face better than she knew her own . . .

She felt something fizzing around her. Something she'd never felt before. A sure knowledge that fate had saved her for this moment.

This moment *right now*.

The images on the screen changed now, the camera switching, and Leila turned away from them. It took every ounce of her strength to pretend what she'd just seen meant nothing. When the truth was that the world had just shifted on its axis.

'You'd better go back,' Tapi said, 'or there'll be trouble.'

He sat down in his seat, pretending to be officious. She saw him reach under his desk for the gun, but she was already shutting the bunker door and quietly wedging the lock shut.

CHAPTER FIFTY-EIGHT

Lace Island, present day

In the stifling heat of the cramped office they'd been left in, Jess jumped, hearing what sounded like a distant gunshot.

'What was that?' she whimpered.

'It's OK,' Suresh said. 'Try and keep calm.'

There was a large desk and chair, but hardly any other furniture, apart from a day bed, which Jess was sitting on now. A gecko scuttled up the wall next to the buzzing bare light bulb.

Suresh was on the other side of the room, inspecting the high window, which had bars on it but no means of escape.

Jess put her face in her hands. 'How can I keep calm? Oh my God. This is all my fault. This is really fucking serious . . .'

Suresh came over and sat next to her, putting his arms round her.

'What if they kill us?' Jess implored.

'If they were going to kill us, they would have done so by now.'

'I'm so scared. That man . . . I met him with Blaise in London. He's the one who must have paid Blaise to find me. This is bad, Suresh . . . really bad . . . I had no idea about the heroin.'

'Come on. We have to think. There must be a way out of here,' Suresh said, but Jess knew he was scared too. She thought of his mobile phone, which was still in the field where the guards had captured them. That guy – the one with the evil eyes – Jess had been convinced he was going to kill them. She'd never experienced fear like it.

Jess felt sick at the thought that Blaise had known about what happened here on Lace Island the whole time. She'd wondered since she'd left Miami why he'd done what he'd done to her, but now she realized just how high the stakes had always been. How terrifying what he was involved in actually was.

They were silent for a moment; Jess stared into Suresh's eyes and she knew that he was thinking the same thing.

'If anything bad happens – really bad, I mean – I want you to know that I'm truly grateful you helped me out, Suresh,' she said, her voice shaking. 'And I'm sorry. I'm sorry for dragging you into all of this—' But she couldn't finish, because his lips were on hers in an urgent kiss. She felt the same feeling rush through her as when she'd first seen him.

'I'm sorry,' he gasped. 'If anything happened and I hadn't kissed you, I would never have forgiven myself. But timing is really not my strong point.'

She grabbed his face, closing her eyes, savouring the sensation of the kiss, her heart hammering.

Suddenly, a stone fell in through the bars behind them and Suresh jumped up. 'What was that?' he said, backing to the wall to look out of the window. 'I think someone is there,' he whispered.

Jess felt her heart hammering, her mind still reeling from Suresh's kiss as she heard something moving over the roof outside. Then silence. She stared at Suresh and they both looked at the door.

The handle was turning.

Very slowly and quietly, the door opened. An Indian woman in dirty trousers and an old army jacket came in. She stared at them, then turned the key, locking herself in with them.

Suresh held out his hands, shielding Jess. 'Please,' he began. 'We mean no harm.'

Jess peered round Suresh to the woman. She looked nervous, her gaze darting to the door. She was filthy, her fingernails black with dirt. She put her fingers to her lips, telling them to talk quietly.

'Do you work here? What is this place?' Jess asked, confused about what was going on.

'This is an illegal heroin plant,' the woman said. She had good English, but with a heavy Indian accent. Her voice was husky and strained. 'It's run by Chan. He will be here soon. He is a very bad man. You are in great danger.'

'We know. We saw him,' Suresh said. 'Can you help us?'

'I can, but first, you must tell me . . . why did you come here?' the woman asked, stepping closer to them now.

'Because—' Jess began, standing next to Suresh.

He frowned at her. 'Don't, Jess,' he said. 'We don't know we can trust her.'

'I don't care. She's here,' Jess told him. 'She might be our only chance.'

She saw the look of understanding pass across his face and he nodded.

Jess turned to the woman. 'We came here because . . . because . . . Oh God, it's complicated, but I was engaged to be married to someone, but I found out that he was trying to marry me because he thought I had some connection to here and that by marrying me . . .' She fizzled out, realizing how crazy she sounded. She turned to Suresh.

'We had no idea that all this was here.'

'This is Suresh, my friend,' Jess explained. 'You cannot imagine the danger I have now put him in, and—' She stopped, startled by the woman's face. Her eyes were shining brightly and she crept towards Jess, holding out her hand.

'It *is* you,' she said, in an awed whisper. 'When I saw you on the camera, I didn't think it was possible, but . . .'

She put her hand to her head and for a moment Jess thought the woman was going to faint. She stared at Suresh, who looked as confused as she felt.

'Hey, are you OK?' Suresh asked, taking the woman's arm. He pulled a face at Jess.

'I have to go,' the woman said suddenly, as if his touch had burnt her. She made for the door.

'Wait,' Jess implored, catching her by the door. 'Please can you help us? This island is privately owned, right? Or at least it was. That's what we know. It was owned by someone called Bibi.'

'And she had a daughter, Leila . . . .' Suresh said slowly.

'Are you . . . are you . . . Leila?' Jess asked, shocked to see now that the woman was crying.

And that's when Jess realized. Without knowing why, she felt her breath catch. 'You're Leila, aren't you?'

The woman nodded wordlessly, then reached inside her jacket. Jess watched as she pulled out a haphazard bundle of well-thumbed photographs in a dirty pink ribbon, which she handed now to Jess, without looking at her.

Jess gasped, the air leaving her lungs as if she'd been hit.

Each photograph was of her. At every age. Loads of them. Ones of her and Angel. In the care home. Even one of her at

Angel's funeral. That guy she'd seen . . . he'd taken a photo of her. She hadn't imagined it.

'How do you have these?' she whispered, staring at Leila, who was half smiling now, tears making her cheeks glisten as she looked at the photos.

'They gave me one a year,' Leila said, but she sounded like she could hardly speak. 'Taken on your birthday. To keep me here. To make me stay. Because as long as I did, you'd be safe.'

Jess could hardly take in what Leila was saying.

'But I don't understand. Does that mean you're . . . you're . . .' she began, but she couldn't say it.

Leila stared at her and nodded, just once.

'Oh my God,' Jess gasped. 'You're my mother?'

CHAPTER FIFTY-NINE

Lace Island, present day

And then it was happening. The thing Leila had feared never would come to pass: she was in her daughter's arms. She felt Jessica's slim arms wrapping around her, as if she was catching Leila from falling, but at the same time, she felt as if she'd been borne up, like she was floating way up in the air.

And to think . . . to think that this might never have happened. That not even an hour ago, she had a gun in her mouth, ready to end everything. Even moments ago, she'd almost lost her nerve. Almost had to run from the shame of the truth. But the truth was out and now . . . now beyond all her wildest dreams . . . *this*.

She was so aware of the time – how little they had of it – but it didn't matter. It felt to Leila as if time had stopped. In the most delicious moment of her life, Leila held her daughter and closed her eyes.

'Is this really happening?' Jess said, pulling away, trying to gasp for air. She shook her head, as if she couldn't take it all in, but Leila felt a new calmness. Nothing else mattered. Only that they were finally together.

'You have your grandmother's eyes, Jessica,' Leila said,

filling her senses with how beautiful her daughter had grown. 'I knew it from when you were tiny. There's that picture of you with that girl . . .' Leila said, pointing to the pictures in Jess's hand.

'Angel.'

'Is that her name? I'm glad you had an angel with you,' Leila said, and she stroked Jessica's face as the tears rolled from her eyes.

'You had all these photos?' she whispered. 'And I never knew?'

'This is all I've had. All I've treasured. All these years. And now you're here.'

'But I don't understand. Why didn't you escape?'

Leila shook her head, stunned now by the magnitude of the task to make her understand.

'How could I? They've locked me up at night. Kept me prisoner for years and years, so they could make me sign everything off and they could carry on their trade. They would be ruined if I left and told anyone what happens here. They ensured I stayed by giving me your pictures. They told me they'd kill you if I didn't do what they said.'

Jessica stared at Suresh, who shook his head, clearly as astonished as she was.

'Jess, we have to get out of here,' Suresh said. 'Leila, can you help me get to a phone that works? A computer with email?'

'What's email?' Leila asked.

Jess and Suresh exchanged a look.

'It doesn't matter,' Suresh said. 'I have to get word out. I have to—'

But at that moment, the door burst open, as if it had been kicked from outside. Leila, Jess and Suresh jumped back.

There was a moment of silence as Leila stared at Chan and Shang. Hakem was close behind.

'Oh look. How touching,' Chan said, and Leila hated him in that moment more than she'd ever hated him. He waved a gun between Leila and Jess. 'Did I miss the reunion?'

'Let them go,' Leila shouted at him. 'Let them go. You have no right—'

'I have every right. What I say happens here.'

He pushed them further into the room. Jess and Suresh had their hands up, but Leila was determined to protect them. Chan didn't scare her. Nothing scared her now. She felt invincible.

She stepped forward to Chan, fronting up to him. He looked at her, clearly startled that she wasn't cowering, as usual. She reached behind her into the waistband of her trousers and gripped Tapi's gun confidently in her hand.

'Why did you do this, Chan? Why did you bring her here?' Leila said, because she saw now that this was just the next step in Chan's awful plan.

'For some insurance,' Shang said, stepping into the room. She saw Jess shrinking back behind Suresh.

'I'm very bored of you and your defiance. So I thought that maybe you might fall off a cliff one of these days, Leila. Or get eaten by a shark. Not that there's ever been any sharks around here.' He laughed and looked across at Shang.

Leila felt something horrifying click into place. A light coming on, illuminating a truth that she'd always known.

'You killed my father,' she said.

'Yes, he was inconvenient,' Chan said, with a shrug. 'And I would have killed you too,' he said, 'if she hadn't run away from her wedding,' he said, nodding at Jess. 'I had everything worked out. Everything transferred legally to Blaise.'

'No,' Leila shouted. 'You don't get to mess with her.'

'Shut up,' Chan said, pointing his gun at Leila, but she felt no fear. This time, the bullet was not going to miss. She pulled the gun round and aimed it at Chan, and with a furious scream, she pulled the trigger.

The sound of the shot was deafening. She watched as Chan clutched his stomach, blood seeping from between his fingers. He stared at her, incomprehension on his face as he looked from his hand to her. His gun clattered to the floor.

'No,' Suresh shouted, as Jess screamed.

Another shot. This time from Shang's gun, and Leila gasped as she saw Suresh slump down.

Jess screamed and now Leila fired a second time, hitting Hakem. He fell in the corridor. Only Shang remained, aiming once more at Leila. She pointed her gun at him, wondering who would fire first.

'Don't kill her. We need her,' Chan said, through gritted teeth.

Leila stared hard at Shang, pointing the gun at him, wanting more than ever to pull the trigger.

'Don't, Leila,' Jess said. Then she launched at Shang with a roundhouse kick, making his gun skitter across the floor, before turning again and punching him in the throat. He fell backwards and staggered against the wall, and Jess pushed him again. He hit his head hard on the door frame and fell down against it.

Leila stared at her daughter, astounded; then she stood over Chan. 'You don't win,' she said.

'Neither do you.'

'Have you any idea how many lives you've ruined?' she spat at him.

'As long as I ruined yours, that's all that matters,' he

replied, falling further back on the floor, blood pooling around him.

'Why? Why have you been so cruel all these years, Chan?' Leila said, kneeling down next to him.

'Because nothing I ever did was good enough.'

'For who?' Leila said.

'For Bibi. Your mother always loved you more than me. No matter what I did for her.'

He coughed now, blood in his mouth. Leila dropped the gun. Her hands were trembling violently. She stared into Chan's face. His brown eyes met hers.

'Her last words were about you.'

'You were there?'

'Of course I was there. I locked her in her bedroom so she'd die from the smoke.'

Leila felt a lump in her throat.

'You thought you started the fire that killed her, but I did,' Chan continued. 'I saw you planting those fireworks. They were useless, Leila. Duds I bought on the market. I planned the explosion, knowing what you were going to do. I heard everything you said to Bibi. I got there first with the dynamite.'

Leila saw that he was telling the truth. She saw now the lighthouse that dreadful night. The explosion. The towering inferno of fire. And she felt a new truth pull everything into clarity. She couldn't possibly have started that fire with the fireworks.

'You let me believe all these years that it was me?' she said. 'You let me blame myself when all along it was you?'

She stayed looking at him, but he never answered. Instead, he had a slow smile on his face. And then he was gone.

She stared at him, hardly able to process what he'd just said.

'Leila. Leila. Help me.' It was Jess. She turned to see Jess cradling Suresh's head. 'Oh God. Oh God, no.'

Leila moved fast, seeing the pallor on the young man's face and the panic on Jess's. Quickly, she went to Suresh, helping to staunch the flow of blood from his chest.

'We need to get him out of here. Let's move him downstairs to the jeep and then to the ship. There'll be a doctor on board,' Leila said, determined now to help her daughter.

Jess nodded, and together, they hauled Suresh up, holding him under his armpits, as he groaned with pain.

They dragged him through the door, and Leila locked Shang inside. Then they made their way down the corridor following a trail of blood. Hakem's. He must have dragged himself away, Leila thought. Gone to get help, no doubt. Which meant the workers would come soon. But Leila would have to worry about that when it happened.

'Be careful,' Jess pleaded.

Leila stared at the sky. Dawn had broken and birds were singing in the palm trees at the front of the house. And then a sound. Distant and then nearer and nearer.

A low helicopter, whipping the tops of the palm trees.

Leila was amazed. She hadn't heard a helicopter on Lace Island for years. How had they got through security? Then she remembered that she'd locked Tapi in the control bunker and cut the wires to his computers.

The door of the helicopter was open, and a man with what looked like a large TV camera was staring down at them, filming.

'It's Kareena's channel,' Suresh said, his voice no more than a whisper, a kind of relieved smile on his face. 'She finally got her story.'

And then he passed out.

CHAPTER SIXTY

Cochin, present day

Jess pinched her eyes, sitting next to the bed in the hospital in Cochin. The monitors round Suresh's bed bleeped, but he lay motionless and asleep. At this time of night, the roar of the traffic on the street outside was hardly noticeable, but Jess still couldn't sleep.

She saw the news come on the TV in the corner and she glanced up at it now.

'In yet more shocking revelations about Lace Island, Cochin's chief of police was arrested today in connection with a huge-scale cover-up that sources say goes right up to government level.'

Jess zoned out. It had been four days since the shootings on Lace Island and the world seemed to have gone crazy. Those first few hours when the helicopter had arrived were still a blur. She'd been in such shock from finding Leila and then Suresh being shot that she'd hardly taken in the news cameras. But then the coastguard had arrived, followed by the police.

The shipment of heroin that had been due to leave Lace Island had been quarantined, and the workers had been rounded up and detained. Mayhem had followed, with multiple arrests, and Leila had remained on Lace Island in police custody, happily answering all their questions. Jess had listened, dumbstruck, as she'd hastily recounted the night of the fire and what had happened and just how many atrocities Chan had been responsible for.

She'd insisted that Jess go to take Suresh to the hospital on the mainland and Jess had left with the news helicopter, still hardly able to believe what had happened.

'We will be together soon,' Leila had said, squeezing Jess's hands. 'I promise. Make sure your friend gets better.'

It touched her that Leila, after everything she'd been through, was so concerned for Suresh. So far, he'd had two operations, and the doctors were hopeful that he'd pull through, but it was by no means certain. Kareena and Suresh's families had all gathered round, fearing the worst.

Jess was happy that they'd let her stay here tonight at the hospital, away from the press pack that had hunted her down since she'd arrived in Cochin. She stood and peeked out of the window, wondering if they were still there.

She knew it wouldn't be long before Kareena returned, and then she'd have to go back to the police station. Two agents from the States were coming to talk to her and she wondered what new bombshell news today would bring. She wasn't sure how much more of these revelations she could take. She knew they wanted to track down Blaise, and despite her exhaustion, she had to do what she could to help them.

She walked over to Suresh in the bed and stared down at him. She prayed to God that he would be OK. That he would be able to walk again.

She knew she shouldn't, but she couldn't stop the memory of the kiss they'd shared when they'd been on Lace Island. She stroked his hair, and then suddenly, she saw his eyelids flickering and he opened his eyes.

Jess gasped, grabbing his hand and leaning in close. She looked towards the door, wondering if she should call the nurse.

'Jess. You're here,' he said.

'Of course I'm here,' she replied, smiling, overjoyed to see the familiar twinkle in his eye. She was so glad that she was here alone with him. That hers was the first face he'd seen. 'How do you feel?'

'I don't know. I can't feel my feet.'

'They say that's normal. It's just where the bullet went near your spine,' she said, hoping not to panic him. 'It'll take some time.'

He nodded, staring at her intently. His eyes had filled with tears. 'Jess. Thank you for saving me.'

'I didn't save you. You saved *me*, remember.'

'Don't tell Kareena,' he said; then he closed his eyes again and went back to sleep.

Jess smoothed her hand over his hair again, wondering what he'd meant. Did he mean that she wasn't to tell Kareena what had happened in that small office? About the shooting, or the kiss? Or both?

He didn't have to worry on that score, Jess thought, pressing a gentle kiss onto his forehead. It wasn't as if she was going to have a heart-to-heart with Kareena anytime soon. Not that she disliked Suresh's fiancée. Quite the opposite. She could see now why Suresh was attracted to her, and his family clearly were totally enamoured with the glamorous newscaster. Rightly so. But to Jess, she was like an emotional bulldozer and Jess found it upsetting how excited Kareena was by the sensational unfolding story on Lace Island. The story that she had taken sole credit for at the news channel that actually wasn't 'a story' at all, but very real and affecting lots of people. Most of all Jess.

Kareena, however, had been relishing every new revelation with wide-eyed awe, while Jess had shrunk back, too out of her depth to criticize.

Besides, she couldn't fault Kareena on how nice she'd been to Jess, insisting that she stay with her at Suresh's apartment. But Jess knew she was keeping her close, waiting for the moment to spring a big interview on her. Which is why Jess had been keeping her at arm's length. It all felt too raw and too soon. She needed to check that Leila and Suresh were safe first before she said anything publicly. And even then, she had no idea what she would say. No idea how she actually felt.

'How is he?' Kareena asked breathlessly, pushing through the door and putting her designer handbag on the chair. Jess sprang away from the bed, feeling her pulse throb in her cheeks. Had Kareena seen her smoothing Suresh's hair or kissing his forehead? 'Sorry I'm late.'

'He woke up. He said a few things,' Jess said.

'That's good. Well, he must hurry up and get better. You'll never guess . . .' Kareena said, her eyes shining.

'What?'

'*Today* magazine have just tripled their fee for photographing the wedding.'

She grinned at Jess over the bed, who put her hands in the pockets of her jeans and tried to smile. She hoped Suresh wasn't listening to any of this. How could Kareena even think about their wedding when he had yet to gain consciousness fully?

But he would regain consciousness, Jess realized. And then he would marry Kareena. She grabbed her bag from the chair, suddenly desperate to get away. She stiffly hugged Kareena goodbye, with promises to call her later, then slipped out into the corridor.

Outside the hospital, Jess felt overwhelmingly tired as she got back into the police car that was waiting for her, ignoring the crowd of press that had gathered and the flashes that went off in her face.

'The agents from the States are already here to see you,' Nev, the police officer who'd been looking after her, explained. She heard the awe in his voice. 'They are exactly like they are on TV,' he added, making Jess smile. This was the biggest news story to hit the station for years and Jess wondered how weird all this was for Nev and his colleagues.

Back at the police headquarters, she followed him through the hot station, where phones were ringing, and she saw through a hatch that there was a room full of people waiting patiently. A whole new day had started already.

What was happening to time? Jess wondered, feeling truly disorientated. Days seemed to be flowing into nights and back into days without stopping. *Would her life ever be normal again?*

She climbed up some stairs and was taken through to a shabby, bare interview room with dark green paint flaking off the walls. A fan was blowing, but it didn't look like it was doing much for the two American men in the room, who rose to shake Jess's hand.

'I'm Senior Special Agent Trebitz, and this is my colleague Agent Stone,' the man with the dark hair explained.

She sat in the chair as Nev fussed, wanting to bring them coffee, although Jess sensed that this was a stretch and that the station didn't usually provide such a service.

Agent Trebitz had shaggy long hair and was sweating in his short-sleeved pink polo shirt. 'I know you have been through a lot, Jess, but time is important right now. We want you to tell us all you can about' – he consulted his pile of papers – 'Blaise Blackmore . . . as you knew him.'

Jess stared at them. 'That wasn't . . . isn't his name?'

'No. He has plenty of identities,' Agent Trebitz explained, showing her a colour photocopy of a montage of passports. All of them had different names. All of them had Blaise's picture.

'Oh my God. Who is he, then?'

'He's an international fixer,' Agent Stone explained, handing over a picture of Blaise, looking entirely different, with a beard and dressed in a suit. He works with an accomplice. His girlfriend, we think.'

'Porscha,' Jess said, as they handed another photo over of Porscha, this time in a blonde wig. She remembered that night in the club when she'd first met her and how she'd felt: small and insignificant – like Porscha held all the power. She should have trusted her gut instinct.

'He's been impossible to trace until now. He has his fingers in every sort of pie – gambling, drugs, arms dealing.'

Everything had been a lie, then. She'd suspected it before, but now finding out just how few scruples Blaise actually had made her feel more foolish than ever. She bit her lip, feeling tears perilously close to the surface.

That day she'd met him on the plane, he'd been there all along to bump into her. And in that apartment in New York, what she'd heard him say on the phone: 'It's her.' It all made sense now.

'You weren't to know,' Agent Stone said, seeing her upset. 'He's a very skilled operator. We've been trying to close in the net around him for years, but he eludes us every time.'

Jess took a deep breath and then told them everything she could – about the trip in Miami and Nacho on the boat, even the guy who had served them soda that day. And about the hired apartment in New York and the trip to Ibiza with Serge and Ivana.

Stone, the bigger of the two men, took notes and shook out his hand, as if the writing were making it ache, but when she mentioned Serge, they both stared at each other.

Agent Stone riffled through his file. 'This guy?' he said, showing her an army mugshot of Serge in younger days.

'That's him. They have this yacht. I went on it in Ibiza. He and Serge went off for a few days together. I have no idea where.'

Another look passed between them.

'If we can link Blaise to Serge, we're in with a shot of trapping them both. We cannot tell you how helpful you've been, Jess,' they told her. 'We know that none of this has been easy.'

Jess felt her head aching as she finished the questions, and Nev, the policeman, came in and nodded.

'Oh,' Agent Stone said to Jess, 'she's here.'

'Who is here?'

'Leila. She's just come in from Lace Island. We wanted to question you both.'

Jess stood now as Leila was brought into the small interview room by a policeman. She looked so different to when Leila had seen her last. She looked smaller and exhausted, as if, like Jess, she'd hardly slept. She was wearing a pair of black trousers and a white shirt, which looked too big for her. Jess realized that Leila probably didn't have any of her own clothes.

Leila rushed over to Jess now and threw her arms round her. It felt weird that her mother was so much smaller than her.

'You're here,' Leila said, sounding so relieved, as if she couldn't believe that Jess were real. She cupped Jess's face, her eyes blazing. 'You must forgive us,' she told the agents after a moment. 'My daughter and I have so much to catch up on.'

Jess saw the agents exchange a look. They were clearly as baffled by Leila as Jess was herself. She felt simultaneously comforted and overwhelmed seeing Leila. She thought back to that moment – the moment Leila had handed her the pile of photographs – the magnitude of it just too great to wrap her head around.

And yes, there had been an instant of complete recognition, when she'd realized Leila was her mother, but it hadn't felt to Jess like she'd expected it to then, and it certainly hadn't since. She felt shy now of this stranger with whom she was sharing the stage so publicly.

'So what is it you want to know?' Leila asked them, proprietorially sitting down in a chair. 'I have been told that I am free to go after this interview, and I want to go and get some breakfast with my daughter. I am so hungry.'

Jess sat down next to her mother, stifling a smile. She liked her blunt manner.

Agent Stone cleared his voice. 'You said in your statement to the police on Lace Island that the shipments were funded by Adam Lonegan.'

Jess saw Leila stiffen at the mention of his name. Who was Adam Lonegan? she wondered. Leila sat ramrod-straight on the chair, all jovial talk of breakfast forgotten.

'Yes.'

'You mean Senator Lonegan?'

'He's rich and American. I heard he was in politics, yes.'

Agent Stone shifted uncomfortably. 'Because these are very serious allegations you've made, Leila. And he's denied any involvement with Lace Island. We've looked into it and nothing we've been able to find can link him with any of the accusations you've made. In fact, there's no paperwork to link him to Lace Island at all.'

'But I was there,' Leila protested, standing up and banging her fist on the table, making Stone jump. 'I saw the papers. He signed the deal with Chan, my stepfather, to make it possible for the shipments to go to New Orleans. He knows everything about Lace Island. It's why he's so rich.'

'Are you sure it's the same Adam Lonegan?' Agent Trebitz asked. 'Because his reputation in the US is faultless.'

He sounded sceptical, as if perhaps Leila was making this all up, and Jess saw Leila's look darken into a furious scowl. This was clearly something very important to her.

'Er, excuse me for interrupting,' Jess said, confused, 'but who is this guy you're talking about?'

Leila took a deep breath and pinched the bridge of her nose. Then she sat down heavily on the chair and looked at the floor.

'Leila?' Jess asked, confused. It was as if every ounce of strength had gone from her mother. She hadn't looked like this ever – not even when she'd shot Chan.

'That is enough,' Leila said, staring up coldly at the agents. 'I have said everything. If you don't believe me, fine. But that's all I'm going to say.'

'But—' Agent Stone began. He looked at his colleague, who looked equally baffled.

Jess put her hand on Leila's shoulder, which she now saw was shaking. Was she crying?

Jess moved in closer, seeing how Leila was sobbing. 'What is it?' she asked. She stared up at the two agents with a confused shrug. 'Leila, let me help.'

But Leila's voice now erupted into a sob. She shook her head. 'I can't. I can't.'

Jess swallowed hard. In the short time she'd known her mother, she'd been so strong, but now she seemed to be falling apart.

'Can we have a moment?' Jess asked the agents. She felt frightened now, but sure that Leila would be more forthcoming without the two Americans staring at her.

'Sure,' Trebitz said, rolling his eyes at Stone. They opened the door and walked into the corridor. 'We'll just be outside.'

Jess knelt on the dirty floor in front of Leila and cupped her wet face. 'Leila,' she whispered. 'Leila, talk to me.'

Jess saw her mother's eyes. They were large, magnified by anguished tears. She shook her head.

'You can tell me anything,' Jess said. 'You know that, right?'

'No. No, I can't.'

Jess took a breath. 'What are you so scared of?'

Tears popped out of Leila's eyes. 'I can't,' she whispered. She sobbed, a huge cry escaping her. 'I can't tell you. I'm so sorry.'

Jess shook her head. She desperately wanted to help Leila, but something was chewing at her that Jess could see was more painful than everything that had happened on Lace Island. What was this new, terrifying secret that was eating up Leila?

'It's OK. We have time,' she said, trying to sound reassuring, but she felt rattled. 'But after everything you've been through, why don't you just tell me why you're so upset? Is it something to do with this Lonegan guy?'

Leila's head shot down again. She wrung her hands together, letting out another anguished cry.

'Leila?' Jess implored, kneeling again by her. 'Tell me. Who is he?'

'He . . .'

Jess held her breath, but there was a long pause. Leila couldn't speak.

'Please. Just tell me.'

'He's . . .' She paused again. Then she exhaled, her blood-shot eyes meeting Jess's, and it looked to Jess like her mother's heart was breaking. 'He's your father.'

CHAPTER SIXTY-ONE

Cochin, present day

There. She'd said it. Leila watched as Jess slumped down now, sitting on her heels, taking in this news.

'He's my father?' she asked. She looked confused and Leila felt the absurdity of it for a moment. That this devastating news was a surprise to her daughter, when Leila had thought of nothing else since they'd first met. That all the way here, she'd told herself that she would never, ever tell Jess the truth.

Certainly not here. Not now. In this police station.

But somehow it had just come too close to the surface to hide anymore. And now it was out. The huge secret was out. Spilling out of Leila's soul, like black oil.

Leila could see Jess trying to work out what it all meant.

'Were you . . . I mean, you must have been young when you had me?' she said.

Leila took a shuddering breath.

Now the test.

Now she had to be honest. If she lost Jess forever, then that would be the price she'd have to pay for her honesty. But she couldn't lie. Not any longer. Not after lying for so long about Lace Island.

'Fourteen.'

'And how old was he, this Lonegan guy?'

'I don't know. Thirty, maybe. He was a guest on the island. An associate of Chan's.'

Jess got to her feet. She looked up at the ceiling and Leila longed to hold her in her arms again, but it was as if every ounce of strength had drained out of her.

'I'm so sorry,' she said, her voice cracking. 'I should never have told you.'

Jess shook her head, turning and facing Leila with Bibi's eyes. 'I don't care about him, Leila,' she said. 'I never even thought about having a dad. Only finding my mum. Only finding you.'

Leila felt her words embracing her like a hug. She took a shuddering breath in. She nodded, acknowledging her words, but there was more to say, and Jess knew it.

'He hurt you, didn't he?' Jess said, and saw that Leila was crying now, but she didn't need her to answer. She could see it in her face.

'I was a virgin. He . . . I . . .' Leila shook her head, engulfed by tears.

Jess stared at her, slowly nodding. There was a long moment. Jess watched Leila's chin wobbling; then she took a breath. 'He raped you, right?'

It was a whisper, but Jess might as well have shouted it. Leila nodded, feeling her heart breaking. She closed her eyes. Wishing she could die. Wishing she had blown her brains out, rather than living to inflict any pain on her darling daughter.

'I'm so sorry,' she mumbled.

But then she felt Jess grab her shoulders, forcing her to open her eyes. Jess's eyes blazed down into hers.

'Don't be sorry. You shouldn't be the sorry one. We'll get

him, Leila. I promise. Together. We'll make him pay for what he did to you.'

'But he's so powerful,' Leila protested. 'You heard them.'

'We just need to prove he was on Lace Island. And then there'll be my DNA, of course.'

Leila nodded, not daring to dream that Jess meant it. That she could be so strong. That once again her daughter had saved her.

'Come here. Don't cry anymore,' Jess said, pulling her into a strong embrace. 'I know how hard that was to tell me. But we have each other now. We'll work it all out.'

And as Jess enfolded her into a hug, they cried together. Then Leila suddenly remembered Sister Mary's face, and something else too.

'I have proof,' she whispered, breathing in suddenly, like she was breathing in life. 'I have proof, Jess.'

'Where?'

'In the place that you were born.'

'Then let's get it. We'll make them believe you, I promise.'

'And Sister Mary often prayed for you,' Sister Singh said, raising her voice over the roadworks outside and smiling at Leila and Jess as she walked through the tarpaulin cover to the dusty chapel beyond. 'She never forgot you. Right until she died.'

Poor Sister Mary, Leila thought, feeling more emotional than she'd imagined. She must have been frightened out of her wits that night Chan and Shang had come. And when Chan had dragged Leila away, never to be heard of again, she must have been worried sick. 'I never forgot her either. She saved my life.'

Leila looked around the derelict chapel, soon to be demolished with the rest of the mission. She stared up at the balcony where the nuns had once sung so beautifully, hearing a far-off echo of voices. It was all so different to how she remembered it, and the mission itself was hardly recognizable. The gardens and Sister Vimla's beehives had gone, replaced by a busy road, and the building works next door looked like they would crush the place. A shower of dust fell now from the ceiling.

'It's here,' Leila said, nodding at the floor and then kneeling to move aside a thick piece of cardboard that covered the floor.

'It's most unlikely . . .' Sister Singh said, glancing at Jessica and Leila.

Leila didn't care if the old nun thought she was crazy. It was as if Jess's strength at the police station had given her new power. She knelt now, examining the floor. There had been a grille there, she was sure of it. She sat back, looking up to where the altar had once been, trying to remember exactly how it had looked when she'd scrubbed this floor all those years ago, casting herself back to the terrified girl she'd once been. Remembering, now, all too clearly, how she'd been convinced that God would strike her down.

But God wasn't that simple in his methods. Leila had learnt that the hard way.

Perhaps the aisle was different? she mused, looking again.

'It's so sad the mission is going. After two hundred years,' Sister Singh was saying to Jessica.

'That's awful.'

'It's the modern world. We're in too prime a location. They've taken all our gardens as it is. They forced us to move.'

'Where will you go?' Jess asked.

'That I don't know. We're still praying for a miracle.'

'That's it,' Leila said, realizing her mistake. 'They've moved the aisle. Come. Help me move this pew,' she said to Jessica, who she was getting used to calling Jess.

Together, she and her daughter moved the heavy wooden pew and then Leila saw it. The grille.

'There. There – I told you,' she said, grinning.

Two minutes later, she pulled out a very dirty carrier bag, blowing off a cloud of dust. She saw Jess and Sister Singh exchange a shocked look.

'This is it,' Leila explained, pulling the leather book from the bag. 'The visitors book from Lace Island.'

She felt a rush of emotion as she opened the book. It felt like she was opening up time and she remembered the hallway in Bibi's house and how the book had stood for years on the lectern. She flipped it open to the last page, her eyes clouding as she saw what she was looking for.

She held the book out for Jess to see. She watched as her beautiful girl read the words.

'There he is,' Leila said, feeling her hackles rising in triumph as she remembered standing on the stairs that day and Bibi making Adam Lonegan sign the visitors book. And now, all these years later, it would be the one thing that finished him.

After they'd said goodbye to the nuns, Leila and Jess were soon back on the street, Jess holding the visitors book carefully.

'I have a surprise for you,' Jess said, looking at her phone. 'Leila, I'm going to take this back to the police station, but first I'm going to drop you somewhere.'

Leila was confused by the grin on her daughter's face. She was so confident and competent, Leila thought. How could she be so together after everything that had happened? It still felt too good to be true: that her baby had not only found her but forgiven her too. Her Jessica, she thought, unable to stop herself touching her as she hailed a cab.

In the back of the air-conditioned car, they sat together and flipped through the pages of the visitors book.

'Teddy and Tina Everdene,' Jess said, tracing the ancient ink with her finger.

'They were the ones who persuaded Bibi to send me to school in England.'

'You went to school in England?' Jess asked, clearly stunned.

Leila laughed, delighting that there was so much she had left to tell her daughter. 'Oh yes. A posh boarding school. Hillmain. I didn't last long.'

'Why?'

'I was dreadfully homesick, and there was a teacher – a PE teacher – who accosted me in the shower. I was horrified.'

Jessica shook her head, as if she couldn't believe what Leila was telling her. 'It doesn't surprise me.'

'Doesn't it?'

'Sadly, there were several people like that in the care homes Angel and I went to,' she said.

'But you survived,' Leila said. 'You survived.'

Jess nodded, but Leila felt choked with an emotion she couldn't name. She should have been there. She should have been there for every minute of her daughter's life. She should never have had to live with strangers. Never have had to think for one minute that her mother had abandoned her.

She felt a familiar surge of hatred towards Chan and she shook her head, as if she could still rail at him.

'He's gone, Leila,' Jess said, and Leila faced her, amazed that she could read her mind so clearly. 'Let it go. We *both* survived, remember? We have to look forward, not back.'

'You're a good girl, Jess. You have a good heart. I see that,' Leila said, patting Jess's hand, wishing she could hold her and smother her in kisses.

They drove on in silence for a moment, and then Jess leant forward and stopped the driver.

'What is this place?' Leila asked, staring out of the window at a very plush-looking building. The driver turned into a curved driveway.

'It's a hotel.'

'It looks very grand,' Leila said.

'Go in there, into the restaurant, and wait for me. I'll be there very soon.'

'I don't want to go on my own,' Leila said, panicking. 'I'll come with you.'

'No. It's good for you to do this,' Jessica insisted. 'Have an adventure. Go on. It's time to start living again.'

She leant over and kissed Leila's cheek. 'I'll see you soon, Mum.'

Leila got out of the taxi and stood on the red carpet outside the circular door of the hotel. She waved to Jess as she headed off, watching the cab disappear.

Mum. The word resonated in her head, making a smile appear on her face. She *was* a Mum again. For real, this time, not just in her mind. She sighed, letting the magnitude of the moment sink in.

The hotel was the poshest place Leila had ever been to and she was nervous as she walked in and asked directions to the restaurant. She expected to be stopped, but a nice man directed her to a table and she sat down, feeling self-conscious. It still took some getting used to, being back in civilization and on show. It amazed her that she was still able to walk out in the world – a free woman – but she was constantly baffled by how much the world had changed in her absence.

She picked up the menu, realizing how hungry she was, hoping Jess wouldn't be long. There was so much she needed to tell her – about Lace Island and everything that had happened in the last four days. She smiled when she saw the illustration on the front – of an elephant and a mahout. '"The Lagoon Restaurant,"' she read out loud.

Something caught her eye, and through the wall of potted palms, she saw a man – clearly a member of staff at the hotel – talking to another man on the reception. She saw him greeting some guests and Leila suddenly felt her heart racing. It couldn't be, could it? That man wasn't . . . *Rasa*?

He disappeared from view and Leila didn't have the courage to turn round, but the hairs on the back of her neck were standing up and she knew then that he was walking towards her. Then he stopped next to her table.

'Hello, Leila,' he said.

Leila couldn't speak. She stared up at his face – the very same face that had been in her mind for so long. He looked older, of course, but she felt a deep sense of recognition as she looked into his hazel eyes. He was just the same.

How had Jess engineered this? How could this be happening? She put down the menu, her throat dry as he sat down opposite her at the table, and for a long moment, they just stared at one another.

'You work here?' she said, eventually.

He nodded. 'I'm the manager.'

'It's a fine place,' Leila said, gripping on to the napkin in her lap. The Lagoon Restaurant. Had he named it that because of their lagoon? Because of his memories of Lace Island?

'Leila,' he said again. 'Oh . . .' His voice was no more than a pent-up sigh, and she saw that his eyes were filling with tears.

'I saw the news, and Jess, your daughter, she emailed me and told me that you'd spoken of me. I've been tormenting myself wondering how I was ever going to tell you how sorry I am.' A tear spilt from his eye and he wiped it away quickly. 'Because I am so, so sorry. I should never, ever have left you. All this time . . . all this time . . . I thought you were dead, but you were there . . .'

Leila shook her head, shocked by how emotional he seemed. She pictured him now, the last time she'd seen him, standing under an umbrella in Maliba's yard, the rain lashing down. She remembered how resolute he'd been and how much he'd hurt her. It seemed like yesterday, but at the same time, it felt like an age had passed. How could she start to explain that the girl he'd loved was long gone?

'I can't begin to imagine the horror you have been through. Oh, Leila,' he said. He reached his arm across the table, but her hands stayed in her lap.

'I'm glad it's over, that's all. And that Chan has gone.'

'He's dead?'

'I shot him, Rasa,' Leila said, staring up at him and giving it to him straight. 'I shot him and killed him, and I would do it again in a heartbeat. And I will have to live with the knowledge that I'm that person. Who could do that.'

'I'm so sorry.'

'He murdered Vijay, you know. He used to taunt me with it. I lived in terror that you would be blamed. He told me that you were on the run. Then he told me you were in jail.'

'I wasn't on the run. I was sulking,' he said, with an ashamed shrug. 'I was busy being an apprentice when I heard about the fire at Lace Island. It was only afterwards that Parva told me what had happened.'

'Parva?' Leila said, gripping the table. 'Parva? But . . . but I thought she'd died in the fire?'

'No. She and Bamu, Mina and Victor and the others got out. Parva still lives near me. She married a nice man and they had five children. The eldest is called Leila.'

Leila felt her own tears then, as a huge wave of emotion hit her. 'Oh . . .'

'She'd like to see you. You know you're quite a celebrity now, but for us . . . for us . . .' He stared at her, his eyes twinkling with tears.

'I'd like that too,' Leila nodded, sniffing. Rasa handed her his handkerchief and she pressed it into her face, recognizing the smell of lavender water. It was all too much.

'Come with me. Let's walk,' he said.

She walked by his side through the restaurant, but she knew he was looking at her. Did he find it as astonishing to see her again as she found it seeing him? She felt ashamed that she hadn't made more of an effort with her appearance. She felt dowdy and old compared to all the glamorous young women in the hotel, with their Western fashions. Or the Indian women, with their dashing silk saris. Leila felt like the washed-up refugee that she was, and seeing Rasa, well, it made her feel more emotionally exposed than she could cope with.

At the back of the restaurant was a large conservatory filled with palm trees. The air was hot and humid, but not unpleasant. If Leila hadn't known better, she might have almost imagined she could be in the grove. They walked together between the palms as he told her more about Parva and her family.

'And what about you? Didn't you marry?' she asked.

'I did once, years ago, but it didn't last. I was married to my job and I messed it up. I guess my heart wasn't in it,' he said.

'You've been successful, then?'

'I've worked hard, and yes, I've done well. I've been OK.'

He'd been OK. Leila sighed and she gratefully accepted his offer of a seat on a wicker chair near a trickling fountain. It was all so much to take in. While she'd been in prison on Lace Island, everyone else had been living their lives. It made her feel somehow foolish – that she hadn't realized. That she hadn't even considered it a possibility.

'What will you do now, Leila?' Rasa asked.

She sighed. 'I am taking each day as it comes,' she said, 'but Lace Island is still legally mine, for the time being. They say there may be some compensation now that I have turned in half the state officials, but that won't be for a long time. I don't know how it will work. Keeping Lace Island, I mean. I won't be able to afford the taxes, so I will probably sell it back to the government. That's what they want me to do.'

'And what do you want?'

She smiled sadly. 'Oh . . . I don't know. I never thought I'd live long enough to see this . . . to feel this. To be alive. And Lace Island is my home. I guess ideally I want to remove every trace of Chan and then rebuild Bibi's house. But I can't go back in time.'

Rasa was silent for a long moment, taking in everything that she'd said.

'Why don't you make the whole place into a luxury resort? Make it like Bibi always wanted it to be.'

Leila laughed at the absurdity of the suggestion. 'Me? I wouldn't know how.'

'But *I* would,' Rasa said.

She stared at him, his words sinking in.

'All it would take would be some time and some hard work. And some money, but that can be arranged. We could build it back, Leila. Just how it was. Only better,' he said.

He meant it. She could see it in his eyes. That restoring Lace Island was as much his dream as it was hers.

'You'd do that? For me?'

'Oh, my Leila,' he said, holding her hand. 'If you only knew how much I have longed for this moment. For a second chance to do the right thing.'

Leila stared at him, too overwhelmed to speak. After a moment, she was aware of Rasa looking past her to someone approaching. Leila turned now and saw Jess.

She stopped and smiled and put her hands together in front of her heart. 'I see you've found each other at last,' she said.

CHAPTER SIXTY-TWO

Lace Island, present day

Jess stood at the top of the aircraft steps and breathed in the hot, tropical air, feeling, as she had done the last time she'd come back to Lace Island, that she was somewhere like nowhere else on the planet.

'You're here!'

She laughed, seeing Leila running across the newly relaid tarmac, waving her arms wildly, and Jess waved back, overjoyed as always at seeing her mother.

And boy, was she getting eccentric, Jess thought. Today, she was wearing orange jeans and a purple kaftan, her hair tied up with a big bow. She'd told Jess that for the rest of her life she was only going to wear clothes that made her happy, and Jess had enjoyed bringing her pieces from around the world. She was looking forward to presenting the kimono she'd picked up in Tokyo last week.

She dropped her bag and let Leila reach up and fold her into a hot hug.

'Where have you been this time?' Leila asked, staring at Jess with unashamed pride, and Jess knew she wasn't annoyed with her. After all, it had been Leila who'd insisted that Jess went back to work.

Jess hadn't wanted to leave her, but six months after Leila had been cleared by the police and the press furore had died down, she'd insisted on coming back to Lace Island and starting again.

Jess had found it weird coming back, her memory haunted by the night Suresh had been shot, but Leila couldn't have been happier. She'd insisted that she'd lived on Lace Island all her life and that there was nothing to be frightened of. The worst had already happened. From now on, there were just good times ahead.

It had helped that Rasa had been with her, of course. Dear, sweet, kind Rasa, who had made it clear that looking after Leila was going to be his life's work from now on. It had made Jess's choice to leave them to their plans a lot easier.

Leila hurried Jess away from the plane and over towards the small Mini Moke she'd driven onto the tarmac.

'Where on earth did you find this thing?' Jess laughed.

'Isn't it marvellous? Rasa fixed it up. Miraculously, it survived the fire. We've been finding all sorts of treasures.'

They drove away from the landing strip and Jess whistled, amazed at what had been going on in her absence. All the poppy fields had been bulldozed, and all the barbed wire had gone. That was nothing compared to the building work up at the house. There were workers all over it, and Leila could see a large, sloping red-tiled roof was already up.

They drove further on, past the new house to the small eco bungalow perched on the top of the red cliff, overlooking the sea. The side was already covered in a flowering vine, as if the natural beauty of Lace Island couldn't wait to reassert itself.

Leila raced inside and to the back, where Rasa was on the terrace. He gave Jess a huge hug, then poured tea for her as she stared out at the magnificent view of the twinkling ocean.

'I can't believe how much you guys have achieved already,' Jess said, smiling at Rasa. 'It's going to be incredible.'

'You wait,' Leila said, grinning. 'I have so much to show you.'

In fact, any chance that Jess was hoping to unpack and unwind was thrown out of the window. Leila insisted that Jess take a tour with her down to the lagoon to see the holiday huts on the new bicycles that had just arrived.

Jess laughed, getting onto the smart-looking bike. She hadn't been on one since she'd been in London and she wondered whether hers was still at the flat.

'Does it feel weird, still being here?' she asked Leila, as they cycled together down the muddy track.

'No, making it into the vision Bibi had is erasing all the bad memories. They still come, of course, at night. But Rasa is there to hold me.'

Jess smiled. 'I'm so happy for you both.'

'I thought it would be strange. That I would be . . . I don't know . . . shy, maybe, but' – Leila shrugged and smiled happily – 'so far so good. I have a lot of catching up to do. But he's a good teacher.' She laughed and Jess laughed too. 'I keep forgetting I'm your mother,' Leila said. 'I'm probably not supposed to talk to you about sex.'

'You can talk to me about anything,' Jess said, meaning it. This relationship was weird and wonderful and new, and Jess was loving every minute of it.

They set off, faster now, Leila whooping like a girl, and Jess laughed too. Leila never failed to surprise her on a minute-by-minute basis. In some ways, Jess guessed that part of Leila would forever be a young girl. Then at other times she was sombre and sad and like an ancient wise old woman. It sometimes felt to Jess that she was more the mother figure than Leila, who pumped her for information about the world away from Lace Island, guffawing over the mobile phone Jess had bought her and making Jess howl with laughter when she learnt to text.

But what she'd never failed on was her unadulterated love for Jess.

It had been overwhelming at first – Leila's mothering obsession. It had felt to Jess like Leila had wanted to go back in time and for Jess to be a little baby. She'd fussed around her and smothered her with hugs and kisses, until Jess had had to pull back and gently explain that they needed time to get to know one another.

The photos had helped, of course, Jess being able to fill in Leila about her past, year by year. The homes, the people who had come and gone – and, of course, Angel. And saying it all, telling Leila about what had happened to her felt cathartic. Like she finally belonged to her history and it had become part of her. She no longer needed to escape it, not when Leila longed for every single detail.

How Leila had put up with such emotional and physical abuse for so long and had come out relatively unscathed was humbling to Jess. But strangely, she didn't seem to be bitter, although Jess knew that killing Chan still weighed heavily on her mind, no matter how many times Jess told her that she'd had no choice.

She skidded to a halt when they came to the lagoon, and Jess braked too, laughing at how girlish Leila seemed. She got off her bike, carefully lowering it to the ground. Then she skipped over to one of the new bungalows.

'This one, we're calling Aunty Parva's,' Leila said, twisting the handle on the door of the cabin. They stepped into the eco bungalow, its glass doors overlooking the lagoon.

Jess admired the bungalow with its simple teak finishes and lovely beige and green decor. A cousin of Rasa's, a very pretty young woman called Mina, had designed all the bungalows, and it seemed as if everyone who had once been connected to Lace Island had come flooding back, bearing their talents and an open heart. And each one had made Leila more and more happy, as if the world could not match her joy.

'So tell me what I want to know,' Leila said, gripping her arm. 'Did you go? Were there elephants and feasts?'

She was talking about Suresh's wedding. Leila and Rasa had been invited, but Leila had refused to leave Lace Island with so much going on.

'Hmm,' Jess said, pulling a face. Then she sighed. 'No. I didn't go.'

'You didn't? But . . .'

She sighed again, knowing that she couldn't hide the truth from Leila. 'I couldn't face it. And I didn't want to remind him of what happened. Or there to be any focus on me. It was their day.'

Leila nodded and was silent for a long time. 'That's the only reason?'

Jess shrugged. Of course it wasn't the only reason, not that she could articulate that to her mother. She couldn't say the unspoken words: that she missed Suresh so much it hurt.

She looked out over the lagoon and the hummingbirds dipping in the water. It was stunningly beautiful, which only made her sadness more profound.

'There's no point. It's too late,' she said.

'It's never too late. Never. Look at us,' Leila said, standing next to Jess and linking her arm into hers, but even though Jess knew she was right, her mother's words of comfort didn't stop the ache she felt inside.

It was hard not to get swept up in Leila's endless enthusiastic plans, and for the next fortnight, it felt to Jess as if the rest of the world had disappeared. On this island, in the middle of the bluest oceans, it was as if time took on a different dimension. She was starting to understand how over twenty-five years could have gone by so quickly for Leila.

This morning, Rasa had told Jess to meet him at his new dive boat on the beach. The equipment had just arrived and he wanted Jess to help him test it out. Both he and Leila had been as jumpy as schoolchildren, babbling and squabbling about the reef and the bit they most wanted to show Jess.

Jess sat on the jetty, her feet dangling over the edge, watching Rasa stacking life vests in the boat. When she'd first met him, he'd looked so much like a professional hotel manager, but here, in shorts, a tatty straw hat on his head, he looked years younger. And like he belonged in this boat.

'You know, it makes her so happy when you're here,' he said, polishing one of the diving dials.

'Me too. I love it here, being with you two. It gets more like paradise every day. It's the first time I've relaxed since . . . well, you know.'

'It'll take a while. You've been through a great deal.'

Jess sighed. 'I know.'

There had been rather a lot to process in the last six months, quite apart from finding Leila. Blaise had been arrested, as had Senator Lonegan in the States. He'd apparently asked to meet Jess, but she had no intention of ever giving him that satisfaction. Leila and Rasa were the only parents she needed.

'How is the job?' he asked.

'It's good. It keeps me busy, but I don't know, lately it's been more tiring, jetting off around the world. Being alone in hotel rooms. I want to be somewhere permanent. It's been lovely being here for a few weeks.'

Rasa glanced up at her from beneath his hat and she knew then that there was another motive for Rasa summoning her here.

'What?' she said, smiling.

'It's just . . . you know that the nuns have agreed to come?'

'They have?'

'From the old mission in Cochin. Leila wants to rehouse them here.'

This was news to Jess. She thought back to that day in the chapel and how the nuns had told her and Leila that they were praying for a miracle.

'We've been drawing up plans for a new building with a rehab centre attached.'

Jess stared at him. 'A rehab centre?'

'Your mother is most insistent, and I agree with her. She needs to help people who have been affected by addiction. People who can still be saved. It's early stages, but I can't manage the hotel and that whole project too. I could do with someone to spearhead it. And to promote it. Make it a place that could really make a difference to people.'

Jess bit her lip, feeling a wave of excitement rush through her. She smiled down at Rasa, who winked at her and she knew then that Leila and he had thought this through. And that Leila had put him up to asking Jess about it.

'I . . . We want you to think about it, Jess. Take your time. We'll talk more about it. Nothing has to be decided now, but . . . you know how much it would mean to us both.'

But Jess's heart already had the answer. She didn't need any time.

Her brain raced over the logistics of it. If they built a centre, she would finally be able to do what she had vowed she would when Angel had died.

'Where is your mother, anyway?' Rasa said. 'We're missing valuable diving time.'

'She said she was expecting some people. I'll go and see where she is.'

Jess got up and skipped down the jetty, staring at the beach, a new hope bursting in her heart.

The mission. Everything made sense. Leila and Rasa had just given her the thing she had most wanted. A real purpose. And she knew without a shadow of a doubt that this is what she'd been destined for all along.

She was so full of ideas that it was a while before she noticed that someone was coming down the beach the other way towards her.

She stopped, shielding her eyes, thinking that it must be a mirage. But it wasn't. She'd recognize that limping gait anywhere.

She ran down the beach just as Suresh arrived past the frog rock, his trousers rolled up, dropping his suit jacket in the sand. He looked exhausted and thirsty, like he had literally just washed up on a desert island. Jess handed him her bottle of water and he drank gratefully.

'Leila said you'd be on the beach, but I walked the long way round,' he said.

'Suresh, what are you doing here? Where's Kareena?' she asked.

He laughed, gazing at her. 'She jilted me.'

'She did *what*?'

'The night before the wedding. Everyone was there. All the festivities were about to start and she called the whole thing off.'

Jess stared at him, open-mouthed with shock. 'But . . . but why?'

'She said that she wanted the real deal, that she wanted to fall in love properly and that she'd changed her mind about our arranged marriage. She couldn't go through with it.'

Jess stared at him, her mind racing over the implications of what he was saying. Of the colossal fallout he must have had to have faced. 'Oh God. I'm so sorry.'

'Are you?' he said, looking alarmed. 'Because personally, I think it's the best, most brilliantly honest thing she's ever said. It helps that she's been offered this amazing job in America and is on her way there now. Uncovering the story of Lace Island totally put her on the map.'

Jess could hardly take it in. How could he be so calm about it? 'Wow.'

'But there was another reason too,' he said, stepping in and breathing deeply to catch his breath. 'She said she couldn't go through with it knowing that I'm in love with someone else.'

There was a long moment and Jess felt her breath catch. 'She did?'

Suresh reached out and touched her hair. 'Because I am in love. With you. I have been since the first second I saw you.'

And as she was swallowed up in his eyes, Jess felt her heart filling up with sunshine and a new lightness, as if a heavy cloak she'd been carrying all this time had fallen away from her. An amazed laugh escaped her as she took in the palm trees against the bluest of skies and the whitest of sand, and she remembered the poster Angel had given her all those years ago.

But best of all was that none of it mattered. The only thing that mattered was him. Just him. And the feeling, the feeling that she'd always wondered about. This joyful love that filled her now.

'So you've got to tell me. Have I got the timing right this time?' he asked, smiling at her, and she laughed, letting him take her in his arms, feeling like she might burst with happiness.

'Yes. Your timing is perfect,' she said. And then she kissed him.

Acknowledgements

This book wouldn't be here without the exceptional team at Pan Macmillan, especially my wonderful editor Wayne Brookes. I'd like to thank everyone who works in editorial services and production, especially the lovely Eloise Wood, as well as the marketing and PR, digital and sales teams. The fabulous Jodie Mullish, Katie James and Stuart Dwyer make Pan Mac a joy to work with, and thank you to James Annal for his lovely cover.

Thanks, as always, to the best agents in town, Vivienne Schuster and Felicity Blunt at Curtis Brown. And thank you to my dearest friends, who always support me through the writing process, especially my early readers Dawn Howarth, Bronwin Wheatley and Katy Whelan. Thanks also to Sally Hepburn for her tips on air crew training. And Emlyn, of course. For everything.

This book is a story about mothers and daughters, and it is a theme that is very dear to my heart. During the writing of this book I lost both my mother-in-law, Anne Rees, and my own mum, Anne Lloyd. Both were inspirational women who helped me enormously, and I will miss them forever. It was my mum who started me on my writing journey when I was six and never stopped encouraging and supporting me. So as well as being dedicated to my beautiful daughter, Tallulah, this one is also for Mum, with my love and gratitude.

extracts reading groups
competitions books new
discounts extracts extracts
competitions discounts
books new events
events books
extracts reading groups
new titles
interviews events new
events extracts extracts books
discounts reading groups
new books events
events new interviews books extracts

www.panmacmillan.com

discounts extracts discounts
extracts events reading groups
competitions books extracts new books